KU-630-505

Karin Baine lives in Northern Ireland with her husband, two sons and her out-of-control notebook collection. Her mother and her grandmother's vast collection of books inspired her love of reading and her dream of becoming a Mills & Boon author. Now she can tell people she has a *proper* job! You can follow Karin on Twitter, @karinbaine1, or visit her website for the latest news—karinbaine.com.

Hopelessly addicted to espresso and HEAs, **Kristine Lynn** pens high-stakes contemporary romances in the wee morning hours before teaching writing at an Arizona university. Luckily, the stakes there aren't as dire. When she's not grading, writing, or searching for the perfect vanilla latte, she can be found on the hiking trails behind her home with her daughter and her puppy. She'd love to connect on Twitter, Instagram, or Facebook.

Also by Karin Baine

Mills & Boon Medical Romance

Royal Docs miniseries

Surgeon Prince's Fake Fiancée
A Mother for His Little Princess

Mills & Boon True Love

Pregnant Princess at the Altar

Also by Kristine Lynn

Brought Together by His Baby

Discover more at millsandboon.co.uk.

AN AMERICAN DOCTOR IN IRELAND

KARIN BAINE

ACCIDENTALLY DATING HIS BOSS

KRISTINE LYNN

MILLS & BOON

All rights reserved including the right of reproduction in whole or in part in any form. This edition is published by arrangement with Harlequin Enterprises ULC.

This is a work of fiction. Names, characters, places, locations and incidents are purely fictional and bear no relationship to any real life individuals, living or dead, or to any actual places, business establishments, locations, events or incidents. Any resemblance is entirely coincidental.

This book is sold subject to the condition that it shall not, by way of trade or otherwise, be lent, resold, hired out or otherwise circulated without the prior consent of the publisher in any form of binding or cover other than that in which it is published and without a similar condition including this condition being imposed on the subsequent purchaser.

® and TM are trademarks owned and used by the trademark owner and/or its licensee. Trademarks marked with ® are registered with the United Kingdom Patent Office and/or the Office for Harmonisation in the Internal Market and in other countries.

First published in Great Britain 2024
by Mills & Boon, an imprint of HarperCollins*Publishers* Ltd,
1 London Bridge Street, London, SE1 9GF

www.harpercollins.co.uk

HarperCollins*Publishers* Macken House, 39/40 Mayor Street Upper, Dublin 1, D01 C9W8, Ireland

An American Doctor in Ireland © 2024 Karin Baine

Accidentally Dating His Boss © 2024 Kristine Lynn

ISBN: 978-0-263-32150-0

02/24

This book contains FSC™ certified paper and other controlled sources to ensure responsible forest management.

For more information visit www.harpercollins.co.uk/green.

Printed and Bound in the UK using 100% Renewable Electricity at CPI Group (UK) Ltd, Croydon, CR0 4YY

AN AMERICAN DOCTOR IN IRELAND

KARIN BAINE

MILLS & BOON

For me,
because I don't give myself nearly enough credit! x

CHAPTER ONE

A SEA OF green spread out before Mae Watters. Well, it was a crowd of people dressed for St Patrick's Day. They didn't dye the River Liffey in Dublin green especially for the occasion, the way they did back home in Boston, but it still reminded her of every seventeenth of March she'd spent with her mother at the parade there. And, when she was old enough, they'd graduated to the Irish-themed pubs to celebrate the day.

A year without her had been difficult. Not least because Mae had had no one to turn to when, humiliatingly, her relationship had come to an end. Being jilted at the altar eight months ago, and being left alone in Ireland to pick up the pieces left of her heart, had left her feeling more alone than ever.

It wasn't as though she had any family left in America to go back to—at least, none who wanted to know her. The father who'd left her when she was little could have started a new family and given her half-brothers and sisters, but she'd never know, as he'd disappeared completely out of her life.

'Excuse us.' A family dressed as leprechauns

squeezed past her on the footpath, keen to get to the best vantage point for the parade. She envied the young couple pushing the double stroller transporting a baby and toddler, giddy with excitement. Not because she wanted children, or even a husband now, but because of the family unit it represented—something she'd never have. She'd lost too much, too many loved ones, ever to open herself up to anyone again and to have a chance of starting a family of her own.

Perhaps she shouldn't have come here today, when her spirits weren't as high as everyone else's. Music was blasting all along the street and people were singing, clapping and waving Irish flags as the floats came past to celebrate the patron saint of Ireland. All she wanted to do was cry. But it was a rare day off before she started her new job, it was her Mum's home city and she'd thought she'd feel closer to her here. The problem was, she had, until she remembered that the cruelty of illness had separated them for ever. It was a cruel irony to specialise in medicine when you couldn't save your own mother.

'Ye—oh!'

She was jostled off-balance by a man carrying a little girl high on his shoulders as they pushed in beside her, dancing to the music. Usually, common sense would have prevented her from confronting a tattooed male with bright-green hair, but today her emotions were all over the place.

'Do you mind?' She bristled, rubbing her elbow, which had been banged in the melee.

'Not at all, love!' He grinned, the twinkling blue eyes and bright-white smile not intimidating in the slightest.

Perhaps that was why she wouldn't drop the issue.

'Well, I do mind. I was standing minding my own business until you rudely pushed past me.'

'Sorry, missus. The wee one wanted to see,' he said without a hint of genuine remorse.

'You should pinch her, Dad.'

'Excuse me?'

'It's a tradition. You're supposed to wear green today to remain invisible to the leprechauns, otherwise you get pinched.'

Despite the man's explanation of why his daughter was so keen for him to assault her, Mae wasn't impressed by his behaviour.

'Perhaps you'd be better teaching her something about manners... And it's *Ms*, actually.' She didn't need the reminder that she hadn't actually got to the part where she'd changed her name, or even got a husband.

'Says it all,' he muttered.

Mae could feel her blood starting to boil at the utter gall of the man insulting her when he was the one in the wrong. If not for the presence of the child, she would've had a few choice words to say to him.

'What does?'

'Well, it's that time of the year, isn't it? When all you Yanks come over thinking you'll bag an Irish husband.'

'How dare you?' she blustered. 'I live here.'

His rude comments made her bypass her usual polite manner when dealing with irascible men, common in her line of work, in which she'd learned to smile and plough on rather than react.

But today she rose to the bait. Probably because she'd finally reached her limit of things she could stand in this wet, miserable country. She had followed her heart here, hoping for the romantic fantasy of living happily ever after with her charming Irish fiancé in the seaside town of Bray, but she'd earned her place with every tear she'd shed since.

Especially when she'd been working to help the inhabitants of this country every day, despite her heartbreak. She'd moved out of the house she'd shared with Diarmuid, of course, but seeing him around the hospital had been too painful a reminder of what he'd done to her. Hopefully her move to the city would help her get over it.

The man took his eyes off the spectacle out on the street to study her. 'Hmm. Then I'd wager you came back to find your Irish roots.'

Mae could feel the heat rising in her body, surely manifesting itself in those tell-tale red splotches that oft appeared on her neck when she was riled, as though the effort of trying to hold her temper threatened to burst right through her skin.

'My mother came from Dublin.' She tried to keep the hysteria from her voice as she attempted to justify her residence in the city.

'Of course she did.'

Mae was getting used to the dry Irish sense of humour, the gentle teasing that came with a nudge in the ribs and a twinkle in the eye. However, there was something about this know-it-all stranger that was really pushing her buttons today and making her want to scream.

She hated the fact that her life had boiled down to that of stereotypical American in Ireland. It said nothing of the heartache and loss she'd gone through to get here. If she was this touchy over a few teasing comments now, it was probably for the best that she went home, before the crowd really started celebrating the day, leaving her even more of an outsider.

It occurred to her that she wasn't beholden to be polite to this man or stand anywhere near him. Arguing back wasn't going to achieve anything other than upsetting her, when she was thinking about her mum. And, if that smile on his face grew any wider, she'd be tempted to smack it off.

In an attempt to avoid a possible assault charge, or an emotional breakdown in front of the most annoying man on earth, she simply turned and walked away.

'Wait. I'm sorry.' Liam had seen the flash of pain in the redhead's jade-green eyes before she turned away.

He hadn't meant to upset her. His big mouth was always getting him into trouble. Today was supposed to be fun for everyone involved and he didn't want to be responsible for spoiling anyone's day. Sometimes his brand of humour didn't translate well with American visitors, earning him a clip around the ear from his mother even at the age of thirty-two, lest he offended any of her customers at the family pub. Which, today, should be welcoming as many tourists as possible.

Although he was first and foremost an A&E doctor in Dublin City Hospital, he was often roped in to collect empty glasses during busy periods in the pub. He and Shannon, his daughter, spent a lot of time there. Not because he was a drinker, but because his parents lived in the flat above the premises, and babysat when he was at work.

Since his partner of nine years, Clodagh, had left him—for his best friend, no less—he'd had to rely on help with the school run and occasionally in the evenings when he was working. Shifts in A&E weren't compatible with the life of a single dad. It wasn't the happy family life he'd planned, or the life he now wanted, and he was burdened with the guilt he'd let down his daughter, as well as asking too much of his parents for the best part of a year. The last thing he needed on his conscience was knowing he'd caused unnecessary upset to someone else.

Liam watched the blaze of red hair bobbing through

the crowd, a beacon in the green tide that made her easily identifiable.

'Da-ad! I can't see the parade,' Shannon complained as he followed the American away from the prime view he'd gone to so much trouble to secure.

'I know, sweetheart. I just need to speak to the lady again.'

'The pretty lady with the red hair?' Shannon kicked her heels into his chest to indicate she wanted to dismount his shoulders. Liam bent down as far as he could, reached up and lifted her down on to the ground. She took off before he could even ask what she was up to.

'Shannon! Don't run away!' he shouted, to no avail, and was forced to chase after the green tutu disappearing into the crowd. In pursuit of his daughter, he dodged mums with prams and men with cans in their hands, his heart pounding with the fear of losing her in the crowd. Although she knew the city well, she was only seven years old. She was his baby. She was all he had. He caught sight of her as she located the American redhead, though she remained out of his reach.

Shannon tugged on the belt of the woman's white wool coat. 'My dad wants to speak to you. I can't see the parade until you talk to him.'

Unfortunately, his offspring had inherited his lack of tact, leaving him cringing as the woman watched him approach.

'I'm so sorry. Both for my daughter accosting you, and for upsetting you earlier. I was joking about the whole "Irish roots" thing.' He took Shannon's hand and discreetly pulled her to his side.

The redhead arched an eyebrow at him. 'No, you weren't. You were enjoying belittling me. Believe it or not, a high percentage of Americans *are* actually of Irish origin. My mother was a Dublin girl. I moved here last year after she died. So, in future please think before you judge people.'

'I apologise for thinking I was being funny.'

'You're not,' the American and his daughter chorused.

'Apparently...' He tucked that little nugget away for future reference, something to add to his list of failures.

'Do you often use your daughter to get women to talk to you?' Red asked, clearly enjoying watching him squirm.

It was the price he'd have to pay for sticking his size tens in it in the first place.

'Not often, no. Again, I can only apologise. If you're ever in O'Conner's in Westmoreland Street, I'll even buy you a pint to say sorry.'

'O'Conner's?'

'My parents own it—and you won't pay Temple Bar prices there.'

'I thought you were buying,' she said, quick as a flash.

'Only the first round. The next one's on you.' Were they flirting? He was so long out of the game, he couldn't tell. Though he wasn't interested in any

Paddy's Day shenanigans, unlike most of the Irish population, he was enjoying the back and forth between them.

'Dad! Dad! There's Ray!'

Before he could get a definitive answer as to whether or not he'd see his new banter partner again, Shannon was tugging on his shirt and pointing towards the parade. Ray, their next-door neighbour, was walking head and shoulders above the rest of the parade. Easily done when he was wearing stilts, dressed as St Patrick in emerald-green robes, wore a mitre on his head, and carried a staff in his hand, chasing several people dressed as snakes.

'A friend of yours?' the American beauty asked as they watched his antics.

'Ray Jackson. My next-door neighbour.' Despite everyone else's enthusiasm, Liam couldn't quite bring himself to join in on the cheering.

'What's wrong? Did he steal your outfit?'

'No. He has an alcohol problem, and it looks very much to me as though he's been drinking already today.' Not a good idea to be drunk in charge of stilts, he was sure.

Right on cue, there was a collective gasp from the crowd as St Patrick began to topple, almost crushing one of the green leotard-clad snakes in the process.

'Can you keep an eye on Shannon for me?' He didn't intend letting his daughter out of his sight, even if he had left her with a trustworthy-looking stranger, but being a doctor wasn't a job that finished at five o'clock, or even stopped on a day off.

'But I...'

With a patient and friend to attend to, he didn't wait around to hear the excuse.

'What are you playing at, Raymondo?' he asked, running over to assess the damage. The music and laughter had ceased now, happy faces etched with concern, fingernails being bitten as St Patrick lay in a heap in the middle of the road.

'I think I lost my balance. I'm getting too old for this.' Ray groaned through gritted teeth.

'You don't say. I'm going to have to take these things off you so I can get a proper look at that leg.' The right leg, which was crumpled under the middle-aged saint, looked to be at an odd angle. Liam gingerly began to undo the stilts fastened around his feet.

'Stop! Don't move him,' a now familiar American twang instructed.

'Can you stay back, please? I've got this. And where is my daughter?' Now that the redhead was walking towards him minus her charge, nausea began to swell in his stomach. He should never have taken his eyes off her.

'She's with her grandmother. Now, please move aside so I can take a look.' She knelt down beside him, regardless that her white coat would be covered in green glitter and paint from the road when she got up again.

At least Shannon was okay, and he was glad his mum

had found time for a break after all—just in time for another spot of babysitting. He glanced over and gave her a thumbs-up when he spotted her hovering at the edge of the crowd. She gestured that she'd take Shannon back with her to the pub, leaving him to focus on the job at hand.

'Thanks, but I've got this,' he insisted. 'I'm a doctor.'

'So am I,' she countered, bringing them to a stalemate.

'Good for you.' He was surprised that an American doctor should have chosen to move to Ireland to work. This wasn't about egos; Raymond was hurt and currently holding up the entire St Patrick's Day parade.

He could feel her bristle beside him. 'You don't look much like a doctor.'

'What happened to not being too judgemental? The green hair was "fun dad" showing up for Shannon today. It's my day off.'

'And the tattoos?'

He was tempted to tell her they were the marks of a misspent youth. It wasn't against the medical oath, or any of her business, how he'd chosen to adorn his body. However, it gave him huge satisfaction, seeing her face when he licked his thumb and smudged the Irish flag he'd drawn on his arm this morning to match the shamrocks he'd painted on Shannon's cheeks.

'Listen, I'm glad I have two doctors fighting over me—but no offence, Liam, I'd prefer the redhead.'

'Not appropriate, Ray,' Liam admonished as he

rolled up the man's trouser leg to uncover a nasty open fracture. The broken bone was sticking up through the wound, the swelling around the area already apparent. Given the fact Ray wasn't writhing in agony, he suspected the alcohol he'd consumed had gone some way to dulling the pain—small mercies.

'I suppose this will get done quicker if we work together. Dr Mae Watters.' She held out her hand for him to shake, which he duly did.

'Dr Liam O'Conner. First things first, we need to call an ambulance.' He knew there were probably medical staff on hand to cover the parade, but Ray was going to need to be transferred to the hospital for treatment.

'I've done that, and we know he's conscious and responsive, if a tad inebriated.'

'Hey! I—I needed some Irish courage,' Ray hiccupped, the stench of booze and stale cigarettes making Liam and Mae recoil.

'We'll have to stabilise that leg.' It was necessary to immobilise the limb to prevent further injury until he reached hospital. Without a sterile dressing to hand, Liam used the green silk stole around Ray's neck to apply pressure to the wound without covering the bone.

'You can use my belt to fashion something with the stilt,' Mae suggested, whipping out the tie from the waistband of her coat.

'Just let us know if it hurts or you start to feel nauseous, Ray. The paramedics will be able to give you something for the pain when they get here,' Mae reassured him as Liam worked quickly to bind the leg to the makeshift splint above and below the fracture, careful not to jar the leg any more than necessary.

'Ah, the good stuff…' Ray trailed off and Liam wondered exactly how much he had drunk this morning. He knew he wouldn't be honest with him about his alcohol consumption—he never was—though Liam heard the rattle of bottles going into the recycling bin every morning. It wouldn't be a good idea to mix painkillers with a skinful of alcohol, and he'd be sure to fill the ambulance crew in on his neighbour's history. At least, what he knew of it, from the drunken ramblings and numerous falls Ray had suffered since his partner had died a couple of years ago.

'We're going to be having another talk about your drinking, Ray.'

Ray batted away his concerns with a tut and an eye-roll. They'd both had their personal problems, but Ray had been a visible warning to Liam not to give into the self-pity which had descended upon him too when Clodagh left him just over a year ago. He hadn't wanted to become another shell of a man who could barely function. Shannon needed more from him than ever. She was the reason he got up every morning, and the reason he didn't drown his sorrows in the bottom of a glass every evening. He felt sorry for his neighbour; he saw the pity in Mae's eyes, and he never wanted anyone to look at him the same way.

As much as he might need to blot out the memory of

Clodagh cheating on him, ending their relationship and walking out on their family, it would be selfish to do so. Even more than pretending his relationship hadn't been in trouble, because that would've meant admitting his failure as a partner and father. A fact which was public knowledge anyway, now that they were separated.

In hindsight, having a family had always been his idea of an idyll, not Clodagh's. They had only been dating a few months when she'd fallen pregnant, before they'd even talked about whether or not they wanted marriage and children. It later became apparent that, unlike him, she hadn't wanted either. Whilst he'd been over the moon at the prospect of becoming a parent, she hadn't been as enthusiastic.

Still in her twenties, Clodagh had always given the impression she resented being tied down to the responsibility of having a child. Liam had done his best to carry most of the load, doing most of the childcare, giving her the freedom to still go out with her friends. Perhaps somewhere along the way he'd pushed her out, creating a strong bond with Shannon that mother and daughter had never quite mirrored. Liam had no doubt she loved Shannon, but even now she seemed an afterthought next to Clodagh's work and personal life. He wished he could forget about Clodagh, and her betrayal, just as easily.

When the sirens sounded, the crowd began to part so the ambulance could get through.

'Yeah, yeah. If you tell me you haven't been tempted

to lose yourself in a bottle since Clodagh left you, then you're a liar,' Ray rambled.

Though Mae didn't comment, Liam could feel her eyes on him. He refused to look up and see that same pity in her eyes for him.

'I've been tempted, Ray, yes. But it doesn't solve anything, does it? Only makes things worse.' Liam was relieved when the ambulance arrived so they could stop discussing his failed relationship under the watchful gaze of the entire city. There was one pair of green eyes in particular before which he didn't want to appear weak. Not when he'd already made such a sterling impression on his new American friend... Despite her being the first woman he'd felt the urge to engage in conversation since Clodagh had left, now he'd be glad to climb into the ambulance and leave her behind.

He relayed Ray's current condition to the medics and waited as they transferred him into the back of the ambulance.

'Who's coming with him?'

'I am,' both Liam and Mae chorused.

'Which hospital are you taking him to?' he enquired, hoping the geography would give Mae a reason to back off.

'Dublin City.'

'That's where I work.' He played his trump card with a flourish.

'Me too.' Mae killed his sense of triumph dead before he'd even had the chance to blow his horn.

Though she looked surprised by the coincidence, there was no sign of her backing down. If anything, she looked smug that she had as much right to accompany the patient as he did.

If this feisty American was going to be his new colleague, work was about to get a lot more interesting.

CHAPTER TWO

LIAM WAS ABLE to fast-track Ray through the Accident and Emergency department thanks to his position and a large dose of charm. Mae followed, keen to see the patient through, regardless of her male counterpart seeming to have things under control—or perhaps in spite of. She hated to think of him having the upper hand and getting rid of her so easily. Yes, it was his neighbour, but they'd both been on scene and, since this was her new place of work, she'd just as much right to be here as Dr O'Conner.

It felt weird to call him that. Yes, she'd been unfairly judgemental about his appearance, but his demeanour around her thus far had left a lot to be desired. Even if he had worked well in a medical crisis.

'You can go home, if you want. I'll stay and make sure Ray is comfortable,' Liam told her outside the cubicle.

'I'd rather be here. I don't like his colour, and if you're right about his drinking.... I noticed distention of his abdomen, which could be due to the release of fluid from his liver, and the swelling in his lower legs

might be fluid retention.' She was familiar with the yel-
lowing complexion in long-term alcohol abusers and
what it meant. All the symptoms she had noticed were
indicative of liver disease—not things which would
clear up of their own accord, and certainly not if the
patient continued to drink heavily.

'I've thought the same thing myself for a long time
but it's been next to impossible getting him to go to
the doctor. That's why I've ordered a battery of tests
while he's here, the full MOT, so I can be fully prepared when I go into battle and try to talk to him about
his drinking problem again.'

Okay, so when he wasn't teasing and making rude,
stereotypical jokes at her expense, he did sound like a
doctor, and a good neighbour. It was one thing to strap
up a broken leg and get someone to the hospital, but
quite another to order up extra blood tests and wait for
the results, on a hunch. Especially when it was his day
off and he had a daughter at home.

Mae had heard the snippet of information about his
personal life revealed by his inebriated friend and she
couldn't help but be curious. Apparently, his partner
had left him too—she hoped in less humiliating circumstances than her ex, though she knew that would
be scant comfort. She knew what it was like to plan a
future, a happy family and a life together with someone. Since he already had a daughter, she supposed
he'd been planning a life together too before the bomb-
shell had dropped. Knowing he'd likely suffered the

same heartbreak and bewilderment she had gave her a new insight into the man she would no doubt run into again in the future, now they were working in the same building.

'I can have a chat to him too, if that would help? I'm a hepatologist, so this is my area of expertise. I have some contacts who can provide him with counselling, or some rehab options.' Addiction wasn't something cured with a prescription or good will. It took a desire on the patient's behalf to want to change, but it also required some outside help at times. She'd referred many of her patients over the years to various services away from the hospital and, whilst it didn't work for everyone, lots of people had benefitted from different forms of therapy.

'Thanks, but I think I'll try and get through to him first. He's a stubborn so-and-so. I know how to handle him.' When he saw her tense at the merest hint she wasn't up to the battle, he added, 'I wouldn't want you to get offended if he goes off on one.'

That comment didn't do anything to appease her. It only served to remind her of their initial meeting. Then she saw the same twinkle in his eye and realised he was goading her. The growl of frustration which came out of her mouth was as unfamiliar to her as it was amusing to him, as she pushed past him back into the cubicle, ignoring the chuckling behind her.

'Mr Jackson, I think we're going to have to keep you in overnight. Do you have anyone we can contact for you?' She watched Liam walk back into the cubicle, waiting for him to challenge her authority. Although she didn't officially start until tomorrow, and technically this was his jurisdiction, she was very much invested in this patient and his future.

A brief frown marked Liam's forehead before it disappeared again. 'We're running a few blood tests while you're here to see if there's anything else going on inside that body of yours.'

'I thought it was a clean break. Surely all I need is a bit of plaster and some crutches?' Ray was already trying to sit up, probably planning his escape to the nearest pub.

'The leg fracture should be a straightforward matter. However, it's your drinking that's causing us concern.'

Ray rolled his eyes at Liam's assessment.

'I'm a liver specialist, Mr Jackson, and I would like to keep you under observation tonight until we get the results of these tests. We might need to do a few body scans too, just so we can get a clearer picture of what's going on inside. Dr O'Conner has told me that alcohol may have been a factor in your fall today and, combined with the colour of your complexion, it gives me reason to think you might have some liver or kidney problems going on.' The whole time Mae was giving her talk, Ray was glaring daggers at Liam for throwing him under the bus.

'So, it's a crime to have a pint now, is it? It's St Patrick's Day, in case you hadn't noticed. The whole country's enjoying a drink today. Well, apart from you two, obviously.' Arms folded across his chest, Ray looked as belligerent as they came, but Mae was used to dealing with people in denial. They usually only ended up under her care because they'd been ignoring the signs of the toll alcohol was taking on their body, completely in the grip of their addiction, until it was obvious to everyone else around them. By the time they reached her door, they were experiencing severe repercussions of their lifestyle choices.

Of course, not all her patients were in the thrall of addiction; many had illnesses or congenital problems they had no control over. That was why she found people like Ray so challenging and frustrating. They'd had choices. Okay, so life wasn't as simple as saying yes or no to a drink or doing drugs, otherwise the world wouldn't be populated with people lost to their vices— but there was still time to turn their lives around. Too often they had no interest in doing so, content to take the easier path they'd grown accustomed to rather than doing the hard work it took to make the change.

'If it was just one drink we wouldn't be worried, Ray, but we all know it's more than that.' Liam was deep into his 'serious doctor' mode now and Mae could only imagine how often he'd first used the friendly approach to try and get his neighbour to slow down the drinking.

'What else have I got to look forward to if I can't have a beer?' he complained.

Mae might never understand that all-consuming desire for the next fix of alcohol or pills, but she knew how it felt to face that dark abyss, believing nothing good was ever going to happen again. After the wedding that never was, she'd spent some time there, wallowing in the grief for her mother and the loss of her relationship; realising she was destined to be on her own for the rest of her life.

Perhaps it was the strength of character she'd inherited from her mother which had pulled her out of that despair, and for that she gave thanks and counted herself lucky to have had such a badass role model. Not everyone was able to claw their way out of that quagmire, and she was sure her mother had languished there herself once upon a time, as a single parent in a foreign country. After all, she'd left behind her life in Ireland to follow her American tourist love, only to be left with a baby in a foreign country when he'd grown tired of family life. Not unlike Mae's situation, though thankfully she didn't have a child to bring up alone.

But the Watters women had managed to pick themselves up, dust themselves off and build up stronger defences than ever, which hopefully would prevent another emotional collapse. Especially now she'd sworn off serious relationships, negating the risk of ever being blindsided, humiliated and rejected by someone who was supposed to love her.

'There is a life outside of the bottle, Ray. I don't mean to sound patronising, but I think if you have a few days of clarity you'll come to the same conclusion yourself.' Mae knew she was playing with fire, especially when they weren't one hundred percent sure how bad Ray's addiction was. Even Liam had seemed surprised that he'd been drinking so early in the day, so perhaps he wasn't aware of the full extent of the man's difficulties. She didn't want to cross the line, especially when she was only starting her new job, but she wanted to help.

'I can't stay. You know I have to get back for Brodie.' Ray deferred to Liam as threw off the bed covers, clearly not intending to stay put.

'His dog,' Liam clarified.

'He's not just some wee dog that can be left alone. Brodie's an Irish Wolfhound who'll probably be wrecking the house as we speak. He doesn't like being left on his own.' It was clear Ray was using his pet as an excuse to leave, but Mae knew if he left now they'd likely never get him back for another investigation.

'I'm sure someone can look in on him—or, failing that, there are places we could phone to take care of him until you're discharged.' She was desperately trying to come up with answers to pacify him, and failing.

Enraged by the suggestion, he was now pulling himself up into a sitting position on the bed, trying to manoeuvre his injured leg so he could stand up. 'There's no way I'm giving my dog up. He's all I have. He's the only reason I get up in the morning. He has a routine and won't do well without me.'

'Wait, Ray. I can look in on him when I go home. Give me your keys and I can feed him and take him for a walk.' Liam's suggestion at least made Ray pause for thought.

'What about when you're at work? You know he likes company. I can't stay. No way.' Now Ray was on his feet and not even Liam, standing blocking his path, appeared to be enough to prevent him from hobbling away.

'I'll help too. I'm sure me and Liam won't always be working at the same time, and it's only going to be for tomorrow, right? I can take a book and sit with him for a while after my shift. These tests are important, Ray.'

Mae surprised herself with the offer, but she was desperate, and she could see by the concern etched on his face that Liam was too. Minding a dog for a few hours didn't seem like a high price to pay if it meant improving the quality of a patient's life. Not that she'd be volunteering to pet-sit for every lonely patient that crossed her path or else she'd end up befriending every cat lady in the city.

Both men were looking at her as though she were mad.

'You would do that?' Ray asked quietly, and it broke her heart to think that giving a few hours of her time to help him out was such a big deal to him.

'Yes.'

'That's settled. Ray, get back onto the bed, and Mae

and I will see to Brodie. Happy St Patrick's Day.' Liam grinned and she couldn't help but think he'd somehow got the better of her.

This had been a bad idea all around. At first Liam had found some satisfaction in the idea of the haughty American trying to wrangle his next-door neighbour's giant mutt. It didn't seem so funny now that she was encroaching into his personal space. With both of them heading the same direction, and having volunteered to look after Ray's beast of a dog, he hadn't had much choice but to travel back with her to pick up Shannon and head home.

'After you.' He held the pub door open for Mae, half-expecting a lecture about how she didn't need anyone holding doors open for her. Instead, she tipped her head to him and walked in as though it was her local, without a hint of trepidation.

'It's not what I expected,' she said, glancing around before taking a seat in one of the booths.

'No? Not enough diddly-dee music or leprechauns leaping about for you?' he teased.

On cue, the traditional Irish penny-whistle music his mother liked to put on for visitors suddenly filled the bar. Mae chuckled, her shoulders heaving with every laugh at his expense.

'It's for the tourists, you know,' he tried to explain, fighting to be heard above the piercing tunes and Mae's deep, warm laugh.

In other circumstances, he might have been embarrassed at being shown up like that. He'd had enough of being made to look foolish when his partner and his best friend had been carrying on an affair right under his nose. It had been difficult to face people in public after that, wondering who'd known, and if people had been laughing at him behind his back.

With Mae, it was different. This game of trying to get the better of one another was a private joke between them—one that he was in on, not the butt of—and so far, this one-upmanship was the basis of their newly formed relationship. For work purposes only, of course. He wasn't interested in anything else so soon after his recent heartbreak.

Apart from anything else, bristly Mae didn't seem the motherly type, and that was something he would definitely be looking for in a potential partner—a sign that he'd found a soul mate who wanted to settle down and emulate his parents' happy marriage, which he envied. He'd thought when Clodagh had fallen pregnant that that would be the beginning of his dream coming true. He'd not realised that, instead of finding someone who wanted to settle down, his partner was someone whose head would be turned by a flash surgeon who only cared about his own wants, with no guilty conscience about splitting up a family.

'Well, you can tell them I'm not a tourist. Not any more.' She fixed him with an intense stare, but beneath it he could see the hint of a smile. This was how they'd butted heads earlier, but thankfully she appeared to have forgiven him for being a clumsy big oaf. Still, it wouldn't hurt to butter her up, in case he needed her help in the future at the hospital, or during their spell of dog-sitting.

'What can I get you to eat and drink? I'm not sure we've got any of the green stout left but I'm sure we've still got some boiled bacon and cabbage.' He couldn't seem to help baiting her, although he knew to stay away from the matter of her own heritage. It was clearly a touchy subject, and no wonder, if she'd recently lost her mother. Liam's family were so supportive of him and Shannon, he'd feel as though he'd lost a limb if anything ever happened to either of his parents.

'I'm fine, thanks. If you just want to take me to Ray's house to meet the famous Brodie…' She clearly couldn't wait to get out of the place but he knew his mother would never forgive him if he didn't make an introduction. She'd be offended if he brought someone into the family business and she didn't have the opportunity to show off her hospitality skills.

'All in good time. There's no way my ma is going to let me go without a feed in me. Besides, I'll have to wait until Shannon has had her tea as well, before I can go. Now, what can I get you to drink?' He wouldn't dare to presume.

'White wine would be great, thank you,' she said, apparently resigned to the fact they were staying for dinner.

'Good choice.' Liam made his way over to the bar,

keen to put their order in before the crowds of hungry tourists descended in earnest after a day in the sunshine.

He also wanted to chat to his mother to explain the circumstances. As someone who was always pushing for him to meet someone else, it would be easy for her to get carried away with the idea Mae was someone more than a new work colleague, and he wanted to nip that notion in the bud.

'How's Shannon been?' he asked, helping himself to a chip out of the basket his father was just plating up with some tasty-looking steaks.

'She's upstairs with your mum having something to eat. I'm glad you're here; I need her down here to help me serve up the food.'

'Shannon?'

'Your mum, you eejit.' His father gave him a good-natured clout around the ear for winding him up. He was never too old to tease them, or for a slap when he deserved it.

'Can I get two plates of pie and champ?' His stomach was rumbling. Usually by now he'd have had sampled most things on the menu, but events had overtaken his appetite, and he hadn't eaten since breakfast.

'Two plates?'

'Yeah, I've got a new work colleague with me. We had to miss most of the parade to go to the hospital.'

'The girls said there'd been an accident. Everything

all right?' His father stopped stirring and slicing long enough to show his concern.

'Ray had one too many before he decided to head up the parade dressed as St Patrick, wearing stilts.'

The busy chef resumed his duties, shaking his head. 'I won't serve him in here any more. He's only hurting himself.'

'I know. I've had a chat with him and we're keeping him in overnight. Meanwhile, I'm helping to look after Brodie.'

His good deed earned a hearty laugh. 'Good luck with that.'

Liam helped himself to another chip. 'I know. Shannon will enjoy it, though. I'm just going to pop upstairs to see her and mum. We're sitting over at table two by the door—the redhead in the white coat.'

As Liam opened the swing door to go upstairs, his father leaned his head round to gawp at his companion, and gave an appreciative whistle and nod.

'She's a colleague, Da,' he reiterated before disappearing upstairs to repeat it all over again.

Mae sat people-watching whilst waiting for Liam to return to the table. It wasn't quite the quiet, reflective day she'd expected to have, but perhaps that wasn't a bad thing, when she'd started to spiral into grief, thinking about her mum before Liam and his daughter had rudely crashed into her self-pity.

She envied the jovial atmosphere the customers

exuded, standing at the bar, waiting impatiently for their drinks. Every now and then the general hubbub was interrupted with raucous laughter or cheering as those dressed head-to-toe in green, or sporting fake ginger beards, egged each other on in stupid drinking games. They were clearly here for 'the craic', as they said around these parts, whereas she'd come to the parade to reminisce about those fun days she'd had with her mother. At least battling with Liam and Ray had taken her mind off more depressing matters.

She watched a man dressed in chef whites walk over, older than the other members of staff behind the bar, carrying a glass of wine and a glass of something dark.

'Thank you.' She accepted the wine as he pushed it across the table but nearly choked on it when he sat down in the seat opposite.

'My boy tells me you work at the hospital.' Ah, so this was Mr O'Conner senior.

Although the realisation that this wasn't an ageing stranger hitting on her helped ease her anxiety a bit, it was clear he'd come to check her out on his son's behalf. She didn't want to be rude, or make a bad impression, but she certainly wasn't in the market for commitment with a man with a small child.

'Yes, I'm a liver specialist. I went with him to make sure Ray, his neighbour, was okay.'

'That's bad business, that,' he said, shaking his head. 'He hasn't been the same since his wife died. A bit like our Liam. Since Clodagh ran off with his best mate, he's focused all his attention on Shannon and work. I mean, he's always been a good dad, but he doesn't make any time for himself, you know. He's still young and, if the women swooning over him in here are anything to go by, he's still a catch, wouldn't you say so?'

It was easy to see where Liam got his charm from, as his father gave her his best crinkly-eyed smile and put her on the spot.

'I, er, yes, I suppose he is attractive.' There was no reason to deny it. She had eyes—the dark hair, blue eyes and hint of scruff around the jaw was certainly an arresting sight. It was when he opened his mouth she found herself spluttering to find words.

'That's nice to know. You're not too bad yourself.' Liam chose the optimum moment to embarrass her, in earshot of the compliment she'd been duped into giving. In that moment, she was too mortified to process the one he'd paid her in return.

He set a plate of food in front of her, and another on the other side of the table. 'Da, you're in my seat.'

His father got up, not a bit put out by the discourtesy of his offspring. 'Sorry, what's your name again?'

'Mae.'

'Nice to meet you, Mae. I'm Paddy.' He held out his hand and waited until she shook it.

'Hello, Paddy.'

'Are you married?'

'Okay, Dad, that's enough of the inquisition. We're just here to get a bite of dinner then go and see to the dog. Don't you have a dinner rush to see to? There's a queue of people waiting to be served over there.' Thankfully, Liam's distraction seemed to work as he drifted back over across the bar floor.

'Nice to meet you, Mae. Hope to see you again.'

She raised her glass to him but he'd already disappeared into the throng.

'My dad,' Liam explained a little too late as he dug heartily into his dinner.

'I figured. I didn't order any food, though.' She looked down at the mound of mashed potatoes and spring onions paired with a huge slice of juicy meat pie.

'I did. We haven't eaten all day, and my parents would never let you leave without a meal anyway. It's champ with steak and ale pie. Eat up.'

Mae poked at the chunks of beef in meaty gravy encased in flaky pastry and cautiously took her first forkful.

'It's delicious.' Though she didn't think she could finish the huge portion, there was no denying the rich, dark steak pieces and creamy mash were tasty.

'See. How long since you've had a home-cooked meal?' he asked once he'd swallowed down his mouthful.

'I cook,' she protested. 'But you know the hours are hectic. I suppose it's been a while since I made anything substantial.'

She had to admit she was more prone to batch cooking once in a wonder, then freezing the results. So, more often than not, dinner was zapped in the micro-wave after a long shift at the hospital.

'Now you know where to come. Especially if you're going to be in the neighbourhood seeing to Brodie.'

'Sure.' She had no intention of running the risk of seeing Liam or his family again. As nice as his father seemed to be, and his mother probably was, she didn't want to be involved in their happy family set-up. She'd been doing just fine on her own this past year.

They both tucked into their meals and Mae realised she was hungrier than she'd thought.

'Sorry about my dad, by the way. Mum will likely be the same. They're not used to me bringing anyone in here. Though I did tell them both we're merely work acquaintances.' He stopped eating long enough to press home the point, fixing her with those piercing eyes.

'It's fine. My mum used to be the same, always try-ing to marry me off to any eligible bachelor.' Perhaps that was why she'd jumped into an engagement so soon after her mother had passed, trying to fulfil her wishes that she'd find a man and settle down. Thank goodness she hadn't been alive to witness the debacle that had been her wedding day.

'I suppose he told you the whole sorry saga about me and Clodagh?' Although he asked the question casu-ally, Mae wasn't sure if he'd be hurt to know his father had indeed been telling a complete stranger about his failed relationship. She certainly wouldn't have wanted hers to be common knowledge. That was part of the reason she'd moved here, so she could be anonymous again, and not the poor, jilted fiancée who'd been left standing at the altar.

In the end she decided to be honest. It wasn't as though Paddy had gone into great detail about his son's personal life. He had no reason to. 'He just mentioned that she'd gone off with your best friend. Sorry.'

She was surprised when he smiled.

'It's not your fault Dad's a blabbermouth, or my partner and best friend were lying cheats. Most people at the hospital know anyway, so I'm sure you would've found out at some point. It's been a year—well, eleven months, two weeks and a day, to be precise. You'd think I'd be over it by now. Although, since we met in here during a karaoke night, it's hard not to think about her every time I set foot in this place.' He was trying to brush it off but Mae could hear the bitterness behind his words.

She recognised it. Although her ex hadn't cheated on her, as far as she was concerned he'd still betrayed her. He could have saved her the humiliation she'd felt in a church full of people they knew if he'd only had the courage to call things off before then. He'd taken some leave since, and actively avoided her, though she'd spotted him once or twice at work. He'd never offered a face-to-face apology, or a full explanation, other than a brief note to say sorry and that he simply wasn't ready for marriage. The actions of a coward she was glad she hadn't married in the end.

Once she'd got over the heartache of their relationship ending so abruptly, their future together being over without her having a say, she'd been left with a seething rage inside her. To this day she would find it hard not to punch him in the face, should she ever set eyes on him again. She wondered how Liam had restrained himself from doing the same to his so-called friend, or if indeed he had.

'It must have been very difficult. Especially when you had a daughter to think about.' Mae considered confiding about her own relationship disaster, so he didn't feel so bad about sharing, but it wasn't something she was ready to talk about yet when it was still so raw.

'At least one of us did,' he muttered under his breath.

'Does she see her mother?' It was none of her business, yet Mae found herself drawn to this little family. Probably because this was the most conversation she'd had outside of work in months.

'Not as often as she should, but it's a little awkward, I guess. She's still with Colm.'

'Ouch.'

'Yeah. Mum and Dad do the handovers every second weekend, so we don't have to see each other, but I know Colm, and he isn't a family man. I can't see him wanting to give up his Saturday nights out to watch cartoons and eat pizza with my daughter.'

'Sounds like my idea of a good time,' Mae joked, when she could see how difficult the whole situation was for Liam to talk about.

She was rewarded with that dazzling smile. 'Mine too. I suppose we'll get into a routine at some point and we'll find our "new normal". It's just taking a while to get used to.'

'When's the last time she saw Shannon?'

Liam screwed up his face, deep in thought, so she knew it hadn't been recently. 'About two months ago, I think. She took her to the cinema. Had her back by lunchtime.'

'At least Shannon still has her mother in her life. I know it must be difficult for you, but it's the best thing for her. I may not have children of my own, but I know what it's like to only have one parent in your life. My dad disappeared out of mine when I was little, so I never knew him. I don't even know what he looks like. I think that's what made losing mum harder— knowing I still have a parent out there, but one who doesn't want to be in my life. Shannon will appreciate you putting your own feelings to one side to accommodate the relationship she still has with her mother when she's older.'

Over the years, she'd sometimes blamed her mum for her father's absence, thinking she could have done more to keep him in their lives, or tried harder to find him. Deep down, Mae had to accept her father simply had no interest in having a daughter, and that was no one's fault but his.

At least Liam was trying to find a solution to his

change of circumstances. All she'd done about her problems was run away from them.

'I hope so. I need a reason for maintaining contact with Clodagh other than some ember of hope that we can still make things work and be that happy family I convinced myself we were.'

Her heart broke for him. That sudden thump of re-alisation that a relationship was over hurt badly, left a person dazed, confused and struggling to figure out what had happened. She couldn't imagine still having to see her ex twice a month and pretend as though he hadn't ripped her heart out and stomped on it. It was the reason she'd moved to the city in the first place. Liam was stronger and more courageous than she could ever hope to be. Or else he was simply just a good father.

The woman who'd identified herself as Shannon's grandmother when Mae had handed her over earlier appeared in the bar with the little girl. Both had Liam's amazing eyes and dark hair, though he'd obviously in-herited his height from his father's side of the family.

'You must be Mae. I'm Moira, Liam's mum. I think you already met Shannon.'

'Yes. Hi again, Shannon. It's good to see you both in nicer circumstances.' The last time she'd seen them, she'd been desperate to get away to treat the injured Ray lying in the middle of the parade. It had been a hasty explanation about how she'd been entrusted with Moira's granddaughter before she'd handed her over and disappeared into the melee.

'I hope he hasn't been making a nuisance of himself and showing us up.'

'Not at all. Liam has been very accommodating.' At least, he had since the hospital.

'You got something to eat and drink, then?'

'I did, thank you. It was delicious.' Mae's compliment drew a flush of pleasure to the woman's cheeks.

'You're welcome to stay for a few drinks. I don't mind Shannon staying overnight if you two want to hit the town.' Moira's gaze flicked between Mae and Liam and his sigh was audible.

'I've told both you and dad, we're just colleagues. Mae's only here to help out with Ray's dog. Now, have you got all of your stuff ready to go, Shannon?' Liam was on his feet, ready to go.

'Everything's in the bag and she's had her dinner.'

'Thanks, Mum.' Liam kissed his mother on the cheek and took the rucksack from her.

'Are we really going to see Brodie?' Shannon asked, her eyes wide with excitement.

'Yes, we need to feed him for Ray. Mae's coming with us, if that's okay? She's going to be looking after him for a while too.'

Mae just knew, if his daughter had had any objection to her being there, Liam wouldn't have hesitated to rule her out of the equation, quite rightly putting Shannon's feelings above all else. She admired that about him, even if there were other aspects of his personality which managed to irritate at times.

'Yay!' Shannon clapped her hands but Mae imagined that was more to do with her excitement over seeing the dog than her accompanying them.

Liam lifted his car keys. 'We're just a few minutes away. My car's parked around the corner.'

'You're driving?' Mae knew the fondness for alcohol on today of all days, and was surprised he'd take the chance of driving his daughter, even if he'd only had a couple of beers.

A puzzled frown marked his forehead. 'Yes. Why wouldn't I?'

'You've been drinking,' she spat out of the side of her mouth, so no one else would hear.

The frown deepened. 'Soft drinks only. Do you really think I would put my daughter in a car with me if I was drunk?'

Liam was almost shaking with the effort it was taking not to explode with rage. She could see it in the tension of his body, the set of his jaw and the flash of anger in his eyes.

She'd messed up.

'Sorry, I just thought with you spending so much time in the pub...' She trailed off, knowing there was no way of justifying the fact she'd jumped to conclusions.

'My Liam's not a big drinker, and I certainly wouldn't let him drive Shannon around if he was.' It appeared she'd managed to upset his mother too with her quick, inaccurate judgement. The last thing she wanted to do was offend the family when they'd been so warm and welcoming to her.

'I know; I'm sorry.'

'It doesn't matter. Come on, Shannon.' Despite his assurance it wasn't a matter worth dwelling on, Liam walked out of the pub without another word, pulling his daughter along by the hand.

'It was lovely to meet you. Thank you for your hospitality.' She gave Moira a weak, apologetic smile before following the pair out of the door.

As Liam buckled Shannon into her car seat in the back of the car, Mae waited patiently on the pavement to attempt another apology. Liam closed the door and turned to her.

'Okay, so now I can see why the stereotype thing was annoying. You're not just a Yank claiming she's Irish because her great-granny once ate some colcannon, and I'm not a drunken Irish lout. Can we start over?'

She was so relieved his anger had been short-lived, and that he'd owned up to being irritating to her this morning. It showed a strength of character she didn't usually come across. She doubted Liam was the sort of man who would have stood her up at the altar and let her find out their relationship was over at the same time as the rest of the congregation. He was the type to be upfront and honest, someone who wore his heart on his sleeve. If she ever thought about dating again, those were the first and foremost qualities she would look for in a potential partner.

But she wasn't, so it didn't matter. And why was she thinking about Liam and dating in the same context? He was a new work colleague, he had a daughter and he clearly got his kicks from pushing her buttons. Everything she should avoid at all costs.

She couldn't work out how she'd ended up in his car, with his daughter in the back seat, on her way to dog-sit for his neighbour, but she did know it was asking for trouble.

CHAPTER THREE

LIAM HESITATED BEFORE turning the key in the lock and took a deep breath, not sure what might be behind the door, or what he and Mae had got themselves in to.

'I have to admit, I haven't been inside Ray's house since his wife died. I have no idea what we might be walking into.'

'How bad can it be, right?' Mae shrugged but she was hanging back on the front step next to Shannon, waiting for him to take the first step inside.

They found out as soon as he opened the door. The stale smell of dog, beer and cigarettes hit them all at the same time.

'Wow.' Liam took a step back.

'Goodness.' Mae held her hand over her nose.

'It stinks in there,' Shannon declared very undiplomatically as she screwed up her nose.

'Let me go in and open a few windows.' The gloomy hall suggested Ray hadn't even opened the curtains, never mind the windows. He meant for Mae and Shannon to wait outside, but they followed him in, so he didn't have time to clear a path through the empty bottles, cans and post all lying in their path.

'He can't come back to this.' Mae began picking up the litter. 'Is there a recycling bin?'

'There should be one out the back. I'll go and get it.' Liam walked through the debris field in the kitchen to retrieve the recycling bin from the yard. The yard hadn't been looked after any better than the inside of the house, three-foot-high weeds sprouting from the cracks in the paving.

'Where's Brodie?' Shannon asked when he returned.

'I don't know. Maybe he's in the lounge. I'll check.' He left them filling the bin with the empties and braced himself for whatever else was in store.

The door was barely open before he found himself flat on his back with a hound licking his face enthusiastically.

'Brodie, I presume?' Mae was standing above him, not trying very hard to keep the smile off her face, whilst his daughter was laughing hysterically beside her.

'Uh-huh. Get off me, you stupid mutt.' It took some effort to prise the beast off him so he could stand, only to have Brodie jump up on him again, his huge paws landing on Liam's shoulders.

'He's not a mutt, he's gorgeous.' Mae ruffled Brodie's scruffy grey fur, earning her a new fan.

'I suppose we should feed him. I'll show you where

everything is then you can go. Shannon and I will walk him.'

Mae's frown stopped him from planning the rest of the rota.

'I'm not going to go now and leave you to tidy this place on your own. We can hardly let Ray come back to this. It's certainly not going to do anything to improve his mood.'

'I can't ask you to clean up this mess.'

'You didn't. I volunteered.'

He was surprised someone as well turned out as Mae would even offer to dirty her hands in a stranger's house. If he'd known it was this bad, he would never have brought her here. In future, he was going to have to keep a closer eye on his neighbour, who obviously wasn't coping well on his own.

'Okay. Shannon, can you play with him while we're in the kitchen?' He didn't have to ask twice. She was already digging into the pile of dog toys in the corner and throwing them for Brodie, who was quick to switch his loyalty.

'Will she be all right with him?' Mae hovered in the doorway, apparently reluctant to leave the scene.

'He's a big softy, honestly. She plays with him all the time. I wouldn't leave her in there otherwise.' Liam was doing his best not to take offence, as it seemed his parenting was being questioned once more, and chose instead to believe Mae was simply concerned.

'I know. Sorry.'

As far as he could tell, she worried a lot about other people. Why else would she be here now, helping to clean a patient's house? Ray wasn't her friend or neighbour, just someone she knew was having some trouble at home. They'd all been complete strangers to her until this morning and there weren't many people who would have got involved outside of their work commitments. It showed she had a big heart, and was possibly as lonely as he was, if she had nothing better to do with her evening.

She hadn't mentioned having to get home to anyone, not even a pet—something most people would've used as an excuse to get out of cleaning, and he wouldn't have blamed her if she had. It was different for him: he knew Ray. He should have realised there was more going on other than him drinking one too many and too frequently. As a doctor, he should have seen the signs of depression, which had obviously set in after his partner had walked out, and the potential signs of liver disease. Perhaps he had been too wrapped up in his own problems and self-pity to notice. Now Mae had helped him to peel back the layers to see what was going on behind the scenes, he felt as though he had a duty to be a better friend and neighbour to Ray.

'So, Brodie's food is in this cupboard, his food bowl stays in the kitchen and his water bowl in the living room.' Liam set about filling the bowl before starting in on the kitchen clean-up.

Mae was brushing up the dog hairs littering the

floor whilst he began the mammoth task of washing the dishes. It looked as though Ray had used every plate and glass in the cupboard without ever thinking to clean one. He shuddered at the thought of whatever germs lingered on the cluttered, dirty surfaces.

'You're quite the domestic god, aren't you?' Mae teased as he scrubbed the pots clean.

'I've had to be, since it's just me and Shannon at home. It wouldn't be fair to have her growing up in this sort of mess. Doing the dishes was always my depart-ment, anyway. Clodagh was afraid of breaking a nail. Although, I will admit to buying a dishwasher since she left; I'm not super-human.'

With only him doing the household chores and tak-ing care of Shannon, he'd had to make better use of his time, as well as asking for help from his parents when he'd needed it. Despite trying to do everything on his own at first, it had soon become apparent that he couldn't juggle parenting and work all on his own.

'I have a dishwasher and I live on my own. Time's too precious in between shifts to waste it washing dirty plates,' replied Mae. That answered one question, at least, though Liam couldn't help but push for more. After all, she'd learned more about his family circum-stances over the course of one day than most people who knew him. He only thought it fair he should know a little more about her too.

'So, what are you doing, wasting it here? It's your day off; you should be out celebrating somewhere.' He wasn't blind, or stupid. Mae was an attractive, success-ful, caring woman. There had to be men, and women, desperate to spend time with her. Liam was sure it wasn't a lack of interest that was keeping her in the singles market and wondered what had happened to make her think it was a better choice than being with someone. It was certainly to do with heartache: he knew the symptoms.

'I've not long moved to the city. I don't know many people yet, and to be honest I'm after a quiet life these days. The past months have been a little fraught, to say the least.' That sad look in her eyes, the sigh of res-ignation and her apparent need to hide away from the world suggested a recent break-up. He'd gone through the same stages after Clodagh and he wondered if she'd reached the rage part of the process yet.

'Oh? New start in the big smoke?' That was one thing they didn't have in common. Born in Dublin, Liam had lived there his entire life, and had never wanted to live anywhere else—except when Clodagh had left, when the moon wouldn't have been far enough away for him to be from she and Colm, his so-called best friend.

Mae, on the other hand, seemed a more adventurous soul, having travelled from America in the first place. He couldn't imagine moving to a different country and not knowing anyone, not having that support system which had got him through some of the darkest days of his existence. Whatever had happened, it must have been serious enough for her to leave what was familiar to her to start all over again in another country.

'Yeah, but not in the exciting "Boston girl moves to Dublin" way you probably think it is. I didn't get sick of the country life, it got sick of me.' She gave a half-hearted attempt at a smile and Liam could almost feel the pain it caused her even to fake it. Kind of like when he'd promised Shannon everything was going to be all right, and desperately tried to hold things together at the same time.

'You want to talk about it?' It had taken him a couple of days before he'd admitted to himself, never mind anyone else, that Clodagh had walked out on him. But, when he had finally confided in his parents, it had been a relief to share the burden—to spill all the hurt and betrayal he'd felt, his fears for the future and worries about Shannon. They'd helped to quell the panic in him, promising to help where they could, and that was when the tide had begun to turn. He'd been able to see a future, albeit different from the one he'd planned with Clodagh. Eventually he'd managed to get some semblance of a life back together, even though the scars would always remain.

Although he couldn't promise to do as much for Mae as his parents had done for him, he hoped a listening ear might go some way to easing the pain. She deserved some help after everything she was doing for Ray.

'No. Yes.' This time he knew the smile was for him. 'I think it's only fair, when you've had all the gory details of my relationship laid bare in the space of a few hours. It puts me on something of a back foot when we're going to be working at the same hospital...'

'I would never say anything!' She had such a look of horror on her face at the mere suggestion she would use any personal information against him that he had to confess, it was simply another attempt to get a rise out of her. He couldn't seem to help himself.

'I'm joking. It's my defence mechanism when I think things are getting too serious. Probably part of the reason Clodagh had enough of me. She always said I needed to grow up. How ironic is that, when she left the father of her daughter to run off with the hospital playboy?' His thoughts began to drift back to the shadows of the past and he was grateful when Mae scooped some suds from the sink and flicked them at him. A distraction from his relationship woes was always welcome.

'I must remember that. It'll save me from losing my temper with you so often.' She nudged his elbow with hers so he could see she hadn't taken offence—this time.

'I am serious about offering a shoulder to lean on. Here, have this one; I'm not using it at the minute.' He slouched one shoulder down and she leaned her head on it for a split second before they both burst out laughing.

It felt good to do that again—to have a brief moment of happiness when he wasn't worrying, or over-thinking. And it was nice to have someone to do it with, even if

Mae was only here because of Ray. If it hadn't been for the accident and her insistence on being involved, he doubted she would even have spoken to him again unless forced into it.

Mae's laughter soon turned back into another sigh. 'It's hard, isn't it, to just pick up and move on? How do they do it? Where do they get the audacity to ruin someone's life and walk away without a care in the world?' Now she really was beginning to get riled, and he was glad this time it wasn't because of something he'd done. That fiery red hair certainly matched her temper, that feisty nature revealing more about her Irish heritage than her DNA.

'I guess some people just don't have a conscience.' He could never have lived with the guilt of cheating on Clodagh, never mind walking away and leaving her to raise their daughter alone. From what he could tell in the short time he'd known Mae, she would never have acted that way either, when she couldn't even imagine letting Ray walk back into a dirty house.

She was quiet for a moment, as if debating internally whether or not to share something. Gazing out of the window, not meeting his eye, she spoke so softly he nearly missed it. 'I was jilted at the altar. Literally.'

Liam didn't know what to say; it was such a shockingly cruel thing to have suffered. He supposed this was how she'd felt when she'd heard about Clodagh's betrayal. No words seemed adequate to convey just how sorry he was that this had happened to her.

'That's awful. I thought that only happened in films. You know, the ones where the heroine gets her revenge in the final act and her deadbeat ex gets his comeuppance?' He didn't know how else to make things right for someone who clearly deserved to be treated better, other than to try and make her smile.

Liam had hoped the image of her ex losing everything, or being humiliated in a similar fashion, would ease the pain a little, but it didn't.

'I wish. Unfortunately, I'm still in the "licking my wounds" phase.'

Sometimes, in his low moments, he fantasised about his ex-best friend being dumped for someone more exciting and carefree to see how he liked it. Not that it achieved anything other than to put Liam in a bad mood. He hadn't reached the stage where he wished any harm to the mother of his daughter, and he wasn't sure he ever would. He was probably still in love with the idea of the little family they'd been, rather than Clodagh. He also had to accept some of the blame for their relationship breaking down, he supposed. The fact he'd remained oblivious to her seeing his friend right under his nose said how little they'd communicated, or had even been involved in each other's lives.

In hindsight, they'd been ships that passed in the night at times, his shifts often clashing with Clodagh's work at the local hotel, though he'd never know if that was intentional or not. He'd been under the mistaken impression they were still working as a team and hadn't realised she was unhappy after eight years together. Perhaps he simply hadn't wanted to believe it, if it would have meant admitting his family wasn't as perfect as he'd imagined. Clodagh had had a point about him never growing up when he'd still believed in the fairy tale and the happy-ever-after, thinking it happened by magic. Not that it took work and communication to maintain a healthy, happy relationship. He was only realising that now, too late.

'It passes—eventually. I'm so sorry he put you through that. Assuming he wasn't a cruel man who intended to embarrass you, I can only assume he simply didn't have the balls to tell you he didn't want to get married. I'm sure it wasn't anything you'd done, or deserved. He must just have left it too late to fix things and you suffered as a result. I think I'm guilty of doing the same thing with Clodagh—ignoring the strains in our relationship until it finally snapped and there was no way of fixing things. By the time I had to face reality, she'd already moved on.'

'Were you married?'

He shook his head. 'I proposed several times, but she said she didn't need a bit of paper to verify our relationship; that having Shannon was proof enough, even though we hadn't planned her. I suppose not wanting to get hitched to me was a blessing in disguise, or a sign she never intended to stick around—I'll never be sure. But I wanted the wedding, and thought we'd even add to our family some day. I guess we were both on different wavelengths. I wanted to settle down and commit, Clodagh was looking for a way out. I just didn't want to see it.'

Mae was listening intently, and he realised giving her a shoulder to lean on had also made him take a closer look at what had happened to Clodagh and him. Yes, she'd broken his heart along with his trust, but there had been signs. On occasion she'd tried to arrange date nights for them to 'talk' on the rare evenings they'd both been at home, but more often than not he'd spent that time at his parents' place. Talking about his feelings hadn't been his strong point—at least up until they'd been ground into the dust. When Clodagh had given up asking him, he'd assumed she was okay with the close relationship he had with his family. That was probably when she'd given up on them, and had moved on to his so-called best friend.

Mae shrugged. 'Perhaps we're both just romantics at heart. Both oblivious to any problems because it would ruin the fantasy. I think the reason I got so upset when you called me out about moving here to find myself a husband was because it was true. I was lost without my mum and, when I met Diarmuid at a medical conference, he represented everything I was missing in my life. I followed him back to Ireland looking for something to fill that void. It was asking too much, apparently, putting pressure on him that he couldn't handle. I learned my lesson about relying on anyone but myself for my own happiness.'

There was a resignation in Mae's voice that he knew was a defence mechanism because he'd just built one himself, determined not to let another person close enough to inflict that level of damage to his heart ever again. He wasn't sure how long he could sustain it, when his tragic heart still held out hope for that happy family he'd always longed for.

'You deserve more, you know.' He stopped washing the dishes to turn and look at her properly, trying to instil his sincerity and that belief into her psyche, willing it to go beyond the insecurities her ex had left behind.

She gave him a wobbly smile. 'We both do.'

Perhaps it was the proximity to one another, or that recognition of one wounded soul finding another, but something seemed to happen between them—as if a switch had been flicked, awareness suddenly crackling between them. Liam knew she was beautiful but in that moment he saw her frailty, her vulnerability, and he found himself inexplicably drawn to her. Especially those sweet lips she'd just parted with the tip of her tongue, as if waiting for him to show her the tenderness she did deserve.

For a moment it seemed to him that the only sound in the room was of their breathing, rapid and ragged. Anticipation and expectation filled the air between them. He was going to kiss her, he wanted to kiss her…and her eyes and lips said she wanted him to kiss her.

Then he heard Brodie bark, Shannon laugh and he came back down to earth with a bump. He'd only met this woman this morning; he had a daughter to think about, and he couldn't go around kissing random women in front of her. She'd been through enough turmoil, for him to start confusing her like that. It wasn't as though he even wanted to start a new relationship with anyone, so kissing Mae was a really bad idea— as tempting as it was.

He stepped back without saying a word and saw Mae compose herself again, the moment over.

They continued with their chores in silence, the unburdening of their souls, and their almost kiss, clearly taking its toll. If he was honest, he was a little embarrassed to have revealed so much personal information to someone he'd only met, and he suspected Mae felt the same way, even if they'd both clearly needed to vent. It was also probably the reason they'd nearly kissed, finding a solace in one another that they hadn't had with anyone else since having their hearts broken.

It was a relief when Shannon and Brodie came charging through the door, breaking the awkward atmosphere that had settled in the kitchen.

'When can we go home, Dad? I'm tired.'

'Very soon. I've just got to feed Brodie.'

'Why don't I do that and let you get Shannon to bed? I can take Brodie for a walk before I go home.' Mae was giving him an excuse to leave, and Liam would take it. He needed some time to regroup, to think about what he had told Mae and, more importantly, why. It was clear they had a lot in common, despite initial impressions, but he didn't want to get into some kind of dysfunctional therapy-based relationship where, every time they saw one another, they'd lapse into introspection about their break-ups, bemoaning their exes…or thinking they'd found the solution with their lips. It wasn't going to help either of them move on.

'You can leave the key under the mat for me when we're done. I'll see to him in the morning.' Then, hopefully they'd only see each other in passing at the hospital.

For someone who'd sworn never to let anyone into his heart again, he'd opened the door wide enough for her to have a peek inside after just one day of getting to know one another. He couldn't afford any more slip-ups.

CHAPTER FOUR

MAE HAD AN emotional hangover. She hadn't slept well and, quite frankly, felt ill thinking about how much she'd shared with Liam yesterday. And what she'd almost shared. It would be easy to put her effusive diatribe about her marital humiliation down to it having been an emotional day for her personally. She'd been upset about having the first St Patrick's Day without her mum, and in her home town.

However, deep down, she knew the reason she'd told Liam all the gory details was because he was another jilted unfortunate. The circumstances might have been different, but they'd both been left hurt, scarred by the betrayal of their trust. In her defence, he had spilled the gossip on his doomed relationship first, and she'd known he wouldn't judge her for having been rejected so publicly. Her greatest fear was that other people would side with her ex, believing he'd had a lucky escape, and that there must have been something wrong with her for him to have walked out on their wedding day.

If anything, Liam had made her see the fault had

been on both sides. He'd accepted some of the guilt for not having seen the signs his relationship had been in trouble and, when she looked back, she could say the same. She'd been the one making all the wedding preparations; Diarmuid had never really got involved. Talk about their future had been a one-sided affair at times, and she'd put that down to cultural differences—Irish men weren't really known for being great at expressing their feelings. Well, she'd been partly right—he simply hadn't been able to tell her he wasn't ready for marriage.

Yesterday had been a revelation. Once they'd got over their first meeting, talking to Liam had felt like talking to a friend. It had been therapeutic, in a way. Being able to confide in him was akin to the valve in a pressure cooker being released. It was as though all the hurt, rage and confusion she'd been left with these past months finally had somewhere to go and it had all come pouring out—unfortunately for Liam. She'd clearly mistaken his empathy for something more and thought he was going to kiss her at one point, embarrassing them both. In the end, she could sense he'd been glad of the excuse to get away from her when she'd offered to walk the dog.

So she didn't understand why he was at Ray's bedside now, knowing she'd be here.

'I know visiting time's over but I sweet-talked the nurses into letting me see Ray. Please don't chuck me out.' He batted long, dark eyelashes at her, which were almost as mesmerising as the bright blue eyes they framed.

She held up her hands. 'I'm just here to give Ray an update.'

'You can say whatever it is that has put that frown on your face in front of Liam. He's the only visitor I've had.' Despite the circumstances, Ray didn't appear to be feeling too sorry for himself. Rather, he seemed resigned to the bad news she'd come to deliver. It was the part of Mae's job she detested, but all too familiar in her line of work. Liver problems weren't often fixed with a prescription and a bandage.

She pulled the curtain around the bed to afford him some privacy and took a seat at his bedside. 'As you know, Mr Jackson—'

'Ray,' he corrected.

'As you know, Ray, we had some concerns about your liver function so we ran some blood tests. Unfortunately, the results of those tests suggest there's something serious, called alcoholic hepatitis, going on. We would like to do an ultrasound to get a better idea of what we're dealing with before we proceed in case there are any complications with the condition, and to rule out things like gallstones. You're also suffering from malnutrition. Alcohol suppresses the appetite, so you're not getting a well-balanced diet. We want to keep you here a little longer for investigation and to make sure you're well enough to go home.'

Ray nodded his head sagely. 'Am I dying?'

'We're nowhere near that conclusion. For now, we just need to see what's happening inside, then we can put a treatment plan in place. At this moment in time, there is no cause for alarm. If you're able to stop drinking completely, the liver can regenerate itself and undo a lot of the damage. We will refer you to a dietitian and a counsellor to help with that.' Although there was clearly an issue, it wasn't going to help having Ray worrying about it. They needed to keep him calm in the meantime.

'What about Brodie? I can't lie about here knowing he's at home alone.'

'He's grand, Ray. Dr Watters and I have been checking in on him. I'm sure another couple of days won't make much difference.' Liam looked to Mae for confirmation that they could make it work, given they both knew how serious Ray's situation could become if left to continue untreated—perhaps even fatal. It was something neither of them would want on their conscience, even if it meant the two of them coming into proximity outside of work for a while longer.

When she realised she'd hesitated too long, she spat out a quick, 'Of course. We'll look after him. I'll go around once my shift is done. He's no trouble at all.'

A little white lie she felt was needed in this situation.

'You rest up, Ray, and don't worry.' Liam rose at the same time as Mae.

'Easier said than done,' Ray grumbled.

'We'll do our best to take care of you, and Brodie,' Mae promised as she left him to rest.

Liam waited for her in the corridor. 'I didn't know it was so serious, otherwise we could have at least provided him with some proper meals.'

It was clear he was feeling guilty, but Mae knew he'd been too busy going through his own personal problems to keep track of his neighbour's health too.

'Does he have any family? I don't see any listed in his file but perhaps you know of someone who could be with him? It might not be a bad idea to have someone close by. He'll need support to give up drinking altogether.'

'None that I know of. He never had any children, and he's never mentioned family. That's probably why he fell apart after his wife died. She was all he had.'

Mae could see how he'd fallen into despair so easily. At least she'd had work to distract her after losing her mum and Diarmuid in the space of a year. If she'd been stuck in the house alone day after day, she might very well have succumbed to the melancholy in some form or another. Losing a loved one affected so many aspects of a person's life, even their personality; she considered grief an illness in itself.

'I guess it's up to us, then.' She didn't see any way to disentangle herself from the situation now. She and Liam were inextricably linked, at least for the duration of Ray's hospital admission. Perhaps even after, depending on whatever ongoing treatment he needed.

Ray might find he was too exhausted after all his appointments to give Brodie the exercise he needed. Liam had admitted he needed extra help to manage Shannon and work, so it would be asking too much to expect him to do everything on his own, especially when Mae had no other commitments. After yesterday's heart to heart, he was aware she had no life outside of work, so she couldn't very well cry off helping now without it seeming as though she was avoiding him. Which was what she would prefer, given all that she'd shared with him last night. It would have been nice to have some breathing room, a little time and space for him to forget the most humiliating details of her personal life, and nearly kissing him, before they'd been thrown together again.

'Sorry. I know I should have asked before volunteering us both for Brodie duty again, but if I hadn't he'd have tried to discharge himself.'

'Not a problem. It's not as though I have anything else to do with my time off than keep an Irish Wolfhound company.' It was absurd, really, that a dog had a better social life than a city doctor but she supposed that had been her decision.

Since moving here only a couple of weeks ago, she'd cocooned herself in her apartment to protect herself from any other men with the capacity to break her heart. Like all her recent decisions, it probably hadn't been the best idea. She hadn't taken that time to meet new acquaintances and now she had no one to call for a chat, or with whom to go for a coffee. Perhaps she'd have to rethink her hermit lifestyle and try to make a few friends in her new job. Otherwise, she was going to have a very small social circle to call on when she needed company, which only included a single father and a needy hound.

'Thanks. Listen, about last night...'

Mae's insides bunched together at the mere mention of their time together, the thought of everything they'd shared in that kitchen coming back to haunt her. 'Let's not talk about it ever again.'

Liam gave a hearty laugh. 'Yeah, it was a bit full-on. I just wanted to say that I'm not usually so...open. I don't want things to be awkward between us when we'll probably see each other here at the hospital from time to time, and now that we're Brodie's full-time carers for the foreseeable future. Rest assured, I won't bend your ear every time I see you about my tragic personal life. That's not me.'

He omitted all mention of the almost-kiss and she was grateful. Hopefully they could put it behind them and pretend it had never happened.

'No, you're more likely to tease me until I lose my temper.' She couldn't resist putting him in his place about their first interaction which seemed much longer than only yesterday—though she was relieved to find Liam was also obviously having regrets over sharing so much yesterday. They'd clearly both needed to talk and had simply found themselves in a moment of weakness. She didn't think either of them would make the same mistake again.

Liam grimaced. 'You're never going to let me live that one down, are you?'

'No.' Not when she enjoyed seeing him squirm.

'Ouch. I guess I deserve it. Anyway, I guess I'll see you tonight.'

'Tonight? I thought it was my turn with Brodie. Aren't you working?'

'Not tonight. My, er, mother has invited you over for dinner. I know, I know, I told her we're just friends, barely even colleagues. I also made the mistake of telling her you're new to the area, and don't know many people here yet, so having a meal with the family is mandatory. Sorry.'

Mae could see from his eyes and the furrowed brow he wasn't any happier than she was about the situation but they were both committed to the event now. If he hadn't issued the invitation, his parents would have been upset, and if she declined they'd be offended. It seemed they were destined to spend another evening in one another's company.

'Hmm. Well, I'll agree on the basis that any talk about exes is off the table. I've done enough soul searching to last a lifetime, so I'd like to just enjoy a nice meal with your family without even thinking about Diarmuid.'

'Done.' Liam held out his hand for her to shake. 'Although, I can't speak for my mother…'

Her washing-machine stomach churned at the prospect of her having been jilted on her wedding day becoming dinner conversation for Liam's whole family. If they were anything like him, they had absolutely no tact or boundaries. Not a good match for a sensitive, self-confessed hermit.

'Thanks for inviting me over, Mr and Mrs O'Conner.' Mae handed over a lovely bouquet of pastel-coloured flowers to his mother, instantly earning her mega brownie points from his already over-keen parents.

Liam had been fielding questions since last night about where she lived, who her parents were and, most importantly to them, if she was single, and if so why. Not that he told them any of the personal information Mae had entrusted him with. He certainly wouldn't have appreciated her sharing anything he'd told her in confidence with anyone else, even if his parents had no such qualms.

'It's lovely of you to come. Doesn't Mae look beautiful, Paddy?' Whilst his mother brought a blush to their guest's cheeks, his father was battling the embarrassment of having to pay someone a compliment.

'Aye. Grand,' he muttered, before shuffling away into the kitchen in the flat above the bar.

Dressed casually in jeans and an off-the-shoulder white fluffy sweater, red wavy hair tumbling loose and wearing a pair of cowboy boots, Mae was beautiful. She also couldn't have looked more American if she'd tried.

Liam could understand why his parents were not so subtly pushing to get them together. On paper she was everything a man could want—beautiful, smart, successful; the list went on and on. It was just a shame neither of them was interested in a relationship after having been so badly burned by their last ones. Not that he was probably even her type, when she found him so irritating. Given what he'd heard about her ex, he imagined Mae's type was all talk no action, cowed by a successful, confident woman and clearly afraid of commitment—about as far removed from Liam's personality as possible.

None of which would dissuade his parents from believing that they should at least try—for his sake and Shannon's. Their belief that all he needed to move on from Clodagh's betrayal was another woman was jarring to say the least. As childhood sweethearts who'd been together for decades, they would never understand what it was like to have their heart ripped out the way he'd had. He was playing along tonight to keep them happy, but had made another attempt to convince them they were merely acquaintances before Mae's arrival.

It hadn't been a fun task, asking her over after last night, and he'd been afraid things would be awkward. Apart from their deep and meaningful conversation, he didn't want her to think he was pushing for more, either romantically or in terms of reaping added personal information. Thankfully Ray had given him an excuse to be in her department, at least, giving them more reason to spend time together. Liam was glad he and Mae had managed to get over any embarrassment and had made an agreement to veto any further talk about exes to make this evening bearable.

'You sit there beside Liam, Mae. Shannon, you sit beside me and Paddy can go at the end of the table.' His mother issued orders for the seating plan at the table in the small living room, leaving Mae and him exchanging a knowing look that said they'd go along with this to keep the peace.

'You really didn't need to go to all this trouble for me!' Mae exclaimed as his father loaded the table with dishes of chips, mash and veg, along with a selection of roast meats. A typical Sunday dinner, especially made midweek for their visitor.

'Liam said you've just moved to the city. This is our way of welcoming you,' his mother insisted as she took Mae's plate and filled it for her.

'But you fed me last night!' Mae laughed.

'Now you're a regular.'

Liam didn't even bother to hide the smirk on his face. His mother had an answer for everything when it came to getting her own way. Now Mae would see how they'd both ended up here tonight again.

She didn't argue any more, simply digging in to the mountain of food which was handed to her. She was learning fast. 'Well, thank you, Mrs O'Conner. You've certainly made me feel welcome.'

'Moira, please.'

'You need some veg, Shannon.' When he spied his daughter's plate consisted mostly of chips, Liam piled on some broccoli, much to Shannon's disgust.

'Don't you just love these?' Mae speared a floret on her fork and studied it intently. 'It's like eating mini trees.' She popped the whole thing in her mouth and chomped down.

Liam observed his daughter watching the whole thing, then she very slowly lifted a piece of broccoli to her lips and bit down. A couple of mouthfuls later, and the whole thing was gone. It was the first time in weeks she hadn't had a temper tantrum at the table when he'd tried to get her to eat anything remotely healthy.

He blamed himself for his daughter's predilection for junk food. When Clodagh had first left, he couldn't face cooking or eating, and it had been easier to order a takeaway for Shannon. Then he'd been trying to over-compensate for all the turmoil she'd gone through in the separation, letting her make her own meal choices for a sense of control and comfort. He'd wanted her to be happy, and he hadn't wanted to be the bad guy, forc-ing her to eat something she didn't like. However, as a doctor, he knew all too well that that would lead to con-sequences later on and meal times had become some-thing of a battleground lately. Something not aided by his mother, who liked to spoil her only grandchild too.

Apparently, all he'd needed was an attractive stranger to make her think there was fun to be had in eating broccoli and she would be converted. He wouldn't complain, but he did wonder if he now needed to have Mae in attendance for all meal times. A good female role model wasn't to be underestimated and, though his mother spent a lot of time with Shannon, he wondered if he would have to rethink his current bachelor status if he was going to avoid further clashes with his daughter. She had yet to hit puberty, when there'd be those turbulent teenage years to come...

Mae gave him a wink across the table and he offered a smile in return, until he noticed his mother watching their interaction. Not wishing to give her any more false hope, he instead focused on clearing his plate.

'How's Ray? Liam said you'll be looking after that dog of his for another few days.'

Liam was relieved his mother's line of questioning wasn't focused on Mae's relationship status, at least.

Mae finished swallowing her food before she answered. 'Yes. We're going to be keeping him in to run a few more tests.'

He knew Mae, as Ray's doctor, wouldn't be comfortable sharing details of her patient's condition without his consent, so he did it for her. 'Ray's in a bad way, Ma. The drinking has caught up with him and he has liver damage. We'll know better once he's had an ultrasound to see how bad he is, and what treatment he'll need.'

He could see the news had shocked his parents, his mother crossing herself and promising to pray for him. His father remained silent but he knew he was simply processing the news. Sometimes it was difficult for his dad to reconcile how he and his mum made their living with the serious drinking culture that seemed to dominate the area. Although Liam knew they didn't serve those who had an obvious problem, some people, like Ray, hid it better, and his family shouldn't feel responsible for grown adults making the wrong decisions.

'Is he going to die, Daddy? What will happen to Brodie?' Shannon, who had been sitting quietly absorbing the conversation around her, now voiced her worries.

'We're going to give Ray the best treatment we can, that's why he has to stay in the hospital for a while longer. So we can make him better.' Mae chose her words carefully, trying to reassure Shannon things would be okay.

Neither of them could promise that Ray wouldn't die if he didn't stop drinking and, as much as Liam wanted to stop Shannon from worrying, it wasn't fair to give her false hope. It could make things more difficult in the long wrong if something did go wrong, and losing his daughter's trust would kill him.

'Mae's his doctor, so you know she'll take good care of him, and we'll look after Brodie for as long as we're needed. We won't leave either of them alone, okay?'

'Thanks, Daddy.' Shannon leaned across to give him a hug, so he knew just how much that meant to her.

He found himself welling up, not only at his daughter's compassion for their neighbour, but also at her display of affection towards him. Sometimes he really just needed a hug—another reminder that being on his own for the rest of his life wasn't something he wanted. One day he'd have to take that chance and risk his heart in the hope the gamble paid off. That he'd get that happy family he'd always dreamed about.

'Don't you worry your head, sweetheart. Mae and your dad will look after Ray, and Brodie,' his mother promised.

Shannon finished her meal, then asked to play games on his phone, and he was pleased that their combined efforts to reassure her everything would be okay appeared to have had the desired effect. He supposed it was better that she'd asked rather than keeping her concerns to herself, but he realised he'd have to be more careful about what he said around her. She'd seen and heard more than she should at her age. Liam was ashamed to admit he hadn't reacted well when he'd discovered Clodagh's cheating, and there had been rows before she'd left. He was trying to make up for it, to be a better father to Shannon, and that meant protecting her from other people's problems where he could. She didn't need to worry about things that were beyond her control.

He could also do with taking a leaf out of his own book. Clodagh had made her decision, and what he'd done, or hadn't done, to contribute to that decision no longer mattered. There was nothing to be gained from continually castigating himself about the past. It was more important to think about the future and the life he and Shannon could still have. Just because things hadn't worked out between her mother and him, it didn't translate they could never have a happy family again with someone else.

What it did mean was that he had to be open to another relationship, had to be brave enough to open his heart again and make sure it was someone who wouldn't hurt his daughter or him again. It was a lot to ask, and a lot of that responsibility to make another relationship work would weigh heavily on his shoulders when he knew he'd been part of the problem in the failure of his relationship with Clodagh.

His talk last night with Mae had at least opened his eyes to the things he could've done differently, so hopefully he would learn for the future. If he'd only been able to talk to Clodagh the way he had with Mae—with honesty and by digging deep into those emotions he'd been afraid to voice out loud for so long—they might have been able to salvage their relationship. Now he could only hope he'd use what he'd learned about himself to improve a relationship he was yet to have.

The next step was to put himself out there again, show willing when it came to dating again—though he was worried that he might end up unravelling about his ex, the way he had with Mae, and put off any potential partners. He was lucky she'd even agreed to come here tonight, but he supposed that was only because they'd both made it clear that it was out of a sense of duty rather than a wish to be with each other. He was safe with Mae.

At least with her he didn't have to pretend he was holding it all together; he wasn't under pressure to impress or perform. Mae had seen him at his most raw, wallowing in self-pity and recriminations. Far from scaring her off, she'd been able to empathise with his situation. And she'd still agreed to come tonight. She must be as lonely as he was.

Despite her initial reservations about accepting Moira's and Paddy's invitation to dinner, Mae had enjoyed it. It was nice to be part of a warm, loving family, even for a little while, and they had made her feel as though she belonged there. It didn't seem to matter that she was an American stranger to them, with no romantic links or otherwise to their family. As an acquaintance of Liam, she'd been accepted regardless, and had been regaled with stories, jokes and an evening of excellent company. She was almost sad to leave, knowing she was going back to a house where she left the TV on constantly simply so there was some noise other than the sound of her own thoughts.

It was this need to replace the comfort of the little family she'd had with her mum that had most likely led her into her relationship with Diarmuid. A rebound of sorts, trying to replace one love in her life with another.

It probably would never have worked long term, because Diarmuid could never have adequately filled the void her mother's death had left inside her. He hadn't been right for her, and eventually she would have seen it too. It just happened that Diarmuid had realised it first, even if he had gone the wrong way about breaking up with her.

Diarmuid had represented an escape from her grief, planning their marriage and future together at a time when she'd been afraid she'd never have one, fearful that she'd be on her own for ever. Now she had to accept once more that that was the more likely scenario than that she'd ever trust enough to share her life, and her heart, with anyone again.

After her father and Diarmuid walking out on her, she didn't trust another man not to do the same. No one could guarantee she wouldn't end up alone and heartbroken again. She'd seen it with her mother time and time again: her dating, falling in love then being left when the man had grown tired of the relationship, until she'd been left alone to deal with her illness. Mae had been there for her, of course, juggling her medical career with her mother's needs, but she'd seen how upset her mum had been because she'd been let down again. Her latest beau had bailed out on her once he'd known she would need a lot of care.

If she did ever date again, it would be a casual thing, in which she wouldn't hand over her heart and trust someone not to stomp it into the ground when they tired of her. She needed to protect herself.

Still, that didn't mean she didn't miss the cosy atmosphere of a family dinner. She'd only known the O'Conners for a couple of days but they were becoming a familiar part of her new life in Dublin. It wouldn't be easy just to walk away and pretend they'd never crossed paths. She would always be drawn here any time she was in this part of the city. Whilst there was no problem in dropping in every now and then to say hi, she had to make sure she didn't confuse her relationship with Liam with her longing to belong…again.

However, Shannon was yawning, and she couldn't very well stay on after Liam went home just to feel part of something again.

'I think I need to go home and lie down after that. I'm full! But thank you for a lovely dinner.' Mae said her goodbyes, sure her waist had expanded a good two inches since she'd arrived.

'Any time, love.' Moira saw her to the door and kissed her on the cheek.

'Nice to see you again,' Paddy added.

'Shannon and I will see you down to the door. Night, Mum and Dad.' Liam hugged his parents and waited until they'd both kissed Shannon goodnight before he opened the door.

The moment they stepped out of the bubble, the noise of the outside world came rushing up the stairs to meet them: screaming, shouting, glasses smashing; it sounded as though war had broken out down below.

'I'll go and see what's happened,' Liam said, trying to usher Mae and Shannon back inside.

Moira took her granddaughter by the shoulders but Mae wasn't going to be so easily restrained. Both she and Paddy followed Liam downstairs.

'What's going on?' he asked the bar staff, who were standing staring at the open door.

'I think a fight has broken out from the pub across the way. Do you want me to close the doors before it spills over into here?' The hipster-looking barman, with a ginger ponytail and beard, clearly wasn't looking to get involved.

'No. There might be people hurt out there.'

'It's not our problem, son.' Paddy tried to dissuade him from getting involved but Liam was already holding open the door, ready to go out into the fray.

'I'm a doctor, Da. Of course it's my problem,' he said, before stepping out.

Mae followed him out, eager not only to help if she was needed, but also to make sure Liam didn't get into any trouble himself. It was clear that this was an ongoing issue between father and son: Paddy ran a self-contained family business he wasn't willing to put at risk for any reason; Liam, on the other hand, couldn't help himself from offering help, as she had seen yesterday at the parade—and probably even when it wasn't wanted or appreciated.

She admired his dedication to his profession, but also his bravery in wading in. If she'd been on her own when a drunken brawl had broken out, she couldn't be certain she'd be heading in the direction they were now. It was only knowing she had Liam as back-up that gave her enough strength to follow him out there.

'Somebody help. He's bleeding!' A clearly distressed and inebriated young woman was standing over a man sitting on the ground, blood pouring from his head turning his once white T-shirt a startling scarlet.

'Yeah? He deserved it. There's more where that came from.' A great, big oaf of a man, his belly drooping from underneath his too-tight football shirt, was staggering about in the middle of the street, waving a broken bottle.

'The Garda are on their way,' someone shouted from the crowd, which had backed away from the man with the makeshift weapon.

'Phone an ambulance too,' Liam commanded, advancing on the feuding pair.

'Liam, be careful.' Mae had no idea what he was planning, but her heart was in her mouth at the thought he was about to get in the middle of this nasty fight. He waved a hand behind him, and she wasn't sure if it was to tell her to be quiet or to stay back. It didn't matter because she didn't intend to do either.

'I just need to check your friend's head wound. I'm a doctor.' Like a zoo keeper trying to wrangle a wild animal, Liam slowly edged forward on his toes, a hand out in front to demonstrate he meant no harm.

'This is none of your business.' The angry man waved the bottle in Liam's direction but the threat did nothing to deter him.

'I'm a doctor. It kind of is.'

'He'll live. That's what he gets for spilling my beer.'

'I'm sure he didn't mean it.' Liam nodded over to the injured victim, presumably trying to get him to make an apology in order to calm the situation.

No such luck.

'It's hard not to bump into him when he's the size of a flaming house.'

'Say that again!' The man lunged forward at the insult, and Liam jumped in between the pair.

Mae didn't want to watch; she couldn't even breathe, thinking that he was going to get himself into real trouble. But she wouldn't leave in case he needed her.

'Just give me the bottle, mate, so no one else gets hurt.' Liam tried again to reason with him.

'I'm not your "mate". I'm nobody's "mate".' The big slug of a man jabbed the bottle at Liam.

Mae let out a scream, but Liam had jumped back at the last minute, so all the man managed to stab was air.

'Hey, you, you big bully, he's only trying to help.' Mae couldn't help herself. It wasn't in her nature to simply stand back and watch as someone got hurt, any more than it was in Liam's. Plus, he wasn't just someone. He was a colleague, and someone she'd begrudgingly become used to having around these past couple of days.

'Mae, what are you doing? Get back.' Liam was staring at her, madder than she'd ever seen him, brow knitted into a serious scowl and jaw clenched so tight, it looked as though he might actually break something.

'He can't just threaten people and get away with it. This man has a daughter, you know. He's a single parent, yet he's waded in here, trying to help. What does he get in return, someone trying to stab him with a broken bottle and take him away from her? What kind of country is this? What kind of man are you?'

Her rant at least distracted the attacker. He was probably wondering if he should make a charge at her to shut her up, but he did take his eyes off Liam and drop his guard for a moment.

It gave Liam the opportunity to make a grab for the bottle, catching him unawares. Although, once the thug realised what Super Doc was trying to do, he fought back, causing a tug of war between the two over the bottle. Seeing the situation was still precarious, and with no one else appearing to want to intervene, Mae launched herself at him. She jumped onto the man's back, digging her boots into his sides, covering his eyes with her hands, and generally trying to disorientate him. The burly guy did his best to shrug her off, but she clung on as though she was riding a bucking bronco, slapping him, kneeing him in the back and desperately trying to get him to drop the weapon. In the end, he had no choice, deciding it was more important to deal with her now.

That was when she realised she could be in trouble. Liam pulled the bottle out of his hand and threw it away, but not before he got a punch to the nose. The sight of the blood streaming down his face was enough to distract Mae and she let up on her assault for a moment, worried that he'd been seriously hurt. Her bronco took the opportunity to fling her off his back as though he was swatting a fly, sending her flying onto the cobbled street below. She landed with a hard thud, her backside taking the brunt of the fall.

Their burly attacker took one look at the chaotic, bloodied scene he'd created and took off, lumbering down the street, pushing people out of the way, but at least he was gone. The immediate threat had passed and, judging by the sound of the police sirens coming closer, it wouldn't be long before the Garda would pick him up.

'I don't know whether to hug you or shout at you for being so stupid.' Liam came over and held out a hand to help her up from the ground, the other pinching the bridge of his nose in an attempt to stem the bleeding.

Whether it was the shock of what had just happened setting in, the genuine concern she saw on his face for her or the sheer relief that he was okay, she didn't know, but she burst into tears all the same.

Liam helped her to her feet and pulled her into a hug. 'I'm going to get blood all over your lovely sweater,' he whispered into her ear, as the crowd gave them a round of applause for their efforts, before filtering back into the various pubs they'd exited to watch the show.

'I don't care. I need a hug.' She buried her head in the crook of his shoulder, luxuriating in the warm, manly feel of him around her. The security of his embrace was everything she needed after the drama and upset.

When the hug lasted a probably inappropriate amount of time for two people who professed to be work colleagues only, Liam let go.

'Er…if you're okay, we should probably go and check on the patient.'

'Yeah. Just a bruised…ego,' she said, patting her backside to make him laugh.

'It's fine, there's no need to fuss,' the man with the very obvious head wound insisted as they approached him.

'Let me clean it up and take a look for myself. We did just take on that maniac with a broken bottle for you,' Liam reminded him.

'Didn't ask you to, did I?'

'Don't be so ungrateful, Mikey. You could have brain damage or anything.' A woman who must have been his girlfriend gave him a slap on the arm, showing the most sense out of the two of them.

'This is all we've got inside, Liam. What the hell happened to you?' Paddy arrived carrying a first aid kit, apparently having missed his son's heroics. It was probably just as well or else he'd likely have joined in.

'It kicked off a bit. You should have seen Annie Oakley here, taking on the big guy wielding the broken bottle.' Liam took the first aid kit and began cleaning the head wound, ignoring his own injuries.

Paddy looked at her with a mixture of surprise and bewilderment. 'You tackled a man brandishing a weapon?' He turned to Liam. 'And you let her?'

'She wouldn't listen.'

'The guy was distracted at the time.' Mae tried to downplay her part in the melee, and the seriousness of it, neglecting to mention he'd been trying to stab Liam when she'd jumped aboard.

'Anyway, it looks as though the Garda have caught up with him.' Liam pointed down the street where the police were chasing down their assailant, tackling him to the ground and forcing handcuffs on him.

Mae was relieved they wouldn't have to worry about him coming back. She'd had enough excitement for one night.

'Let's get you sorted, then.' She moved over to where Liam was tending the patient.

'That's going to need stitches.'

'I'm not going to hospital. Sod that.'

'If you don't, that's going to keep opening up. We can only patch it up for now.' Liam dabbed around the wound with an antibacterial wipe, drawing a sharp intake of breath from his reluctant patient.

'It's a deep wound. Dr O'Conner is right, it needs stitches. An open wound could get easily infected and lead to more problems. Best to get it treated now.' Mae retrieved a sterile dressing from the first aid box and taped it over the large gash in his skull.

All they received in response for their efforts was a grunt, although his girlfriend did offer to buy them both a beer. By the time the paramedics arrived on scene, Mae was glad they were relieved of their responsibility.

'What about you, sir? You look as though you've been in the wars too. You might need a check over too.' One of the ambulance crew tried to persuade Liam to have some treatment, which she could have told him was a waste of breath.

'It's just a bloody nose. We're both doctors, so I'm sure we can sort it ourselves, can't we, Mae?' He looked at her to confirm he didn't warrant an ambulance ride and a wait in Accident and Emergency, despite the blow he'd taken.

Though she was tempted to throw him under the bus, both to tick him off and make sure he was all right, she knew he didn't want the hassle.

'Sure,' she said, with more enthusiasm than was believable, earning her a glare from Liam.

'Well, you don't want to go back in there. You'll scare Shannon.' Paddy used typical Irish humour to disguise any concerns he would have had over his son's involvement in the brawl.

'I know. Best not tell my ma, either,' Liam made him promise. 'I've got the keys for Ray's house and we have to sort the dog out anyway. I'll get myself cleaned up then come back for Shannon.'

'I'll pass on your details to the guards if you're sure you're both okay?' Paddy looked at Mae for reassurance before he was content to go back into the pub without them.

'We're grand,' she said, attempting her best Irish accent.

Paddy gave her a thumbs-up, leaving the scene at the same time as the paramedics with their uncooperative passenger. Now that the two of them were alone in the middle of the street, it seemed as if the whole thing had been a figment of their imagination. Except for the blood covering Liam's face and shirt and the bruises she could feel forming on her butt cheeks.

'So… Ray's house?' Mae packed up the rest of the first aid kit to take with them, hoping they wouldn't need to use anything other than some antibacterial wipes to clean Liam's face. The blood appeared to have stopped streaming at least since she'd plugged his nose with some cotton.

'Ray's house,' Liam confirmed, pulling the key from his pocket and waving it so close to her face she had to slap his hand away.

'You can be so annoying, you know.'

'Yeah, but you love it. Why else do you keep coming back for more?' Liam grinned.

Why indeed? Though she was grateful no longer to be so concerned about his wellbeing she felt physically sick, Mae knew there was a reason she was drawn to Liam. She did like him, regardless that he could push her buttons. He was that elusive combination of being fun and a friend—both of which had been missing in her life for some time. Liam and his family were refilling the well of good times and company that had been empty for too long, bar fight notwithstanding. It did mean they were going to be spending more time together alone, when the feelings she'd been having during the tussle tonight had been definitcly more than a passing concern.

As long as he kept up this annoying man-child version of himself, she'd survive. Hopefully.

CHAPTER FIVE

'HELLO, BOY.' LIAM scratched Brodie behind the ears as he came to meet them at the door. 'I think we'll bring him in next door for a change of scenery while I get changed. I don't want to drip blood all over Ray's house. Can you grab Brodie's lead and food bowls?'

Mae located the dog's belongings, leaving Liam to wrangle on the lead and pour some food from the giant bag into the bowl, which she carried next door. Liam led them all to his house. As he turned the key in the lock, Mae experienced a little flutter in her belly as she was allowed over the threshold into Liam's inner sanctum. There was a certain intimacy in entering someone's home for the first time—a trust that she had yet to place in anyone sufficiently to let them breach the sanctuary of her new place. Despite Liam having shared so much with her yesterday, she got the impression he valued his privacy. This was a privilege, even if she'd only been invited in because of the events tonight.

She followed him down the hall, where he flicked on the light, illuminating the homely kitchen. It was tidy except for the childish drawings and pots of paint littering the farmhouse-style table: the mark of a man who took pride in his home, yet wasn't afraid to let his daughter have fun expressing herself.

He took the lead off Brodie, which resulted in the dog doing a mad dash around the small kitchen, knocking over one of the dining chairs, before returning to jump up and lick Liam's face.

'Who's such a good dog?' Mae muscled in on the action, fighting for the wolfhound's attention. He was another one she was getting used to having in her life.

Brodie left Liam's attentions to enjoy Mae's cuddles. Ray hadn't mentioned any house rules so, after Liam and Shannon had gone home last night, she'd spent her first dog-sitting shift cuddled up on the sofa with Brodie, watching TV. He wasn't a fan of wildlife programmes, it turned out, restlessly looking for the animals who'd had the audacity to come into his house. However, he'd settled down when she'd put on her soap operas. Clearly he found it as comforting as she did that the people in the kitchen sink dramas had more problems than her.

Neither she nor Brodie would have expected to see each other again so soon.

'You're so fickle,' Liam chastised Brodie, who was standing on his hind legs, feet on her shoulders, nuzzling his head into her neck, not caring a jot what Liam thought about his swapping allegiance so quickly and easily.

'Ah, he loves me.'

'Huh,' Liam grunted. 'He loves anyone who'll feed him and pay him attention.'

'Me too.' Mae grinned.

'Then you must be head over heels for me.' Liam tossed the comment over his shoulder as he made his way past the love-in going on between Mae and Brodie.

It brought Mae up short. Whilst she wasn't head over her heels for Liam, she knew she liked him. She just didn't want him to know that.

'For your family, maybe. Your dad can cook, your mum is *very* attentive and your daughter is super-cute. I'm afraid you're none of those things. Just…irritating.' She wanted to get the message across that she was *not* falling for him, then she set down Brodie's dinner so he'd love her a little bit more.

'Irritating, huh?'

'Also frustrating, and reckless when it comes to getting involved in fights that have nothing to do with you.' She added that one on behalf of his parents and daughter, who would've given him grief over his actions if they'd known what he was up to at the time.

'Ah, but never boring.' Without warning, he stripped off his shirt and ran it under the cold-water tap in a vain attempt to rinse the blood out of it.

She didn't know where to look. Well, she knew where she wanted to look. Her eyes were drawn to his broad back and the smooth muscles of his arms and, if she tipped her head forward a little bit, she could see the pert pectoral muscles.

'Do you want me to give you the full show?' He'd caught her red-handed. Her embarrassment was only topped by the provocative dance he proceeded to do, hands behind his head, thrusting his hips towards her.

Despite the heat infusing her face, she was enjoying the full, uninterrupted view of his lean torso. Then Brodie nudged her arm with his wet nose to remind her what she was supposed to be doing here, and it wasn't ogling a new work colleague.

'Get over yourself. I simply hadn't expected you to be getting naked. Some warning would have been nice or, you know, you could have stripped off in another room.' She huffed.

'I would still be half-naked, so…'

'Maybe I should just strip off my top half and expect you not to be surprised.' It was so unfair men got to whip off their shirts at the drop of a hat and everyone was supposed to be cool with it. What if she hadn't wanted to know what body was beneath the tight shirts? It wouldn't have kept her up all night wondering. Now she knew exactly what he looked like naked from the waist up, sleep definitely wasn't going to come easily. For someone who apparently ate very hearty, carb-laden meals, he had no business looking that good.

'Feel free. I'm not about to stop you.' He leaned back against the sink, arms folded, with that smug look on his face that almost made her want to call his bluff, to make him blush and bluster and think about nothing else but her being naked too. Except she couldn't promise that would happen. Whether he'd be turned off by her curves, wrinkling his nose in disgust, or they got into a game of one-upmanship that led to them both ending up stripping off completely, she couldn't take the risk.

'Pig.' It was the only comeback she could come up with in the moment. Not particularly witty or relevant, but hopefully it would end any expectation that she might whip off her sweater just to prove a point.

'Spoilsport.'

Grr. She just knew he was grinning behind her back.

Liam always used humour to deflect when he was uncomfortable and this was no exception. It had given him a thrill to catch her watching him like that, with undisguised interest in his body, and boosted his ego. That was something he needed after having been unceremoniously dumped, apparently found lacking in personality and physicality. Okay, so Mae had called him irritating, but he knew she enjoyed their banter as much as he did, otherwise she wouldn't have accepted the dinner invitation tonight.

Of course he hadn't anticipated them being caught up in a bar fight, and having to bring her home to patch him up—another step further into his private life and a big deal for him, when the only other woman who'd been in this house, except his mum, was Clodagh.

It was the threat, or promise, of her stripping off which had nearly been his undoing. His imagination had run away with him in that moment, thinking about where that could lead, until his head had been full of kissing, of hands caressing each other's bodies then ripping the rest of one another's clothes off... That was when he deployed the humour missile, knowing that teasing her would defuse any heat before it even had a chance to catch light.

He gave them both some time to cool down and washed up the couple of dishes he'd left in the sink before he fetched the first-aid kit, along with a clean shirt, and started to clean himself up. The first splash of cold water over his face stung his nostrils and filled the sink with swirls of raspberry-coloured streams of water. The intake of air through his gritted teeth drew Mae's attention back to him from Brodie's dinner.

'Let me tend to that. You can't even see what you're doing,' Mae tsked, clearly still irked by him, but her nurturing instinct was too strong to ignore his plight. He'd take it. It wouldn't do to tick her off so much she wouldn't help him with the dog any more. Plus, she made his evenings much more interesting.

Liam hadn't realised how staid his life had become of late until Mae had appeared, shaken things up, and given him a reason to leave his house other than to feed the next-door neighbour's dog or go to his parents' pub, which was only a few minutes' drive away.

He and Shannon had been hurting so hard, trying to find a new normal, get into a different routine from the one they'd been used to, that they'd locked themselves away from the world. Perhaps it was a defence mechanism—keeping out all the bad stuff, staying where they felt safe. It had taken an uptight, smart-mouthed American to show him the error of his ways. He still had a life to live, and so did Shannon, and he couldn't take away her freedom, even if he was trying to protect her in the process.

Taking her to the parade yesterday had been the first time they'd done anything fun and spontaneous since her mother had left. Although Ray's antics had ended their day out prematurely, there had been snatches of the old them, just Daddy and daughter enjoying their time together, instead of being bogged down in worry about their future without Clodagh. He knew Shannon missed her mother, but she mentioned her less now as she got used to it being the two of them.

Mae had helped to extend their socialising, even if it had just been going to his parents and next door. At least that meant they still felt comfortable, being in familiar surroundings, regardless that Mae was brand new to them. He was surprised how easily his mum, dad and Shannon had taken to her. It made it so much easier to be around her, knowing they felt comfortable around her too. Even if he was feeling distinctly uncomfortable now.

He silently thanked them for providing him with another opportunity to see and talk to her again outside of the workplace. She was becoming the brightest parts of his days, which had been pretty damn miserable until recently.

They sat down at the kitchen table, which they'd cleared of all Shannon's art work. Mae took some cotton and was now dabbing away the rest of the blood around his nose. It was the tender look in her eyes, her gentle touch, that he was struggling with most.

He had his parents' love, of course, but that physical and emotional connection as she tended to him was something he'd been missing, probably long before his relationship had collapsed.

The intimacy between Clodagh and him had virtually disappeared. They'd barely been in the same room even to accidentally touch one another, never mind do anything else. He'd put it down to over work and stress on both parts. Long shifts and looking after a child was all-consuming, even harder when there was only one parent in the household. He'd spent so much time these last months being a doctor, father and jilted partner, he'd forgotten what it was like simply to be a man. To have feelings that weren't negative, or wrapped up in someone else's, was new, exhilarating.

What was more, Mae was no longer looking at him as though he was merely an irritant, or a patient, but a man. She was studying him the same way he was watching her—with interest. He offered a smile and received one in return, albeit slightly hesitant.

'Thank you, Mae. For Ray, for yesterday and for

this.' For making him feel like a normal man, attractive and wanted, with desires of his own.

She held his gaze for a while, and with every second the air between them grew thicker with anticipation and tension. That same urge to kiss her as he'd had last night came rushing forward and it was all he could do not to act on it. Then she turned away on the pretence that she had to pack away the first-aid things right there and then and saved him from making a fool of himself.

'You should probably put on a shirt. You don't want to add pneumonia to your list of ailments. I doubt you can afford to get sick when you have so much on your plate.' She flitted around the kitchen like a nervy butterfly, putting the used cotton ball in the rubbish and cleaning the sink.

This skittish version of her was new to him. She'd been so self-assured, both in combat with him and in a medical setting. It was clear she felt unsettled and he was sure he was the cause. They'd both been left hurting after their last relationships had spectacularly imploded, but he didn't think they should suffer for their partners' decisions for ever. They hadn't deserved the way they'd been treated in the past, and they didn't deserve to be punished now, afraid to open themselves up to anyone else in the fear they'd be hurt all over again.

A little flirtation, acknowledging an attraction, shouldn't be something to fear. It wasn't going to help them open up emotionally in the future if they saw it as something destructive. Not communicating had been his downfall in the past and he didn't want that to continue for ever. Not when he still had hopes that some day he'd be in a happy, healthy relationship, raising the family he'd always wanted.

'I thought you liked this look.' He'd neglected to put on the clean shirt under the pretence that he didn't want to get blood on it until he was all cleaned up. Now he knew it was because he liked to see that look in her eyes, that appreciation of his body, and the ego boost it gave him. He moved over to where she stood, knowing he was invading her personal space, waiting for her to push him away or draw him closer.

'Stop it. Please.'

To Liam's horror, there were tears in Mae's eyes as she quietly pleaded with him.

'I'm sorry. I didn't mean to upset you.' He always took things too far and now he'd crossed the line, mistaking her kindness for something more. Immediately stepping away, he tugged the shirt on over his head and covered himself up. As much as he wanted to comfort her, hold her and apologise profusely, he knew she probably just wanted to leave.

'You didn't. I mean…it's not you.' She angrily wiped away the tears before they dared to fall. 'I just can't handle anyone else playing with my emotions.'

'I wasn't… I didn't mean to…' He threaded his fingers through his hair and tugged, deserving every second of the self-inflicted pain and more. Guilty of only thinking about himself as usual, he'd neglected to re-alise she hadn't been having as much fun as he had during the exchange.

'I know you were only teasing but I'm still a bit raw after Diarmuid. Having these…feelings isn't some-thing I'd planned. I know I'm just the silly American but please don't make fun of me.' She was shredding the wrapper from the antiseptic wipe she'd used to clean him up, obviously fretting about what had nearly happened. But he'd been right about her feeling the attraction between them too. Her tears and the flight re-sponse was the manifestation of her fear at admitting it.

'I wasn't making fun of you. I promise.' Suddenly, the anger over their situation welled up inside him until he wanted to smash things, though it wouldn't have done anything only upset her more. It seemed so un-fair. Clodagh and Diarmuid weren't likely to beat them-selves up over their failures. Especially when Clodagh had moved on to the next relationship before she'd had the courtesy to tell him theirs was over.

He had to make do with pacing the floor like a cap-tive animal as he raged about the unfairness of it all. 'Why should we feel guilty or ashamed that we might actually fancy one another? We're not kids, nor are we the ones in the wrong.'

Now he knew that Mae wanted the same thing as he did, but was too afraid of making a fool of herself, he knew it was down to him to make the move. He crossed the distance between them in one step. Mae tilted up her chin to meet him as though she'd been waiting for him to come and claim her, and he did.

He captured her face in his hands, her mouth with his, and kissed her as though they were free from all the worry that seemed to dictate their every move, every thought. For those few seconds, free from consequences and future regret, he kissed her with every ounce of passion he felt for her, channelling every one of those hopes and dreams that his future wouldn't be marred by the failure of one relationship into one kiss.

Mae latched her lips onto his, tentatively dipping her tongue into his mouth to meet him, letting her hands slide under his shirt and around his waist, mirroring every one of his movements, until their bodies were entwined like jungle vines, stronger together than in isolation.

A need for more of this freedom from the usual intrusive thoughts in his head, more of Mae and this rush of passion she'd awakened inside him, spurred Liam's libido. This wasn't the time for over-analysing and worrying about the future; he wanted to stay in the moment. And the moment was telling him to be with Mae.

'Should we be doing this?' she asked breathlessly as he kissed his way along the curve of her neck, brushing her hair away so he could continue his pursuit across her shoulder.

She gasped when he dipped his head lower and pulled her jumper down to expose the swell of her breasts in her lacy white bra, but he knew she didn't want him to stop. Not when she peeled off his jacket and just this moment unbuckled his belt. That jolt of awareness slammed into him as her fingers traced the buttons of his fly and he had to take a moment to remember to breathe, to try and clear his head a little, before he embarrassed himself.

'Probably not.' His laugh was a little shaky, much like his legs and his breathing.

This had been unexpected, exciting, and he was going back for more.

With extra urgency their mouths clashed together and their hands tugged at one another's clothes, their breathing ragged, their want evident. Mae couldn't even think straight, and she didn't want to if it meant putting an end to this. She was enjoying it too much.

It was nice to feel wanted, to know she hadn't got carried away again imagining something that wasn't there. Okay, so this was never going to be her romantic fantasy come true. They'd spent half their time winding each other up, plus he was a single dad, both of which were not keys to a successful relationship. No, kissing Liam was simply a chemical reaction and nothing else. He was right: she shouldn't beat herself up because she found someone attractive; she hadn't taken a vow of chastity, or broken any laws. They were two adults enjoying each other's company.

It helped that he was an amazing kisser. She didn't know from one second to the next whether to expect him to be soft and tender, or hard and demanding, but she was enjoying both aspects of his attentions to her lips. It made her think of what he was capable of in other areas, and she found herself keen to find out first-hand, caution be damned. Neither of them wanted anything serious; both were likely on the rebound and in need of a serious ego boost, not to mention a physical release. She was sure it had been some time for both of them since they'd last had anything resembling a sex life.

The loud ring of Liam's phone had him break off the kiss as though he'd been scorched, spinning round to discreetly adjust his clothes as he answered the call, as though they'd been busted by someone walking in un-announced. Mae busied herself wringing the last of the water out of his T-shirt on the draining board, hoping she didn't look as dishevelled with lust as she felt. She was dizzy from the sudden cold turkey she was now undergoing after the withdrawal of Liam's lips from hers. It was surprising how quickly she'd got used to kissing him. It had been intoxicating.

'Yes, Dad, I'm fine. I'm, er, just cleaning myself up. Yes, you can bring her over. No, I'm not going to scare her. Okay, I'll see you soon.'

Mae scrubbed at the blood on Liam's shirt rather than try and make eye contact.

'Dad's on his way over with Shannon,' he said.

'I should probably leave before they get here.' Before she did anything else likely to get her into trouble.

'Are you really still going to pretend that this isn't happening?' He was so close she could feel his warm breath on her skin. Enough contact, apparently, for her body to go into meltdown.

He opened his mouth and she assumed it was because he was about to make another wise crack. She hadn't expected him to kiss her again. Her eyes fluttered shut, her heart picked up an extra beat and her lips parted to accept him, as though her body was already pre-programmed to welcome him at the drop of a hat—or a T-shirt. This time the kiss was fleeting, barely there, and possibly the most frustrating moment of her life. Give or take coming to terms with her ex's behaviour, and inability to have spoken to her at any point in time before she'd made it down the aisle.

He took a step back and smiled. 'See? You want this. You want me.'

Still worked up by the kiss, and waiting for the next instalment, her body was inclined to agree.

'You're so full of yourself.' She dipped into her bag of self-protecting aides and pulled out a handful of sarcasm to chuck back at him.

'I'm only stating the truth.' He reached out and brushed a lock of hair away from her face.

Mae's eyes fluttered shut and she revelled in the brief contact. 'But what would it achieve?'

So they had chemistry, but falling into bed after knowing one another only a couple of days would be asking for trouble. Especially when they had to work at the same hospital.

'Er…how about fun? Remember that?'

'Remind me. It's been a while.'

Now that she thought about it, it was something that hadn't been in abundance even before the ultimate rejection. The weeks and months leading up to the wedding had been spent agonising over every detail, worrying that everything would go to plan. There hadn't been much room to do anything fun in between work and organising the big day.

Perhaps that had been a large part of the problem between Diarmuid and her. Even if he had complained they weren't spending enough quality time together, she probably wouldn't have done anything about it, because her attention had been completely consumed with the wedding, on having the best day of her life and proving the romantic fantasy had come true. She'd neglected the reality of their situation too long and their relationship had flatlined as a result.

A good time hadn't been high on her list of priorities since then. That spot had gone to simply surviving.

'No commitment other than to make each other feel good.' He dotted tiny, ghost-like kisses down her neck, sending goose bumps popping up all over her skin.

'That does feel…sound nice.' He was scrambling her brain with every touch of his lips on her body.

'Mmm-hmm. Doesn't it?'

'But Shannon… Your dad…' As nice as this was,

the pair were going to be here soon, and there was no way there would be time to fit in everything she wanted to do with Liam in that small window. If anything, it would leave her frustrated to start something they couldn't finish properly.

'I know. Tonight's out of the question. So, I have a proposition.' He stopped kissing her and retreated back into his own personal space, leaving her dazed and confused.

She needed the breathing room because she was so disorientated and under his spell right now, she would agree to anything.

'What?' Even to her ears she sounded breathless, as though she'd just run a marathon. Her heart was racing too, the exhilaration of the moment doing more to fuel the adrenaline in her body than any form of exercise. Well, almost any… Her thoughts drifted to whatever indecent proposal he had in mind and whether or not her heart could take it.

'Neither of us are in the market for a serious, long-term relationship. Let's face it, we'd probably drive each other up the wall. But, it's also clear there's an attraction here. One we would be acting on right now if my dad hadn't interrupted.' The devilish glint in his eyes only upped the level of Mae's frustration, unaided by the fact he'd yet to get to the point.

'Yes, and he's going to be here soon with your daughter.' *So get on with it!*

'I know we haven't known each other that long, that

we're going to be working at the same hospital and have Ray as a mutual connection. Sleeping together could make things complicated. If we let it.'

'What are you suggesting?' She had been trying not to think beyond tonight, or let herself feel anything that wasn't in the moment. Now Liam was ruining the mood by talking about the future consequences.

Liam cleared his throat. 'A fling.'

'Excuse me?' For a moment Mae thought she'd misheard him.

'I don't see why we should deny ourselves some fun. We haven't done anything wrong and we deserve some happiness. But I also know we're both still hurting from our last relationships. I thought perhaps, if you agree, we could keep things casual. You know? See each other in private.'

'You want to be my booty call?' The idea had its appeal.

'We would be each other's booty call. No strings, or expectations, other than having a good time.'

'That's a big promise.'

Liam ducked his head with a grin, almost bashfully. It was nice to see that perhaps he wasn't as confident as he often portrayed. She liked seeing that softer side of him. It represented him opening up, letting that brash exterior slip so she could see a more vulnerable Liam. The one who didn't want to risk getting hurt again either.

'I just know we would have a really good time together.' He pulled her close, capturing the gasp of surprise on her lips with his. The kissing alone was sufficient to prove his point.

Except she wasn't usually that kind of girl. At least, not one who got involved with fathers of young children. He was showing her a way round that, so the level of commitment that would normally have required wasn't an issue. But she was already so involved with his family, it seemed impossible to separate, or juggle, those relationships. After Diarmuid, she'd made a promise to herself not to get involved with someone she could lose her heart to so easily. She didn't want to lose herself in that commitment to a relationship and, seeing how close he was to his daughter, Liam seemed the worst person to rebound with. Even if he was suggesting something a lot more intriguing than potential heartbreak. Although the thought of exploring all kinds of possibilities with Liam was tempting, she just wasn't sure it would be worth taking the risk.

'I don't know, Liam. It's one thing getting carried away in the heat of the moment, but this is a crazy idea you're asking me to make a logical decision about.' Now she'd been given time to think, all the red flags were waving in her face. She certainly didn't want to agree to something now, when she was wound so tightly with arousal for him, only to regret it when her brain wasn't so fried by lust.

There was a rap on the back door as Paddy appeared with Shannon.

'Sleep on it. We can talk about it tomorrow,' Liam whispered, before going to greet his daughter and reassure her everything was okay.

There were so many things wrong with that last comment, but they wouldn't have the privacy to go over her fears now the rest of Liam's family was here.

Namely that there was no way she'd sleep tonight with erotic images of Liam in various stages of undress roaming unbidden in her head, and the prospect of more if she chose. Plus, she didn't think she could face talking about it again tomorrow without being affected by what had happened here tonight. Common sense told her she should put a stop to any romantic notions now and rule this as an error of judgement, a moment of madness which definitely should not be extended indefinitely. However, deep down she knew she wasn't strong enough to say no to this once-in-a-lifetime opportunity.

CHAPTER SIX

MAE HAD BEEN ignoring his texts. Liam had briefly considered calling and leaving a voice message when she invariably didn't answer his call, then decided it would seem too needy—the opposite of the arrangement he'd proposed. He still couldn't quite believe that he'd suggested a fling, or that she'd even agreed to consider it. Clearly his libido had been doing the talking last night, afraid that he wouldn't get to finish what they'd started.

He wasn't sure how this would work on a practical level when they would have to co-ordinate work and his responsibility as a father. It wasn't as if he could parade Mae through the house in the mornings and not expect Shannon to notice. The logistics would be difficult, though he couldn't bring himself to regret anything when she'd said she'd contemplate the idea of a fling.

It had been a last grasp to maintain the momentum which had sprung between them in the kitchen—not the most romantic place on earth, but it hadn't stopped them from engaging in one of the most passionate encounters he'd ever experienced. It was all he'd been able to think about, along with the possibility of having something more with Mae.

He knew a relationship was off the cards. Neither of them was emotionally ready to jump into anything serious, but it was clear they still had needs. A fling seemed the easy solution to fulfil their want for one another, and the ego boost might even help them when they were ready to move onto another relationship. They could avoid all the complications of family getting involved in their personal business by keeping it quiet, and it would give him something more than dinner with his parents to look forward to.

The only problem with his sexual master plan was the growing suspicion that, in the cold light of day, Mae had changed her mind and decided she didn't even want a casual fling with him. If she was agreeable to the idea in theory, he was willing to find a solution to ensure they could spend time together. Whether that meant meeting at her place, or booking rooms by the hour when Shannon was in school, he wanted to make this work.

From the second he'd made the suggestion, he hadn't been able to think about anything else other than being with Mae. Although a rejection from her wouldn't be the same as Clodagh leaving him for his best mate, it would still hurt. It would also make things awkward when he had to consult her on a patient and he still hadn't had her answer. That wasn't the sign of someone who couldn't wait to embark on a racy, passionate fling.

'Is there any update on Dr Watters?' he asked the head nurse, who'd been the one to put in the call requesting Mae's expertise. Whilst Liam knew Mae wouldn't have blown him off when it came to a patient—she was too professional—his behaviour last night had been anything but, and he could only hope that wasn't the reason she'd been avoiding him.

'Why don't you ask her yourself?' Liam's A&E colleague nodded to the space behind him.

He took a split second to compose himself, to brace for the look of contempt that was likely there on her face, before he turned around. But she was too hard to read when she was in doctor mode. Hair tied back, not a strand out of place, wearing a smart skirt and blouse, she looked immaculate. A far cry from the flushed, dishevelled version of Mae from last night. He knew which one he preferred: the Mae who couldn't keep her hands off him, not the one standing here with an indifferent expression on her face.

'I'm here. What do you need me for?'

It wasn't a loaded question for anyone but him. He needed her for company, for kissing, for feeding his ego, and hopefully for more. Although, judging by this cool reception and her refusal to reply to his messages, he'd be lucky if she even let on she knew him.

'We have a patient coming in who's taken an overdose of Paracetamol. I can handle it, but I thought it would be good to get your input to try and limit the liver damage.' He'd known Mae was in today. They'd cross-checked their schedules to work out the times for looking after Brodie and he remembered there was a brief cross-over period this afternoon when they would both be in attendance.

Though he didn't take any joy in the fact someone had felt so desperate they'd thought to end their life, it gave him a chance to see Mae. She was also the best person to have on hand in this instance. An overdose of Paracetamol could result in potentially fatal liver damage. They only had a very small window of time to help and they were all lucky to be able to utilise Mae's expertise.

He'd seen more than his fair share of drug overdoses due to prescription and illegal drugs in the emergency department, accidental or otherwise. Some had been too late for medical intervention no matter how hard the staff had tried to provide assistance. Those were the cases he took home with him, the names and faces he couldn't forget because he felt as though he'd failed them. Even if Mae didn't want to speak to him personally, he'd willingly set aside his pride to have her here if it meant saving someone's life.

That invisible hum of tension before an emergency admission hung in the air. Everyone waited to launch into action the moment the doors swung open, powerless until they did. When the familiar fluorescent jackets of the ambulance crew blazed brightly as they crashed into the department with their patient on a stretcher, the hospital staff circled, ready to take over.

They quickly transferred the patient onto a hospital bed, accepting the responsibility for the young woman's life, and relieving the ambulance crew so they could move on to their next job.

'Twenty-six-year-old female: Anne Marie Hagen. History of depression. Found unconscious by her best friend after breaking up with her boyfriend. Apparently surrounded by empty Paracetamol packets. She's breathing but hasn't retained consciousness.'

As always, the initial transfer was noisy and busy, getting all the details of the case, and doing a preliminary assessment.

'Do we know how long ago this happened?' Mae asked.

'Her friend saw her about two hours ago, so it can't be that long.'

'Okay, thanks. We're lucky we got to her so quickly. Anything past eight hours would have limited what we can do.' She went on to order the usual bloods and urine sample, with the most important results being the liver function.

'Are you happy to go ahead with administering activated charcoal?' Liam asked, monitoring Anne Marie's blood pressure and pulse to make sure she didn't suddenly deteriorate.

He hadn't asked Mae to attend just so he could take over. He trusted her judgement, an expert in this field, but he wanted to be useful.

'Yes, and can we get an IV of acetylcysteine set up,

please? Given that we're still within that time frame, we should be able to prevent serious hepatotoxicity.'

It didn't matter that this girl had tried to take her own life; they would work together to save her as best they could. She was a patient, someone who'd clearly been so distressed she hadn't seen any point in continuing. It was always difficult when such young people were involved: they should have had their whole lives ahead of them. Now, thanks to Mae and everyone else involved, she still did. Of course, Anne Marie would have to be referred to the mental health team, but that was for her own benefit. Hopefully they would help her move past whatever issues had led her to make this choice, so she wouldn't ever try this again.

Although they couldn't know for certain if a break-up had been the catalyst for this, Liam understood how totally devastated she must have been to have attempted to end her life. When he'd discovered Clodagh and Colm in bed, he'd thought his life was over too. He hadn't seen a way past it and it was only having to look after Shannon which had forced him to get up out of the doldrums every morning and go through the motions of a functioning adult. Inside, though, he might as well have died. Suddenly his whole life had been taken away from him. He didn't know who he was any more, or what to do without Clodagh there. There had been a grieving period; it was only natural after the loss of a relationship.

He was still in the angry phase, and he just knew

Anne Marie would get there too once she'd had a little time to think things through. The overdose had probably been an impulse reaction, a way to shut down the pain. Perhaps, as in some cases, it had been a cry for help—a signal to those around her that she wasn't doing okay and needed more support. With Mae's assistance, and a follow-up treatment plan, he hoped Anne Marie would eventually be able to put the whole thing behind her and start over, the way he had.

Yes, he still had some kinks to work out when it came to his love life—namely that he needed to find the courage to invest in another relationship. He imagined that would happen faster if Mae agreed to this crazy arrangement where they could have all the benefits of a relationship without having to commit their hearts to it, playing it safe.

'Okay, that should keep her stabilised for now. I'll want to see the results of the liver function test to see what we're dealing with, and she'll need a referral to psych.' Mae was winding down her part in procedures and Liam knew she wasn't going to stick around longer than necessary, to avoid talking to him. He didn't want to let that happen without a chance at least to clear the air in case he never got to speak to her again.

Mae was ready to leave, to get away from the sad circumstances of the patient that had hit too close to home, and the man she hadn't been able to get out of her head since he'd kissed her.

Suddenly, alarms were going off and medical staff swarming back around the bed again.

'She's gone into cardiac arrest!' one of the nurses shouted, forcing Mae immediately to turn back.

'We need a defibrillator over here!' Liam yelled, waiting as the patient's clothes were cut open to give access to her chest.

He started chest compressions, keeping the blood pumping around her body until they could apply electric shocks. After a while he stopped to check for a response, but it was soon clear they would have to use the defibrillator to try and restart the woman's heart. Once pads had been attached, Mae took up the paddles. 'Stand clear.'

Making sure no one was touching the patient or her bed, liable to get a shock themselves, Mae delivered the first shock. She waited to check the heart rhythm but, with no improvement, responsibility transferred back to Liam.

Again, hands locked, arms straight, he began more chest compressions. He flicked a glance at Mae, which she didn't want to acknowledge. It was concern that they weren't going to bring this patient back after all. Mae had to retain a certain professional detachment at work, but in circumstances like these it was impossible not to be affected.

This was a young woman who'd had her whole world in front of her. Yet, she had come to think, for whatever reason, that her life was no longer worth living. Mae

knew that feeling. Running from the church, after realising Diarmuid wasn't going to turn up, it had crossed
her mind to throw herself in front of the nearest bus.
Then she wouldn't have had to deal with the loss, the
humiliation and the heartbreak her fiancé's actions had
caused. If she hadn't had her mother's strength, the
outcome of those first few days after their break-up
could've been very different.

These painful personal dramas, which seemed so
all encompassing at the time, did eventually become
easier to live with. She only hoped Anne Marie got the
opportunity to realise that, to see she could still lead
a very full life.

Liam stopped CPR to check the patient's heart
rhythm, then it was Mae's turn again.

'Stand clear.' She delivered another shock with the
paddles, watching Anne Marie's body jerk as she did
so.

It seemed like such a violent act, but she'd seen
time and time again how it often gave people a second
chance at life, and she only hoped this woman would
be one of them. Life was short. Certainly too short to
give up on it at such a young age.

She thought of Diarmuid and herself. In a way, she'd
been guilty of giving up her life for him, even though
she was still functioning on an outward level. Moving
away had been a start, as had getting herself a new
job, but in terms of her personal life she might as well
have died. It was only natural she'd wanted to protect

herself, but she'd basically let Diarmuid win. She'd decided that he was the only man who could ever mean anything to her. She really didn't want to live with that for ever. He'd gone on to have another life. They both deserved the same—to move on from the heartbreak and start living again.

Suddenly, the expectant air around the cubicle was filled with the steady beep of Anne Marie's heart, and Mae had to fight back tears. They'd done it. Now this woman had been given another chance at life, it would be down to her to move on from the past and look to her future. Mae knew she had to do the same.

'Let's get her stabilised.' The medical team swung into action, getting her settled again, though she would probably be transferred to the intensive care unit once she was stabilised so they could keep a close eye on her. Hopefully, once they got all the toxins out of her body, she would be well on her way to recovery.

'Thanks for your assistance, Mae... Dr Watters,' Liam said to her once their job was done and the nurses took over the responsibility for the rest of their patient's care. Mae found some satisfaction in him stumbling over her name, and suspected that he'd found the circumstances more difficult than usual too.

'Just doing my job.' Her slightly quivering voice and bottom lip weren't in keeping with the self-assured comment. At times it was much more than a job, it was a reminder of her own vulnerabilities, and today especially had been something of a wake-up call.

However, she didn't intend to make a show of herself by crying in front of the team. Apart from Liam, they wouldn't understand why she'd get so emotional over a random patient. It wouldn't look good or do anything for her reputation at her new place of work if they thought she couldn't cope with any vulnerable cases. So she turned on her heel and walked away, not looking back, hoping she'd at least managed to portray someone in charge of her emotions.

Liam could see Mae was upset even if she'd acted professionally and efficiently with him to get their patient back. He checked with the rest of the team that they had everything in place for Anne Marie before he ducked out for a few minutes.

'Mae,' he called down the corridor, jogging towards her. She could have pretended not to hear him, so he appreciated that she waited for him, though he supposed it was only out of propriety rather than a favour to him. She couldn't very well refuse his company for a few moments without people sensing there was something going on and jumping to conclusions.

They walked in silence out of the department and down the dimly lit corridor in the old part of the hospital which afforded them a little privacy. Liam pulled her aside under a staircase, away from prying eyes and listening ears.

'Are you okay?' The question which had been hov-

ering on his lips since she'd left A&E finally burst
from his mouth.

Mae nodded, her wide, glistening eyes and chewed
bottom lip saying otherwise.

'You can talk to me. I'm not going to make any
judgement because you got upset over a vulnerable,
young patient. You're only human, Mae.' He wanted to
reach out to her, to give her a hug and offer some comfort, but he didn't want to overstep the mark…again.

She swallowed hard and he could see the effort it
was taking her not to cry. As much as he wanted to tell
her it was okay to show emotion, Liam knew Mae was
too proud to be seen so vulnerable at work.

'Knowing Anne Marie was in so much pain that
she thought ending her life was the only option available triggered a lot for me. I'll be okay…don't worry.'

Liam dismissed her attempt to fob him off. It was
obvious she was in pain too. 'I've been there too, after
Clodagh. We all have our dark days. What's important
is that we pick ourselves up again, eventually, and move
on. Hopefully Anne Marie will be able to do the same
once she realises nothing is worth ending a life for.'

'But have we moved on, Liam? Yes, we're getting up,
going to work and acting like normal human beings,
but we're still holding back from being with anyone
else. Instead of protecting our hearts, aren't we punishing ourselves by holding back?'

Liam smiled. 'Isn't that what I've been saying? I

don't want to be alone for ever, and yes, we run the risk of getting hurt again. But if we don't even try...'

'I know. I'm beginning to realise that I still deserve a love life. I don't want to end up sad and lonely, thinking that's all there is for me.'

'Having someone who thinks you're beautiful and amazing does not necessarily mean he's going to hurt you. I kissed you because I like you, because I think we could have something special together.'

He was about to apologise for getting things so very wrong when Mae got there first.

'I'm sorry I didn't answer your messages. I just... Last night was very confusing for me.'

'I get that. It sort of crept up on us both then completely consumed us.' Even now, the passion which had swept them away was bubbling back up to the surface now that he was so close to her again.

'When I had time to mull things over, consider your proposal, I thought perhaps it was short-changing us both. That we were worth more than a purely physical relationship and we'd only be doing it because our exes had battered our confidence.'

'And now?' The hesitation he saw in her eyes, and the fact she hadn't tried to move away from him, led him to believe she might just have had a change of heart.

'Seeing Anne Marie, what she was prepared to do, to give up... We all deserve better. I don't need any more heartache, or another man to throw my life away on, but I'm not dead yet.'

'And I don't have room in my life for anything serious that will take my attention from my daughter. But we both have needs.' At least they were on that page together.

Mae inched closer and danced her fingertips along the buttons on his shirt, making his skin burn without even touching him. 'But I think you were right about what you said last night—we deserve to have a little fun. Neither Diarmuid or Clodagh are going to rule the rest of our lives. Choosing how we do this is our route to freedom.'

Liam liked this decisive Mae, and not just because she was giving him what he wanted. She was taking control of the situation, of her life. He didn't mind, when the whole thing had been his idea in the first place and he'd certainly be reaping the benefits if she agreed to be with him for any amount of time.

'So, really, sleeping together is our first step to independence.' Liam nuzzled into her neck, luxuriating in the scent of vanilla and summer berries clinging to her skin. The pulse in her throat beat hard against his lips and he knew she was as turned on as he was already.

'Uh-huh. Really, we're doing each other a favour...' She gasped as he slid his hand beneath her shirt to touch the bare skin of her back.

'And I do like to be helpful.'

'I have noticed this about you. One good turn deserves another and all that.' She took him by surprise then, kissing him hard on the lips, tangling her fingers in his hair and bringing every nerve end to attention.

The buzz of her pager which eventually broke through their erotic haze to remind them where they were.

'Sorry. I have an appointment to get to,' she said with a grimace.

Liam reached out to trace the smudged lipstick around her lips. 'You might want to redo your make-up beforehand.'

There was that rosy glow in her cheeks again. 'I might just do that.'

She went to walk away, then stopped and turned back. 'So, how are we going to do this?'

They needed a plan about how they would actually get the time alone needed for this secret fling. Even a casual arrangement required some planning when he had to juggle his job, his daughter and dog-sitting an Irish wolfhound.

At least he had tonight covered.

'Mum and Dad promised Shannon she could sleep over later.'

The smile on Mae's face at that news gave him a warm glow inside, knowing he'd been the one to put it there. He hoped by the end of the night she'd be grinning from ear to ear.

'You are sexy. You are wanted. You are fierce. You are an independent woman who does not need a man in her life for anything other than sex. You do not need to see him as anything other than a sex object. You are not, under any circumstances, to fall for him,' Mae told the woman in the mirror with a wag of her finger, but she doubted even the stern look was enough to convince her of any of that.

Well, maybe the being wanted part. Liam had made it pretty clear he was physically attracted to her even if he didn't want any emotional entanglements—which, she reminded herself, was something she needed to avoid too.

She'd spent all last night and most of today vacillating about whether or not she should take this leap into sexual freedom with Liam. That was what it would be for her. An affair free from the emotional restraints of a relationship. She wasn't even sure she was ready for that. But after the way Liam had kissed her, the way she'd felt today when they'd been alone, she was willing to try.

Even now she shivered with the anticipation of what the night had in store. She was standing in her underwear, still deciding what to wear. She lifted the body-skimming polka-dot wiggle dress and held it against her body, then dismissed it. It was sexy, but she worried it would look like she was trying too hard when this was supposed to be a casual hook-up. Now she rethought the red lacy lingerie in case it looked too obvious, too desperate—too 'my fiancé jilted me and I need someone to find me attractive so I can feel good about myself'. But she remembered this was just about sex, so there was no need for subtlety.

The doorbell rang and she grabbed her second-choice outfit from the bed—a white boho dress with flowers, which she couldn't have worn out in the Irish March weather, but which hopefully showed enough leg to capture Liam's interest.

One last swipe of lip gloss, a quick tidy of the bedroom and she padded downstairs barefoot to answer the door. A deep breath, shaky release and she came face to face with the man who'd been stalking her every thought recently.

'Hi.' That grin was enough to make her believe she'd done the right thing by taking the risk with this crazy scheme.

'Hey, you. Come in.' Mae peered outside to see if anyone had witnessed his arrival. Although she barely knew anyone in the street, she had a feeling that everyone was watching, knowing she was about to embark on a scandalous sex fest...hopefully.

He side-stepped into the hall, one hand behind his back, seemingly feeling as awkward about this as she was. She took comfort in the fact he obviously didn't make a habit of this sort of thing. It was apparent he hadn't been with anyone since Clodagh, but that didn't mean he hadn't been a playboy in his youth.

'Is everything okay, Liam?'

'Yeah, sure.'

'It's just, you're acting kind of weird. If you've

changed your mind...' The thought that he might be trying to find a way to let her down gently hit her hard, deflating her ego immediately. It told her just how much she'd been looking forward to being with him when the disappointment settled into her very bones.

He suddenly thrust forward a bunch of flowers. 'I bought these on the way over, then I thought it might seem a bit much, since this isn't really a date. I didn't want you to read too much into it and think I was trying to turn this into something more already. I just thought I should bring you a gift.'

'Thank you. They're beautiful.' Sheer relief made her want to laugh but she bit her lip, not wishing to offend him. It was a sweet gesture—yes, totally unnecessary, but it proved that he wasn't used to this any more than she was.

'So are you.'

Her heart melted at the whole first-date vibe that was going on, expectation thrumming between them as they skirted around the reason he was here.

'I'll just go and put them in some water.' She needed some too, her mouth suddenly dry, the tension becoming too intense to bear in the cramped entrance hall.

'You've got a nice place here. Not too far from the hospital,' he said, following her to the kitchen.

'Yes, I like it.' The conversation was weirdly formal and stilted, so unlike their usual verbal encounters. Discussing their commute to work wasn't in keeping with the idea that this was going to be fun and exciting. A passionate fling, to her mind, shouldn't involve small talk and gifts: it was supposed to be ripping one another's clothes off, too busy kissing to waste time speaking.

She stood at the sink to fill the vase, wondering if this had been a good idea. If it turned into a disaster it would only make things worse. It was supposed to be an ego boost to make them feel better about themselves after being dumped. An awkward, unsatisfactory fumble wasn't going to help her move on. If anything, it would put her off getting involved in any capacity with another man.

She poured herself a glass of water and sighed as she took a sip. The fantasy had been nice while it had lasted. Before Mae had a chance to voice her second thoughts, Liam came to stand behind her, slipping his arms around her waist.

'I've been waiting all day for this,' he whispered into her ear, melting any concerns that this wasn't going to live up to her expectations. His breath against her neck brought her body back to full attention, as though it had been waiting just for him.

As her heart kicked into overdrive, her nipples tightened and arousal burst through the dam walls, she knew she needed Liam.

'Me too.' She could hardly speak, her body entirely focused on Liam's touch—including her brain.

He kissed her neck where the hairs were already standing to attention, her body hyper-aware of him being so close. A soft sigh escaped her lips, which she soon caught again with an intake of breath when he slid his hands under her dress. Skin on skin, he travelled up her thighs, slowly, carefully and confidently. He paused when he reached her panties and she held her breath, waiting to see what he would do next. Much to her dismay he didn't rip them off and toss them aside, but kept skimming the sides of her body until he reached her chest. He pressed himself closer so she could feel how turned on he was, his hardness nestled against her backside. She didn't think she'd ever been so aroused when still fully clothed.

Then he yanked down her bra and the front of her dress, exposing her breasts to the cool air and his strong hands. Her entire being was straining now for his attention, that aching need taking her over completely. When he cupped her breasts and tugged her nipples, she almost orgasmed right there and then.

Unable to remain passive, Mae spun around to kiss him. She began to pull at his T-shirt, desperate to expose his body too, but she had to give up on her quest when he refused to relinquish his quest to drive her insane. He lowered his head and caught her nipple in his mouth, sucking as he kneaded her breasts with both hands. Mae braced herself against the kitchen work top because her legs had apparently stopped working.

He licked, sucked and played with her until she was begging him to give her some release. 'Liam, please...'

She didn't have to ask again. Without hesitation, he

put his hands up her dress and whipped her underwear down her legs. Mae was so wet by then, his fingers slid easily inside her. She had to cling on to him for support now that he was totally in control of what was happening to her body. He literally had her at his fingertips. Slow strokes, quick circles and his steady persistence brought her hurtling to release. Liam maintained eye contact as she climaxed, making it all the more intense.

It surprised her, overwhelmed her, as she came again and again. Only when every tremor had finished rippling through her body did he finally release her.

'Are you okay?' he asked softly.

'Uh-huh.' She didn't even know what words were any more.

Liam grinned. 'I'll take that as a yes. You want to take this upstairs?'

She nodded, though even that took effort. Her body no longer felt like hers, more like a marionette manipulated by Liam, and without him she didn't know how to move any more. He took her hand, but they'd only taken a couple of steps when her knees buckled and she had to grab hold of him to remain upright.

'Although I'm not sure if I can.' She was no virgin and, though it had been a while, she still remembered every lover she'd ever had. None had had this effect on her, making her orgasm so hard, so quickly, it left her incapacitated. Especially when they hadn't even slept together. If this was just a taste of the power he could have over, how they could be together, Mae already knew she wouldn't want this to end between them.

That definitely wasn't in keeping with their casual agreement.

Liam caught her before she fell and swept her up in his arms, ignoring her protests that she was too heavy. 'Sure, there's nothing of you.'

To prove his point, he carried her straight upstairs with a swagger to his step, which might have been caused by the pride of bringing Mae to climax so easily, or by the erection pressing against his fly as she nuzzled into his chest. Either way, the encounter had bolstered him mentally and physically and he couldn't wait for more. As long as Mae was up to it.

She seemed wiped out. He supposed it was a lot to process after being on her own for such a long time. He could only imagine how he was going to feel after the same, not that it was making his jeans any more comfortable. The last people they'd slept with were people they'd been in relationships with, partners they'd loved and who'd ultimately found them lacking in some way. This might only be a sexual release for both of them now, but that didn't mean there wouldn't be some emotional involvement. If not with each other, at least for themselves. They needed it—to know they were normal, they were wanted and that they were able to move on from their pasts.

'That one.' Mae pointed towards the door at the end of the landing.

He nudged it open, taking her into a room filled with photos and trinkets of her life in Boston, a little nest of comfort she'd built for herself in this new country. The fact that she was giving him permission to enter into this sanctuary showed how much trust she was putting in him not to hurt her—another reason this couldn't go beyond a non-meaningful fling. Mae deserved someone who would put her feelings above everyone else's, and he couldn't prioritise her over Shannon. All he could do was make her feel good, make her feel appreciated and wanted, for as long as they had together.

He set her down on the mattress, nestled in the bank of cushions adorning the bed. With an impatient swipe of her hands, Mae nudged them onto the floor, then proceeded to strip her dress over her head. She tossed it on the floor with her bra, so she was lying there beautifully naked waiting for him, the red hair spread around her making her look like Venus come to life.

Liam had a sudden moment of imposter syndrome, believing he wasn't worthy of being here with her. That he was as bad as her ex, using her to satiate his needs without considering her feelings enough. Those negative thoughts only lasted until she hooked her fingers into the belt loops on his jeans and pulled him closer.

'Aren't you going to join me?' Despite her bravado, he could see her nervously worrying her bottom lip with her teeth and realised she needed this as much as he did.

'If you insist.' As eager as he was to get naked with her, he took his time undressing, watching the appreciation and desire turn her eyes to glittering jade. The T-shirt went first, joining the pile of clothes and cushions on the floor. He reached for her hand and moved it over his chest, down his stomach and briefly over his crotch.

'I like it when you touch me.' His honesty manifested itself almost as a growl, his voice so thick with arousal and lust for her.

Mae sat up, alert once more, the weariness dissipating as she took her cue. Kneeling on the bed, she unbuckled his belt, every deliberate movement extending the foreplay. When she popped open the buttons on his fly, it was all he could do to restrain himself, but he wasn't going to rush the best thing to happen to him in months. Instead, he stood tall, clinging on to his resolve as she pushed his jeans away and teased his erection through his boxers. She gripped him through the cotton fabric and he gritted his teeth together, fighting every natural urge that came rushing forward at her touch.

When she pulled his underwear down and exclaimed, 'Well, hello, soldier!', all bets were off. He loved this playful, flirtatious side to Mae. Along with her touch, it helped him forget about everything his ex had done to him and simply enjoy the moment with her.

In a hurry to kick off the rest of his clothes, he almost stumbled onto the bed with her, spurred on by her little giggle. Lying face to face, Liam kissed her, luxuriating in the soft, welcoming feel of her lips against his. She'd become his sanctuary.

Something between them seemed to have shifted in those few seconds. The frenzied passion was now a sensual exploration as they caressed each other's naked bodies, the kisses tender and softer than before, as if they were drawing comfort from one another rather than embarking on what was supposed to be a wild, reckless shag-a-thon.

Mae must have thought the same, as her gentle strokes along his shaft now became insistent and demanding, until he couldn't think straight, forcing all his energy into not embarrassing himself, and also wanting her with a hunger that was eating him from the inside out.

He moved so she was underneath him, her soft breasts pushed so temptingly against him he couldn't resist, especially when she was so responsive every time he touched her there. With one breast cupped in his palm, he grazed his teeth over the sensitive bud atop, tugging on it until she was groaning and writhing with a mixture of frustration and pleasure. He knew, because he felt it too. He was enjoying all the sensations, wanting instant gratification but also wanting to make this last for ever. The horny excitement, the restlessness and stimulation of being together and not yet consummating their relationship, were all preferable to feeling miserable, analysing where he'd gone wrong and worrying about the future.

Mae liked him, and clearly wanted him, and that was enough for now. She grabbed his backside and pulled him flush against her—a woman who knew her own mind and wasn't afraid to show him what was on it.

'I need to get some protection.' He'd bought a packet of condoms in preparation and, though he was loath to move from his current position, they were lying in the heap of clothes on the floor.

'In my night stand. Hold on.' Mae rummaged one-handed in the drawer beside the bed and produced a foil packet.

He raised an eyebrow. 'I don't mean to be judgemental, but I was under the impression you hadn't been with anyone since…you know.'

He hated himself for even thinking it, never mind saying it. It was none of his business if she'd been in bed with half the country, but he found himself irrationally hating anyone who'd been here with her before him. Part of the reason he'd bonded with Mae was that they'd been in similar circumstances relationship-wise and, to him, that included post-break-up celibacy, so they'd experience this breakthrough in their emotional and physical development together.

Ugh. So much for 'no strings' if he was jealous of anyone she potentially could have slept with before they'd even met.

'Sorry. Sorry. I have no right to say anything about your love life.'

Mae held his face in her hands and locked her eyes on to his. 'I haven't been with anyone since my non-wedding day. I haven't wanted to be with anyone until you. And I haven't any intention of sleeping with anyone but you for the near future, okay? I bought them especially. I mean, if we're embarking on some sort of sex-fest until we're both rendered incapable of walking and talking, we don't want to run out, right?'

'Right. I'm sorry...'

Mae placed a finger on his lips. 'No apologies. Just fun.'

'Just fun,' he muttered against her finger before drawing it into his mouth and sucking it hard.

Mae continued the battle of one-upmanship by putting the condom on him herself, Liam breaking out in a sweat as he fought so hard to maintain his composure.

'You do not play fair at all, Dr Watters.' Pinning her hands to the bed, he kissed the smug smile of satisfaction from her lips.

He nudged her knees apart and positioned himself between her legs, entering her in one swift move that seemed to stun them both. It certainly took him a long, hot minute to recompose himself, once the fireworks had stopped going off in his head. Mae's little gasp when he entered her soon turned to a sigh of satisfaction as he moved inside her. Every time they joined together was a test of his restraint when he just wanted to give himself over to the euphoria he was experiencing. Dipping in and out of her felt like a new reward every time.

Greedy for more, he hooked her legs over his shoulders and pushed deeper, harder, faster. Mae's gasps became louder, quicker, more ragged. Then he realised his breathing was rapid too, that pressure to give in to his release becoming so intense, he thought he'd explode.

He watched where their bodies were joined as he slid in and out of this beautiful woman, realising how privileged he was to be in this position. To be with Mae. He kissed her, long and passionately, showing her how grateful he was with every thrust of his hips. He waited until she tightened around him, clutching at his back as her orgasm hit, until he found complete satisfaction too. Mae's cry was drowned out by his roar of triumph, their bodies rocking together until they had nothing left to give and his throat was raw.

Yet he found himself reluctant to move away when it was all over, only doing so when his knees were too weak to hold him up any longer.

'This might just kill me,' he said, rolling over beside her.

'Yeah, but you'll die happy.' Mae turned on her side and kissed him.

'Amen.' He lay on his back, fighting to get his breath back and praying this wouldn't be the last time they had this. That it was only the beginning. He needed this feeling, needed Mae, to help him forget all the bad stuff and, yes, make him happy. It was a long time since he'd had anything in his life to smile about and now it would be hard to wipe the grin off his face.

'What are you smiling about?'

'This. You, and how you make me feel like a king,' he said honestly. There was no point in hiding it, not when communication had been his downfall in the past and he wanted this to last with Mae for as long as possible.

'I think you did all the hard work…this time.' Mae stood up and walked towards the bathroom, giving him an envious view of her pert backside. Though he was sorry she was leaving him in bed without her, he kept hold of her words, the twinkle in her eye and the promise that they would do this all over again.

CHAPTER SEVEN

MAE STARED AT the reflection in the bathroom mirror. She didn't recognise the flushed face staring back or the twinkle back in her eyes, and her hair made her look as though she'd been thoroughly ravished in bed. Which she had. The wanton woman smiled back at her. This was exactly what she needed: fun; an ego boost... Liam.

And it felt safe, knowing he couldn't break her heart, because she wasn't going to give it to him. He could have her body; she'd give it willingly after he'd showed her exactly what he could do with it. The rest she intended to keep under lock and key, knowing she couldn't trust anyone not to damage it—including herself.

That said, she wasn't in a rush for their tryst to end just yet. She splashed some water over her face and freshened up before going back into the room. The sight of Liam stretched out naked on her bed convinced her that, just because this was supposed to be casual, it didn't mean he shouldn't stay a little while longer. Since Shannon was staying at his parents' place, and he didn't seem to be in a hurry to leave either, Mae slid back into bed next to him.

'No taxi waiting for you?'

'No…sorry, do you want me to leave?' He sat up immediately and reached down for his clothes, clearly mistaking her teasing for a hint he should leave.

'No. Not at all. I just thought that might be how these things work—you know?—wham, bam.'

'There was no "wham bam" involved, but I do thank you, ma'am—very, very much.' Liam punctuated the words with kisses dotted along her collarbone, making her feel she never wanted him to leave.

'I just… I don't do this. I guess I'm just trying to figure out what the rules are.' She didn't want to misstep and have it end when she was already enjoying the benefits.

'We make our own rules. If we want to cuddle after, hey, that's normal—I think. As long as we're both comfortable with what's happening, I don't see any reason to bolt the second the deed is done.'

'The deed?' She chuckled.

'You know what I mean. We're only here for one thing.' He let his hand drift along the curve of her waist, barely touching her, but her body responded all the same, ready to accept him all over again.

'Yeah, but there's no rush, is there? Shannon's with your mum and dad, and it seems foolish for us both to spend the night alone in separate houses. Not that I'm expecting you to stay over, or anything. But, you know, we can hang out, order takeaway and watch trash TV. If that doesn't seem too much like breaking the rules?' She didn't want to frighten him off but it would be nice to have some company. Since moving in, she'd spent every night on her own, and it seemed a little churlish to send him home simply because it breached the 'hook-up and done' code.

'Look.' He turned onto his side, giving her a serious look. 'We both know the score. Neither of us is going to read more into what's happening than what we've agreed to. I'd actually enjoy doing something normal, like ordering some food and vegging out in front of the telly. In company, for once. No, this probably isn't like any other casual relationship because we already know each other, and we work together. As long as we are both happy, I don't see the problem. If that changes, then we'll reconsider our arrangement. Deal?'

'Deal.' Mae shook his outstretched hand. It didn't seem odd at all to make a deal whilst lying naked with a co-worker, the way her life had been going lately. Infinitely preferable to moving halfway across the world and being dumped on her wedding day.

'Okay, so... Chinese, Indian, burgers...?' Liam lifted his phone and began scrolling.

'Chinese,' she said without hesitation, her stomach rumbling, having been too nervous to eat anything before their date.

He held the screen so she could see the menu and

pick what she wanted to eat, then he added his order, along with extra portions of rice and noodles. 'Done.'

When Mae saw the size of the order he'd just put in, she began to get concerned. 'The way you've been feeding me recently, I'm going to end up the size of a house.'

She'd already put on a little weight on after the wedding, during her comfort eating stage.

'I like your curves,' he said, grabbing hold of her backside and pulling her flush against him. 'Besides, we can always work off a few calories.'

'Yeah?' With his eyes darkening with desire, it was clear how he planned to work out. His idea of exercise sure beat those dreaded early-morning gym trips. She might just cancel her membership and employ him as her personal trainer instead.

'Well, the app says delivery is going to take at least an hour. I think we could squeeze in a good workout, you know? Build up an appetite.' He was moving over her again, covering her with his body and rolling her onto her back. Mae submitted completely and willingly.

'We wouldn't want to get lazy. It's important to balance diet and exercise for your wellbeing,' she muttered as he dipped his head to capture her mouth once more.

Mae sighed into the kiss, reaching up to wind her fingers in Liam's hair and claim him as hers for a little while longer. This was all temporary—a fantasy she was allowed to indulge in to make her feel better about herself. It was working. When she was with Liam, he

treated her like a goddess. She was no longer the rejected bride not worthy of love but a sexy, confident
single woman embarking on a passionate fling. Liam
O'Conner was just the tonic she needed.

'You want another beer?' Mae shouted from the
kitchen.

'Why not? I can always walk home.' Whilst he had
no intention of going to work with a hangover tomorrow, he was enjoying the evening.

Eating a takeaway while watching soap operas was
a normal night. Liam did it all the time. So why did
it feel so special just because he was doing it with
Mae? Probably because it felt comfortable, knowing
she was happy to do it. Even on the nights he and Clodagh had been at home together, she hadn't wanted to
sit in with him, preferring to go out with 'the girls'.
He'd been too boring, too staid, because he'd simply
wanted family time together. Secrecy was a big part of
his arrangement with Mae, for everyone's sake. It also
meant there wasn't any pressure to go out clubbing, or
try to be someone he wasn't. This was enough for her,
and so was he.

'There's enough food left to feed the street.' She
tossed him a beer and curled up beside him on the sofa.

'We can box it up and put it in the fridge once it's
cooled down. I'll have it for breakfast.'

'Yuk.' She screwed up her nose and took a slug of

beer from her bottle. 'I don't know how you can eat so much and still look so good.'

'I do have to work at it. I've got a home gym, and eat salads in between parent visits usually. I've made an exception for you this week, but it's nice to know you think I'm hot.' He was teasing her but she was definitely giving him an ego boost. Not only with her comments, but the way she'd responded to him in bed, where he knew he was most definitely doing something right.

Liam supposed sex had kind of taken a back seat between Clodagh and him due to shift clashes and, if he was honest, a lack of interest. They hadn't made enough time, or effort. Yet he seemed to be able to find both for Mae. Perhaps he'd known deep down that he and Clodagh were over and had checked out long before she had.

In which case, he couldn't blame her for having gone elsewhere. It was being with Mae that showed him all that had been missing in the relationship—passion, fun and enjoying one another. He'd settled for less because he wanted to save his family, provide some stability in Shannon's life and be the good parent he'd had growing up, but family life had been far from perfect. Some day he hoped he could have it all: a romantic, fun relationship that also nurtured a loving environment for his daughter to grow up in.

'You know you are. Confidence is not something you seem to have a problem with.'

'A common misconception about me. Yes, I'm an extrovert, but that doesn't mean I don't have hang-ups like everyone else. You know how it feels when you've been rejected—it hurts.'

He saw her wince and mentally kicked himself for bringing up her past relationship woes and spoiling the evening. 'Sorry. I just mean we're here together tonight because we're too afraid to commit to a proper relationship again. This is safe until we're ready to trust someone with our hearts some day.'

Mae scrambled to sit upright, her legs tucked under her to bring her up to the same height as Liam. 'So you think you'll want to do the whole serious relationship again? That's not for me.'

'No? Never, ever?' He let out a long breath. 'I don't think I could do that. I need to be with someone.'

'Why is it so important? You're doing okay, just you and Shannon. Why do you need to bring a third party in to make you happy, knowing they could do the opposite?'

He had to think on that one for a bit, knowing her fears were justified. It wasn't that he hadn't considered it: it was why they were keeping this secret, after all. He didn't want Shannon to get hurt, and by keeping things casual with Mae he was protecting his own heart. Especially knowing she didn't want another serious relationship. Ultimately, though, he thought the risk would be worth taking if he could still find that special someone to share his life with.

'I know a lot of people resent their parents, or choose partners that are the complete opposite to who they were, but you've met my mum and dad. They're great, right?'

She nodded with a smile. 'Yes, they are.'

'Growing up in that place was the happiest time of my life. I know it's unconventional, and it was noisy, and they were always working, but they always made time for me and each other. Family was the most important thing, and I still believe that. I just want that sort of security for Shannon, as well as for me. I know she has me and her grandparents, even her mother on occasion, but it's not the same. I want someone to share the parenting with, to cook dinner with after work, to go on holiday and make plans for the future with. Maybe even have more kids some day. I don't want one failed relationship to take all of that away for ever.'

Mae watched him with something he was sure was a mixture of surprise and sadness. As though she didn't believe he could still want all of that, and sure she was too afraid to.

'I can sort of see where you're coming from, even if my childhood has given me a different perspective on that. I never knew my father: he split when I was little, leaving Mum to raise me. I loved her so much. She was like my best friend, you know? So strong and independent and caring. Losing her... Well, it was devastating.' Her voice faltered. 'I tried the serious relationship thing with Diarmuid, but in hindsight I think

I was just looking for a replacement—something to fill the void the loss of my mother had created. I realise now I'm not going to find that with anyone. She's simply irreplaceable.'

Liam saw through her smile to the heartbreak and loneliness inside her. At least he had Shannon and his parents to keep him buoyed, and remind him he was loved. Mae had no one and it was a shame she wanted to keep it that way.

'By your own admission, your marriage was probably a mistake. Something you rushed into. That doesn't mean there isn't someone out there who's perfect for you, that you could be happy with. Didn't you ever want a family of your own?'

It was a simple enough question, but it packed a powerful punch straight through Mae's defences and straight to her heart. Liam *saw* her.

'I did, at one point. I mean, when you grow up in a one-parent family always struggling for money, it's the dream to have the whole family package, including a dad to love and support you. When I met Diarmuid, I thought we would have that too. I guess it was better he left me when he did, rather than walk away later on an entire family. It's made me think about what a lucky escape I've had and how careful I need to be in future. I don't want to inflict a difficult childhood on an innocent child because I got carried away in a romantic fantasy.

'The reality of life is that relationships don't work out. I've accepted that. I mean, if you'd known Clodagh was going to leave, would you have started a family?' Mae threw the question back at him even though she knew she was treading on dangerous ground, because Shannon was everything to Liam. She just wanted him to realise the gravity behind her making that kind of decision—choosing to protect potential offspring before they even came into existence.

The uncharacteristic scowl suggested perhaps she had strayed too far beyond those blurred lines between a fling and something more personal. She doubted a no-strings arrangement included deep and meaningful conversations about their life choices and motivations.

'We can't live our lives on "ifs" and "buts", Mae, or we'd never accomplish anything. Okay, so it didn't work out between Clodagh and I, but I wouldn't be without Shannon. Would I have done things differently given a chance? Yes. Perhaps I was more invested in the idea of family than putting in the work to make sure we stayed together, but I don't regret becoming a father. I regret letting her and Clodagh down by not doing enough to make the relationship work, but I'm not going to let it steal my future from me. I've learned some lessons, and hope it will help me if I do ever get into another long-term relationship, but there's no point in looking back any more. Being with you has shown me that.' He grabbed hold of her feet and pulled her, so she slid down the couch towards him, and kissed her.

Mae's eyes fluttered shut and she let the feel of his lips dictate her mood instead of the noise currently buzzing in her head. She wanted to focus on Liam kissing her, on being together right now, instead of worrying about the future.

Except she couldn't put his words to the back of her mind just yet. He still wanted marriage, a family and everything she'd thought was possible once upon a time. She wished she had his optimism, or even that she could be 'the one' for him and that they'd all live happily ever after. Life had cruelly illustrated to her that it wasn't a realistic expectation, even if Liam did make a good argument.

Fear held her back from being with someone. From being with Liam. She was scared of being rejected again, of her heart taking another beating, of planning a future together and having it whipped away from her again. The only thing worse than having to go through that again, of losing someone else she loved, would be having a child live through it too. She wouldn't be able to live with the guilt of that. Yet the way Liam talked about his daughter, the love he obviously had for her, made her heart ache a little more. It was as though she'd lost an entire family because of Diarmuid, because she could never let anyone get close to her again after the way he'd treated her.

In moments like this, being with Liam, she was beginning to have second thoughts about remaining alone. 'For ever' seemed like a long time, especially if it meant not having company like this, with someone who knew her. What she had with Liam wasn't something she'd be able to replicate in the future. A casual fling with some random guy she met in a bar or club was never going to have the same depth as this thing with Liam. She knew that after only one day. This wasn't just sex, it was amazing sex, and she wondered if that was because they knew more about each other than two strangers who'd simply hooked up one night.

The passion and desire had likely built up from seeing each other at work and not being able to touch one another. She wondered if that was sustainable. It certainly felt like it, when they were already pulling at each other's clothes again, impatient to experience that ecstasy together all over again.

More frighteningly, perhaps she was beginning to ask herself if this could be more than stealing a few hours together. Liam had been open about wanting a partner willing to settle down and raise a family with him and, whilst Mae didn't know if she was open to that possibility, she had definitely grown close to Liam and his daughter.

The question now was whether or not she was willing to risk her peace of mind for more time with Liam.

Liam was wrapped around Mae's naked body, trying to get his breath back—again. This time they hadn't made it to the bedroom and, despite the uncomfortable confines of the sofa, his body was finally getting weary. He was in danger of falling into a food and sex coma, having over-indulged in both. Not that he was complaining. He just needed a little time before he was ready for action again.

'I should probably go,' he muttered into the back of her neck as they lay spooning on the couch.

Mae groaned and wriggled against him, not doing anything to persuade him he should leave.

'We both need some sleep.' He half-heartedly tried again to convince them both to move, but he was pleasantly exhausted, and quite happy to remain in situ with Mae in his arms.

'You could stay. I mean, it's too late to walk home, if you could even manage to stand right now, and it seems pointless paying for a taxi when your car's outside...'

'I don't know...'

'I just thought, you know, if you wanted to stay on the couch for the night. Sorry... I didn't mean to overstep any boundaries.' Mae sat up, extracting herself from his arms and grabbing the clothes she'd discarded earlier.

'Hey. I know you were only thinking of me. Don't worry. It's just that I don't have a toothbrush and I don't want to spoil the illusion of this erotic fantasy with my very real morning breath.'

Liam didn't want her to feel bad because he hadn't immediately jumped at her invitation. He'd hesitated because it had crossed his mind that staying the night wasn't in keeping with the idea of 'just sex', but he supposed they'd crossed that line some time ago. Having dinner and discussing their past relationships over drinks probably wasn't the norm for this kind of set-up.

It wasn't that he didn't want to stay the night: it would be easier, and it would mean he didn't have to go home to an empty house. He was merely worried that staying over with Mae might become too comfortable. This felt more like the beginning of a relationship than something that wasn't supposed to have any emotional attachment for them. He already knew he had feelings for Mae that went beyond the physical—a bad move when she'd told him in no uncertain terms she didn't want a commitment.

Yet, they were electric together, and that wasn't something he could easily walk away from. Especially when his legs were like jelly after all his exertions tonight.

'I'm sure I have a spare in the bathroom. If you want to stay…if it's not breaking the rules…'

'I'm not going to stay on the sofa, Mae.'

'Oh. Okay. Do you need me to order a cab?' She looked a little crestfallen and Liam almost felt bad about teasing her.

'If I'm sleeping here tonight, I want to do it in your bed. These bones of mine are getting too old to spend the night anywhere but in a nice, comfy bed.' That definitely wasn't in keeping with the idea of just sex, but they'd already crossed so many boundaries that others might consider casual that it hardly mattered now. Not if it meant waking up in Mae's arms. Who knew when they'd next get to spend time together, never mind an entire night? Liam intended to make the most of his child-free time.

Although Mae was smiling, seemingly pleased by his decision, he did sense some hesitation before she took it when he held out his hand to her.

'I only meant to sleep. I don't believe you can have too much of a good thing, but I do think some recovery time is necessary before you indulge again.' Liam grinned, fully intending to indulge again before he finally had to leave. He knew they were both exhausted, with jobs and lives of their own to go back to tomorrow, but they could let the fantasy go on a little bit longer.

'A sleep, a shower and some breakfast in the morning should set us both to rights again.' Mae led the way back upstairs, with Liam keen to follow.

'That sounds like a plan.' And an excellent way to start a new day. It was a shame this was probably only a one-off when the thought of waking up in Mae's bed, with her naked beside him, was likely something he could easily get used to.

The sound of his phone buzzing roused Liam from a deep sleep. It took him a few seconds to come to in the dark and realise where he was. Then Mae stirred beside him and he was tempted to ignore the call and snuggle back under the sheets with her. Instead, one glance at the screen and he was straight out of bed, phone in hand.

'Dad? What's wrong?' It was three o'clock in the morning and he knew his parents wouldn't have called him unless something was seriously amiss.

'Sorry to wake you, son, but it's Shannon.'

Liam's stomach plummeted through the floor. 'What's happened?'

He bounded down the stairs and grabbed his clothes from the floor, dressing one-handed while waiting to hear whatever bad news his father was about to impart.

'Now, don't panic…'

The very words were guaranteed to make him panic. 'Is she all right?'

'She's had a fall. I'm not sure if she was disoriented in the dark, or if she was sleep walking, but she fell down the stairs. The poor lamb knocked herself out for a bit and I think she might have broken her arm. I've phoned for an ambulance but I thought maybe you could get here quicker to take a look and reassure her.'

He could have, if he hadn't been drinking at Mae's house, but he didn't want to tell them that and complicate the situation any further.

'I'll be there as quick as I can.' Liam hung up so he could order a taxi, cursing himself for taking his eyes off the ball. In paying more heed to his libido than his daughter, he'd failed her and left her to get hurt whilst he'd been out pretending he was a single man with no responsibilities.

Liam lifted one of his shoes and fired it across the room, watching it ricochet off the kitchen door. A pointless exercise, since he had to go and pick it up again or he couldn't leave the house, and it did nothing to alleviate the guilt and frustration he was experiencing. He was angry at himself for going against everything he'd promised himself and Shannon after Clodagh had left. Spending the night with Mae hadn't been putting his daughter's needs first, and it certainly hadn't been the action of a man trying to be a better father. It had been selfish and foolish, and now his daughter was going to pay the price for his mistakes, again.

'Is there something wrong?' Mae appeared in the doorway, hair in disarray, eyes half-closed with sleep, tying the belt of her dressing gown around her waist.

Liam clenched his teeth together, trying to ignore the fact that her bare legs seemed to go on for ever and that he knew exactly what was under that robe. 'Shannon fell down the stairs and hurt herself. I have to get to the pub.'

'I'm so sorry. Let me come with you.'

'The taxi's on its way. I'm not waiting for you. My daughter needs me and I've already let her down tonight.'

'I swear I'll be two minutes. Let me help. If I'm not down when the cab comes, you can go without me.' She hovered in the doorway, waiting for him to give her the nod, to let her know things were okay between them.

Although he was regretting leaving Shannon tonight,

it wasn't Mae's fault. She'd done everything right. That was the problem. He hadn't wanted to leave, and he knew that was bad news for the future. A fling between them was always going to be complicated and he simply couldn't afford this level of distraction taking him away from his daughter.

He also knew turning up together would cause problems. His parents weren't stupid; they'd know they'd spent the night together. Since he was already having second thoughts about continuing whatever this was with Mae, explaining the circumstances was not going to put him in a good light with anyone. He would need to come up with a pretty good excuse as to why she was with him at this time of the morning if he was to avoid embarrassing everyone involved.

However, if the ambulance was too far away and Shannon had been seriously hurt, he might need an extra pair of medical hands. His daughter's welfare had to come before his personal problems—something he should have remembered before he let her get hurt. Now he would simply have to swallow his pride and get to his daughter as fast as possible. Any difficult conversations to be had with his parents and Mae would have to wait until he knew Shannon was all right.

'Two minutes,' he said gruffly, hoping it expressed both his impatience and a hint that this was already over between them.

Mae raced back upstairs and he opened the door, waiting for the glare of the taxi headlights to turn into the street, part of him hoping it would appear before Mae did, so he didn't have to face the problem of her being there. Mae would understand if he went without her. After all, a single dad called away to deal with his daughter in the middle of the night wasn't the fun he'd promised. It represented the sort of commitment she'd told him she didn't want in her life.

When she did bounce back downstairs ready to go, clad in jeans, sweater and pulling on a pair of running shoes, it prompted him to ask himself why. If Mae was prepared to involve herself in his domestic dramas, it had to be because she was more invested in Shannon and him than she'd even realised. Whilst ultimately that was what he wanted, someone who'd be there for Shannon and him, he knew that wasn't the future Mae saw for herself.

There was no point in fooling themselves that this was going to work. It wouldn't be fair to anyone when it inevitably ended, no one satisfied with what they'd settled for. They would have to put this down to what it was—a one-night stand with added complications— and go back to their own separate lives. It had been nice while it lasted, a brief respite from beating himself up over his personal failures. Once he was assured Shannon was okay, it would be back to business as usual.

The cab ride over to the pub was excruciating. Liam hadn't spoken to her since they'd left the house and she knew it was because he regretted everything that had happened between them. If they hadn't been so caught up in one another, Liam would have been at home with Shannon and she wouldn't have hurt herself. For someone who'd been so careful to protect his daughter until now, he'd be devastated by these events.

Mae could have let him go to deal with the situation himself, but she'd feared if she did she might never see him again, at least outside of a professional capacity. She still wasn't ready for their time to end just yet and hoped by showing him she cared about Shannon too they might be able to salvage something between them.

Although she'd sworn not to commit to anything or anyone capable of breaking her heart somewhere down the line, she was already in too deep with Liam to walk away now. If they couldn't manage to keep things casual, she hoped they could at least take things slowly if she was to venture back into a relationship.

Talking tonight, enjoying each other's company, making love and going to bed together at the end of the day were all things she'd been missing in her life. Liam had shown her what she could still have if she was brave enough to open up her life, and her heart, to the possibility of being with someone again.

Yes, it was scary embarking on something with a man who had such a great responsibility as a father but, if being a part of his family was what it took for him to continue seeing one another, Mae was willing to try. As long as they went into it with their eyes open, aware of how they'd both been scarred in the past, and promising never to reopen those old wounds with actions of their own, they might stand a chance.

'Thanks.'

Liam threw some money at the driver outside the pub before getting out of the car without even looking back to see if Mae was following. Obviously his primary concern was for Shannon, but it still hurt she didn't warrant a smidge of his attention.

'She's inside. We thought we'd keep her downstairs so the paramedics could get to her easier.' Paddy met them at the entrance of the dark pub, which seemed so eerie at this time of the morning with no one else around, the noise of customers seemingly a distant memory.

They crossed the rain-soaked cobbles and rushed inside, both praying Shannon wasn't too badly injured.

'The ambulance is on the way. We loaned the car to Sean tonight so he could go to the cash and carry for us in the morning, otherwise we would have driven her ourselves.' They found his mother cradling Shannon in one of the booths in which only a few hours ago people would've been sitting, drinking and having fun.

'It's fine. We're here now. Daddy's here, sweetie.' Liam moved so Shannon was resting her head on his lap instead of his mother's.

Mae saw the look Moira gave Liam and her, but she made no comment and received no explanation, though it must've been obvious what had gone on. She must look a mess with mega bedhead, not to mention her make-up sweated off after her sex session with Liam, wearing the first clothes that came to hand. That alone would've signalled what they'd been up to, even if arriving together in the early hours of the morning hadn't.

She felt herself heat up under Moira's scrutiny and ducked into the other side of the booth from Liam, out of harm's way. 'How is she?'

'There's quite a bad gash at her temple. Is your head hurting, sweetie?' Liam brushed her blood-matted hair away from her face, the look of love in his eyes for his daughter so intense, it made Mae want to weep.

It was a promise to love and protect her at all costs. Mae had never had any man look at her that way, parent or partner. Nor was she likely to if she didn't open up her life, and her heart, to let someone close enough to love her like that. At this moment in time, she was tempted to go against everything she'd promised herself and take a risk on love again if it meant Liam might look at her like that some day.

'Where were you, Daddy? I had a bad dream and I couldn't find you.'

Mae didn't know which was worse to witness—the little girl's distress, or the cloud of guilt that moved over her father's face. She wanted to reach out and hug both of them, but knew that would be over-stepping so many boundaries in front of Liam's family and he wouldn't appreciate it.

'I know, Shannon. I'm sorry. I'll never leave you on

your own again, okay? Now, can you be a big, brave girl and let me see where you're hurt?'

Shannon nodded slowly, naturally wary but trusting her father not to do anything to cause her any unnecessary pain. Liam would blame himself for Shannon getting hurt, of course—that was the nature of a good parent—but it was an accident that no one could have prevented. Mae wasn't ashamed to admit she envied their relationship when it had been missing in her life for too long. She'd never had it with her father and, now that her mother was gone, there was no one in her life she could trust implicitly always to look out for her like that. If she didn't take a few risks, she never would.

'Could you put some more lights on, Paddy, please? And Moira, could you pass me the first-aid kit?' If she was going to be seen here tonight as someone other than the harlot who'd tempted a good dad away from his daughter, then Mae needed to earn her place.

Immediately, Paddy and Moira sprang into action, and she was sure they were simply glad to have a part to play too. Now that they could better see what they were dealing with, Liam helped Shannon on to the table.

Mae began cleaning the wound on the little girl's temple. 'This might sting a little bit, Shannon, but we have to clean the area to see how deep the cut is.'

'I need to see this arm too, love.' Liam tried to persuade her to let him assess what damage had been done there, but Shannon cradled the limp limb closer to her body, refusing his request.

Once Mae had finished dressing the head wound, she moved around to join Liam at the end of the table to face Shannon. 'You're lucky. You have two doctors who want to help you feel better. Won't you let us take a look? It won't heal unless we do, and you don't want to go about with one wing for ever, do you?'

That made Shannon smile, especially when Liam quacked at her. 'You're my little lame duck, aren't you, Shannon?'

'Quack, quack,' she responded, and tentatively held out her arm for Liam to look at it.

'Good girl.'

Carefully, Liam felt along the bruised arm, Shannon flinching when he reached her elbow. 'Okay, I think there's a fracture there. We need to stabilise that until the paramedics get here. Is there any update on that?'

'I'll phone again.' Paddy disappeared back behind the bar.

'Moira, do you have anything we could use as a splint? Like a piece of wood, or even a rolled-up newspaper would do for now. We could tie that around her arm temporarily to immobilise it.'

Mae wanted to do something other than sit waiting for someone else to help Shannon. She hated to see her in pain, as much as she disliked watching her father's anguish. It was important to her that she could be there for them and Mae realised that she'd already made that commitment she was so afraid of. Once Shannon was treated at the hospital and they knew she was all right, Mae would discuss the matter with Liam. If he was on board, she'd like to take that first step back into the relationship world with him.

'Here you go. I brought a couple of towels too.' Moira returned with some makeshift medical supplies for Mae to use whilst Liam reassured his daughter they were working in her best interests.

'Shannon, if you can hold your arm out, Mae is going to tie some things around it to keep it straight. We need you to stay still until she's all done.' Liam had one arm around Shannon's waist, holding her close, with the other presenting the broken limb for Mae to work on.

She was grateful he was allowing her to be of some assistance when she knew he was quite capable of doing all this on his own. Hopefully it was a sign that he was ready for her to be part of their lives too.

'When you get to the hospital they'll put a proper cast on it for you, but we're just going to tie this on now so it doesn't hurt any more when you move it.' Mae used the bandages in the first-aid kit to hold the temporary fix in place, but she was relieved when she heard the sirens outside.

'I'll go and direct them in.' Paddy, still in his pyjamas, rushed out into the street so they didn't waste any time trying to locate their patient. A short time later, he returned with two paramedics, carrying their first-aid gear.

'Over here.' Liam waved them over and Mae moved out of the way so they had full access to examine Shannon.

'It looks as though someone has beat us to it,' one of the men commented on seeing Shannon's home-made splint.

'We're both doctors, but unfortunately we didn't have the means to get her to hospital ourselves tonight. Shannon had a fall down the stairs while she was staying with my parents. She had a bad knock to the head, and was briefly unconscious, but she's responsive and seems fine at the moment.'

'No sickness or dizzy spells?'

'No. She was out cold for a few moments, the longest time of my life. We just didn't want to do anything that might do her more harm than good.' Moira was hovering by the table, understandably concerned with her granddaughter's welfare, and no doubt blaming herself as much as Liam for the accident.

'That's fine. We'll do an X-ray on that arm at the hospital, Shannon, and try and make you more comfortable, but there's nothing to worry about. Is Mum or Dad coming with us in the ambulance?'

'I'm her dad. Mae's just a friend.' Liam asserted his position, and Mae's at the same time, as he scooped Shannon up into his arms, ready to leave.

'I guess I'll phone a cab to take me home.' Despite

her role in the drama, Mae was left feeling like a spare part with no real reason to be here, with Liam willing to leave her with his parents in an awkward post-hook-up situation.

'That's probably for the best. I'll call you later.'

The promise to get back in touch was the only thing saving her from total humiliation. It wouldn't do to get too needy; Liam was always going to put his daughter first. He was that kind of man, and if he hadn't been she probably wouldn't even be thinking of venturing into something beyond casual with him. It was precisely because he was loyal and loving that made her want to take that risk.

'I have the number of a local firm,' Moira informed her with a pat on the arm Mae hoped was more out of friendship than pity.

'Okay, sweetheart, I'll just be downstairs if you need me.' Liam tucked Shannon under the covers and edged towards the door. She'd wanted to sleep in his bed, and after the night they'd had and the guilt he was still carrying he couldn't say no.

'I just have to make a phone call then I promise I'll be right up again.' He didn't want to leave her, even though he knew she was safe and would likely be asleep before he reached the bottom of the stairs. It had been a long night for everyone. But he had also promised to call Mae.

Although it was late—technically speaking, it was

early morning, but since no one had slept he still counted it as night—he suspected Mae would be up. She'd been great tonight, helping with Shannon, and he was sure she'd want to be kept up to date with her progress. He'd already called his parents to let them know Shannon was fine, with no sign of concussion and a cast on her arm to show off in school that day. Their profuse apologies hadn't been necessary when it was his fault he'd left Shannon there, his only thoughts having been of the time he'd get to spend with Mae. He hoped his reassurances would help them get some sleep.

This call was going to be a little more difficult and painful. He'd waited until he'd come home to give him some space to think things over first, and to afford some privacy. Mae had been upfront about not wanting anything serious, so she deserved the same respect when it came to ending things.

She answered the call the second it rang. 'How is she?'

The concern in her voice made Liam ache all the more for the life he really wanted with Mae and Shannon. If only he could be sure that it would work between them, that she could commit to his family, he wouldn't have to choose between his daughter and her. It was a contest she could never win.

'They put a cast on her arm, but other than that she's fine. Currently asleep in my bed. She's understandably clingy and didn't even want me to come down and phone you.'

'In that case, I won't keep you. I just wanted to know she was okay.' Mae was about to end the call but that wasn't what Liam wanted—none of this was. But, if he didn't have this conversation now, he'd have to do it at work and it wouldn't be fair to ambush her like that.

'Listen, Mae, tonight has really opened my eyes. I just don't think a casual fling is going to work for me...'

'I was thinking the same thing.'

Good, at least they were on the same page. It should make things easier if, as he thought, she'd realised the responsibility of looking after his daughter would be more commitment than she was ready to give.

'So, we'll just put this down to a lapse of judgement? A very, very nice one while it lasted, but I can't justify the time away from my daughter. I should have been with her tonight. She was looking for me when she fell, and I just can't let her down like that again. It's probably best we just go back to being work colleagues. I hope you understand.' It wouldn't do to beg her to consider something long term and more serious when he wasn't sure either of them could commit to that. He'd already messed up, and it had only been one day, so the damage he could manage to inflict on his relationship with his daughter was unimaginable and not worth the risk.

'Of course,' she said eventually, letting him breathe a sigh of relief.

'Okay, then… I guess I'll see you around.'

'I guess so.'

'Bye, Mae. I'm sorry things didn't work out.'

'Me too, Liam.' Her voice was quiet but she was the first to hang up.

Liam didn't have much practice at ending relationships; his last experience had been him on the other end of that conversation. It hadn't been his intention to cause Mae any pain, though she seemed to sympathise with the position he was in. He hadn't wanted her to get upset or feel rejected.

But, if he was honest, her stoic response stung. It was as if what they'd had together tonight didn't really matter. In other circumstances, he knew they could have had something really special, mostly because they already had. To find she was able to simply forget it so easily was not only a knock to his ego, but confirmation that she wasn't the one for him after all. If he was ever going to let someone back into his life permanently, it would have to be someone who would fight for them, who would show a commitment to Shannon and him that Mae obviously didn't want.

CHAPTER EIGHT

'AT LEAST YOU love me, Brodie, eh?' Mae cuddled her furry friend closely and shared her bag of crisps with him. Though he didn't seem interested in the soppy movie she'd selected for the evening's entertainment, he was enjoying the hugs and attention. It didn't even matter about the slobber and crumbs he'd got all over her leisure wear, as long as she had him to hug tonight instead of being completely on her own.

She'd substituted an Irish wolfhound for Liam: that was how great a hole had been left in her life in just a matter of days. It was her fault for breaking her own rules. No matter how short the fling, she apparently couldn't separate her emotions from a physical relationship. Although, sleeping with someone she would see on a regular basis had always been asking for trouble. Having dinner with his family and getting to know his daughter were extra red flags she'd chosen to ignore. Little wonder then that, when he prioritised Shannon's welfare over some fun with her, Mae had been bereft.

She had hoped they'd have a chance to explore their relationship a little more, but he'd made it clear he wasn't interested beyond the one night. At least she'd been able to walk away with her dignity intact, if not her heart. She'd known the score; it wasn't Liam's fault she couldn't control her emotions because she'd only gone and fallen for him.

In the short space of time she'd got to know him, she'd opened her heart and had been preparing to share a little bit more with him. He and Shannon had showed her what she was missing out on by shutting herself off from the possibility of love and family. She didn't feel any better now after a brief, albeit passionate, tryst with Liam than she had after a serious relationship with Diarmuid.

'Perhaps I should just give up on men altogether and become a dog lady,' she said to Brodie, who licked away her tears then snatched the last crisp out of her hand. Betrayed by another male.

For a little while she'd been able to believe that a future with someone was possible—a relationship, maybe even a family some day. Being dropped like a hot potato the second his daughter had needed him, though understandable, had been nonetheless crushing. It simply reiterated the notion that everyone left her eventually. Although, in this case it had happened pretty darn quick. Maybe this time she would learn her lesson and not give her heart to anyone again. She couldn't trust anyone with it, not even herself.

All the lies she'd told herself about not getting emotionally involved with Liam, knowing she liked him, had just been to cover the fact she wanted to be with him. Now here she was, crying and pouring her heart out to a dog, when her fling with Liam was supposed to have been just a bit of fun. Apparently, she wasn't capable of that without losing her heart and her mind over a man. Over Liam.

The tears started again and she buried her face in Brodie's fur, drawing some comfort from his warmth. It said a lot about her life that she was spending her evening with a dog because she was so lonely, a feeling that had only been exacerbated by having spent time with Liam and his family. She hadn't just lost him but Paddy, Moira and Shannon too. Once Ray was out of hospital, she wouldn't even have Brodie.

It would be easy to pack up and move on somewhere else where she wouldn't run the risk of seeing Liam again and endure the pain of knowing they couldn't be together. But she couldn't keep doing that after every failed romance. She wanted to settle down and be happy, even if that meant being on her own.

'You're very grumpy tonight, Daddy.' Shannon pouted at him.

'Am I? Sorry, sweetheart, I just have a lot on my mind.' Mostly a certain woman he couldn't stop thinking about.

It had been a couple of days since he'd ended things and, though it had ultimately been his decision, he missed Mae. It was funny how close they'd become in such a short space of time and how much impact she'd had on his family. His parents and Shannon had been asking after her ever since. He'd excused her absence as a clash of shifts but he couldn't use that line for ever. It was awkward when his mum and dad knew they'd slept together; that'd been obvious when they'd both arrived in the early hours after Shannon's accident. It was more difficult still when they knew he didn't just hook up with anyone.

No one since Clodagh, in fact. Mae was special, they all knew that, but they respected him enough to make his own mistakes and not throw it back in his face. He'd done enough self-flagellation about losing her to suffice. Although, he had noticed his mum phoning to check in with him more often, sending home-made comfort food with Shannon every day. As much as he was indulging heavily in the baked goods and carbs, none of it could replace the feel-good endorphins he'd only had when he'd been with Mae.

He was beginning to wonder if he'd jumped the gun. If they might have been able to work something out that suited them both so he hadn't had to lose her altogether. She'd been quick to accept the end of their arrangement without quibble, so he supposed there was no compromise to be had. In hindsight, telling someone who'd been burned so badly in a relationship that he'd only accept a partner who'd be there for him and his daughter might have been overkill. Those high expectations were never going to be attainable after only one night together but it was too late now to go back.

Yes, he had regrets and, given some time to think things through more clearly, he would've done things differently. Right now, he'd do anything to have Mae back in his life in whatever capacity he could. She'd helped with Ray and Shannon, not to mention the fracas outside the pub. They'd worked as a team.

More than that, she'd been there for him when he'd needed it. Liam had found a peace with Mae that he hadn't had in a long time, and their short-lived fling had been the explosive candle on the cake. It was no wonder Shannon thought he was grumpy when he'd been mad at himself these past days for throwing all that away. They were both missing her, and ending things hadn't achieved anything in the long run when they were hurting anyway.

'I miss Mae too.' His daughter was more astute than he gave her credit for, though he didn't want to get into a conversation about why Mae was no longer in the picture. Shannon was too young to fully understand the intricacies of adult relationships. Apparently, so was he. He was still trying to understand his own actions and could only think that his knee-jerk reaction in ending things with Mae had been his defences kicking in. When Shannon had been hurt, that was all he'd been able to think of, and how he was to blame. It was something he was too used to doing since Clodagh had left him doing the sole parenting, but he realised now, too late, that he was entitled to live a life of his own, just like Shannon's mother.

'We're both busy people. You're my main girl, Shannon, and don't you forget it.' He put an arm around her shoulders and gave her a squeeze before opening the back door. It was then he realised he must have left it unlocked after their last visit. Thankfully, Brodie made an excellent burglar deterrent, and he would have heard him bark if a stranger had attempted to get in.

Shannon shrugged him off. 'Da-ad. I'm not going to be a kid for ever, you know. You really do need to get yourself a life.'

She flounced off into Ray's house, giving him a glimpse of the teenage years yet to come, and he knew she was right. Some day she wasn't going to want him anywhere near her and then where would he be? Likely sitting drowning his sorrows in his parents' place, lamenting a lost love that he let get away.

'You're such an eejit,' he chastised himself, only for his daughter's squeal coming from the living room to make him forget all his recent bad decisions for a moment.

'Shannon? What's wrong?' He burst through the door, half-expecting to see her lying hurt somewhere.

Instead, he was met with the sight of her hugging Mae, with Brodie jumping on both of them, trying to be a part of the happy reunion.

'Hey,' Mae said quietly when she spotted him, furtively glancing around the living room, as if he'd caught her doing something she shouldn't. There was an empty family-sized bag of crisps lying on the sofa in between the pile of cushions, her shoes had been kicked off onto the floor and the credits of a movie were playing on the TV. She'd obviously been here for a while. If he'd known that, he might have come over earlier.

'Hey. Sorry. I didn't think you'd still be coming over to see to Brodie.' He had assumed she would have ditched the dog-sitting, in an attempt to avoid him, when it was as much a favour to him as to Ray.

'Of course I would. I promised Ray. I wouldn't leave Brodie on his own simply because we'd agreed not to see each other.' She frowned at him and he realised immediately what an injustice he'd done even to think that of her. Mae would never have purposely left anyone in the lurch. She was too good a person. Perhaps deep down he'd known that and had come over tonight because there was a chance of running into her like this.

'Did you and Daddy fall out? Is that why you've been crying, Mae?' Shannon asked, eyeballing the two of them before Liam had a chance to apologise to Mae for underestimating her.

'I haven't—'

'That's adult business.' He managed to talk over Mae in his lame attempt to distract his daughter. 'Sorry, I didn't mean to interrupt.'

'I was just saying I haven't been crying. It, er, must be my allergies.'

'What did you do, Daddy?' Shannon, not fooled by

either of them, was fairly and correctly putting the blame on his shoulders for any upset Mae had suffered.

Now that Shannon had pointed it out, he could see the red rings around Mae's usually bright and clear green eyes, and she didn't look at all like her normal glam self. She was wearing pale-pink sweatpants and a matching baggy sweater, without a trace of make-up on her face. Whilst he still thought her beautiful, it was apparent that she hadn't put in her usual effort with her appearance.

He was guilty of the same tonight, dressing for comfort rather than style because it didn't seem important. Nothing did against the ache in his heart, which had been growing stronger since the last time he'd seen Mae. He almost hoped that her casual attire was an outward reflection of her heartache too, so that he knew he'd meant more to her than a one-night stand.

'He didn't do anything, Shannon. Your daddy just wants to spend all the time he can with you.' Mae stepped in to save his blushes, as his daughter was probably gearing up to give him a stern telling off.

'I see him every day,' Shannon said, rolling her eyes to make them both laugh. There he was, trying to be present in her life, when it seemed as though he was nothing but a nuisance. Perhaps he should let Shannon make all the important decisions in their lives from now on. She certainly wouldn't have let Mae walk away so easily.

'That's because he's a very good dad. I haven't seen

my father since I was a little girl. You're very lucky you have someone so lovely taking care of you.' Mae was fixing Shannon's braid over her shoulder and Liam knew she was feeling the loss of her mother all over again. She was someone who should never have been on her own when she had so much love to give. It was clear in the way she was with Shannon, so loving and tender, that she would have made a great mum. If only men like him had treated her better, she might have believed it too.

'Did your daddy go away, like my mummy?'

'Yes, he did, but aren't you lucky you still get to see your mummy?'

The hitch in Mae's voice hinted at the pain she was still going through at the loss of her own mother, something he thankfully had no experience of, but sympathised with. After all, he'd fallen apart when a loved one had simply moved out of the house and the relationship; he could only imagine losing someone for ever. He had spent these past days thinking of nothing else and he knew he couldn't waste the second chance he'd been given. Opportunities to reconnect didn't come around often and he didn't want to spend the rest of his life hating himself for not grabbing it with both hands.

'Not every day, but I see daddy all the time when he's not at work.' Blissfully oblivious to Mae's distress, Shannon was very philosophical about her circumstances, showing just how much she'd adapted to the new dynamic already. Better than her father, it seemed.

'That's what makes him such a good daddy. He wants to be there for you all the time so you never, ever get hurt again.' Mae gently touched the cast on Shannon's arm, and Liam got the impression she felt as guilty that it had happened as he did.

It occurred to him that accepting responsibility for an accident that had been beyond her control was ridiculous, yet that was exactly what he'd done. He'd blamed himself for something he could never have prevented, to the extent he'd thought he had to stay glued to his daughter's side—a notion she clearly wasn't a fan of and, now he could see the situation from a different point of view, something completely unnecessary.

'That's just silly. He's not with me when I'm at school, or asleep.' She had a point. There was nothing to say she wouldn't fall or have an accident when he was at work or in a different room. He couldn't be in two different places at once and it was stupid to think otherwise. It was time he stopped using his daughter as an excuse to keep Mae at a distance and make that leap of faith.

'Shannon, could you go into the kitchen and give Brodie some water? I'd like to talk to Mae.' He wanted a little privacy so he didn't embarrass Mae, or himself, if she wasn't interested in anything more between them, and if he'd imagined the lingering embers of their passion still glowing, waiting to be stoked once more.

Shannon skipped off with Brodie galloping behind her. Mae faced him, her arms wrapped around her body, hugging herself in an expression of self-defence and anxiety. She wasn't the same spiky American he'd sparred with during their first meeting. Although she'd let down those protective barriers and let him in, he'd wounded her with his actions, and he was sorry for that.

'Sorry. I wasn't expecting anyone over. Ray will probably be home tomorrow, so I was just saying my goodbyes to Brodie. I'll tidy up before I leave.' She glanced around at the evidence of her pity party. Liam recognised the signs, since he'd left a similar scene be-hind at home—his wallowing illustrated by chocolate wrappers and empty coffee cups.

He shook his head. 'That's not what I wanted to talk to you about. I, er, I missed you.'

She gave him a half-smile which he wasn't sure came from pity or something else. 'I missed you too.'

He wanted to say more, but instead he gathered her into his arms and held her tight. He felt huge relief when she wrapped her arms around him in response, instead of recoiling or pushing him away, which she would have had every right to do.

Eventually Mae let go. 'How's Shannon? She seems okay. No permanent psychological damage?'

He could tell by the way she was biting her lip that she was teasing him.

'Okay, so I was being a little bit over-protective and a tad over the top.'

'Just a tad. But I understand why. She's your daughter. You feel responsible, and you're afraid that she'll get hurt because of your actions.'

'Exactly.' And Mae's grasp of his situation, her empathy, was why he wanted to fight for her.

'I would never want her to get hurt either. You have to do what's best.'

'Yes…yes, I do. For once, I want to do whatever's best for me, and I think that's to have you back in my life. I know you don't want anything serious, Mae, but do you think we could still see each other? You know, maybe go out every now and then?' It wouldn't be the instant happy family he'd dreamed of, but he was willing to take things slowly if it meant he would still have Mae around.

'With Shannon?'

'Not if you don't want that…' He didn't want to frighten her off if she was even considering forgiving him and wanting to try again.

'I think maybe it's time we both stopped being afraid of being with each other. We can't hide away for ever, living in fear that we'll get hurt again, and letting the good things slip away from us. We're good together.' She slid her arms back around his waist, that connection making him remember their night together, and promising the thrill of more.

'That we are. So… I can stop pretending to Shannon and my parents that we're only colleagues?' If Mae was willing to try again, it seemed plausible that they should be open about it this time.

She cocked her head to one side. 'You really think we ever had them fooled?'

He thought about it for a split second. 'Nah. I think they knew before we even did.'

'We better prepare ourselves for the "we told you so" conversation.'

'It's fine. I can handle it. It's better than the, "you eejit, why did you let her go?" one I've been having with myself.'

'You are an eejit, but you're my eejit.' Mae tilted her face up to his and sealed their new beginning with a tender kiss.

'Always,' he replied, knowing he'd found the woman he'd been missing in his life long before they'd even known each other. It had taken them some time to work out that they were meant to be together but, now they had, Liam would do everything it took to make the relationship work.

He and Mae had finally found in one another the family they'd both been searching for.

EPILOGUE

'SHANNON, DON'T GO too far. Stay where we can see you!' Mae shouted after the little girl as she ran ahead into the woods.

'As if we could miss that dog, and since it's glued to her side there isn't much chance of losing either of them. It gives us a few minutes' peace, at least. Maybe even time to make out.' Liam nuzzled into her neck, his warm breath on her skin already making her wish they hadn't got out of bed this morning.

They'd only been together six months, but it was enough time for both of them to know it was what they both wanted and needed. She'd moved in with Liam and Shannon after a few weeks of dating, neither of them having wanted to waste any time that could've been spent together. It made practical sense too, making sure there was usually someone at home for Shannon, and saving on the travelling. On the odd occasion they were both working, Paddy and Moira were only too happy to babysit. Mae felt as though she was part of a real family now. Especially on those Sunday afternoons when Liam's parents cooked them a roast dinner that couldn't be beaten.

They'd even got the dog to complete the family picture. Technically he was still Ray's but it had made sense for them to take Brodie on a more permanent basis while Ray was working to overcome his alcohol issue. Ray was attending support meetings, and stopping drinking had definitely improved his health. Although his condition was irreversible, abstaining from alcohol would give him a longer life expectancy than if he'd continued to drink. He'd even put on a little weight since he'd started eating better, aided by the home-cooked meals Liam's parents sent round for him. Mae and Liam had him round for dinner every now and then to check in with him and give him some company.

Ray kept Brodie with him during the day, but mostly it was down to Liam and Mae to feed and walk the wolfhound. Shannon was absolutely besotted with the mutt, and Mae was sure he had helped her adjust to the upheaval when she'd moved in. She still saw her mother on occasion, which gave Mae and Liam some alone time.

They were very much still in the honeymoon stage, but the way he made her melt every time he touched her convinced her it would always be the same for them. In and out of the bedroom they made a good team, and she was thankful that both she and Liam had taken that leap of faith in one another to try and make things work.

'Not the kissing *again*.' Shannon voiced her disgust at the kissing they'd progressed to, so engrossed in one another, they hadn't heard her come back.

In typical Liam style, he responded by planting a smacker on his daughter's cheek. 'I wouldn't want you to feel left out. You're still my number one girl.'

'Ew!' Shannon wiped away all trace of him with the back of her hand. 'Can we go and have dinner now, Daddy? You said we could go out to celebrate.'

'Oh? That's the first I've heard.' Mae turned to Liam, wondering what they were celebrating, other than having an afternoon off together.

Out of the corner of her eye she saw him gesturing to Shannon to zip her lips. He was always surprising her with romantic meals or movie nights, working hard to ensure they weren't just parenting Shannon together but constantly investing in their relationship. She appreciated that, along with the daily conversations that kept them a part of each other's lives even during those busier times. He was doing everything to make sure this relationship worked and keep her happy, though he only had to be in her orbit to do that. She'd never felt so safe and loved.

'I have something for you. Or, rather, Brodie does. Come here, boy!' He called the dog, which bounded over, and on Liam's direction jumped up on Mae, his front paws resting on her shoulders.

'What is it?' She was too busy fending off Brodie's

kisses and trying to keep her balance to understand what was going on.

'On his collar.'

There, attached to Brodie's name tag, was a beautiful diamond ring. She looked at Liam, her mouth open, eyes wide, afraid to believe what was happening. When he knelt down in the pile of leaves on the ground and took her hand, she just about stopped breathing.

'Mae Watters, I know we haven't been together long, but this feels too right not to act on it. Will you please be my wife and make our little family complete?'

It was all too much, and she felt the tears pricking the back of her eyes at the pure love for her this man emanated. Even Shannon was clapping beside him, apparently in on this plot and accepting it, which was much more important. They hadn't discussed marriage. After Diarmuid and her last doomed wedding day, she hadn't thought she'd ever want to make that level of commitment again. But these past months with Liam and Shannon had been the happiest of her life, and she was ready for more. Ready to commit herself to this family.

'Yes! Yes, I will, Liam O'Conner.' She held out her hand whilst he wrestled the ring off the dog to place it on her finger. 'I guess you were pretty confident I was going to say yes if you already planned a celebratory dinner?'

'If that didn't work, I was hoping I could kiss you into submission.'

This time Shannon cheered when they kissed, and they didn't care who was watching.

Mae couldn't help but think her mum would be proud she'd discovered her Irish roots after all.

* * * * *

ACCIDENTALLY
DATING HIS BOSS

KRISTINE LYNN

MILLS & BOON

To Kiera.

For your friendship, sisterhood,
words of wisdom, and laughter.

You're the teacher, mother, and friend I hope to be.

CHAPTER ONE

MARY POPPINS WAS full of crap.

Because no amount of sugar—or booze or miles on a solitary beach run—was going to make this easier to swallow.

Dr. Owen Rhys groaned into his steaming cup of coffee before taking a sip.

"Son of a—" he hissed. It was so hot it numbed his lips, but not before scorching them.

Come on, he pleaded with the universe. *Give me at least one break today.*

He was a doctor; he knew better than to sip coffee straight out of the pot in the same way he knew not to overthink an email. But thinking logically about the latest missive polluting his inbox wasn't possible, not with his mind spinning a thousand curt responses he'd like to fire back. If he wanted to jump-start unemployment, that is. He scanned the email again, his eyes finding the most egregious parts to hone in on.

…moving the meeting back until ten to put out some fires…
…time to shake up the way we do things at Mercy…
…need to be innovative with the ways we invite the press into our practices…

The email was system-wide, sent to every chief, doc, surgeon and resident, but the last line in the second-to-last paragraph seemed like it was written directly to him.

No department is immune to the changes coming our way. Not even those that bring in the most revenue or whose notoriety has given this hospital a certain reputation with elite clients.

It might as well have said, *Dr. Rhys, pay special attention to this part. Because it's your fault for sleeping with Emma Hartley in the first place. Maybe if you hadn't, she wouldn't have come to you for help and our hospital wouldn't be front-page news next to "botched surgery" in last week's paper. Ciao!*

Without thinking, Owen took another sip of his coffee, which hadn't cooled since he'd tried to singe his skin off thirty seconds earlier. He cursed and put the cup down. Caffeine wasn't gonna make this email disappear anyway. His gaze shifted from his computer to the front page of the *Los Angeles Daily News*. It wasn't any better.

Emma-freaking-Hartley.

Chalk it up to another idea that seemed good at the time but decidedly…wasn't. Despite his no-dating directive—a by-product of chronically disappointing people in his life—he'd let their one night together stretch into a few months of fun. It lasted as long as "fun" in Hollywood usually lasted, and he and the A-list actress had parted ways amicably. So, when she came to him for help with a scar from a surgery that had gone bad at a no-name clinic in the Valley, of course he was going to help her.

Regret came swift and heavy. Sure, he was the one who helped Emma lessen the scar, but of course, some photographer had followed her to his office and the news had gone nuts with speculation.

Had Owen caused the original scar? Was he sneaking her in after hours to fix his own mistake? And other asinine questions.

It was a damn nightmare.

Never mind the personal boundaries they'd crossed to get the photos—the paparazzi's invasive presence brought Owen's past screaming back into the present.

Owen shuddered as the memories assaulted his subconscious.

He sat down, his knees weak as he recalled his brother Sam being hounded by a reporter after his accident—an accident Owen caused when he left a boiling pot of water unattended on the stove. In an attempt to finish the dinner Owen started, his younger brother accidentally hit the pot, sending the scalding liquid over his neck and torso.

Even now, Owen could still hear his brother's screams of terror when he tossed and turned at night…was still plagued by Sam's weakened shouts from the hospital bed when the reporter had snuck in.

He rubbed his arms, suddenly chilled.

Then there was the court case where his family sued the overzealous reporter for harassment of a minor in his hospital room, his home and on his way to school. His family had won, but at what cost?

Sam had spent two years after his injury afraid to go outside. His parents spent every waking hour tending to Sam's health behind shuttered windows. Meanwhile, Owen lived as a ghost in his own home, haunting dark rooms with guilt-ridden silence until he was old enough to drive, which meant old enough to go to parties. If he was going to live life invisible to the people he loved the most, his future smothered by remorse, he wasn't gonna be sober for it.

Owen rubbed at an ache behind his ribcage; if it weren't for that one party, that one neighbor talking some sense into Owen…who knew where he'd be now?

Even though he'd pulled himself out of a spiral, it had been too late for his family. The uneasy feeling of prying eyes followed them everywhere they went until Sam moved away, as if his younger brother's injury wasn't enough to endure. They'd never recovered.

And now, twenty years later, the same thing was happening with Emma.

Her affair with Owen—and her original surgery—were splashed all over the news thanks to his notoriety as a plastic surgeon and her starlet fame. No matter how many times Owen commented publicly that her botched surgery was *not* performed by him, or anywhere near Mercy, his face was splashed all over the media.

Exactly what he'd been trying to avoid his entire career.

"Dammit," he cursed. He'd never see the media as anything other than a cancer of modern society.

Sure, a degree of notoriety helped book the surgeries he needed to keep his public career afloat, but that work only mattered because it funded the pro bono medical work he did anonymously for the nonprofit he'd created. Since Sam's accident, his ability to help burn victims and domestic abuse survivors who couldn't afford medical insurance would always be his priority. He couldn't stop the accidents themselves, or the media that covered them, but he sure as hell could help the patients who needed him most. Each save was a pound added to the scales of justice.

And the "Emma situation" had put it all at risk.

Until, out of the blue, the story was washed away with a one-liner from Emma's PR team, and then buried in the side column of today's paper like it'd never happened.

The curt statement thanked Owen for his work to help the actress and *boom*—just like that, his name was cleared. For that, anyway.

So why was the headline next to the front-page article worse somehow?

Mercy Hospital—Known as the "Hospital to the Stars" by Greater Hollywood—Revamps its Image with a New CMO at the Helm.

Because it could do more damage to my nonprofit than the Emma story did, and the anonymous work I do after leaving Mercy each day is about to fall under scrutiny. Not to mention I'm just now finding out this new chief medical officer's plan at the same time "greater Hollywood" is.

The story beneath the headline was worse still. Dr. Kris Offerman—his new boss—flaunted her plans for a new trauma center at Mercy that would do the same work Owen was doing. She'd invited local police officers harmed in the line of duty to her announcement; they'd be the first to receive free, world-class medical attention the minute the center opened. In return, their stories would be shared as part of an ongoing *Changing the Face of Medicine* docuseries in a partnership with LATV.

On the surface, the tweak to Mercy's business model seemed like a move that would finally synchronize Owen's medical practices. He could move his nonprofit patients to Mercy and give them the best standard of care at one of the premier hospitals on the West Coast.

But, again, *at what cost*?

The patients he saw at the clinic didn't want their names dragged through a news cycle. They just wanted help and to go home and live normal, scar-free lives like his brother should have been able to do.

Bottom line? The outreach was a good thing, the fact that Offerman needed to advertise it, a whole other. If she pursued the media part of the trauma center plan, he wouldn't be a part of it.

He'd give her the benefit of the doubt, but the story in the news didn't bode well.

Dammit.

He raked his palms down his stubble-lined cheeks. What was he supposed to do if she marched ahead with this foolhardy plan?

The way he saw it, he had two choices.

First, he could hold tight to his moral compass—the one

pointing him in the direction of doing good for the sake of doing good, rather than for the accolades it drummed up— and fire off a resignation letter to his boss. He had enough money saved up that he could keep the nonprofit clinic open for almost a year.

What then?

He was a damn good surgeon, but good enough to withstand the questions from future employers about why he'd quit the most coveted job in the country?

He reread the email, stopping at the part where Offerman mentioned needing everyone on board for this to work. He hadn't even met the woman in person and she was already living up to her name. Dex, his best friend and Chief of Psychiatry at Mercy, had called her "*a fixer*," which translated to a *hard-ass*.

Owen's second choice was more complicated. He could stick around for a few months and see what came of the trauma center. Maybe if he was on the inside, he could exact meaningful change with the way Offerman saw their patients. Maybe he could convince her to practice like he did—out of the public's eye and with only the patient's well-being in mind.

Hmmm. He reached for his coffee again, but decided against a third scalding.

The thing was, Owen started off his career wanting to help burn victims like Sam—patients who didn't have the resources Emma did. But he kept that part of his life quiet on purpose. It wasn't for show; it was to change lives. Hell, he'd even let the Mercy Telegraph—what he called the gossip train at the hospital—believe he left work early to party or vacation or whatever else they drummed up instead of what he was actually doing. Namely more surgeries for people who could never afford American healthcare's steep prices.

It wasn't any of their business how he spent his time if his work was getting done.

Until now. He had a sinking feeling Dr. Offerman would make it her business.

What will it mean if I stay at Mercy, if I move the nonprofit over and Offerman publicizes it?

A spotlight wouldn't just be on his clinic and his patients, but on *him*, too. For years—since he was a teen in the aftermath of making the biggest mistake of his life—he'd operated in the shadows. There, he could do the work without expecting praise or accolades he neither deserved nor wanted. He did what he did because circumstances demanded it. End of story.

"Ugh…" he groaned.

"Spoonful of sugar," my a—

A chime from the laptop interrupted his less-than-kind thoughts about his new boss. Because that particular chime he'd handpicked for one notification and one notification only. A new message from @ladydoc.

A shiver ran up his spine the way it always did when he heard that sound. Funny that over the past six months, that feeling hadn't dissipated at all. If anything, he'd grown more excited when he heard from her.

Which was silly if he thought too much about it. He didn't know her real name, where she lived or even what she looked like. But since the day they'd met on DocTalk, a forum for anyone in the medical field to chat about frustrations, network, even date, he'd been drawn to @ladydoc. They agreed to stay friends when it became pretty obvious both of them needed one, and that was more than enough for Owen, who definitely didn't do relationships. He barely even did friends.

Online, he could talk freely without worrying what it would do to his image or career. The distance of anonymity also allowed him to keep her at arm's length. From there, he couldn't hurt her like he'd hurt everyone else he let in. From a distance, she wouldn't be able to see his flaws; up close they were terrifying to reckon with and impossible to see past. Everyone—his

parents, Sam, even Emma—was better off with him staying
in the shadows.

Nothing was at stake with @ladydoc, so just about anything was possible.

Yeah, but what if she saw past your mistakes? his subconscious asked.

He shook his head. *Nope.* Because then he'd have to learn
to forgive himself and there weren't enough patients left to
save in the city for that balancing act to happen.

He clicked open the message.

Hey there, @makingadifference. Wanted to thank you for the
doughnut recommendation. I live at DK's now, if you ever
want to find me, haha.

He smiled. DK's, huh? He'd given her three doughnut places
to choose from and she'd visited the one two blocks from his
house. She was closer than he thought. They'd never broached
the subject of meeting up in person, but now that he was 99
percent certain she lived in northwest LA, the possibility hit
him upside the chest like three hundred volts from a defibrillator.

He typed out a response, his blood pressure spiking. Not a
good sign for a surgeon, but another chronic symptom every
time he eased into what had become hour-long chats each
morning and evening.

Glad you liked it. It's the best-kept secret in LA, so keep it
close to your chest. We don't need tourists finding out how
good we have it, haha.

Was he the kind of man who added *haha* to the end of a
sentence? Apparently, he was. He hit Send and then stared
at the screen while he waited for a response. He was also the

kind of guy who stared at the three "typing" dots instead of going on with his day.

It wasn't like he didn't have anything to do. He was chief of plastic surgery at one of the premier hospitals in California for one. Not to mention he had a laundry list of issues facing him at said place of employment.

Largely because he'd come close to breaking his only rule— *no dating, just work*—with Emma, putting the rest of his life in the spotlight. His rules existed for a reason. Life was simpler that way; he couldn't hurt someone who didn't exist.

Which was what made the whole six-month exchange with @ladydoc even more interesting. Being online friends meant a veil was dropped between them, protecting them both from the possibility of attachment, of romance, of *more*. *More* was a four-letter word to Owen.

Yet, knowing she was so close cracked open the door of possibility. Maybe his four-p.m. scrimmage with Dexter could provide some clarity.

Finally, the chime he'd been waiting for rang loud against his vaulted ceiling.

Greedily, he read it out loud.

"'My lips are sealed. Well, about this, anyway. ;) Any chance you have an equally good Thai restaurant recommendation? I figure a city this big has to have a hidden gem there, too. I'll owe you one…'"

Owen's eyes widened even though there was no one to ask *Do you see this? Did she just flirt with me?* For not the first time, he wished he hadn't kept @ladydoc a secret from Sam and Dex. At least then he could dissect this conversation with them.

But then again, sharing her was out of the question, too. She was the one unencumbered part of his life, the only person beside Dex who knew about the accident with his brother and how, after a spiral that almost took his life, it catapulted Owen into the type of medicine he practiced. The only one aware of his estrangement with his parents, and why he kept everyone at arm's length because of it. Yet, she agreed that being alone saved you and everyone else from more heartache. That way, no one had to forgive unforgiveable offenses, no one had to pretend to be happy to see someone who'd ruined their lives and no one had to worry about what you'd be capable of next. Not even Dex was aware of that blossom of shame growing in the darkest parts of Owen's heart, where he didn't let in any light. Just @ladydoc.

She was special. And the only thing that was *his*.

Instead, maybe Dex could help him pick apart a piece of correspondence from another woman he'd never met, but whose emails were infinitely less enjoyable—their new boss.

Owen glanced at his watch. *Damn.* He was twenty minutes behind.

Try Thai Palace on Twenty-Fourth and Kelly. You won't regret anything except having a new addiction. Thank me later? ;)

Did he just flirt back? Owen smacked his head with the heel of his palm.

You got it. Gotta run to a thing I really wish I didn't have to go to. But you made my dinner plans worth looking forward to. Talk soon?

He resisted the urge to ask if she wanted to grab food together at Thai Palace that evening, just as friends. Instead he wrote back.

Looking forward to it. Gotta go, too. Rough day at the office. Wish you were here—might not be as bad then.

Owen hesitated before sending the chat message. *"Wish you were here"* was awfully close to *I'd like to meet up.*

He hit Reply before he could back out and grabbed his coffee thermos, briefcase and phone. Time to get this circus over with.

He remote-started his Audi A8 and let the seat adjust to him. Just as he was pulling out of his driveway, the phone rang over the speakers, filling the small space.

He chuckled when he saw the name on the dash.

"I was just thinking about you," he said.

"Oh, yeah? You have another erotic dream about me I should know about?"

"Just because you get to hear about sex dreams all day doesn't mean you're the cause of mine, my friend," Owen said, laughing.

"Ha! You *are* having sex dreams. I knew it. Told you this 'no-dating' thing was bad for you."

"So's sleeping with people if the situation with Emma is any proof. Anyway, you know the only time you show up in my thoughts is when I'm figuring out ways to school you on the court."

"Any luck with that lately?"

"None. I'm screwed. I seriously think you hang out with the Lakers in your free time."

"What free time? You see our schedules for this week? We have dinners planned now. *Dinners.* You know what that's gonna do to my social life?"

"Move it back a few hours? Besides, you just broke up with Kelsey. Give it time before you go back to paying half your salary for a woman you don't plan on waking up next to."

Owen's best friend was a serial dater, the yin to Owen's yang. Making it worse was the fact that Dex had left his only long-term relationship because she'd adopted a child—a deal breaker where Dex was concerned. Now that he was back on the market, no female was immune to his interest.

"You've got a point there."

"Besides, don't you leave for Africa soon?"

"All the more reason to fill my love cup now."

"Your 'love cup'? Do you hear yourself?"

"What's wrong with liking women? Just because you don't—"

"I like women just fine. I just have no desire to—"

"Invite one into my life so I can hurt them eventually," Dex finished for him, albeit in a nasally teasing tone. Owen had been repeating that a lot lately, hadn't he?

"Touché."

Owen turned left out of his gated community, throwing a wave to Percy, the security guard. He made a mental note to stop on his way back in tonight and ask Percy how new fatherhood was treating the man. He and his wife had been trying for two years before their infant, Jill, came along.

"Siri, schedule a gift for Percy."

"Isn't that the guy who works the gate at the Estates?" Dex asked when the task was complete.

"Yep. Just had a new baby."

"Gross. I'm perpetually glad I skipped that part of life."

"That you know of. Anyway, you've let me ramble on about sex nightmares, the Lakers and now my security guard. You wanna tell me why you called?"

Because it wasn't like Dex not to get to the point.

"I, um, wanted to let you know the morning medical staff meeting was postponed."

"I know. I got the email. Not off to a good start if she's already pushing agendas back and having us rearrange patient care."

There was a beat of silence where all Owen heard was the gentle purr of his engine. It felt ominous since Dex was never this quiet.

"That's the thing," Dex finally said. "She pushed it back again to have a one-on-one with the head of plastics."

"With me?" Owen glanced down at his iwatch and frowned. The only thing on his calendar was the delayed staff meeting where they'd formally introduce Dr. Offerman as the CMO, and that was still an hour out. "Are you sure?"

"Pretty sure. She came by my office just now and asked what I knew about you with respect to pro bono work and if I thought you'd be interested in taking part in the TV special."

Owen barked out a laugh. "I hope you told her there isn't a chance. I'm a physician, not an actor. And our patients aren't extras—they're people with lives and jobs and families. I'm struggling to see how this is going to be helpful."

"So you're a no, then."

"Hell yeah, I'm a no. I mean, it goes against everything I practice medicine for."

Especially after everything the media had done to his family.

"I get why you feel the way you do, but I don't think you can afford to feel that way at the cost of everyone's jobs."

"Excuse me?"

"I'm just saying, it costs money to keep our hospital running and her series will generate what we need to do that. Maybe just hear her out. Not everyone in Hollywood is like that guy who violated your brother's privacy."

Owen's grip on the steering wheel tightened. Needles of frustration pierced his skin.

"Whose side are you on?" Dex had never challenged Owen like this.

"My patients'. My department will be eviscerated without better funding."

Owen wasn't prone to anger—what did he really have to be angry about when the world hadn't been particularly cruel to him like it had been to his brother Sam? But he felt the unfamiliar and unwelcome emotion rise like bile in the back of his throat.

"Fine." Owen caught a sigh on the other end of the line. It

wasn't Dex's fault this was happening, but it didn't feel good hearing about it from his best friend, either.

"Listen, don't shoot the messenger, Owen. I wasn't even supposed to tell you. I'm just saying, keep an open mind and keep me updated, too." Owen gritted his teeth as the car in front of him slammed on its brakes. Of course the LA traffic would come to a standstill a mile from the hospital. His day had turned from crap to a dumpster fire pretty quick. "You know, you could tell her about the work you're doing at the—"

"No. That's none of her business. I do it because it'll help folks, not save my skin. I'll think of something."

"Better do it quick."

Owen glanced out the window at the looming shadow of the place he used to consider home.

"Right. Well, I should go," Owen mumbled. Now he was a man who mumbled instead of standing firm and confident like he'd earned the right to be. Great. He didn't dare wonder what else the day could hold for him in case it came too close to tempting fate.

"See you on the court later? I leave next Monday for the Africa trip and want to kick your ass one more time."

"Sure," Owen said, then clicked off the call. For the ump-teenth time that morning, he wished for two things.

One, that he'd never checked his email that morning.

And two, that he'd had the forethought to ask @ladydoc for her phone number. As he headed into the lion's den at Mercy Hospital that morning, he could really use a friendly voice.

CHAPTER TWO

DR. KRIS OFFERMAN closed the chat app on her phone but her smile remained. The last message from @makingadifference flashed repeatedly in her thoughts like a beacon of light, despite the darkness of upcoming meetings that threatened it. Each time she replayed it, the emphasis was placed somewhere new, changing the meaning ever so slightly.

Wish you were *here*…

Wish you *were* here…

Wish *you* were here…

She knew what it actually was—a question thrown out like bait to see if she was ready to meet him. As in, meet in person with no ability to hide behind a screen, making it her first "date" since James. Her heart slammed against her chest, begging the question…

Am I ready for that?

James had done a number on her—twice, actually. First, when she'd discovered he slept with half the residents at their hospital while they were dating. Though that wasn't near as damning as the second discovery that he'd taken the internship research she conducted under his mentorship and passed it off as his own at a conference, winning him a Lasker Award. She'd barely been twenty-three and the experience jaded her to the possibility of love and a career being able to exist simultaneously. In fact, that particular betrayal almost changed her mind about wanting to practice medicine at all.

Almost.

Instead, she'd put *everything* the past decade—every shred of time, energy and heart—into her own work, work she kept secret and tight to her chest so nothing could threaten her happiness again. Maybe if it'd just been James's deception, she'd have stayed naive a little longer, let the hope of love win out in the end. James might have obliterated her trust, but before that, her parents' deaths left her to fend off waking nightmares in the foster system; and now Alice...

She swallowed a sob. Alice, the person who'd saved her from giving up her career after James, was gone now, too.

Kris was alone again.

She shook her head as if realizing the fundamental truth for the first time. It wasn't fun, but being alone was safer.

No men, no girls' trips to exotic locales, not even a book club. That meant no loss, no heartache, no fear of being abandoned again.

Just her career remained now. And it made her happy. Mostly, anyway.

But as her thoughts meandered back over her six months of chats with @makingadifference, her smile deepened with each memory.

There was the night he'd stayed up for four hours as she contemplated moving to a new city halfway across the country for work.

"Is it work you could imagine making you jump out of bed each day?" he'd asked her.

Not once had he asked about the pay or benefits, just whether she'd be happy.

A month later he'd told her—without details of course, abiding by the rules they'd set early on—about how his brother's childhood injury inspired him to go into medicine in the first place. About the patients he helped pro bono at a free clinic.

"Why not just do those out of your own hospital?" she'd asked.

"It's not about the notoriety. I do it to help, and to be honest, the credit would only make people look at me instead of my work. If I do it for the credit, my motivations are kind of corrupt, aren't they? I'd rather focus on the patients."

His selflessness had blown her away, though she'd wondered what else he wasn't saying. Because he could focus on the patients at a hospital, too. And yet…the vulnerability of what came next had been a major shift in opening herself up to him.

"I feel like I let him down by settling for the bigger paycheck, the flashier job, though."

"Doesn't your day job fund the work you do behind the scenes?"

"True—I just wonder if it's enough."

"It's never too late," she'd replied.

And that had marked another shift, this time in how he opened up to her. All this time, she'd wondered what he meant by enough, though. What scales did he feel the need to balance?

Their degree of anonymity meant a veil of safety for her work and ideas, but also in allowing her to ask herself the tough questions without the risk of ridicule or duplicity.

She laughed as another memory popped up, replacing the heavier one. He loved to pepper their more serious conversations about work with goofy medical humor. The joke he'd told her yesterday had her giggling like she'd inhaled laughing gas.

"Did I tell you about my neighbor who had to take her dalmatian to the eye doctor?" he'd asked her.

By then she should have known his silly sense of humor, but she'd taken the bait.

"No! Is he okay? Poor pup."

"Poor pup, indeed. But he had to go in since he kept seeing spots."

She'd laughed for a solid minute before writing him back and playfully admonishing him for tricking her like that.

Yeah, she supposed she was ready to meet @makingadifference.

Maybe.

As long as it remained platonic so she didn't run the risk of falling for yet another doctor who might put his own success first if given the chance. Not that she thought *he* was capable of that, but she couldn't risk it—not with what was at stake now.

Her trauma center.

The growth she'd made after—and despite—all her personal loss.

She'd thought finding Alice after being orphaned as a teen was the magical fix, the bandage that would close the open wounds crippling her. And that mentor-turned-friendship had helped heal her, for a while anyway. But losing Alice to cancer last year had reopened the injuries from her youth. In the end, it didn't really matter how successful or accomplished Kris was—people she loved could still leave her.

Needless to say, she could use a little goofy.

Oh, but Alice. You'd know what to do about @makingadifference.

The Alice-shaped space in Kris's heart throbbed in the silence. No answer came. Just more memories, more emotions with them.

She'd met Alice at a medical school conference in Tampa, gosh—was it almost fifteen years ago?—when Kris forgot her badge at her hotel room before her presentation about sickle cell anemia. Alice was the next in line to enter and instead of making Kris feel bad for holding everyone up, she made a scene demanding that Kris be let in and issued a new credential.

Using the same guerilla warfare tactics, she all but bullied her way into Kris's life, despite Kris's vehement opposition to anything resembling outside support. By then Kris's parents had been gone eight years, she'd aged out of foster care and didn't think she needed anyone else. Didn't want anyone else, because losing another person close to her might just do her in.

Alice had proved her wrong, of course. No matter how much her loss had hurt, how close it brought her to reliving the grief of losing her parents, Kris knew without a doubt she wouldn't be the successful woman she was today without Alice's love and guidance. Especially after the James debacle.

"No emotions on the job, hon. That's the only way to make it as a woman in healthcare. Cry at home and with people who care about you. Your colleagues never will, so don't let them beyond your walls."

But in the end, she'd still lost Alice.

Kris bit her bottom lip to keep the emotion out of the job today. Of all days, it was vital to keep the air of professionalism she maintained so she'd never be tainted with *"maybe she's not good enough"* again. Especially on her first official day.

Two nurses walked by her window, laughing hard enough about something that had one of them wiping at her eyes, and Kris's heartstrings pulled.

Alice was right. There'd be no silliness, no tears, no laughter on her end—not with these colleagues, anyway. Just with @makingadifference. He posed no danger if she abided by their "no details" referendum. He couldn't hurt her like James had, and he couldn't leave her like Alice did. It was a win-win as far as friendships went.

So…maybe they shouldn't meet just yet. She needed a second to get acclimated at Mercy, especially with the particular staff member on his way to her office.

Dr. Owen Rhys, the chief of plastics. His reputation preceded him in more ways than one.

On one hand, he had the reputation of being a brilliant surgeon, even if the type of surgeries he specialized in wasn't her forte. Who was she to judge? He seemed more than competent and he was one of the only reasons the hospital had any operating capital at all.

On the other hand, his HR file and surgical record indicated he didn't do anything above and beyond his ten-a.m. to four-p.m. surgical day, and she needed a team player. Word around the hospital was that he was a bit of a playboy who liked to have fun at the expense of his professional time, and image. *That*, she could judge, though she'd have to be careful as to how she fielded the conversation. Rhys was smart and accomplished with a wide patient base. Keeping him on her side was paramount for her plan to work.

Largely because she hoped to convince him to donate some of the time he was rumored to spend chatting women up at bars to helping burn victims and public-service-related injuries. For free, no less.

It's not going to be easy.

Nothing was. With the exception of conversations with @makingadifference in the private DocTalk chat room, anyway.

While she waited for Dr. Rhys to arrive, she inhaled the scent of the new-to-her office, which was tinged with pine wood cleaner and a hint of acrid smoke. Paired with the lines in the carpet, an old vacuum must have been in there within the past day. She exhaled so she could allow the scent of fresh possibilities to worm its way into her chest.

Two years ago, she might've tapped out a string of worries with the end of her pen on her new desk. Worry a solely administrative job was too far outside her comfort zone after a decade of practicing trauma medicine. Worry that Owen was every bit the unprofessional playboy she'd heard he was. Which would lead to concern that this time, she wouldn't be able to keep her anger at bay, or her emotions out of the job.

But she'd lost Alice since then, and there just wasn't the space for self-flagellation anymore, not when there wasn't anyone left to help her overcome it.

It didn't mean she was without doubts; she just didn't have time for the guilt that came with them anymore. She was successful even though her parents would never know it, and Alice wouldn't ever be there to congratulate the new victories.

She was on her own, for better or worse.

Just that morning, she'd had to give herself a little pep talk.

C'mon, Kris. You've dealt with indifferent men like that before. You've also had harder fixes than his media mess or the hospital's low cash flow. Remember sewing wounds in Angola when a warlord tried to forcibly remove you from the country? Those were tough days. This you can do with your eyes closed.

And that was it. What used to take her a day to work through only took the span of time it took to eat a piece of toast and chug her coffee.

She sat on the corner of the desk, her awards and accolades lining one full side of the sepulchral room. And yet, it still seemed empty. Why did anyone think a hospital administrator needed so much space? A shower *and* a reading nook? When she'd practiced trauma in Angola, she'd seen three generations of family living in spaces half this size.

A small shred of doubt had lingered, but not about her skill level.

Because @makingadifference wasn't the only one who'd sold out. She'd taken this high-paying admin position, leaving her crew in Angola behind. It was a hard truth that had settled in her chest like a stone, but she had plans, and when she finished the trauma center, she'd leave "The Fixer" behind for good. Yeah, she knew what her colleagues and staff called her behind her back, but there were worse nicknames for a female exec in the healthcare business.

Besides, with Alice's connections, there was no way Mercy's new trauma center—*her* new trauma center—wasn't going to be profitable, if not downright lucrative.

She picked up the newspaper in front of her. The photo on the front page no longer boasted Owen Rhys's frown, but rather a photo of Kris in front of Mercy, three police officers who were injured in the line of duty beside her. It was a far better look for the hospital already.

Thankfully, her trauma plan had turned the news cycle around to something more positive for all parties involved.

As for Dr. Rhys, hopefully he'd appreciate that she'd cleared his reputation as a surgeon. Then maybe he wouldn't be as mad about what she had to tell him. Namely that the best spot for the trauma center meant taking over half the overly huge, space-wasting plastics wing.

A wing overseen and built by Dr. Owen Rhys.

Of course, this was news she had no intention of sharing until he played ball and joined her in her initiative.

She stole a glance at her Cartier watch, noting he was two minutes late. Not a good start.

Kris pressed the sides of her temple in the hopes it would alleviate the first-day pressure building behind her eyes.

A loud rap on the door surprised her and she dropped the pen she'd been holding. It clattered to the hardwood floor and as she bent down to retrieve it, she knocked her head on the equally hard wood of the desk. The resounding crack was enough to make the partial headache that had been brewing behind her eyes a full-blown brain compressor.

"Son of a—"

"I can come back if this isn't a good time," a deep voice said. She froze, her head still below her desk, her butt sticking up like the brown stink bugs littering the dirt roads in Angola. The thick timbre of the words lathered her skin in warmth at the same time sending an unfamiliar jolt of energy through her veins akin to an adrenaline shot.

Was it possible that a voice could sound like sex smiling down on her? If it were, that's the impression she got. Not convenient. Not one bit. She maneuvered as gracefully as she could out of her tight spot, smoothing her skirt that had risen a good three inches in her dive for the pen.

"Do you always walk in without being invited?" she asked her mystery guest.

"No. But I'm not usually late to a meeting I didn't know was happening until I saw the note on my office door. I figured I'd not waste any more of your time."

Owen Rhys.

A few errant curls had dislodged themselves from her hastily made topknot, so she gave them a tuck behind her ear and focused on the man in front of her.

And immediately regretted it.

Because if his voice sounded like sex incarnate, his physique sealed the deal.

Muscles pressed against his Ralph Lauren button-down as though they were trapped.

Thick chestnut hair looked like waves sculpted from clay.

A jaw that frat boys would envy because it looked strong enough to open a beer bottle twitched in a half smile.

He was handsome as a movie star—something of a cross between old-time Hollywood and front-page rebel. But with... *gray* eyes? So help her, she actually squinted so she could be sure, but, yeah.

He has slate-gray eyes. With flecks of baby blue.

She gulped in the hopes of dislodging whatever was stuck in her throat and preventing her from saying something— anything—to him.

"I'm Dr. Owen Rhys." He extended his hand and she shook it. Why was it so warm and firm? "And you must be Dr. Offerman?"

She nodded, grateful he'd taken the lead so she didn't have to embarrass herself by trying to remember who she was while she was still processing the steely eyes staring back at her. When his gaze narrowed and his lips turned up in an off-kilter smile, it broke whatever trance she was in and the full weight of who she was crashed down around her.

Not only was she this man's *boss*, but she needed him to

help secure the first phase of her project—a place to build the trauma center and a team of doctors to staff it.

She shook her head, the fog he'd created between his voice and physical presence evaporating under this new recognition. His eyes and muscles and smile didn't matter one measly bit. In fact, it would be better for everyone if she forgot them entirely. Even though her unruly libido offered a different opinion.

"Dr. Rhys. Sorry for that. I'm just settling into the office and time change and I imagine both will take some getting used to. Go ahead and have a seat."

"It's a nice space." He remained standing.

"It is. It's more space than I need, but I guess that comes with the title."

Shut! Up! her brain shouted at her, and she didn't disagree with it.

"I'm sure that's what the board thought."

"Anyway, I'd love to spend a couple minutes getting to know each other. Why don't you pull up a chair and we can talk." She gestured to the plush armchair in front of her desk and took the seat next to it so he wasn't put off by the formality of the desk.

He wasn't in trouble. And yet…

His smile disappeared as suddenly as he'd arrived in her office, and with it, the warmth left the room.

"Is there a reason we're doing this one-on-one instead of in a group setting? I wasn't exactly excited to find out I'm the reason you pushed back our weekly staff meeting."

Yep, there was a chill in here, all right. But with the shiver that raced down her spine, she was reminded that the man who'd ignored her invitations to sit and left her feeling like an interloper in her own office stood between her and everything she'd had to fight to bring to fruition.

"There is a reason. And I'll share it when you sit."

That the man didn't often hear no wasn't her concern.

In case he thought she was kidding, she met his gaze—

cold steel indeed—and leaned back in the chair, arms crossed over her chest.

She gestured to the seat again and this time, without breaking her gaze, he sat down.

"Thank you. I'd like to start over, Dr. Rhys. I'm Dr. Kris Offerman, Mercy's new chief medical officer."

Your boss.

She extended her hand and he took it, his jaw set and showing off a small muscle tic in his cheek. He held her hand and stared longer than what made her comfortable. An energy not unlike the kind that zapped her when she saw him for the first time buzzed between their palms until she dropped his hand. She resisted the urge to shake whatever was making her hand tingle out of her system.

"Nice to meet you." His thin smile said he didn't mean it. "I know you're new here—welcome, by the way—but I don't appreciate having to shuffle my patients around last minute."

"I can understand that and I apologize. This was time sensitive or I would have given more notice." She forced a smile. What a sanctimonious little… She'd checked his schedule and all he had on his surgical calendar was *personal* after three-p.m., and only one patient at noon before that. Like hell she was caving to give his carefree schedule precedence over one that would put his highly paid talents to work. Time to break out the big guns. "So, I'll get to the point. I need you on board for my first initiative at Mercy, a state-of-the-art trauma center that will primarily cater to first responders and members of the community who need free access to restorative surgeries and recovery. We won't take insurance because this will be entirely privately funded at no cost to the patients."

Where she expected, if not excitement, at least curiosity, she was met instead with his brows pulled in and a stiff jaw.

"What's your motive?" he asked.

Now it was her turn to be confused.

"I'm sorry?"

"Your motive. For the trauma center."

"I'm not sure I need a motive to create a groundbreaking, innovative solution to LA's lack of accessible, affordable trauma care."

His lips twisted into a smirk. "Tell me that again without the party line, boss. I saw the front-page spread about your TV special and Dex Shaw called to let me know your plan for having me on camera."

She winced. Maybe she shouldn't have jumped the gun and run that story before she talked to Dr. Rhys. She had her reasons—twelve of them, all members of the board—but she hadn't accounted for her staff reading the news before hearing it from her. This wasn't shaping up to be a good first meeting.

"That's only partially true. What I'd really like from you is to—"

"Treat me like one of your pawns to make you look good for the board of directors?"

The nerve of this man. She forced a smile again. "Let me backtrack. I want to start off by thanking you for what your... *services*...have brought to the hospital. I recognize that you're a big reason our cash flow isn't as low as it could be—however, you're aware it doesn't buy you out of any ethics mandates issued by Mercy." He bristled but she ignored him and continued. "That said, my job as CMO is to help bring Mercy some extra funding and a fresh image. I figured you wouldn't mind getting some positive attention for your medical achievements while we use the income from the show to propel the initiative forward." He opened his mouth to reply but she kept going.

"I could use your expertise in burn treatment, scar tissue mitigation and birth defects, but if you've ever worked with on-the-job traumas, I'd like to use you there, too. You'd be donating your time, of course, but the supplies and patient stays would be covered by my administrative department."

She reached back to her desk and procured a single sheet

of paper with the core budget that would ensure Mercy Hospital remained the superpower it was.

"Take a look."

As he read it his jaw tightened and his eyes became laser focused.

The plush, swanky office wasn't immune to the late morning traffic sounds of downtown LA. Cars honked, alarms went off and congestion made its own creaks and screeches that were endemic to the city. Finally, Dr. Rhys handed the paper back to her.

"It's impressive. But you're wrong. The last thing I'd want is to put myself, or my patients, into the unnecessary spotlight."

She froze. Well, that wasn't expected. She opened her mouth to reply, but shut it again when she realized she had no way to combat his argument. That he didn't want to spend his time giving free surgeries, sure. But his protectiveness over his patients wasn't even on her radar.

Most doctors she worked with clamored to get front and center in the limelight to flaunt their successes. It was part of the same ego that made them brilliant doctors. Was this part of his general apathy she saw in his short workdays and lack of anything resembling an altruistic ethic of care?

"However," he continued, "your plan sounds good, at least on paper. I'd like to consult on what the burn center would need and how to orient the suites to ensure privacy and optimal healing. Then, when it's up and running, I'll help as much as you need with the surgeries and long-term care plans *if* you can guarantee the patients I bring in won't be filmed. I'm firm on that point."

"I'll bring in the patients, Dr. Rhys. You won't be required to troll for the surgeries. And it will be up to them to decide whether they want to take part in the docuseries."

She chuckled. Where would a world-class plastic surgeon find patients for her trauma clinic anyway?

Dr. Rhys's brows lifted like he found her humor distasteful.

"Can you guarantee my terms, or not?"

"I'll consider it as the build is underway, but we'll have to discuss it more once the board asks for our final staffing numbers. Until then, do you support this initiative?"

"The center, yes. It actually fills a need I've been thinking of for some time." His forehead pulled tight again. "But the fact that you want to bring a film crew to chronicle the trauma people have endured I'll never get behind."

"You mean to say if we can get consenting patients to help spread the word and bring this hospital revenue, you still won't support it?"

"It may not seem like it, but you and I are a lot alike, Dr. Offerman." His voice grew thick and gravely like new pavement. From experience, she'd place a bet this was personal to him. But how? Nothing in his personnel file indicated anything traumatic, or even trauma adjacent. There wasn't actually much in his personnel file, period. "I know what people say about me, but I don't care. I work hard at what I do and the only thing—the *only* thing—I care about is my patients and their well-being. I get the sense that if you weren't the new suit for Mercy you'd be the same and that's the only reason I'm agreeing to help. But if I think for one minute you're putting the needs of your reality show or even this hospital above my patients? I'll be gone quicker than you can rip off a bandage."

What the—?

The door swung open before she could comment. She spun around, shock making her slower than usual. The president of the board and CEO of Mercy Hospital stormed in. There was no other way to describe the hurricane of emotion on Keith Masterson's face, or in his clenched fists. She steeled herself. The ire on his pursed lips and sweaty brow she'd expected; his barging into her office was not.

"Keith, I'm in a meeting. You know—"

"Dr. Rhys. Good to see you. Pardon the interruption, but—" He wheeled on her, anger showing in his trembling lips. "Did you really announce the half-baked plan you mentioned in passing to me to the *whole state of California?*"

A small bead of spit stuck to his lip.

"I did. And it's not half-baked. I assumed that your nod of approval was just that."

A small lie. She'd been vague on purpose. The hospital, like most, was in debt and she'd run the numbers a hundred ways from Tuesday. Her trauma center was the best way to come out on top without losing half the staff. That it helped her accomplish her dream of building a community-serving project—the same kind she and Alice were working on before Alice died—was just the cherry on a pretty legit sundae.

"No. Nowhere in that plan did you mention you were building a *trauma center?* And in the *plastics* wing?" She winced. He must've talked to the builder she'd hired to do the estimate. There went that element of surprise. Owen Rhys, to his credit, barely blinked at the news. "It's the one place in this hospital that actually covers its own costs *and* pays for people outside of its department."

Keith's face had gone from pale to white with red splotches that indicated elevated blood pressure, likely due to stress. She'd bring up her medical suggestion for treatment another time; something told her he wouldn't appreciate the free advice just then.

"Yes. And I know. However, you gave me a budget and a staff and told me to '*increase our cash flow,*' so I am, Keith. This is me fixing it in the best way I know how, a way that will hopefully be sustainable long after you and I retire."

Retiring, coincidentally, was part of the treatment plan she was going to suggest to Keith. It was either leave the stress of being CEO of a hospital behind or face the devastating consequences.

"But this is gonna cost triple the budget I set out for you."

"It will. But, Keith, you've heard the saying, you've got to spend money to make money?"

He frowned and wiped his brow with a handkerchief that'd seen better days.

"I always despised that saying," he muttered.

"You saw my CV, saw the budget reports on the last three hospitals I worked for, right?"

Keith nodded, glancing at Owen, who simply sat there, arms crossed over his chest, a hint of a smile playing at his lips. He didn't faze easily, she'd give him that.

"So you know I'm good at what I do." He nodded again, this time, with resignation sagging his shoulders. "Which is why you hired me, because you trust me to do this well, am I correct?"

"It's awfully risky as your first move," Keith said.

"I agree, but that's how much I believe in this plan. Which I can support with research and projections and everything else you'll need to sell the center to the board."

"Why didn't I get those first?"

She smiled. "Because you never would have allowed it to happen."

And last time I waited to share my plan, a man stole all the credit. A man I thought I loved.

No way she was making that mistake again.

The red splotches on his cheeks turned purple. He poked a finger in her direction. "I want that on my desk by eight a.m. tomorrow morning."

"I'll do you one better. You'll have them before happy hour today, Keith." He nodded curtly and headed back toward the door. She took a single sheet of paper off her desk, the same one she'd made a copy of for Dr. Rhys to convince him of her plan. "But the only one you'll need to see is the payout for the documentary and the nonprofits that are jumping on board to collaborate—deep-pocket nonprofits." She handed it over, biting back a smile. When he looked over the page, his eyes widening with each line his gaze traveled over, she swallowed an *I told you so.*

Professionalism really was a drag sometimes.

"Are we okay till the board meeting?"

His gaze didn't leave the paper. He ran a hand along the balding spot on the back of his head, whistling out a breath.

"Um, yeah. We're good. I'll be in contact."

When the door shut behind him, Kris turned back to Owen.

"Where were we?" she asked, more to herself.

"We were at the part where you were going to tell me just how you plan to make me give up half my suite space to accommodate this insane plan of yours, and why I should even let you try."

"I'm sorry you had to hear that way."

"There's a lot of that going around this morning, Dr. Offerman, but no one actually seems sorry." He stood up. "Thanks for your time and it was nice meeting you. But I've got patients to see. Good luck with the rest of your first day."

"Dr. Rhys, we're not done. I'd like to go through your average week and decide on a schedule for the pro bono surgeries once the center is up and running."

He took the pen she'd been using, the one she'd dropped when he entered, and clicked it a few times.

"I assure you we're done here. If you want me to keep making you money and plan a whole new trauma surgical suite while you demolish mine, I need to leave this office before I say something I'll regret."

"It's more complicated than simply demolishing your suites—" she tried again. He waved her off.

"I don't do complicated. Just tell me what to do and I'll do it. But in the future, that can all be said in an email. I'm a busy man and right now I have a patient consultation waiting."

She stood, too, her cheeks flushed hot with frustration.

"Dr. Rhys," she said, channeling all her female boss energy, "I want to make it clear, because there seems to be some confusion about who's in charge here, but I'm the new CMO, and the one in control of your hospital privileges."

"Oh, believe me, that much I got." Just as he got to the door, he turned back to face her and all signs he was as agitated as her were wiped clean off his face. Replacing them was a smug grin and eyes that danced with her discomfort. "Nice to meet you, boss. I'll be looking forward to that email."

Owen walked out of her office, the soft close of the door in stark relief to the chaotic energy left in his wake.

What the hell had just happened, and how had that man—a man she'd spent less than twenty minutes with—gotten her to break her one rule?

"Don't show emotion, especially anger, or that's where they have you."

Kris had never forgotten Alice's parting words to her before Kris took up residency in Minnesota. Not even when James had stolen all that was dear to her.

Until now.

Meeting Owen Rhys had taken a decade of building a life according to one rule and snapped it cleanly in half. Because not only was she angry—livid, actually—she was pretty darn sure he knew it, too.

CHAPTER THREE

LIKE HELL OWEN was going to consider Dr. Offerman his boss. In terms of practicing medicine, sure. But telling him who he could and couldn't bring in as a patient? When she clearly needed his help to get this thing off the ground?

Yeah, not gonna happen.

It was not like she was asking him to do something he wasn't already doing at his clinic. But the gall in asking—nay, *demanding*—as much? With an unspoken but very much assumed *or else* attached to the end of her "request"?

Abso-effing-lutely not.

He needed something to calm his nerves. He'd never let anyone rile him like this, largely because he prided himself in putting his own emotions on the back burner to do what was right.

So why are you so pissed right now? You've worked with bigger hard-asses your whole career and they never stopped you from getting anything done.

Why was he so mad? An image of Offerman's stiff stance and flat, narrowed eyes pierced his resolve. It was a look he was familiar with—disappointment and resentment. He sighed and raked his hands through his hair as the truth settled low in his abdomen.

It was the same look his parents had every time they'd seen him after the accident, coming home drunk from a party or driving a little too recklessly. They'd all but kicked him out and told him to get his act together but he'd heard the thing they really wanted to say, that had been on the tips of their tongues every time they passed him on the way to Sam's room, to make Sam breakfast, to take Sam to an appointment.

What happened to Sam was your fault.

Not just the accident, but the ramifications all the way through the court case against the reporter. None of it would have happened if Owen hadn't left the water boiling so he could go talk to a girl, then forgotten all about it until his brother's screams of agony had broken through his teenage lust. He'd upended not only Sam's life, but their whole family's.

Drinking and reckless behavior hadn't solved his guilt. When he was pinned up against the garage by a neighbor after he'd mowed down their daughter's bicycle, the guy had said one thing to him. *"Make your life count for something, son. Don't be a waste of potential, okay?"*

That'd been all it took to switch tacks and do something productive with his reckless emotions. He'd buckled down, gotten into college, graduated with honors and received early acceptance to medical school, where he'd won every award residents and surgical fellows could earn. Though he kept up a relationship with Sam, he hadn't done more than send cards and gifts to his parents for holidays. How could he, when they only brought judgment—judgment he had plenty of for himself? Not that he deserved any less... He'd only go back home when he'd made up for what he'd done. It was a mantra that guided him.

One more person—just save one more.

Owen shivered.

Anyway, since then, he'd done over two hundred pro bono surgeries off the books. He couldn't take back what'd happened to Sam and his folks, but he could damn well try and make up for it by sacrificing his future for others.

And now all of that might come to a grinding halt thanks

to a woman who'd made up her mind about him based on reputation alone.

He stormed back to his office, his fists clenched, his jaw wired so tight he wasn't sure he'd be able to finish his now-cold coffee. Who did Kris Offerman think she was? God of everything?

Owen dumped the coffee down the granite sink in his en suite office bathroom and went out to make an espresso. Scooping the grounds, he replayed the "meeting"—dressing down would be a more appropriate term—with Dr. Offerman. With her backside up in the air, her head buried beneath her desk, she'd diffused the tension right away.

Until she'd stood up. It's not like he'd wanted to stare, but… how could he have pulled his gaze from her athletic curves wrapped in a black knee-length skirt and matching V-neck sleeveless top? Especially when her strong, shapely calves led to black pumps with a peep toe, showing off red polish. Why did that one detail—fire-engine red that her authoritative personality didn't match—throw him off? His carefully practiced speech had evaporated like the morning fog under a hot summer LA sun.

Scalding water poured over his hand and he dropped his mug, which shattered at his feet.

"Dammit!" Owen surveyed the damage to the mug and his hand. The mug was done for, but his hand would recover, thankfully. He depended too much on the instrument to injure it doing something stupid.

Never—not once—did he lose focus; it was devastating in his line of work. Leave it to Kris to cause him to break that streak on her first damned day on the job.

A feral scream built in the back of his throat but he tamped it by imagining the photo on the lock screen of his phone. It represented his end goal, his vision board of sorts. It was only a candid picture of the person who mattered most to Owen, but it was enough.

Sam.

Speaking of the guy, it had been a while since he'd caught up with his brother. He dug his phone out of his pocket, but it took him three times to hit Call, his hands were shaking so badly.

While the phone rang on the other end, Owen ran his hand under cold water in the bathroom. It stung but faded to a dull ache after a few seconds.

"Gotta be kidding me," he grumbled.

"About what? You're the one who called me."

"Hey, Sam. Sorry. Just hurt my hand."

"Oh, damn. You okay?"

"Yeah. Anyway, I'm just checking in. How's life in SLO?"

His younger brother Sam had moved up to San Luis Obispo when he was old enough to be on his own. The Central Coast, with its mild temperatures and humidity, was just what Sam's damaged skin needed. The wine country and epic surfing didn't hurt. Nor did his parents following suit and moving closer to Sam.

"Great. Waves were overhead this weekend. When you gonna ditch the smog and traffic and come join me? The Rhys brothers together up here? We'd dominate."

Owen laughed. "Maybe someday."

"So why'd you really call? Because you just checked in three days ago and not that I don't love hearing from you, bro, but there's not much on my end to share. So spill."

Owen sighed and leaned against the door to his office before sliding down to the hardwood floor.

"You ever just have one of those days?" he asked.

"This about the front page of the *Daily News*?"

"You saw that, huh?"

Sam chuckled, the sound somehow restorative even though it was aimed at Owen's misfortune. Between Sam's injury and the expensive, drawn-out procedures to fix what little the surgeons could, Sam hadn't had much cause to laugh in his life.

That didn't stop him from doing it, though. In fact, Sam was the happiest man he knew, which frustrated Owen as much as it inspired him. He'd love to learn to appreciate life the way his little brother did.

"Hard not to recognize that monstrosity of a hospital when it's life-size on my home page. And a reality show, huh? You need to talk about it?"

Owen shook his head even though Sam couldn't see it. "A docuseries, and no. Not about that."

An image of Dr. Offerman's chestnut curls framing her face, her brows furrowed and her lips in a frown sprung up like an unwanted weed.

"Oh, yeah? Now you gotta share. Who is she?"

"Why are you so sure there's a she?" Owen asked. But he knew the answer. His brother had an uncanny knack for sniffing out details about their family before anyone was willing to share them.

"Lemme guess."

Please don't, Owen wanted to say.

"The female in question is that new boss you've been dreading and now you realize you're right but not because she'll make your work life a living hell, even though she might do that, too, but because…" He paused for dramatic effect. If he were standing there, Owen would have slugged him for being a know-it-all. "She's *fine*. Am I close?"

Owen gulped back the weird heat mixed with twisting discomfort that had plagued him since he'd first seen Dr. Offerman in all her—yes, *fine*—glory. It was probably just the stress of everything going on but it needed to go away. Now.

"Close. But it's not like I don't see a dozen beautiful women a day, Sam. And this one's just more of the same but in a frustrating, stubborn package." Except his frustration with Dr. Offerman was partly *because* he was so damned attracted to her. From his medical perspective—with perky C-cups, a slim waist and toned, shapely legs—she was a cosmetic surgeon's nightmare. There wasn't a thing he'd offer to change about her. And he appreciated that with the same parts of himself he shouldn't be listening to right now.

"Yeah, but you ever come across one that thinks like you?"

"How do you know she thinks like me?"

"For starters, I read the article. She's doing the same thing you are, but without slinking in the shadows all moody and brooding like Batman." Owen frowned. "And what'd you say? Stubborn? Frustrating? Sounds familiar."

"Watch it. Anyway, enough about her. We can talk women this weekend. I'll try to come up."

"Heard that before, so forgive me if I don't hold my breath, big brother."

"Yeah, yeah. Hey, you, uh, hear anything from the folks?"

There was a beat of silence on the other end of the line before Sam spoke up, though his voice sounded uncharacteristically strained.

"They're still on their cruise. Retirement suits them, I think. They asked about you, you know."

"Oh, yeah?" Owen pressed the heel of his palm to his eye to alleviate the sudden heat that arose there. Half the time he thought Sam made up these little moments where their folks actually cared about the kid who'd almost killed their youngest child. The rest of the time, he tried to keep the hope from blossoming. The thing was, if he didn't face them, he wouldn't know either way, and most days, that was okay with him, the not knowing. It meant keeping their blame at bay, which in turn curbed his guilt just enough he could pretend it wasn't throbbing behind his heart, malignant.

"They don't blame you any more than I do, Owen. They just miss you."

Owen coughed back a wave of emotion that threatened everything he'd built to keep it in check. That was the downside to keeping his distance. He didn't deserve to be missed, not by people whose lives he'd ruined.

"I've got to run, Sam. But I'm glad you're doing well. I'll be up no matter what at the end of the month for the California Polytechnic State University conference, so save some wine, women, and waves for me, 'kay?"

"No promises on the women. I can't beat 'em off with a stick. See ya."

Sam clicked out of the call, leaving Owen more frustrated than before.

Aside from that unpleasant stroll down memory lane, there was something else bothering Owen. Why did Offerman make him so uncomfortable when, like Sam said, she was just doing what he was, albeit out in the open?

The chime he usually looked forward to buzzed in his pocket. Instead of excitement, the first thing he felt was a familiar emotion that made him queasy.

Guilt.

Knock it off. You're not cheating on a woman you've never met by thinking about one who looks good in a skirt suit.

Thinking about Offerman didn't cheapen what he had with @ladydoc. Besides, they were just friends, remember?

He swiped open the chat and smiled.

You ever have one of those days?

That was what her message asked, echoing his question to Sam.

Boy, have I ever. This Monday started with too few cups of coffee and will end with too much tequila, he sent back.

God, I wish I could join you. That sounds terrific, as long as the tequila comes in small, single servings. None of this lime juice nonsense.

Okay, he loved this woman. Objectively, of course.

Now you're talking. Too bad my workday isn't over for an-other...oh, eternity. Ten hours, if I'm actually counting, but that's too depressing. Sorry yours is rough, too.

For a split second he almost asked if she wanted to vent, but then he remembered the one rule they'd made—no details about specific job positions, hospitals or staff they worked with. The medical community was too small and the likeli-hood they knew the same people too big.

It's okay...and expected, I guess. I just wish I could say what I mean and do the good I set out to do when I became a doc before it got buried beneath protocol, bureaucracy and other people's screwups.

If that wasn't the truth he'd been wrestling with the past, well, decade, he didn't know what was. Owen walked to the window where he was treated with a view the hospital paid exorbitantly for. The Santa Monica Mountains rose behind the city he'd called home since med school, the Pacific Ocean off to the left. The sun had burned off the morning fog, leaving shards of light dancing across the water. He loved it here and couldn't imagine uprooting to another place. This was home.

Well said. The sad thing is, I'm more the doctor I wanted to be outside the walls of this place. I'd give just about anything to combine the two worlds, but...

But what?
Dex was the only person at Mercy who knew about his pro bono work at the clinic for a reason. Unless he came clean, he was stuck as Dr. Owen Rhys, Plastic Surgeon to the Stars. And the crappy thing was, he had the opportunity to come clean *and* keep doing that work—but not on his terms.

The three little dots that indicated she was typing a response blinked on and off three times and then disappeared. Disappointment rattled him as it always did when their conversations tapered off.

Exactly. I started this to prove myself and maybe a little to absolve the feelings of not being good enough for my foster parents, my ex, everyone else. But now that it's just me... I need to figure out what I want my life and career to look like. Anyhoo, gotta run, but have a good day. I have a sneaking suspicion this will be the best part of mine.

It would be for him, too.

That was confirmed when a notification on his phone showed an email from Dr. Offerman. He groaned back a complaint he didn't have time to make.

Dr. Rhys. Here is the email you requested.

He chuckled to himself even though not a damned bit of this was humorous. She'd called his bluff and now her whole strategy was in writing, meaning he couldn't pretend not to have heard her.

Good play, Offerman. One point to you, zero for me. For now.

He kept reading even though each line was worse than the next.

In this document, you'll find my plan for the trauma center and your role in it, should you choose to stay at Mercy, outlined in severe enough detail it leaves no room for misinterpretation. However, as the CMO of Mercy Hospital, my door is always open should you have any lingering questions. Unless I hear back from you about a specific aspect of the below strategy, I'll assume you accept this as the binding contract it is intended to be.

Owen read the "contract" with growing distaste. The words were like acid on his tongue, made worse because he read the whole email in her voice, which had the strange effect of making him half hard and wholly pissed. Screw points, she'd changed the whole game. And left him without a clue what move to make next.

She ended the email with a schedule of press engagements, Mercy board meetings and a litany of other tasks that would have every minute of his time aside from surgeries and patient consults booked.

Anger flashed hot against his skin. She didn't hear a damn thing he said about involving the press in his medical practice and to make matters worse, she was encroaching on his time with the clinic patients who counted on him to fix what no one else would.

Begrudgingly, Owen walked the almost regal hallway to the plastics wing he'd designed. Second only to the obstetrics wing, that saw many of the same patients Owen did, his office and the neighboring recovery suites were the nicest rooms on Mercy's campus. And the most expensive—after all, how could he and Mercy Hospital recruit some of the biggest names in Hollywood with suites that couldn't compete with a Hollywood Boulevard hotel?

He slumped in an oversize leather armchair that he'd used only once before when his office was taken over by the entourage of a reality television star having her breast enhancement filmed as part of her show. He'd hated that surgery for so many reasons, including her need to show off her private life to the public, and his part in that sham. Was that just a sliver of what he'd feel if Kris went ahead with her media outreach?

Despite that being a rhetorical question, the answer didn't sit well with him.

Owen's phone chimed in his pocket and even though it wasn't the telltale sign of a certain person he wanted to talk to, his pulse still went wild.

Certainly @ladydoc was the only real thing in his life. The irony that they had no details about one another's lives wasn't lost on him. But still. Just one errant thought about her and he couldn't keep the smile off his face. He was his most authentic self talking to her, but what made him happier was knowing he could, in some small way, add joy to her day.

It fell almost immediately after seeing the notification, though. It was another message from Kris, this time to the core group of Mercy attendings.

Please come hungry to our six p.m. meeting with Mercy's other admin. I'm ordering in, so any allergy concerns you need me to address would be appreciated.

Great. Dinner with suits. The icing on the cake was the place she listed as the caterer.

Thai Palace. He groaned and sat back against the cool leather. The food sounded good, of course, but he'd rather eat there with @ladydoc, not his warden of a boss and some union goons deciding his and his clinic patients' futures.

He typed out a message to @ladydoc, his fingers flying over the glass keyboard. It may not have been the smartest move in his playbook, but it was the only way he could think to get the acrid taste of every interaction with Kris off his tongue.

Owen read and reread what he'd written and though it was a ballsy move, one he couldn't take back, he couldn't find a good enough reason not to hit Send. The first part was a blur, but the last line flashed like a Vegas sign.

So, what do you say, friend? Meet me there? I'll wait for you to let me know when. No rush… ;)

The gentle *whoosh* of the message leaving his phone acted like an alarm alerting him to the potential consequences.

Holy crap.

Had he really just asked @ladydoc to meet up? Why now, when their easy conversation was the only good part of his days?

What if...? his brain conjured. No, he'd already countered that argument a dozen times before. If it wasn't the same in person, he'd roll with it. It was not like he could have anything more than friendship with her anyway.

He stood up and started piling books on his desk that he'd never actually read but kept on display anyway so people might think he had. Time to start making room for what mattered.

And it certainly wasn't the image his boss had of him. That Kris had stirred something in Owen's chest was nothing more than his body's visceral reaction to a beautiful woman. It didn't—*couldn't*—mean anything more because the woman herself was infuriating as hell and just as bent on putting him in his place as he was on seeing her out the door she had breezed through. Besides, she was his boss. Anything other than an ardent, clinical appreciation of her physicality was so off-limits it might as well be illegal.

Owen tried to brush off a crippling sense of doom that filled his chest, suffocating him.

If he wrecked things now, he had no one to blame but himself.

With that thought in mind, Owen put his phone on the desk in front of him and turned the volume up so he'd know the minute @ladydoc responded. Waiting was one area of his life he'd never get accustomed to, but right now, it seemed his only option.

CHAPTER FOUR

KRIS GRABBED HER CLIPBOARD and slipped into her white lab coat. She still wasn't used to seeing Chief Medical Officer underneath her name. Would she ever be?

As a trauma and peds doc by trade, being an admin—at least for now—was a snug fit, as if the shirt she wore was a size too small and constricted her breathing.

At least today would be spent medicine adjacent. She snuck a peek at her multistep plan for the hospital, typed, printed and in protected sleeves. Alice would be proud.

The woman had trained Kris well in foolproof ways to stay organized, as well as how to give the middle finger to anyone who got in her way. The plan in Kris's hands reflected both.

1: Familiarize yourself with the ethics/current management system and build up peer review culture.

Check. She'd done that before she stepped foot in LA. The peer review would allow physicians to hold each other accountable for exemplary standard of care, the first step in creating a viable hospital workplace.

2: Implement Phase One of the trauma center.

Check. The board had overwhelmingly voted to start construction of the center when she'd shared the proposed budget. No one wanted to pass up the opportunity to have their pet projects funded by the money the center would generate. Unsurprisingly, Owen was the only one opposed to the film crew documenting the progress. Most of the doctors were chomping at the bit for airtime and he still adamantly refused.

Which led to point three.

3: Observe attending physicians; create action plans for each one based on bedside manner, best practices etc.

It was the asterisk beneath step three that had her scowling into her tea.

> **Start with Plastic Surgery, so you know who will be a good fit for the burn center.*

It meant a whole day alongside Owen-freaking-Rhys. Too bad Alice wasn't here to help Kris handle this particular item.

She put her tea down, hugged the clipboard between her knees and tied her unruly curls into a loose ponytail. The likelihood she'd be observing any major surgeries was low—his case list showed a couple consultations for lipo, one breast augmentation and two Botox appointments—but she wanted to be ready.

Emotionally, that was a hard sell. All day with the doc who infuriated her to no end. All day watching *him* talk to patients instead of practicing on her own. All day telling her body its ardent appreciation of him wasn't welcome.

The only silver lining was the fact that she couldn't have her phone out while she observed, so she couldn't reread the week-old message from @makingadifference, dissect it and mull over the consequences of accepting or declining his offer.

Hey, @ladydoc. Thanks for the advice about my secret medical stuff. I think I found a way to do both, even with you-know-who on my back.

She'd laughed at that. Bad bosses were the worst. She was lucky to have had Alice guiding her through med school and a slew of horrible supervisors, including James. Her loss poked at the gaping, raw hole in Kris's chest—a wound first opened by losing her parents. Usually she could ignore the pain, but today it thrummed.

Anyway, I was thinking about our friendship and realized there's something missing... Tea. You said it's your favorite, and while the chai at Tea Haus was good...okay, fine, it was exceptional, even if it won't steer me away from my espresso addiction...it isn't the same as having it with a friend. So, what do you say, friend? Meet me there? I'll wait for you to let me know when. No rush... ;)

Her first impulse had been to write back in all caps an emphatic *yes* with one too many exclamation points. But then the familiar doubt had crept in, this time in Alice's voice.

You've been breaking a lot of your rules since you got here.

The voice, coming from somewhere deep inside her chest, wasn't wrong, but couldn't Kris afford to show a little emotion in her personal life, especially since she'd finally earned a seat at the table?

Alice chimed in again via Kris's subconscious.

As a CMO you have the power to exact change—real change that comes from building a world-class, nonprofit trauma center. It could help three times the patients, including those from areas outside Hollywood and Bel Air. Put @makingadifference on the back burner for now. Concentrate on work.

She was so close to realizing her singular dream since first deciding to be a doctor the night her parents died. She'd watched the dedicated team who'd cared for them until the end with awe. Her trauma center would bring that kind of medicine to the people who needed it most.

And every person I care for leaves anyway... Do I really want to risk that again?

No, she didn't. So, no. No emotion yet, if ever.

When Kris had her trauma center up and running, she could exhale and hopefully @makingadifference would be patient enough to wait.

With that thought buoying her mood ever so slightly, Kris shut the office door and walked down the long hallway leading to the plastics wing.

Dr. Rhys awaited her like a stoic, frustrated statue under the entryway.

Make that a gorgeous, rugged statue. *Oof.* She needed to get over her personal feelings for the man, and fast. If she didn't, she'd give her subordinate the power to undermine all her hard work and self-sacrifice. It would be like James all over again, but this time, as the boss, she had the power to control the outcome.

"Thanks for meeting me, Dr. Rhys."

His gaze was sharp, per usual, but as she approached him, she noticed the steely gray color had softened to a pale silver like clouds just before a storm.

"Dr. Offerman," he said, his voice even as he held out a hand and she shook it firmly. His palm against hers sent a trail of heat from her stomach south, disrupting her nerves and replacing them with something worse. Something unmentionable. "I'd like to welcome you to LA's most sought-after, exclusive plastic surgery center."

"Thank you. It's a beautiful building." She chose not to comment on how they'd lost 10 percent of their elective surgeries this week, probably residual fallout from the Emma situation. Today wasn't about that; it was about Dr. Rhys's practice, another check in her box.

Owen held her gaze. Confusion flashed across his face, but evaporated before she could react. Finally, he released her hand and welcomed her into the foyer of the center.

Kris concentrated on the warmth radiating from her palm

in the hopes it would temper the other, less welcome, feelings building in her chest.

She'd been to the plastics wing before, during the campus visit that was part of her hiring process. But being led by the man partially responsible for designing it she noticed different details.

The lighting caught her attention first. It was soft and pleasant, so unlike the harsh and bright ED lights she was used to working under. Also missing were the pervasive beeping and clicking from machines like she heard daily in other parts of the hospital.

It was *quiet*. Not eerily so, but enough to draw notice. As much as the machines were a gentle purr instead of a screeching alert, the voices were muted as well. In fact, from the pale white walls with white modern art pieces, to the white leather couches in the waiting room, and the tranquil music playing overhead, the whole place reeked of calm.

Frankly, she preferred the clatter and clamor of the emergency department. At least it felt like a hospital. This was something otherworldly, a place akin to the maternity ward Dr. Gaines ran next door but sans the cries of newborn infants and homey feel.

But it would be good for this influence to be part of the recovery suites in the trauma center; patients would feel cared for, enveloped by warmth. She took mental notes, trying to ignore the unease in her chest.

It wasn't so much the landscape as the man leading the way that threw her sense of balance off. Because Owen wasn't soft or pristine, or even welcoming like the space he inhabited. He was all hard edges and strength. She added some distance between them as they walked.

"What's on your docket today?" she asked, even though she had a printed copy of his schedule in her briefcase.

"I had a couple routine appointments, but one canceled, so I brought in a consult from the LAFD."

"The fire department?" Now it was Kris's turn to be confused.

"They called ahead and asked if we'd see their captain," he told her, pushing through another set of double doors.

"Why did they call you? Was it because of the newspaper article?" Excitement flourished where the unease had been earlier. That was part of her plan—garner interest before the doors opened so the official start went seamlessly.

"You mean, why did they call the doc who just works on tits and ass?"

Kris frowned. "That's not what I said. I've never had a problem with the types of surgeries you do."

"Just how I spend my time when I'm not bringing in revenue for Mercy?"

Kris opened her mouth to respond, but paused, an excuse tangled around her tongue. He was right. But it wasn't just about him, not entirely.

"I apologize. That's not the message I meant to convey. I'll do my best to leave my feelings at the door. I just want to make sure you'll give the time and dedication to the trauma center it deserves."

What she didn't say was, *My feelings about you somehow stirred up emotions I plastered behind thick walls in my heart and I can't figure out why. About Alice, my parents. Being part of a family...*

If there was something more, something deeper than just finding Owen handsome, well, then, she didn't want any part of that. Her set of rules were there to keep men like Owen— serious, confident, alluring, but also potentially career damaging—from changing her course for her. Again.

She'd fallen for a colleague before and he'd taken the credit for her success. She'd never let that happen again. Medicine was all she had left and it was fulfilling enough. No demands other than her hard work, no vulnerability except what she shared with her patients. No loss except what she couldn't prevent in the OR.

"Thanks. I know I've got a lot of ground to gain with you, but I appreciate the time to do that. Anyway, would you like to meet our patient?"

Kris nodded and even allowed the hint of a smile to play on her lips. Actual medicine? An actual patient? Yeah, she was in.

"I'd love that. But I want you to work like I'm not here, okay? I'm just meant to observe."

Owen nodded and strode through a large wooden door, Kris at his heels.

She blinked back surprise when her eyes adjusted to the muted light in the space. It had the same overall feel as the rest of the wing, but there was a personality to the room that didn't exist outside it. The walls were lined with photos of laughing men and women, and even a few children. Only on closer inspection could she see hints of imperfections in the images.

An off-kilter smile because of a thin, almost invisible scar along the top lip of a young woman.

Tightness around a man's eyes that belied slight scarring.

A child's hairline just a hint higher on one side than the other.

All of them were beautiful and full of a life Kris hadn't seen on this side of the hospital. But then, she hadn't really been looking, had she? Guilt bubbled up from deep in her abdomen.

Never mind the rest of the plastics wing, she wanted her trauma center to look like *this*, to feel this homey.

"Hey there, Chuck. Before we start, I want to introduce Mercy's CMO, Dr. Kris Offerman." Chuck dipped his chin and smiled. "How you doing today?" Owen asked the man sitting on top of the medical recliner in the center of the room. Kris didn't need to look any closer to see the obvious scarring along the man's shoulder and neck, but based on the color and texture, it was likely much milder than the original injury.

"Still breathing, so I'll take it as a win."

Owen chuckled and nodded. His smile was unexpected and added to the discomfort she'd felt around him since they met outside the surgery center. Was that the purpose of this whole day? To throw her off? Or was she giving herself too much credit in his life? Chances were much higher that her insistent thoughts of him were one-sided.

"I hear you there. Let's take a look at how that scar is healing." Owen helped his patient lift his arm out of his sleeve, letting the shirt hang around Chuck's neck. Why wasn't he in a hospital gown? Kris slipped open her notebook to jot down the suggestion just as Owen said, "And if this is uncomfortable, we still have a gown for you, Chuck."

"Not a chance. You know I hate those things." Turning his attention to Kris, Chuck added, "You're the boss around here, right?"

Kris nodded. "I am. What can I do for you, sir?"

Chuck laughed heartily. "You can start by calling me Chuck. Also, we're a quarter through the twenty-first century. Tell me there are hospital gowns out there that don't make us patients look like we're in a bad episode of *M*A*S*H**."

Kris found herself smiling. "I wish that were the case, but if there are, some company's keeping them secret. I'll dig around, though."

"Thanks. This guy makes me wear one for procedures, but I'm grateful he's not a stickler for the rules in visits like this. I wouldn't want to make a bad impression the first time meeting such a gorgeous woman like yourself."

Kris warmed at the compliment but Owen's skin flashed with color and he coughed loud enough to halt that line of conversation.

The thing was, when it came to making the patients comfortable, she agreed with Chuck. While it was standard operating procedure to have patients dress in gowns in case they needed to be wheeled into surgery, with patients like Chuck, why make them do something unnecessary? Owen had put his patient first, a good thing regardless of standard procedure.

"So, Chuck," Owen continued, his voice a little gruffer than usual, "it's looking good. The skin is still pink and inflamed around the middle of the injury, but I think we're on track for the final surgery. Should I schedule you in for next week?"

"Damn, Doc. That'd be great." Chuck looked up at Kris again, but this time, his eyes appeared damp and his smile wavered. "You know this guy's doing this surgery—"

"Soon. I'm doing it soon, so you can get back to doing what you love." Owen cut his patient off.

"Uh, yeah. Right." Chuck shot Owen a wink. Kris's skin prickled with awareness. Owen was already working with the LAFD? Why didn't she see that on his surgical records? "Oh, and thanks for letting me opt out of the whole filming thing. I'm not comfortable with the public knowing who I am, especially since it wouldn't take much to figure out what firehouse I'm part of. Don't wanna do anything that'll put my guys at risk. This injury did enough of that."

"Don't worry about it. Thanks for signing the waiver, though, and I appreciate you considering it."

"No sweat. It's a cool idea and I'll bet a lot of guys won't mind. I'm just not the TV type."

Owen chuckled. "Nah, me neither. Now, twist your shoulder for me. I want to see your range of motion."

Kris kept her gaze on Owen but his focus was pinned to Chuck's injury, measuring it and jotting down notes on a tablet.

He wouldn't sell you out like James.

She wanted to believe the small voice since he'd followed the protocol she'd set up with the waivers and hadn't said anything to her. How many more surprises did he have up his sleeve?

James acted like he was on my side long enough to screw me, though—both inside and outside the bedroom.

Good or bad, she didn't want any surprises where Owen was concerned. He unnerved her enough as it was, especially for an employee on her payroll.

"I'll go over the rest of the surgical details with you this afternoon," Owen said.

The rest?

"Shoot. I didn't get you in trouble with the boss, did I?"

Owen tossed Kris a glance that shot straight to her chest and stalled her breathing. His gray eyes needed to be registered as deadly weapons since they'd slayed her more than once.

"No more than I'm already in. Okay, Chuck, bend your elbow for me."

Chuck did as he was instructed while Kris watched on.

"This hurt at all?" Owen asked Chuck.

"Nope. Just tight."

"That should go away after the next surgery. I'm hoping you'll be back to ninety or ninety-five percent mobility six weeks post-op."

"That's a promise I can hang my helmet on. That's all I wanted, you know."

"I do," Owen replied. His voice was thick and Kris's pulse sped up in response.

Chuck coughed like Owen had earlier and met Kris with a sideways glance. "I don't care about the scar. I'm too old to get tripped up over people's stares. But this guy's making it possible for me to get back to work, and I didn't think that was ever gonna happen. He's good people, Boss."

A wave of emotion crashed into Kris's chest.

"I know," she said, staring at Owen until his gaze settled on her.

"Hey, Chuck, what award do you give a firefighter?"

"Oh, Doc. You're the best, but your jokes are more painful than the last three surgeries."

"C'mon. You gotta give me something. And while you're at it, you can put your shirt back on. Things look good."

"Thanks. And I don't have a clue what award."

"Most extinguished." Chuck barked out a laugh and shook his head. "Too soon?" Owen asked.

"Nah. I'm gonna tell the guys that one, actually."

Kris watched as Owen finished up with his patient. The joke tugged at a recent memory, one where @makingadifference had shared a similar dad joke with her about doctors. Surely it was a coincidence, right? Still, what she called her "finely tuned doctor gauge" was dialed in.

After he'd input his final notes to the tablet and the nurse had met with them to discuss pre-op instructions, Chuck left and Kris was alone with Owen.

"What didn't you want him to say?" Kris asked.

Owen whistled, shifting on his feet.

"I'm covering the cost of Chuck's surgery myself," Owen said. "I'd never expect the hospital to pay for the space. But—" He paused, gazing into her eyes with questions in his. "I was already working with him. I can appreciate what you're trying to do with the center, but I'd like to keep the patients I have already without passing them off to another plastics doc over there."

"Patients, as in plural? Are you working with another hospital?"

"I'd like to keep that information to myself to protect my patients. It's not a breach of contract to work outside Mercy."

Kris nodded. Agreeing with Owen wasn't par for the course, but this was different. He was giving people their lives back and she wanted to be a part of it. The question was, why didn't he say anything earlier?

You keep your work to yourself. You may not be the only one.

As she silenced her subconscious, another memory surfaced.

@makingadifference did pro bono work after hours to help atone for guilt he felt for his role in his brother's health issues, which meant he didn't want anyone—but her—to know about it.

Kris's stomach flipped. There was no way...*was there*?

She cleared her throat. "I'll comp the surgical suites and recovery rooms if you'll donate your time. We'll call it a precursor to the trauma center, a test run of sorts. I'll see if I can move up some of the funding."

"Okay. Thanks. I know it would mean a lot to Chuck to have a recovery room so he didn't inconvenience his family."

"Have you," she hedged her words, careful not to spook Owen when they'd just somehow stumbled into a tenuous peace. "Have you done a lot of work with the LAFD?"

He nodded. "A bit." The corner of his mouth kicked up into—*was that a smile*? "And yes, since I see you waiting to ask, I've worked with vets and the PD, too. We wouldn't be trolling for any patients to get this off the ground, Dr. Offerman. Kris."

Kris's pulse raced like she'd been jabbed with a shot of adrenaline when he used her name. It had the effect of warming her from the inside out and wasn't entirely uncomfortable. But it didn't help the constant demand she made of her body to ignore the man's effect on it. Or the question sitting in the back of her throat: Who are you?

Ask him the joke. The one about doctors.

No, she couldn't. She—she didn't want to know. Not yet.

"And you aren't doing the surgeries here because…?"

He shrugged and gestured to the center of the hospital where the CEO and board offices were. "Not exactly a crowd that would've gone for it."

So this whole time…she'd been wrong about him? A rogue wave of an emotion she couldn't quite name—desire? Confusion?—crashed against her chest. She had so many questions, but the last thing she wanted was for this day to become an interview.

"Owen," she steeled herself and bet on the calm air between them. "Would you consider letting me share the surgery with the press? Not the patient's name or any of the particulars, but the fact that we're making headway on the trauma center while we've barely broken ground. It might do the trick to—"

"No," Owen shot back. His eyes flashed dark gray before they lightened again. They really were as temperamental as the LA weather, weren't they? A stone dropped from her chest, weighing her down. Yeah, that wasn't anything like the man she knew online, the oscillating emotions that, if they weren't kept in check, might derail what she'd worked so hard for. At least she'd put that question to bed. "Absolutely not. That's not why I'm doing it and Chuck just told you—he doesn't need the media attention when he just got his life back." Fire danced in his eyes and his taut lips arched into a frown. She'd struck a nerve.

"Letting the public know we're doing good work helps us be able to do more good work, Owen. Believe it or not, it doesn't have anything to do with you, but with the care itself."

A flash of something hard and steely passed over his features but dissipated quickly.

"Not in my opinion. Good work begets good work, no matter who knows about it. Anything else is just a distraction."

Kris frowned but nodded.

"Fine. I understand." *Sort of.* This man could help catapult Mercy's finances with a few surgeries like Chuck's being shared with the press and he wasn't going to take the easy way out. Why not, when he was already doing the work? "So, um, what's the story with those photos?" she asked, turning the conversation to benign territory. "They don't exactly fit the aesthetic of the rest of the center."

Owen gave a sardonic laugh, but at least the lines around his eyes relaxed.

"No, they don't. I put them here because I don't think my cosmetic patients appreciate being faced with any kind of imperfection."

"Who are they? The people in the photos?"

Owen sighed and his gaze slid over each one with an almost reverent attention.

"Patients. People who were hurt but who I was able to help get back some semblance of normalcy. I didn't want to forget their joy, so I commissioned this series from the same photographer that takes the newborn photos in Dr. Gaines's OB office."

"They're beautiful. You...surprised me today," Kris said. Heat prickled her skin.

"That wouldn't be the case if you got to know me before passing judgment," he said, then shook his head. "Sorry. I don't know why I can't keep thoughts like that to myself around you."

"That's fine. I haven't exactly been easy on you, either. I'd like to know more about your work outside cosmetics after the observation if that's okay."

"Sure. Why don't we meet after my shift? I know a place nearby."

Something about the way he worded his question, the "*why don't we meet*" part, made Kris stop and regulate her pulse with careful breathing. It had immediately reminded her of @makingadifference and, more so, reminded her that her online "friend" had asked a similar question she had yet to answer.

Was saying yes to a drink opening herself up to the same mistake she'd made with James? A mistake that had almost cost her the career she'd worked so hard for?

Not for the first time, it was as if Owen read her thoughts.

"Just as a way to unwind and go over your results. I know getting some time with the boss can be difficult, but since I have it now—"

Kris struggled to keep the frown off her face. Why did she care if he threw their working relationship at her? It wasn't like she was remotely interested in the man in any way other than professionally. And not just because of her rules.

Owen wasn't her type. Not at all. Handsome, yes. Intriguing, absolutely. But too stubborn for his own good—and the good of the hospital, which would always be her first priority. Her work was her lifeline when the rest of the world fell apart around her, as it always did. More than once her career had kept her afloat, and even as lonely as she was some nights, could she say that about a relationship?

All that and the fact that she *was*, *indeed*, his boss meant more reasons why dating him could never happen. That would be tethering him to her safety rope, which would likely strangle her at some point.

"Um, thanks for the offer. But I'm buried under work. Rain check?" she asked.

Owen's smile faltered for a split second, then went back to being bright as the sun in July. "Sure. How about we meet in the cafeteria for lunch then? It's innocuous enough and you have to eat, right?" He glanced at his watch. "I'm actually starving and I've got a break between patients."

"Yeah. Sure." She controlled the flood of heat that rose in her chest after accepting his invitation. "I'll go ahead and make sure the staff saves us a table."

"Great. I'll see you in a sec. I just need to check in with the nurses."

Kris nodded as he took off the opposite way down the hall. Before she left the plastic surgery wing, she took one last glance behind her. She'd seen more than she bargained for today with Owen's attention to his patient…and to her.

The thing was, he'd treated her like she was special, and what little she knew about him still said that wasn't something he dished out to everyone.

The possibility of finding out even more about her brooding plastic surgeon kept the smile on her face all the way to the exit. She'd come into today expecting a dumpster fire that refused to be put out and was left with no more than mild apprehension only two hours in. She'd been surprised in a good way by someone at work—something that didn't happen often.

Only a small chill of trepidation ran along her skin. She was still going full steam ahead with her plan for the trauma center, media presence included. Owen had clearly been working with trauma surgeries a long time, so his patient care would be an incredible asset. But Kris was a chameleon, a surgeon-turned-administrator, so she knew better than anyone else it wasn't just the patients that made a hospital thrive.

Which meant sometimes the cuts that needed to be made weren't to flesh, but processes and comfort zones. Could he handle that when the time came for her to make the slices she needed to save the hospital's life?

One thing was for certain; one way or another, the fragile peace between them wouldn't last long.

CHAPTER FIVE

OWEN WANTED TO WHACK his head against the wall. Had he really done that? Had he actually asked out his new boss?

It's fine. I'm just bummed @ladydoc hasn't gotten back to me. We've gotten close and I miss that—that's all.

He desperately hoped his conscience was right, because if it was anything else…he was in trouble. Big trouble of the sort he'd been avoiding.

Nah. If he thought about it, he missed talking to @ladydoc, missed finding out about her day and telling her about his. He missed the advice she gave him when things had seemed hopeless. She was a helluva friend to bounce ideas off, but how were they supposed to go beyond that? They'd agreed no details, which meant no photos, no phone calls.

No intimacy. No vulnerability. Both things he was pretty dang sure two people needed if they were going to make a go of it. Besides, there was no hint that she was remotely interested in him that way—hell, she hadn't even gotten back to him about meeting up as friends.

Well, what did he expect? If he kept himself at arm's length, everyone stayed on the other end of his fingertips.

"Jesus. Didn't I learn anything from Emma?" he grumbled. Look how badly that had gone and she hadn't been his boss.

He groaned and a nurse moved to the other side of the hallway to give him a wider berth. Kris had turned him down nice enough, but that wasn't what ate away at his thoughts as he slowed his pace to the cafeteria.

Why had he asked Kris out? She was cute, sure. Well, okay, whatever. She was more than cute; in fact, she was stunning in a terrifying way that had actually woken him up from a dead sleep the other night. He'd been dreaming of walking around downtown LA, hand in hand with someone he couldn't see, but it had *felt* right, like he was meant to be there. When his dream self had looked up and his gaze had landed on Kris in a sexy pale blue sundress, he'd shot awake and…turned on like none other. Which, of course, had pissed him off. What the hell was his body thinking, reacting like that to his *boss*?

More than just his body's reaction to hers terrified him. It was the way his chest ached when he thought of her that was gonna make him do some stupid crap if he wasn't careful.

He'd quipped about wanting time with "the boss" as a way to make Kris feel better about the invitation. But then, right after the ridiculous words had left his mouth, he'd wished he could take them back. Because…he kinda wished he had the freedom to ask Kris out for real. As anything but her employee.

Again, *why*? She'd opened up a little today, but she still had the power to cut him off at the knees if he didn't play ball under the limelight with her, to draw the same sense of self-loathing out of him that he'd felt from his parents. He had the nagging sense of playing catch-up every time he was around her, which didn't exactly a relationship make.

But he'd told her the truth about his pro bono surgeries, or a version of it at least. There had to be something to that. Not that it meant he was ready to open up and let someone in— someone who could wound him, sure, but worse? Someone else he could hurt.

Even if he *was* ready, Kris was the last person he should be thinking about romantically. If he hurt his boss… A chill rolled through him. It would kill his chances to make the kind of change he'd set out to make. And that was the only thing that mattered—his work at the clinic; it was the only thing keeping him from drowning in regret and guilt.

He raked his hands through his hair before smoothing it out again.

Jesus.

What he needed was a good game of basketball with Dex to set him straight where the fairer sex was concerned but his friend was in Africa for a mental health medical summit. And he was meeting Kris on a lunch date where all eyes in the hospital would be on them and he couldn't keep thoughts of her professional to save his life.

Great. As bonehead moves go, you're killing it.

Owen pushed through the cafeteria entrance and his eyes scanned the tables looking for a familiar face. He saw plenty of docs and nurses he worked with each day, but when his gaze settled on the brunette curls framing a face that had literally haunted his sleep, he fought to keep the grin off his face. No use advertising how he felt about her when he wasn't even sure himself.

"I already ordered," Kris told him, a spread of pale pink coloring her cheeks. "Sorry—I'm just not very nice when I haven't eaten."

Owen opened his mouth to make a quip about how if he'd known that earlier, he'd have shown up to her office with a Snickers the other day, but she shook her head.

"I know what you're about to say, Owen Rhys and don't you dare. You caught me with my backside in the air while you already had home court advantage. I was entitled to a little curtness."

He closed his mouth, which ended up in a toothy grin. This woman was getting under his skin, and he didn't really mind. He could enjoy her and keep his distance; he was a functioning adult, after all.

"Fair enough. I also could have been a tad more gracious."

"A tad?"

"Call it even, then?" he asked, chuckling. She nodded. "Okay, then. What'd you order for lunch?"

"The Waldorf salad."

"A salad, huh? Would you believe I had a joke about salad once, but I tossed it?"

Kris groaned, but the smile she wore said she at least somewhat appreciated his dad joke. Only a brief flash of something—surprise?—strained her features, but it vanished just as quickly.

"That was horrible. Like, ten out of ten cringy. Luckily my food will make up for it."

"Well, I'm not gonna pass judgment on a doctor keeping her fiber up, but at some point, you've got to try the club sandwich. The waffle fries alone are worth it."

Kris pretended to gawk, her mouth wide in mock surprise, her hand pressed against her chest, drawing attention to the subtle V-neck of her shirt that left the top of her curves exposed. Maybe he'd order a water, too. For some reason his mouth and throat had gone dry.

"Waffle fries? What will your patients think?" Her salad was slid in front of her, a mountain of greens, walnuts and apples tossed in a light vinaigrette.

He shrugged and reached over, grabbing a slice of apple from her plate and tossing it into his mouth.

"That I run six miles a day?"

"You know, those of us who could run the LA Marathon every morning and still have to watch what we eat hate you right now. Besides, I found a new doughnut place and I'm sorry to say I'm in a relationship with their vanilla glazed. So, salad it is for the rest of my meals."

Her eyes were playful, but the way she fiddled with her napkin belied a vulnerability he hadn't caught in her before. Owen sat beside her after giving the cafeteria staff his order.

God, sometimes he wanted to leave the city that demanded perfection from already gorgeous people. The tragedy of it all was that in shaping bodies to be symmetrical and Instagram worthy, he was reaffirming some of his patients' beliefs that they weren't good enough as they were.

That was his double-edged sword. He wanted to exclusively use his skills to help public servants like Chuck, or his brother, but then what would fund the time he spent at the free clinic? Those surgeries could only happen if he took on the plastics work he did at Mercy. For now, anyway. Kris's trauma center would be the perfect solution if—and only if—she didn't make him work with a film crew watching over his very private patients.

"Though I wish I could eat doughnuts for lunch instead."

"You should try DK's," he said. "They make a jelly filled that'll make you swear you've seen God."

She peered over at him with that same look from earlier. It wasn't just the surprise in her pulled brows or the way she nibbled on the corner of her lips. It was like she was sussing him out, trying to put the pieces of a puzzle together.

He was hit with the realization that no one had looked at him like that in a while. Maybe ever.

"Um…yeah. That's where I go. A—" Her lips twisted like the napkin in her hand. "A friend recommended it to me."

A friend.

He'd been so blinded asking her out after one semi-cordial interaction he hadn't stopped to consider if she might be seeing someone.

But then, hadn't he recommended DK's to a "friend"?

Wait…

His pulse raced until he took a steadying breath and willed it to calm down so he didn't end up in the ED chasing some wild accusation his brain had conjured up.

But the alignment nagged at him, refusing to let go.

She was new to town, and so was @ladydoc. She'd gone to DK's at the suggestion of a friend and he'd suggested DK's to @ladydoc.

A few similarities he could chalk up to circumstantial evidence. It didn't mean they were the same person, because— because that would be too damn ironic. Falling for a woman who turned out to be the heinous boss he complained about?

He chuckled, then grew serious as he watched her eat a small bite of salad.

"You know, I hate the pressure of chauvinistic perfection this damned city puts on everyone. Not just actors, either. You're beautiful how you are, whether or not you eat a couple carbs."

Where did that come from?

His mind wanted to know. He wasn't sure, only that it was the truth.

Her cheeks showed the effects of the compliment and he wished he had a few more up his sleeve if that was the result.

"Thanks. I'm a little too used to self-deprecation after..." She paused. Who had hurt her? But a server arrived with his food and she just shook her head. "You're right. That does look incredible."

Stealing a play from his book, she snatched a fry from his plate, smothered it in ketchup and tossed it in her mouth. Well, now he couldn't keep his gaze from her smile, especially after she licked her lips clean, her tongue slowly trailing each one, leaving them glistening.

Where was that water he'd ordered?

"After?" he pushed. He gave her another fry and she tossed it in her mouth.

Her brows pulled together as if considering what she wanted to say. He didn't blame her for taking a beat; after all, as he'd pointed out, she was his boss, not an actual date.

"An ex," she finally said. "When I was a teen, I moved into...into a home that made me feel less than. And when I was an intern, an attending capitalized on that."

Anger boiled in Owen's veins. "How so?" he managed to ask through gritted teeth.

"I don't know. I was smart, but he always found a way to put me down in front of my peers. He said it was because he didn't want them to figure out we were seeing each other, but—" She worried on her bottom lip. "Anyway, he stole my research and won a grant with it, so it was pretty clear he knew I was smarter than him all along."

She shrugged and stole another fry off his plate, but the blush on her cheeks had turned crimson. He was pretty sure his were, too.

"What a dick," he said. "He didn't deserve to be an attending and he sure as hell didn't deserve you."

She smiled, but shook her head like she didn't believe him. Man, if she weren't who she was and he weren't…who he was…he'd have liked to try to prove it to her. But unfortunately for him, that would be some luckier man's job.

Kris missed a small bead of ketchup in the corner of her mouth and Owen stared at it, his brows furrowed. He had a sudden urge to run the pad of his thumb along her lip and remove the small teardrop of red.

No, that wasn't the predominant thought he had. What he really wanted to do was take that whole bottom lip of hers, ketchup and all, into his mouth and taste her. Owen gulped back a crushing wave of desire that had no place at work, and certainly not when it was aimed at his boss. His boss with whom, until a few moments ago, he'd shared only a few neutral exchanges, the rest tainted with animosity.

And then there was his no-dating order. He couldn't give anyone what he didn't possess. Namely his heart. It had shattered years ago when he'd been just a teen and had made the worst mistake of his life. A mistake his brother still paid for. Intimacy and vulnerability and the perks that came with them were for people who hadn't disappointed everyone they'd ever loved.

"Um…you…uh…missed a spot." He pointed to the corner of her lip and when her tongue slid over the stain and removed it, he wished he hadn't said anything. Because for some damned reason, regardless of not wanting a relationship, especially after the one time he'd tried to give it a go with Emma and it had spectacularly backfired, he couldn't stop wanting *her*.

Kris.

It wasn't at all helpful that she'd opened up and shared part of who she was outside this place. It...humanized her and piqued his curiosity.

Think of the clinic. Of your practice.

They were the only things that eased the pulsing ache in his chest, that calmed his guilt ever so slightly. Therefore, they were the only things that mattered.

The quick save from his head worked, but barely. He'd need more fortification if he was going to keep Kris off his mind.

"Dr. Offerman," a man's voice said above them. Owen had been so focused on Kris's heart-shaped mouth, then trying to forget about her heart-shaped mouth, he hadn't noticed anyone approaching their table. It was Clive Warren, one of the ER docs.

"Dr. Warren, good to see you again. How can I help you?" Kris asked.

"Excuse the interruption of your lunch, but I need you to consult in the ED."

Owen resisted the urge to roll his eyes. Kris was the CMO, not an ER doc, and Clive was interrupting what had been a nice time, the sexual tension in Owen's chest notwithstanding.

A small stab of hot, green jealousy prickled Owen's skin. It wasn't because Kris was smiling up at Clive in a way she'd never smiled at Owen. Because again, why should he care how Kris smiled at anyone?

"Sure. What's the workup?"

Clive pulled out a chair and Owen frowned. No one had invited the guy to sit with them.

"Ten years old, acute respiratory distress. Temp fluctuates

between a buck and one-oh-three. No history of asthma and a clear chest CT."

"You get a consult from Frey?" Owen asked, even though Clive had all but ignored him since he walked up. Dr. Frey was their chief of peds and one of the most recognized pediatric surgeons in the country.

Clive shook his head. "She's been in surgery with the transplant since eight and probably has three hours left. Dr. Offerman, if we don't figure something out soon, I'm afraid the kid doesn't have three hours."

Kris stood up, leaving her lunch on the table, barely touched. "Okay. Let me change into some scrubs and I'll meet you downstairs. Dr. Rhys, do you mind if I take a rain check for the observation?"

Owen was about to protest but what could he say that wouldn't sound petty compared to potentially saving a child's life?

"You should come along, too," Clive said to Owen, finally acknowledging him once Kris had boxed up her salad and told Clive she'd see him shortly. "Kid's got some burns I'd like you to check out."

"Sounds good. Lead the way." Owen dumped his fries, but carried the sandwich with him as he walked. "Hey, why'd you ask Kri—Dr. Offerman to consult? She's the CMO, not med staff."

Clive shot him a look that said Owen had missed something important. "Well, since she's one of the best peds trauma docs in the country, I figured it was worth a shot if it'll save the kid. He doesn't care what her title is now. He just wants to go home with his family."

"She is?"

"You didn't know that? We had to weasel her out of Angola so we could use her talents here. She's double board certified in trauma surgery and peds. The CMO gig was just the way to get her here so she could fix the budget, then she was going to practice part-time. Who knew she'd build the trauma center and set two bones with one cast?"

Owen let that settle in as he polished off the last two mouthfuls of his sandwich. Kris was a peds trauma surgeon by trade? How didn't he know that?

Because you refused to believe she was anything but a suit. A stubborn, rule-following suit. What're you gonna do now that you know better?

His subconscious—also stubborn, but not wrong—had a point. He didn't know what this new information meant for his perception of Kris, just that she kept surprising him, and not in a bad way.

Owen had a sudden inclination to write @ladydoc and let her know his boss wasn't the monster he'd made her out to be, but his head gave a gentle nudge to his heart.

She hasn't responded to your request to meet.

He sighed. Even if she had, why did it feel superfluous now that some of the excitement and passion he'd felt talking to her had been redistributed to his boss?

It kinda felt like cheating on @ladydoc, but then again, he wasn't the one ghosting her.

They arrived at the ED and Owen stopped to wash his hands and glove up. Somehow, Kris had beaten them there and was waiting outside the doors to the trauma bays. Owen's chest clutched at the sight of her in scrubs, her hair pulled back in a loose ponytail.

It'd never occurred to him to look for a relationship, even simple friendship, in a fellow physician until he'd met @ladydoc on the chat site. But now an ache echoed in the empty space of his chest that should have been filled with friends and colleagues. Turns out if he pushed everyone away, they stayed that way. But maybe…maybe he could loosen up a little. Find some balance and make some friends other than Dex.

For once, the little voice that usually chimed in from the

darkest parts of his mind reminding him that he was a good doctor, but terrible friend, was silent.

"Thanks for meeting us here, Dr. Offerman," Clive told Kris.

She nodded but jutted her chin over at Owen. "You could have finished lunch. I'll connect with you about rescheduling your observation this evening."

"I'm here to consult as well."

"Oh, okay. Well, Dr. Warren, lead the way, then."

Owen recognized a familiar look on Kris's face. It was the same look he got from most folks when they found out he was a plastic surgeon—the "you're not a real doctor" one. Anger bubbled in his stomach, but as he was accustomed to, he ignored it. The kid had burns that he could help with, that *only* he could help with.

He didn't need colleagues passing judgment on his work any more than he needed his family's approval for why he did what he did. Sam said they didn't blame him, but what else was he supposed to assume from their silence? Becoming a trauma surgeon, albeit with a plastics specialty, wasn't enough to get them to visit, to call, to forgive him. Not that he deserved any of that. Especially when he couldn't find a way to forgive himself—how could he expect it from others?

So why does Kris's dismissal sting?

Because I respect her and it's not reciprocated.

And there's your fortification—no matter how much she values what you do for Chuck and patients like him, she'll never see you as an equal.

He shook off the doubts and concentrated on the job at hand. Their patient needed him focused.

When they were at the child's bedside, though, all his reasons for training in burn reconstruction came rushing headlong into Owen's subconscious, pummeling him with memories. The patient—Remy Thompson—had cropped brown hair that fell over his eyes, which were icy blue and filled with pain.

Burns were raked over his exposed chest and shoulder and the pinkness combined with the slight swelling indicated they were relatively recent.

A lump formed in Owen's throat. *Sam.* He looked so much like Sam had in those first months after his injury. He'd seen injured kids before, but none that bore such a strong resemblance to his brother.

Kris checked Remy's breathing while Owen examined the wounds covering what looked to be over a fifth of the boy's chest and back. He looked up and shared a glance with Kris that said *this isn't good.* She nodded her agreement and turned to address the parents.

"His breathing is shallow, with limited respiratory sounds on his right. I'd worry about the burns being the cause of the constriction, but they're not on the same side. Can you talk me through how long this has been going on?"

The parents listed off Remy's symptoms, which had deteriorated over the past ten hours or so, until they felt they had to bring him in.

"Hmmm. I want a BiPAP and two mils of dexamethasone and a repeat CT every two hours."

"Are you thinking acidosis?" Owen asked.

"I am."

"That's rare in kids, isn't it?"

She nodded but before she could respond, the monitors went wild, all the alarms triggered at the same time.

"He's got low oxygenation and a bradycardic pulse. Scratch the BiPap. I want a mask and vent set up, and push the dexa, stat."

A team of nurses rushed to Remy's side and worked on him while Owen assisted with the ventilator. Remy lost consciousness midway through the intubation which was probably better for him, but his parents stood off to the side, their eyes wet and wide with terror. Before now, Owen hadn't noticed the two small children at their feet. Remy's siblings were watching as their brother coded on the table.

Oh, hell, no.

"Someone help his family to the waiting room," he commanded. "Now."

They were whisked away by a nurse, and just in time as Remy's monitors flashed again, this time with a flatline.

"He's asystolic. Start compressions," Owen called out, not waiting for Kris. They had to save this kid, dammit. They had to.

On the second round of compressions and epi pushed into Remy's IV, the incessant wailing of the monitors slowed to a steady beep. Owen released a breath he hadn't realized he'd been holding.

"We've got sinus rhythm," Kris announced. "Good work," she said to Owen.

Pride washed through him but was followed by a smack of reality. That had been close. Too close. And they weren't out of the woods yet. He couldn't help with the wounds while Remy was still so touch and go, but hopefully the meds would do their magic and he could work out a surgical plan to remove the heavier scarring in a week or two.

He stripped his gloves and walked out of the room, shoving himself through to the stairwell before collapsing on the bottom stair. His head sank to his hands as images of Sam pelted the backs of his eyelids. Had just one thing gone differently, his brother might not have made it. They'd been too close back then as well.

God, would the worry that plagued Owen ever go away? Not the passing of two decades or the miraculous recovery Sam had made worked in lessening the fear Owen felt for his brother. Or the guilt for being the cause of his pain.

Time slipped past him until a hand rested gently on his lower back, steadying him.

"Take your time," Kris said. Her voice washed over him

like a balm and his pulse slowed. Finally, he stood up, facing her. Her gaze, kind and calming, sparked an energy that radiated from his chest outward.

The intimacy tugged at his flight or fight response, challenging it. He didn't move, though, settling into the comfort Kris offered instead. As he did, dust from around his heart crumbled. A small crack in the stony exterior let in some pride and self-forgiveness.

But he couldn't allow more. Not without letting loose the torrent of heat building behind his eyes.

And yet, when she whispered, "That was hard," he found himself agreeing.

"It's why I didn't go into pediatrics. I can't stand to see kids like that—" He stopped himself before he said too much. As it was, he'd never told anyone that he'd have liked to go into pediatrics like her, but didn't have the fortitude. Not after Sam. What was it about this woman that drew his unspoken truths from him like a drug?

"I know what you mean. There are days in my career that are burned into the backs of my eyelids and sometimes I'm not sure how I'll keep going."

"That kid…" Owen said. "He's so—"

"Hurt, yes. But he'll recover. We've got a damn good team that'll take care of him and when he's stable, you'll help with his scarring." Kris continued to peer up at him, her eyes soft and welcoming. He could so easily fall into their depths and lose himself there, but that wasn't an option, no matter how tempting it was.

"I will. Of course I will." After all, that was part of his penance, wasn't it? Fix the mistakes he'd made until the regret abated?

"I'm not saying it'll be an easy road, but he'll make it."

Owen nodded his agreement.

No, the boy's path wasn't an easy road at all. Owen knew that firsthand. It would mean doctors' appointments every week once he was released from the hospital. It meant surgeries upon surgeries to correct the scarring and make sure the internal damage wasn't too great. For Remy's two siblings, their lives would be marred by their brother's illness and recovery; even if the accident hadn't been their fault the way Owen was responsible for his brother's lifelong healing, the other kids' needs would fall by the wayside so the parents could focus on saving this child.

It wasn't fair, but it was what needed to be done. Owen knew it and any blame he might have had for being ignored throughout his own childhood was overshadowed by the necrotic guilt that ate away at him for causing the accident in the first place.

"Yeah. I guess you're right," he replied. Because what else could he say? Even though they'd shared a moment of understanding, Kris wasn't his friend.

If only her scent—jasmine and grapefruit bathed in warmth—didn't wrap around his good sense, strangling it. She'd moved closer, so much so that all he needed to do was dip his chin and claim her mouth with his. The temptation to give in to that desire beat against his chest like a feral beast wanting to be fed.

But his mind shut that down, reminding him of his promise to himself.

No dating, no romance and certainly no love.

Keeping that promise meant keeping people safe from his inevitable screwups. Which also meant keeping his clinic safe in this case.

@ladydoc had begun to sneak past his defenses, but he'd been able to hide behind their anonymity and agreement to stay friends. He couldn't hide from what he was starting to feel for Kris, though. Not with her invading his space and claiming it with the longing she brought out in him.

His body and heart warred with his mind, arguing that he could open up to her, that their connection—even if it was just physical—meant something. That *he* meant something.

Really? Would that be true if you told her to take her media plan and shove it?

He swallowed a groan.

His attraction to Kris Offerman compounded all the reasons he needed to stay away from her.

"I know it's bad timing, but I need to take a couple personal days. There's something I've got to do."

And someone I need to take a break from.

If Kris was concerned about his sudden change of heart, she didn't show it. She stepped back and the space between them opened like a crevasse ready to swallow him whole. His body buzzed where she'd touched it.

"What about your patients?"

"I don't have any surgeries scheduled until Friday of next week and my team can handle rounding on my patients in recovery. I'll push back consults until after the time off if that's all right."

The clinic patients would have to wait, but that couldn't be helped.

"Okay. We've got a meeting with the media team that morning, so I need you back by then."

"I can do that. Thanks."

"Hey, Owen?" Kris asked.

He gazed down at her, ignoring the clutch of his heart as it registered the concern etched in her half smile.

"Yeah?"

"You doing okay?"

No. I'm not.

"I'll be fine," he said, and turned away from her so he could catch his breath.

Owen started to walk up the stairs toward the plastics center, but his legs felt heavy and encumbered. His mind, though, was untethered as the rest of his week's to-do lists evaporated and left him without something nagging his professional life for the first time since med school. A mistake, he realized, since Kris and @ladydoc both snuck through and settled in comfortably.

What will you do with the time off?

He should go make right what he could with Sam, with his family, even if that meant opening up old wounds. It was well past time. However, the idea sent heat followed by chills racing along his skin. All his adult life, the only thing he'd felt brewing beneath his stony exterior was guilt and an endless ache for the damage he'd inflicted; what would it take to set that aside? And what, pray tell, would take its place?

Maybe something better, something beautiful.

But…was he ready for that? Was his family?

Even if he didn't head up to SLO, he needed to think through how these two women worked through his no-emotions-allowed barrier, leaving him open to questions he didn't have answers to.

Because if he didn't find a way to shore up whatever crack they'd slipped through, he had a feeling the whole damned wall would come crumbling down, burying him in the wreckage.

CHAPTER SIX

KRIS SAT AT the end of the long, elegant conference table, her shoulders relaxed even if the rest of her wasn't. The past three weeks since she'd started at Mercy were some of the longest days in her career and the worst part was, very little of it had included practicing any medicine. Doing a walk-through of the construction that was—miraculously—60 percent done, yes. Building the trauma staff, yes. But patient care? Not once.

She missed the feel of a patient's hand in hers, the look of pleading in their eyes that dissipated as she promised to help them at whatever cost. Helping tame Remy's infection had re-minded her just how much medicine—not just medical sys-tems—meant to her.

She'd done such good work in her career—work she could be proud of, work that made a difference in those lives she helped. And now?

Ha! Now she was the only one left in the conference room after yet another soul-sucking meeting with finance about the operating budget, where their team had issued an unveiled threat about what it would do to the hospital if the trauma cen-ter failed. They would go under, plain and simple. And then all Kris's plans would be for nothing.

What would she have, then? She'd buried herself so deeply in work it had led to immeasurable success in her professional life, but at such a steep cost. If it was gone the next day, what did she have to show for all the years of pushing everyone but Alice aside? She'd be alone, with no one to blame but herself.

A small, humorless laugh escaped her throat.

It was ironic since she dove into work to avoid the loneliness of all the loss stacked up against her heart, suffocating it. All this time, she'd assumed she was living a full, dedicated life, but where was the balance, the sense of what all of it was for?

Tipping the scales ever so slightly was her online friend. His easy friendship, sans the familiar worry it would expose her, showed how much she craved human connection—not that she'd admit that outside the digital world she and @makingadifference shared.

Not when that might leave her open to other, less safe "friendships."

She sighed, gazing out over the LA skyline that the conference room put on full display with its floor-to-ceiling windows and backlighting. Right now the only man on her mind—and frustratingly so since he was as off-limits as a man could be—was Dr. Rhys. So very unsafe for her heart.

He was also the only one who'd looked less than enthused to be part of that meeting. Before he walked away from work the day Remy almost died, he'd been kind and even friendly toward her. Then, there'd even been a moment where she worried he might bend down to kiss her.

It was not like it would have been totally unrequited, but that was precisely why the panic had set in. She'd let herself get close—too close. It was as if she was twenty-three again and back in her first year of residency. Kris had been hoodwinked into falling for more than just a colleague that time; she'd had the bad fortune to fall for James Finnick, a plastics attending with a secret affection for med students. She had been one in a long line of silly affairs the man partook in. But it hadn't been silly to her. Then the complete jerk had stolen her research to top off her mortification.

If it weren't for Alice—and a couple bottles of the good

rioja she'd brought back from Spain—Kris would have done something rash and career ending. Alice taught her how to lock her feelings away while she worked, then took Kris under her wing once she matched at Minneapolis General for her residency. She'd have thought with her background in trauma, a hospital like Boston Gen might've wanted her more, but the matching process—where a physician's specialty and personality were fitted with a hospital advertising the same needs in a resident—had done her an unexpected favor. Kris's dear friend became her mentor, sealing her role as the only one in Kris's life who mattered outside the job.

Until Alice lost her battle with pancreatic cancer while Kris was in Angola, anyway. The woman might be gone too soon, but Alice's lessons remained and had gotten Kris through a lot of tough times.

Enter Owen Rhys. Now Kris was a bundle of unwanted emotions, only one of which was frustration. That, she could have tackled in a nanosecond. The rest, though? Lust, attraction, desire…those were getting too heavy to carry. So was the unnamed ache in her chest that grew larger each day Owen had been gone and didn't check in with the hospital. She could use Alice's wisdom now more than ever.

Kris tapped her pen on the mahogany table, the sound deafening in the silence.

Thankfully, Owen had returned that morning, but with a wall built up around him again. He'd breezed right past her, barely offering her a wan smile before taking his seat at the other end of the conference table. Whatever tenuous amiability had existed between them before he left was gone now.

His usually sharp gaze was dulled, and dare she add distracted?

And that worried her more than anything. James had gone cold like that right before he stole her research, using it to secure a Lasker Award and two-million-dollar grant.

Was Owen biding his time until he could move his patients

to her trauma center and claim credit, if not for the idea, then for sliding in at the eleventh hour and making sure it went off without a hitch? If that was the case, she didn't know what she'd do.

She was "The Fixer," but it was impossible to fix a man who was hell-bent on her destruction, especially a man she'd come to respect, if not care for.

At least the lunch she'd purchased for the meeting had been good. Fortunately @makingadifference had been a hundred percent right about the food; it was hands-down the best Thai she'd had outside the country of Thailand. The unfortunate thing was, she couldn't even tell him because then she'd have to ignore or respond to his request to meet up and both seemed impossible without more clarity.

She pulled her phone out and reread his message for the hundredth time before slipping it back into her suit pocket and pretending it wasn't humming against her heart, asking to be heard.

Maybe that was what bothered her—without the ability to write @makingadifference like she wanted to, her mind was free to wander to other, less desirable topics.

Like how a brooding Owen somehow made her stomach flip faster and more frequently than a kind, quiet Owen. Or how she itched to ask him what was wrong, until her mind reminded her it wasn't her job as his boss.

No. Personal. Feelings.

The three-word mandate seemed more like a prison sentence now.

Ugh.

Kris wanted to scream into the void that was the conference room, but that would be breaking cardinal work rule number one, wouldn't it? No anger, no matter how justified it was. Still, frustration and indecision brewed beneath her outwardly calm exterior, numbing her thoughts.

It was time to clean up and head to her next observation—

an army physician who might be a good fit for the trauma center—but she was paralyzed with exhaustion.

When the door to the conference room opened, causing a shift in the air around her, Kris looked up. Her face was passive, expecting to see a member of the board or a resident coming in to study for their upcoming boards.

Instead, her breath hitched in her chest as she gazed up at the most ridiculously handsome man she'd ever seen. And in her travels, she'd seen some beautiful men.

Owen stood there, arms crossed over his chest, his suit jacket discarded somewhere, leaving his rolled-up shirtsleeves and oh-so-strong forearms on display. She gulped back a wave of very unappreciated lust.

"How can I help you, Dr. Rhys?" she asked, making a move to stand.

He waved her off. "Don't get up for me. I'm just—" He looked conflicted, like he wasn't sure what he wanted to say. "I wanted to know if you'd like to see my clinic. I'm headed there now for some consultations and I thought you might want to tag along. If you're not busy."

"No. Not at all, I mean… I'd love to go and no, I'm not busy."

She took out her phone and tried to hide the way her hands trembled with him that close, his sea-air-infused scent snaking around her.

"Let me just jot an email and I'll be ready to go."

"We can do it another day—"

"No." She rushed. "I want to come. Do you have a minute? Or I could meet you there."

"I'll wait."

In a gesture so unlike him, he sat in the chair beside her. Like, right beside her. Her body buzzed with recognition, something she was aware of as a medical professional, but had never experienced as a woman.

Well, that's inconvenient.

She didn't dare let her gaze wander down his frame, but even in her peripheral vision she registered the tension he carried in every cell. She hit Send and put her phone away.

"I'm good," she said. They both got up at the same time and their chests collided. He went left to let her out, but she happened to go the same direction and they stayed in the über-close holding pattern. Finally, he put a hand on her hip and nudged her the opposite way to where he was going. Her skin burned under his touch, an irony since he made a living saving burn victims and yet seemed to scorch her every time he was near.

What the hell is it about this man?

"Do you mind if I drive?"

"Sure."

As they made their way to the parking lot, curiosity about the man overwhelmed her. What he drove, where he worked after hours, how he lived... Did he eat standing at the counter? Did he sleep in the nude? Did his skin taste how it smelled, like fresh soap and citrus?

She gulped back a flash of heat, thankful he wasn't looking at her and couldn't see the way her skin prickled with goose pimples.

Careful. Those are questions a woman with way more than just professional interest would ask.

And yet...

She couldn't help the burgeoning desire to know everything about Owen Rhys, professional or otherwise. He'd mentioned steering clear of pediatrics, and that one invitation into the psyche of a man she was fascinated by had been all she needed to garner a thousand more questions for him. God, she missed Alice; a good dish session was in order, the topic of course being the stupidly handsome and impossible-to-read plastics doc.

The drive was short—only two city blocks. Two city blocks that transported her to a world she hadn't known existed. When they pulled up and went in, Kris felt her jaw drop. Owen had used the word *clinic*, so she expected an underfunded, over-populated, dilapidated building where Owen risked his health for that of his patients.

The truth was nothing close. This building, with its tall, clean windows offering natural light, vibrant green plants in stained wood boxes hanging from the mezzanine and water feature in the center of the lobby, was...*perfect*. The whole design was tasteful and homey, yet spoke of understated elegance. Much the same as Owen's office where he'd treated Chuck.

"It's incredible. It's—"

Exactly what I want my trauma center to look like, to feel like.

And it was starting to, thanks to Owen's design. Had he helped here, too? Or borrowed from the plans?

"Thank you."

"How didn't I know this was here?"

Owen shrugged and took her hand like it was something he did every day. His fingers threaded in hers and she was suddenly very aware of how warm her hand was. His smile was softer, his eyes fuller and brighter than she'd ever seen them. He looked at home here.

"Come on—I'll show you around and you can ask any questions you want. But for starters, we don't advertise. There are nonprofit groups we work with to bring in patients and donors refer as needed. You wouldn't have heard of us unless you were a patient."

"But—" she started, shaking her head as he walked her through the lobby. How did she phrase this without sounding like an idiot? "But how do you get funding if you don't advertise?"

Because it was the one aspect she was struggling with at Mercy and it might be the one thing that sank her if she wasn't careful.

"We apply for grants, reach out to wealthy donors with an interest in the kind of medicine we're practicing and I donate my time with the money I make at Mercy."

She squeezed his hand, impressed to say the least.

"How many patients a day?"

"Roughly four, but there are times we have every bed full between pre-op, surgery and then post-op and recovery."

"How many beds?"

"Twenty."

"*Twenty?*" she shouted, then giggled and covered her mouth when the word echoed in the cavernous space. Excitement coursed through her. "That's not a clinic, Owen. That's a small hospital."

"Dedicated only to patients who can't afford cosmetic surgery to heal wounds and deformations. So…sorta."

She whistled as they walked up the steps, still grasping his hand. Nerves fluttered across her chest cavity. She hadn't held a man's hand in a *long* time.

Not since the other plastics doc. James.

She shoved that thought out of her head because Owen wasn't like James, but others filled the space.

You work better alone. Alone means no one can leave you behind.

A deep sigh built in her lungs, anguish blocking it from escaping. She knew why she'd made the choice to keep everyone at arm's length, but gosh, it was lonely at times, especially when something simple like holding a man's hand—a man whom she'd begun to think of more fondly—brought so much joy.

That's why you have @makingadifference. So you can have the companionship without the risk.

True, her heart spoke up. *But is there true companionship without risk?*

She kept that question close as Owen led her around.

"It's wonderful, what you're doing, Owen. Really it is. How long have you been moonlighting here?" she asked.

"Can I answer like you're a curious colleague, not my boss?"

A smile broke loose. She hadn't allowed herself to be a friend or colleague for some time. That someone thought of her that way—someone whose opinion had begun to matter to her—was nice.

"Yeah. Go for it."

"I don't moonlight here so much as at Mercy. I keep that job to help fund my surgical time so I don't have to bill my donors for it here, but uh, this is *my* clinic, as in I own and operate it. I'm here every free chance I get making sure patients get the care they need."

Recognition of the stark similarity between her and Owen flicked her heart with awareness. All this time she'd been worried about his reputation.

That he worked as hard as her, that he poured his heart into his career like she did slammed against her like three hundred volts from an AED. It was incredible, but it also reminded her of what they both risked if she fell for her subordinate. He would have the clinic to fall back on if it went to hell, but what would she have?

She needed to focus and build her own dream before she invited anyone into it. Then, if they left, she wouldn't be without that, at least.

She spun around, taking Owen's dream in.

"So you're not really at bars or trolling for women on adult dating sites?" She barked out a laugh, because the rumors were so egregious and he'd—he'd *let* them fester to keep this secret. *Why?*

"Not exactly, no." His smile was thin.

"So why'd you let people believe that about you, especially when the truth is so much better?"

Owen led them into an empty recovery room. The bed boasted leather head- and footboards and thick satin sheets.

There was an en suite bathroom with a wheelchair-access shower and tub, a closet for guests' items and even a pullout couch for them to stay with their loved ones. As stunning as the lobby was, this was even more so.

"I'd think by now you know I don't do anything for the attention, Kris. It isn't important to me what people think. It's important that my patients are well cared for."

She cleared her throat. His message was clear—*I don't approve of your strategy for the trauma center.*

"Yes, but you can do both, you know. Talk about your success *and* provide exceptional ethic of care. In fact, most of the best docs and surgeons do."

"Sure, maybe you're right." *That*, she wasn't expecting. "But this particular project was important to keep to myself. Too many surgeons take your idea and go overboard, flaunting every tiny thing to pump up their oversize egos. I wanted this free of that kind of scrutiny."

Another hit from the paddles, this time at four hundred.

"Why?" she asked. He bit his bottom lip and another question formed in her head. "Do you think it minimizes the good you do if you claim credit?"

"Wha—?" His eyes went big. "I…um… I guess. Yeah. Medicine isn't meant to be flaunted, but somewhere along the way, it became that. I practice for personal reasons, and yeah, claiming credit for my successes would minimize them."

"It wouldn't," she countered. "The good is done, either way."

Owen only shrugged.

"Anyway, this clinic is a nonprofit?" she asked, changing the subject. She tucked the other one away for now, adding it to what she knew of the man. He was so much more than she'd imagined. But she was at a loss for what to do with that information.

He nodded, his hands tucked deep in his slacks pockets.

"Aside from the media partnership, it's not that different from what you mapped out for Mercy."

"When did you start this?" she asked, amazement dripping from her words. The place was stunning—small, but more in an efficient way than lacking in space. Every spare inch was put to use and function, from the retractable surgical trays to the transformable couch.

"We opened our doors ten years ago, but I'd been working toward it since I got my medical license."

She ran a finger along the leather footpost of the recovery suite bed, marveling at his attention to detail.

"You designed it?" she wondered aloud.

"Yep. My…my brother helped, but it was just the two of us."

His brother. A ping of awareness echoed in a part of her head that had been silent for a couple weeks now.

"Is he a doctor?" she asked. It was an innocent enough question, one a curious colleague would have asked. Yet, her intentions were anything but. She asked as @ladydoc.

"Veterinarian, actually. But he had a vested interest in my work."

Kris nodded. She bit her lip to keep it from trembling and giving away what she thought she knew, even with his vague answer. Unless she was wildly off base, Owen was @makingadifference, the man she'd fallen for, message by message over the past six months. He had to be. Between the jokes, the pro bono work on the side…his brother… It all added up, but the equation still stumped her as much as it terrified her.

Because she'd been falling for the desire pulsing between her and Owen, too. The main thing keeping her from acting on that desire—aside from her fear of losing not just him, but her best surgeon for the trauma center—was her adamant belief that they could never share values, or be friends outside that physical attraction.

But if he and @makingadifference were one and the same…

Good grief—what was she supposed to do if she was right? Her hands shook. How was she meant to keep her distance now? And she had to, right? Of course she did.

So, agree to meet @makingadifference.

That would prove what she suspected one way or another, but it didn't answer the question. What would she want to come of that meeting?

I honestly don't know.

Well, she'd better be sure before she decided. Because it would change everything. And yet... A whisper of a thrill danced on her skin.

Imagine...

She'd fallen for the easy friendship, the supportive guidance and the listening ear of @makingadifference. What would that turn into with the added fiery inferno of the physical attraction that boiled just below the surface when she was anywhere near Owen? Separately, she could temper the temptation, but if they were indeed the same man...

God, it would be unstoppable. Life-changing. Passion *and* friendship. Hard work *and* physical desire.

But...she wasn't anywhere near wanting her life to change in that way.

I'm still his boss... And he's still a plastics doc who has the power to unravel my carefully stitched plan for Mercy.

Besides, if he knew, if she told him what she suspected, who was to say he'd want that? He'd been brutally honest with his feelings about his boss as @makingadifference. If she shared that she was both the confidante and the Cruella he'd talked about, chances were the news wouldn't be near as exciting for him. He'd be disappointed and then her worst fears would come true—she'd lose yet another person she cared about.

When he met her gaze, holding it with a question in his eyes, she wasn't sure that was true. But there was too much at risk for a "maybe."

"What?" she asked when he didn't move or blink, just stared at her.

"Why did you take a job where you're acting more like a PR agent than a CMO?" He put up a hand when she opened her mouth. At least the question distracted her from thinking about @makingadifference. "Before you get defensive, I just mean… I saw you in the ED and you were…you were brilliant. This job is beneath you."

Kris studied Owen, the way he met her gaze and didn't waver. It wasn't cocky, it was…curious.

"I lost someone close to me and this was our dream—to open a trauma center for patients like those we treated in Angola. Kinda like what you're doing—people without healthcare, funding or access. People who serve their country or city or even kids caught in the crossfire of someone else's war. We just wanted to help and this was our plan."

"And the TV show?" He sat down across from her.

Kris sighed. "Her idea. We ran the numbers and there didn't seem to be a way to get the word out and keep funding interests with the rising medical costs today."

He rested his chin on his hands and his elbows on his knees. He leaned in closer to her, and she held in a breath. Her skin itched with discomfort this close to him. Not because she didn't feel safe. No, it was something else. She felt transparent the closer he got, like he would see right through to her deepest, darkest secrets and expose them.

"It's not that I don't agree with what you're doing, obviously." He gestured around him. "I just know you're capable of more."

In an effort to shift the balance, she deflected.

"Where did you go, Owen?"

"Up north. To think through some things."

The fact that he issued an answer at all threw her off her game.

"Why? I mean, what happened with Remy that made you so…despondent?"

His gaze was a thousand miles away again.

"That's not important. It won't happen again."

"Do you treat kids who show up here? Or was that your first pediatric patient?"

His jaw twitched but he held her gaze. "It wasn't my first and like I said, it won't happen again."

"I know. I trust you, Owen." Saying it out loud seemed to surprise them both.

His knee drifted and rested against hers. She tried to swallow the gasp at the way her stomach went all squishy as they touched.

"I trust you, too. You're the only one besides my brother and my...friend who knows about this place. Well, Dex knows, too. But he doesn't count since he's so wrapped up in his own drama."

Kris laughed and wondered if he'd notice if her hand dropped to the outside of her leg so it could graze his thigh. She was also suddenly curious about what Owen's frustratingly set jaw would feel like under her palm.

You're his boss.

Yeah, *yeah*, she told her intrusive thoughts.

She was well aware. But that didn't seem to do a damn thing to decrease her wanting.

"Your *friend*?" she teased, nudging his knee. He linked her pinky with his. "If you have a friend, why did you ask me out that day we met Chuck?"

That, she asked as Kris, not @ladydoc.

The question seemed to throw him off, as he stammered through an answer.

"There is someone I've been talking to online, but she's just a friend. And maybe I should have said something since I didn't want you to think I wanted more from you that day."

She leaned in so their shoulders were touching. She filed the admission about having an online friend away with the rest of the circumstantial evidence.

"Just that day?" Her voice was thick and filled with longing. For the first time since residency, her head stepped back and made room for her heart.

"I wouldn't mind if you thought I wanted more now. Against my better judgment, I do—"

His finger tipped her chin up and his gaze simmered close. Her pulse went tachycardiac and her lips couldn't stop trembling to save her life, but she didn't care. All that mattered was the infinitesimal space between them that closed each second he leaned in.

Just as his lips brushed against hers, branding them with the taste of vanilla and coffee, the door to the recovery room swung open.

Owen shot back like he'd been jolted by a defibrillator.

"What's up, Paul?" he asked the receptionist who'd met them on the way in.

Kris struggled to catch her breath while Paul, looking breathless as well, dove in.

"There's a fire in the Malibu hills that's got a team of firefighters trapped," he said, drawing in another long breath. "EMTs have already brought in four guys with burns and some crush injuries. More are incoming."

"Where are they headed?" Owen stood up and started snatching everything he could get his hands on. Kris saw three debridement kits, a box of surgical gloves and a bag of what looked like gauze and antibiotic cream. She followed suit, grabbing another box of gloves and two kits.

"That's what they want to know. They asked if they could bring them here."

"Here?" He stopped dead in his tracks. "How—" But his face went white.

"Yeah, it's Chuck's men. He called over."

"Dammit," Owen muttered, slamming his hand on the mattress. "This place isn't set up for massive trauma. Burns, yeah, but not the kind of stuff they'll need. Mercy's the closest, but they don't have a dedicated—"

"What about the trauma center?" she asked. "It's sixty per-cent finished as of this morning."

"Is that enough?" he asked.

Her breaths came short and fast. "It has to be. We can use your surgical suites for overload, and the rooms that are al-ready completed will get a test run."

"Okay. Yeah. That'll work. But—"

"I won't call the media," she said as they all made their way out the door, Owen and Kris running toward the exit. "I promise."

"Thank you."

She nodded. It wouldn't be at all appropriate to have them there; in fact, imagining a reporter up in the faces of criti-cally—maybe fatally—injured firefighters made Kris queasy. But then, if it wasn't appropriate now, when would it be?

It wasn't the time or place to share the admission she felt growing in her heart with Owen, but she no longer thought the docuseries was the only way to survive this rebuild.

No matter what, this visit to Owen's clinic showed her there had to be another way. There just had to be. And if not, maybe she wasn't as cut out for this job as both she and Alice had hoped.

CHAPTER SEVEN

OWEN TORE OFF the plastic sheath separating the construction zone from the fully ready suites and flipped on all the lights. Kris had called ahead and made sure it was all-hands-on-deck for the triage. Everyone who wasn't already in a patient room in the full ER was sent over and nurses and docs were called in from their days off. This kind of community emergency needed every soul present and willing to pitch in.

Kris's eyes were bright, focused and poised, like the rest of her. She was back in scrubs—something he'd give himself time to appreciate when the crisis was over. Along with figuring out why the hell he'd thought it was a good idea to kiss his boss, a woman who'd barely acquiesced about not having the media present for this mess. Thank God Paul interrupted what would have been an unmitigated disaster. His bad decisions were like wind against the house of cards he'd built his life out of. One strong gust and the whole thing would topple.

"I can operate if I'm needed," she said.

I need you...

Goddammit. He *did*, though—or part of him did, anyway, the part that wasn't diametrically opposed to what it meant to want her, need her—and that concerned him as much as anything else. That his body was acting against its own best interest.

As if to prove a point, he paused and, without overthinking it, pulled her behind a shelving system stocked with bandages, debriding kits and other items they'd likely run out of by the end of the day. He rubbed her arms, the warmth from her thin smile heating his core.

She'd been stubborn and maybe a little bossy and inflexible when he'd met her, but she was the boss, so of course, that made sense. When push came to shove, however, she'd come through.

She hadn't pried, hadn't judged. Just listened. Not unlike @ladydoc.

So much for being emotionally untouchable. Selfishly, he wanted to see what it might look like to let go and let someone in. But that meant letting go of some long-held beliefs about the world, his role in it and what his future was allowed to look like—and that would take more than her crooked smile.

God, is this what self-doubt feels like?

He'd been too used to self-flagellation and crushing guilt to recognize anything else that might rear its ugly head at the least opportune time.

He looked around and no one's eyes were even close to paying attention to them. So he dipped his chin and kissed her, the consequences be damned. Just once, and nothing more than a closed-mouth kiss, but it sent a shock wave through his veins anyway. She had such a visceral effect on him.

His deck of cards wavered. "What was that for?" she asked. The same wave looked like it'd crashed over her, too.

"I just wanted you to know you're amazing and deserve everything after pulling this off—roses lining your path and a red carpet rolled out, too. This center will save a lot of lives tonight."

"Thanks, Owen. And for the record, I'm more a wildflower-and-daisy person than roses."

"Good to know. Hey, how do you criticize your boss?"

She shot him a frosty glare, but her smile remained.

"How?"

He kissed her cheek this time, lingering by her ear. "Very quietly so she can't hear you."

She smiled and turned her head so her lips met his. He inhaled sharply, but when she opened her mouth just enough that he could taste the mint from her gum, the gasp turned to a moan.

"Um…yeah. So, we should head out," she said, pulling away and biting her bottom lip. Her eyes shone and her smile could have powered the new wing by itself. Desire welled up in Owen's chest, but he shoved it down.

"Agreed. I'll go check in with the families and find out what we're dealing with then I'll let you know."

Kris shook her head and the air in the small space shifted. "No. I've actually got that. You should make a round of the trauma rooms and see what we need."

Owen sighed. They were wasting time over semantics. He could do both. "I've worked with these firefighters, Kris. They know and trust me, so I should swing by. It'll only take a minute." He squeezed her shoulder and headed out, but she called after him.

"Dr. Rhys, stop." He did but wasn't expecting the stern, thin-lipped woman in place of the trusting, smiling one he'd kissed a moment ago. "I'm the CMO of Mercy, so I'll be the face of this hospital and the new center. Okay?"

"Yeah. But Kris—"

"And it's Dr. Offerman while we're working. Is that clear?" *What?*

They'd made so much progress. He'd…he'd *kissed* her. And she'd kissed him back. Where was this sudden change coming from?

And then it hit him like a shot of adrenaline.

"Wait. Are you worried I'll steal the thunder?" She hesitated, but the dip in her gaze answered for her. "Or that I'll steal patients." She bit her bottom lip. Where had her distrust of everyone come from? Her ex? "Kris, I might be a stubborn jerk sometimes, but I believe in what you're doing. Look at this place. It's doing what mine couldn't. Hell, maybe after things calm down we can talk about a partnership, where the surgeries happen here and those who need prolonged care can get it at the clinic. But no, I won't sabotage you. Only the patients matter, and they need us both."

And you don't need her? She doesn't matter?

He ignored his conscience.

"Let's discuss this later, okay?"

"Kri— Dr. Offerman. I'm sorry. But you need to know I'm not that guy."

"What guy?" she asked. Her arms were crossed over her chest creating a wall where there'd been openness a moment ago.

"The other doctor who hurt you and made you feel like you weren't good enough. I'm not him and I'm not going to do anything to screw you over. I just want to—"

The doors hissed open, cutting him off.

"You should—*we* should get to work. We can talk when we're done."

Owen nodded, unsure of how he could apologize. He wasn't trying to step on her toes, but she had to trust him if they were ever going to make strides as colleagues. Or friends, which he hoped would happen.

Bull. You want more than that.

He ignored his conscience. Time to get to work.

Grabbing a clipboard, she took off toward the nurses' station. Owen heard her calling out assignments and issuing orders for tests, but her voice was kind and firm. Exactly what a leader should be. If only she could see that. It would also be nice if she saw that he wasn't gunning for her job. He only wanted to support her.

Then show her. You can let her in—it's the only way to make her feel safe enough to trust you.

But how did he do that? It would take some introspection on his part, that was for damn sure.

Something inside his chest cracked open, letting light in. A small voice, one he hadn't heard in a while, whispered, *It's going to be okay. You're going to be okay.*

He wasn't sure he believed it, but he'd cross that bridge after their current crisis was averted.

"Over here," he called out to the EMTs bringing another stretcher in. "We're headed to Trauma One."

That was the last time he thought about Kris for the next four hours. His mind was wholly focused on debriding second- and third-degree burns, setting bones and intubating smoke inhalation patients. Well, maybe not *wholly*.

He did wonder what it would look like to merge his clinic with Kris's trauma center. It would be nice to have the backing of a major hospital, but then again, he'd be beholden to a major hospital's board. It was a lot to think about, but as the recovery suites filled, there was definitely a need to consider.

When he'd sent the last patient on his wing to get cleared by CT, he swung by the waiting room. As he'd expected, Chuck was there, bent over in a chair and wringing his hands. Owen should have come sooner.

"Chuck," he said, putting a hand on the man's shoulder. He didn't move.

"I should've been there," Chuck groaned. Owen sat beside him.

"No, you shouldn't have. You were last time something this big cropped up and you're still paying the price."

Chuck sat up. "But they're *my* men. I'm some of these guys' only family. Hell, I'm Jones's kids' godfather. And he's so—" Chuck released a sob that only a man who'd incurred the kinds of loss he had could make. "He's never gonna walk again, is he?"

Owen was bound by HIPAA laws that prevented him from

being able to say anything about a patient's care without Jones's permission. But he owed Chuck something.

"Like you said, he's your guy. Which means he's strong as hell and when patients are that strong, they've got a heckuva better chance of healing."

"God, I hope so." He sniffled and Owen reached into his pocket where he'd kept some paper towels that were left over from his last cleanup. He offered them to Chuck. "Thanks, but I got one here."

He pulled out a handkerchief that had the DWB—Doctors Without Borders—logo on an African print.

"Where'd you get that?" Owen asked. His pulse kicked up a notch.

"The new boss lady I met the other day in your office. She came by to check on me a little bit ago and got pizzas for the families and other guys who came to wait. 'Course I was blubbering like a newborn, so she gave me her handkerchief."

Owen beamed. She'd come through for Chuck and his team in a way he wouldn't have even thought of if he were in her position. She was made for this gig, no matter how good she was in the OR. Lucky for Mercy, they'd get her for both.

What about you? What do you get from her?

God, his brain wouldn't let up tonight, would it?

"That's great. I'm glad she came by."

"Me, too. She's doing a good thing."

"She is," Owen said. His heartbeat accelerated a degree.

"I like what you've got going at your place, but this is a damn good facility and the fact that it'll be cost-free is all we could ask for. I'm not saying people are excited to be filmed, but for medical help like this? It might just be worth it."

Owen glanced around. His surgical center was set up for cleft palates, burns and other plastic reconstructive surgeries, but it couldn't meet the niche of people in LA who needed good trauma care at no cost. Was the media presence worth having everything Mercy offered?

"You make a good point," he conceded.

Chuck patted him on the arm and stood up. "Gonna grab some pizza. Thanks for taking care of my guys."

"Of course."

Owen sighed, sitting back in the chair. Maybe it was time he gave a little. He didn't believe a camera should be anywhere near his patients, especially those like Chuck or Remy, but maybe he could put his own hang-ups aside and offer an interview for the documentary. There was no harm in sharing some of what he did for Mercy, was there? Especially when it would keep the trauma center solvent, which would, in turn, keep Kris at Mercy.

You're really pretending this is an altruistic move? his subconscious wanted to know. *'Cause I think you're doing this because you want to sleep with the boss.*

Maybe. If she was even interested. Her kiss said she was attracted to him at least, but…it was not like he could see it through anyway. Not until he fixed the mess he'd made before the emergency tonight, both with the kiss, then inadvertently stepping over a line she'd made in the sand.

But even if he did that, and she rejected him anyway, his clinic was at risk. And no matter what, that *had* to be his priority. Not sex, not women, not even—

He cringed. Kris had him in such a tailspin, he forgot what was going on with @ladydoc. She hadn't responded and he had to respect that. But maybe it was time to reach out.

Because for the first time since he'd asked her to slide into a private chat room, he hadn't gone to bed thinking of her, she hadn't entered his dreams nor had he woken up with her on his mind. For almost a week, it was as if she'd vanished altogether.

Replacing the space @ladydoc used to occupy in his heart and thoughts, he'd imagined what Kris's skin would feel like if he were to run his fingers along the shape of her and what secrets he might find hidden beneath the fabric of her suit.

The doors hissed open again and Owen stood up, prepared to follow the EMTs to another room, but it was only another family member of one of the injured firefighters. He glanced through the waiting room windows and watched as Kris crossed the span of the ER, her scrubs stained, meaning she'd taken on some of the workload herself. She was pretty damn amazing, wasn't she?

But if he put aside the magnetic way her physicality woke him up in more ways than one, the woman was a walking, breathing pain.

The meeting with Chuck a couple weeks ago had shifted their perpetual distaste where the other was concerned to something less...antagonistic. That morning had taken it even further. Somehow, it'd led to him kissing his boss. And wanting more—so much more.

Which, again, was a problem for so many reasons.

Owen grabbed his phone, a frown etched on his face as he walked to the staff kitchen to start the IV line of coffee he'd need to survive the rest of the day. His job was done here, but he still had two surgeries that evening at the clinic.

Eff it.

He swiped into the app and shot off a quick message to @ladydoc. There was no guarantee she'd respond anyway. He opened with something kind, but vague. After all, she'd been his first real friend outside Sam and Dex, both of whom were stuck with Owen for better or worse.

Been thinking about you. I had a pretty great—well, fulfilling—day at work and I couldn't have gotten there if you hadn't inspired me to take what I've been doing at the clinic and test the waters at the hospital. So, thanks. Hope you're well...

Maybe the ellipsis was too much, like an invitation that he wasn't prepared to back up. But he hit Send anyway and washed his hands before grabbing a coffee mug. None of them were near big enough for his needs. At least it was Friday.

When Owen's phone chimed with a notification, he almost didn't hear it over the din of the espresso machine. He swiped it open and smiled. She'd written back and his heart slammed against his chest. He'd forgotten the feeling a chime from her gave him.

Hey there, stranger! Sorry for the delay in writing back. I'd blame work, since I'm beyond slammed, but the truth is, I'm still considering your offer. It isn't that I don't want to meet, but more so I'm wondering what that might do to the amazing friendship we've built. I'm not sure about what you think, but talking to you was the best part of every day. I don't want to lose that.

Owen glanced up at his reflection in the microwave above the espresso machine. His smile faltered. Her message confirmed they could only be friends. To him, at least. Because the best part of his day used to be talking to her, but now he looked forward to seeing and talking to the brilliant, stunning, flesh-and-blood woman just a few rooms away.

For the time being, it didn't matter, though. He couldn't have anyone as more than a friend.

He shot off another message.

I've appreciated your friendship more than you know. But I actually can't meet anymore anyway. I can't say why, but I value having someone I can trust to confide in. I don't want to lose that.

His phone buzzed in his hands.

I agree. I'm glad you can trust me.

Stress evaporated off his shoulders, lifting the weight they'd borne for a while now.

Speaking of trust, do you mind if I get some advice? No details, I promise.

Of course. Shoot.

He thought through how to phrase his issue without giving away too much about where he worked or in what department. There were only a handful of plastics docs in LA County who did as much work as he did at Mercy and the clinic. It wouldn't be hard to place him with one or two haphazardly dropped details.

My Stephen King character of a boss turned out to be more—better?—than I thought. They're starting an initiative at our place of employment that'll meet a pretty underserved need in the community and I have the ability to be a part of it. Only if I do I'll have to abandon some of my most important principles. But it would help a ton of people. Thoughts?

The blinking three dots as @ladydoc typed her response were too hard to watch, so Owen finished making his coffee, sat down, and scrolled through his social media. He didn't follow many people and no one really followed him, so after a few minutes, he clicked out and just sat there, listening to the bustle of the ER quiet as families were updated and went home until the next day. He didn't see Kris anymore, but that was to be expected. She had much more on her plate today than he did.

Per usual, @ladydoc's response was just what he needed to hear.

Dang. I wish we hadn't made the "no details" pact. I know why we did, and I think it's important, but I have about a million questions, like "Why are your principles not in alignment with something that could help a lot of people?" Here's my advice—use your strengths to the best of your abilities. That's all you have control of and in the end, it will push your patients' needs to the forefront. You'll know what to do when it matters most.

Hmmm. It wasn't a bad plan. Another text came in.

Mind if I pick your brain as well?

He smiled. They were edging back to normal friendship and it felt good.

Ask away. Be warned—I may offer some unsolicited advice, like making sure you try the new ice-cream joint on Fourth. Trust me—it's worth the calories.

The three dots disappeared quicker this time.

That sounds like just what the doctor ordered. Though I guess you really did order it, didn't you? Haha. Bad medical jokes aren't just your thing. ;) Anyway, I've got... How do I say this? I've got feelings for someone at work, a staff member of mine. Hope it's okay to mention this. I stood my ground when I felt they'd crossed a line, but I also took their advice and put myself in the patient's shoes. I even gave away my favorite bandana that I got from a mentor of mine. I'm just afraid if I make a move he'll sprint away, since before today we kinda frustrated each other. And I'm his boss. Would you ever date anyone you had a power gap with? Advice?

Owen ran a hand along the back of his neck, which had just begun to sweat.

What the—? Kris?

He'd suspected it before, but the suspicion had gone unfounded while he worked out other feelings for the woman. But there was no denying it now.

He put the phone down, as if it might change the words blinking back at him like a warning of some kind. What was he supposed to do? Say? So many realizations came crashing down around him like stones tumbling down the Pacific Coast Highway after a flood.

The first was a boulder: Kris and @ladydoc were the same person. Which meant…he had both the friendship and the passion with one person this whole time and hadn't known.

Which led to another boulder, maybe a bigger one: Kris liked *him*. At least, after their kiss a few hours ago, he assumed it was him she was asking advice about.

The last was a softball-sized rock in the form of a question that whacked him straight in the chest, knocking the wind out of him. Did she know who he was? And if not, should he tell her he knew?

He raked a hand through his hair, which needed a good wash. Jesus. This was a mess.

A hot, holy hell, you-got-what-you-wanted mess.

Owen picked up his phone and sent back a reply.

Mind if I think on it? I'm heading into work now and I want to give it the thought it deserves.

Which wasn't really a lie, was it? He needed time to process this.

The reply came instantly.

Of course. Have a great evening and thanks for reaching out.

Owen poured his double-shot espresso in a paper cup and headed out of the staff room. The noise and chaos of the hospital was now a gentle buzz of overnight nurse staff and the last of the doctors writing up reports.

They'd done it; they'd saved every last firefighter who'd been brought in and on 60 percent capacity, too. The center, save for a few small hiccups, had performed like it was meant to and he had no doubt their success was largely because of Kris's ingenuity. That he'd helped even in a small way with the design filled him with a pride he normally didn't afford himself.

If Sam could see him now… That made him think of his parents, though, and he didn't need that kind of negative thinking if he was going to make the strides he needed to.

Baby steps.

Talk to Sam, then his folks, then figure out his complicated feelings for his boss. Because on one hand, he ached to see her, to hold her and congratulate her and pick up where they'd left off before the first patient arrived. But on the other hand, so much had to happen first. Starting with finding a way to fully forgive himself for the sins of his past so he could have any kind of future unburdened by the guilt and regret he'd been carrying.

Until then, he could at least offer her some of his coffee and a hug to say how well she'd done, right? Maybe let her know he'd *never* take credit for a single of her successes and see if she wanted to talk? No harm in that…

But where was she? He'd checked all the common spaces—the nurses' stations, the staff rooms, even outside the restrooms—and she wasn't anywhere. He walked outside, appreciating the cool undertone of the evening since LA didn't get many of those.

Anticipation rolled over his skin as he scanned the exit for a sign of Kris.

He strode over to the parking lot in case she'd taken off,

but her G-Class was still there. When he turned back toward the ER entrance, a flashing light caught his attention in his periphery.

Squinting, he frowned. Were those…*cameras*? His pace and stride were clipped, getting him to the outside of the fray in seconds, but he stayed hidden in the shadows.

Sure enough, there was a camera—six, in fact—as well as more than half a dozen reporters. At the end of their microphones was Kris. Anger rolled through him, hot and acidic.

She broke her promise. One damn day and her word was worth eff all.

Didn't you just say you might have to give a little?

Yeah, but this? This was more than a little.

Though he couldn't hear everything she said from his dark recess, she was animatedly pointing toward the entrance of the hospital. He moved out to stop the interview, to tell her how off base she was, when he froze.

Chuck was beside her, a solemn look on his face, his arms crossed. He didn't talk, just nodded every now and then.

Oh, that's it.

Owen didn't care who Kris was online or at the hospital. She'd crossed a line and broken his trust, just as he'd finally accepted that they might have a fighting chance at building a medical partnership, if not more, together.

But how was he supposed to do that when the woman he'd come to care about had lied to him?

CHAPTER EIGHT

OWEN'S GAZE WAS sharp and hard and...*focused* when he walked through the door of the hospital the next morning. It was Saturday, but all hands were still on deck after the emergency their community had endured the previous evening. Meanwhile, her thoughts were of the damn-does-this-man-know-how-to-dress-to-his-strengths variety. The danger of her body's reaction to him raced across her skin like an out-of-control fever. While Owen greeted the hospital's security staff and head of nursing, Kris allowed her gaze to travel over him.

He'd chosen—wisely—a slate-gray suit with a light gray tie, which meant his eyes were framed in matching tones, their intensity on full display. When his gaze shifted to her, the *ping-ping-ping* she'd been hearing stopped, as did her breathing. The cerulean pocket square Owen had chosen was just the pop of color needed to highlight small flecks of pale blue in his eyes, adding a depth to them that just wasn't necessary. She got it. He was...*something.* A word that escaped her at the moment as she wrestled to get out from under his penetrating gaze.

Her skin itched under his scrutiny.

Strength.

Her mind finally procured the right word just as the doors shut behind him. Owen personified strength and exuded it as effortlessly as most people inhaled and exhaled. Why did it feel like he was the one in charge today, and that she was just an interloper in a lab coat with the wrong title?

She waved, but he only sent her a curt nod, then shot up the stairs to the plastic surgery suites, taking them two at a time.

Hmm... Why didn't he head in the direction of her office?

And why hadn't he waited for her after wrapping up their patients the night before? She'd expected at least a celebratory high five, but wouldn't have minded seeing where that kiss they'd shared might lead.

Even if it was the single worst idea she'd had outside dating James back in the day. Because Owen was her subordinate. Messing up with him would be career ending and her career was all she had at the end of the day.

Still…

That kiss was hot. Sure, if she'd seen it happen to someone else, she might have called it soft, tender even. But it'd happened to her and—not that she'd admit this to anyone, even @makingadifference—she hadn't recovered. Her stomach had lived in a permanent fluid state since and she'd all but forgotten about Alice's rules. Because how could what she was feeling for Owen be a bad thing? Even knowing she was his boss didn't temper it.

And it wasn't just physical. Knowing now who he was—both on and offline—and how their friendship had grown without the drama of work to complicate it, she was certain she'd found a partner capable of allowing her to set down her fear of loss.

So yeah, so much for keeping her emotions at bay. She liked the man something fierce. In fact, she'd hinted at it in her interaction with @makingadifference last night, testing the waters to see if he'd be okay dating someone who held a higher position at work.

What about his reaction just now?

It wasn't at all what she expected this morning. Was it a result of her standing her ground about her role at Mercy? He had to understand why she'd done that. After all, she'd told him what James had done to her, something only Alice was aware of before she'd shared the experience with Owen.

Worry replaced the excitement she'd felt before he walked into Mercy. She steeled herself against it and strode in the same direction he'd gone. At his door, she knocked and a gruff voice called out, "Come in."

"Hey," she said, walking in. He didn't meet her gaze and his jaw set like it had turned to stone. "What's up, Owen? Did I do something?"

"You did your job to the letter last night. In fact, I'd say you did exactly what you've been saying you'd do since you got here."

His words were kind, bordering on deferential, but the dark glint in his eyes, like the moon reflecting off metal, distracted her.

"Owen," she tried, and even though he turned around to face her, his gaze stayed pinned above her head. "Tell me what's wrong. You and I were—we were great last night and then this morning it's like we're back to day one. Is this about me talking to the firefighters or do you regret the kiss—"

"Yes," he answered without hesitation. Her heart stuttered. *Oh, my God. What did I do?*

She was a workaholic without any personal relationships and suddenly she was the boss who kissed her employee. "But not for the reason you think."

"Then, why?"

A low grumble emanated from his chest. He flattened his palms on the mahogany desk, every muscle in his forearms tense. "You broke your promise last night, Kris. Right in front of my face, and worse yet? You dragged Chuck into it after he expressly said he didn't want to talk to the press."

"Oh," she said.

"Yeah. *Oh.*"

She frowned. He must've seen her talking to the crowd of

reporters who'd gotten wind of where the firefighters were taken the night before. But he hadn't heard what she'd said, clearly.

"Listen, whatever you think—"

"I get it." Owen was curt, his voice as sharp as his gaze. "You can't help who you are any more than I can. But that doesn't mean I have to accept it, either. I made my stance clear and you put our community at risk. Now, if you'll excuse me, I have a patient consultation this afternoon that I can't cancel."

Kris's skin crawled as Owen inhaled deeply and made his face into one of abject solemnity.

She repeated Alice's number-one rule in her head—*Don't get angry. It won't get you anywhere with him.*

Never had her friend's loss been so profound. She would give almost anything to have insight or advice... And a hug. Something to keep from giving in to the fear that clawed at her heart.

"Owen," Kris said, her voice soft. She needed to dig deep and put on her game face, her feelings about Owen notwithstanding. She cleared her throat, noting how dry it was all of a sudden. He wouldn't hear her no matter how she spelled out the truth. Yes, she'd talked to the press, but only because if she didn't, who knows who they would have accosted to get the story and then where would they be? At least she'd mitigated the damage, thanks to Chuck, who'd volunteered to help her give the barest details to shut down the story. "There's going to be good press and bad press no matter what in this business. Yes, I talked to the reporters, but you haven't even asked what I said."

"Because I don't care what you said. You promised you wouldn't and Chuck didn't want to be a part of it, ever. You can't put aside what's best for you and the hospital, can you? Even if it's what's best for our patients?"

He sighed, his shoulders falling along with his chin and Kris realized something. Owen wasn't James—he wouldn't sell her out like James did—but he might as well be with how little he was willing to listen to her. And therein lay the problem Alice had warned her about. As a female executive, if she wanted to exact change, she needed to keep *all* of her emotions out of the equation. She'd assumed that meant anger, but it included lust and love. Especially those two, actually.

It would be lonely, but hadn't she lived that way since she was a teenager?

The coffee and overly sweet scent of pastries from the patient waiting room just outside his door swirled with the nerves floating in her abdomen and she swallowed back bile.

"Okay. I can see you're upset so I'll give you space. But I'd like to talk about this at some point."

Maybe when you've had a chance to read the story in the news and calm down.

"I don't know that I'll have time. I'm meeting with the LAFD and LAPD to talk about using the clinic as a first stop post-trauma and what I'll need to renovate to make that happen."

Okay, maybe he was more like James than she thought.

That's my job, she wanted to shout. *What right do you have to take this from me? From Mercy?*

Anger boiled just below the surface of her skin. Alice would have advice for how to calm herself down, but alone it seemed impossible. Next to Owen it *was* impossible.

Owen, who stood there, set on making her pay while he looked like sin on a cracker. Something dangerous brewed beneath his stony exterior. And yet… Her heart pounded as she imagined what would happen if she ran a finger along his chin, used her lips to release some of the pressure she could see built up there.

Kris's skin and mind hummed with emotion. She'd talked to the press, yes. But did she deserve this? Absolutely not.

The worst part, though, was that attraction topped all of her feelings, even the anger. Watching Owen fight to help people without dragging them through a vicious news cycle was alluring as hell.

But it didn't matter. He was getting in the way of the one thing she wanted more—the trauma center.

"And just what do you plan to do? Steal any patient that comes to Mercy out of spite?"

"No. I plan to open my doors to patients who need access to good care and who value their privacy. I can't help it that no one wants to take part in your docuseries."

What docuseries? she wanted to ask.

She'd announced its termination the evening before, not that Owen was giving her the chance to explain all that to him. That would get in the way of the grown-up temper tantrum he was throwing.

If he thinks you lied to him about this, imagine how he'll feel when you tell him who you are online.

Her subconscious was right; Owen made it abundantly clear he wouldn't appreciate what she'd discovered and kept to herself.

She swallowed a sigh.

"We're on the same team, Owen, and when you realize that, my doors will be open so we can talk about how to best help the community we live in without tearing at each other's throats." She inhaled on a three count and exhaled as slowly before she continued. "There is more than one way to serve our patients and yes, you're right, there are a great many who won't want their story documented and shared. But there are people out there who want to ensure others don't have to go through what they did and if sharing their challenges will help someone else, they'd gladly do it."

Owen's gaze was unreadable, but his jaw twitched.

"I'm not the bad guy here. I'm sorry if I hurt you and I'm equally sorry if I crossed a line in kissing you. But I won't apologize for doing things differently than you." She made it to the door before turning around. "And if you want to talk to Chuck about his involvement, I think he'd be open to discussing it with you."

With that, Kris walked out of Owen's office. What followed wasn't regret or frustration about opening herself up to him. She'd done her best and opened herself to vulnerability and an intimacy she'd never experienced. What she felt was a profound disappointment that she'd lost her friend @makingadifference with the loss of Owen. Because she couldn't pretend to be okay with a man who liked the online version of her, but despised the real-life version. They were both her—the woman in need of companionship and the one dedicated to her career.

If Owen Rhys couldn't see that, then it was his loss.

CHAPTER NINE

OWEN MANAGED TO THROW himself into work for almost a week, but was plagued by Kris's words to him: *"There is more than one way to serve our patients."* Every patient he saw, every surgery he performed, those words—that his way was not the only acceptable way—hung over him.

He knew that, of course he did. But at some point, he'd become inflexible as the world bent around him. And at this point, he had another choice: he needed to jump in line or jump ship. Not because Kris demanded it, but because he couldn't keep this up.

Were multiple days of distance just what he needed, or was something else responsible for his shift in perspective?

You know damn well it has nothing to do with the time and everything to do with her. You miss her, no matter what promise she broke.

His conscience had hit the mark, but he also kinda saw what Kris was talking about. What he would do with that information still eluded him, though.

Owen bent down to tie his running shoe, his breathing challenged after the punishing four-mile speed run he'd just subjected himself to.

Dammit, Dex. You had to leave when all this was going down?

He silently chastised his friend who'd gone to a four-month mental health summit in Africa on behalf of Mercy and to make a clean break from his ex Kelsey. It wasn't his fault, though, even if Dex was the only one besides Sam who Owen could talk to about both his clinic work and his boss who had snuck past his defenses and forced him to grow outside his comfort zone. It was cold and windy out there and he just wanted the comfort of the familiar again.

You've been hiding out in the familiar for a while.

Yeah, because of what happened to Sam. How could Owen subject any of his patients to that? They wouldn't likely get the same payout Sam had.

His brother had convinced Owen he wanted to use the money to invest in Owen's clinic as a silent partner because he didn't want anyone to know where the money had come from. Owen had kept that secret and grown the practice with other donations from patients with similar stories.

And somewhere along the line, he'd adopted that mantra—privacy equals the highest ethic of care—without realizing the truth, which was much closer to Kris's speech the week prior.

It wasn't the only way to do things. And to boldly assume that the way he felt—feelings he couldn't even be sure were his beliefs and not a dogma he'd adopted to keep himself emotionally distant—was the only way of doing things meant he was ignoring a huge proportion of the community he claimed to want to serve.

Looking behind him on the trail, Owen took off again, grateful for the beach path as a respite to all that ailed him. His feet pounded the wood boardwalk, echoing his own disappointment with himself. He'd shut out Kris for no reason except his perception of what had happened, and in doing so he'd lost the two women—or two sides to one complex, alluring woman—he cared about most.

@ladydoc hadn't reached out, confirming his suspicions about who she was. Which begged the question, if she was radio silent, had she sussed out who he was, too? If she had, why hadn't she said anything?

You didn't, either.

No, his annoying subconscious was right. He hadn't, and he regretted it.

Why?

Because he was still holding back, still stuck in a rut of his own making. If only he could reach out, talk to his parents and get some closure there—

But that was terrifying. Crippling. Impossible.

Then get used to living alone.

He pushed harder on the boardwalk, the arches of his feet aching with the pressure. Better than his proverbial heart.

Something else was bothering him, too. The first morning after his fight with Kris, he'd avoided reading the story on the fire, or listening to it on the news because he liked his job at Mercy and was afraid he'd march in and quit then and there.

Since then, he hadn't looked it up because he was afraid it would be a big, public "I told you so." He didn't know if his actual heart could take that blow. He'd rather be shocked by a faulty AED.

Slowing to a walking pace, he waited to catch his breath, then dialed Chuck's number.

"Hey there, Doc. I was just talking about you."

"Oh, yeah? All good things, I hope."

"Of course, of course. I'm with Dr. Offerman in Jones's room. While he gets a sponge bath, the lucky SOB, she and I are talking about how to get some of our guys to your recovery suites for more long-term care."

They were? Kris still wanted to use his clinic after all he'd done?

"Um…that's awesome. And I'm glad Jones is doing better."

"He may not be able to join active duty, but he'll see his son grow up, so that's something to celebrate."

"It sure is. Um, can you tell Kris I'll reach out in the next day or so and drum up a proposal?"

"Will do. Now, what else can I do ya for, Doc?"

"Just a quick question, Chuck, then I'll let you get back to your guys. But do you mind stepping into the hall? I'd like to keep this private."

Owen heard the door shut behind Chuck on the other line. "Okay, what's up?"

"What happened that night outside the hospital after I saw you? I thought you didn't want to talk to the press?"

Chuck exhaled. "Yeah, I thought I didn't, until I saw 'em try to sneak in through a back door." Owen's damp skin went cold as old memories from his childhood surfaced. "Anyway, I found Dr. Offerman and told her I'd like to issue a statement that would get them off my guys' backs."

He chuckled, then continued. "Well, she wasn't too excited about that. Said she'd made a promise not to talk to the press, but when she heard me out, she agreed it needed to be done and there was a way to make it beneficial for both the families and her hospital."

Owen cringed. The hospital hadn't needed protecting—the patients had. But he listened.

"Okay. Walk me through it if you don't mind."

"You didn't read the story? I was pretty proud of us."

"No, I didn't yet. But I will right now. Thanks, Chuck. Tell Jones I'll see him in the clinic this week to make a cost-free surgical plan so we can minimize his scarring."

"You bet, Doc."

Chuck hung up and Owen found a bench on the side of the boardwalk and sat. The sun was high and there was glare, but he pulled up the local news story on the fire. His skin warmed again when Kris's voice came through the phone's speaker.

"We ask that you keep the firefighters and their families' needs as a priority right now as they heal from a profound trauma."

"What about the docuseries?" a reporter asked.

"There won't be one anymore. We're committed to sharing the stories of the patients who want their healing to help

*others, but we can't ask that an entire community get behind
what was an initial plan for funding this cost-free center."*

"So, what will you do, then? Close your doors?"

*"No. Not if we can avoid it. I'm committed to finding alter-
nate sources to finance this important endeavor and I'm making a public plea to the governor and mayor of LA to match us
with support from the state. Los Angeles is a town that houses
Hollywood and fairy tales for many individuals, but for others,
it's expensive, dangerous and doesn't support access to basic
needs. We need to do better for our firefighters, police, veter-
ans and children. Mercy is doing its part. What will you do?"*

The reporters all went wild as a commentator added speculation as to what the public officials would decide. Owen sank
back on the bench, his fingers laced behind his head as he realized what she'd done. She'd leveraged her position and the
media to make a public call to action to support the patients
Owen cared about most.

And he'd treated her like crap for it instead of listening to
her.

But the worst part about all of this—the press release, the
way it made his dream job more possible instead of closing
those doors—was that he wanted one thing more.

Kris Offerman. @ladydoc. Whoever she was, he wanted
her.

Like, hands on her naked body, mouth on hers, tangled-in-
sheets kind of wanting. He wanted it every day. But he also
wanted the kind of challenging but supportive conversations
he'd had with her online persona. She was a whole, complete
woman, and he'd gone and treated her like the individual parts
of herself.

Screw the governor. *He* needed to do better.

His phone rang and it sounded like it was coming from
inside his skull. He flipped it to Answer without looking at
who'd interrupted his thoughts.

"Yeah," he said.

"Well, hello to you, too. I catch you at a bad time?"

"Hey, Sam." Owen leaned back in his chair and stared at the waves crashing against the pale yellow shoreline dotted with beachcombers, surfers and kids building hopes in sand castles that would only wash away with the tide. Most days, Sam's voice was maybe the only thing on earth that could talk him off the ledges he found himself peering over. It didn't make a dent today, though. "Sorry. Just me being an idiot, but nothing that can't wait. What's up?"

"Just wanted to touch base about this weekend. Mom and Dad are stoked to see you so I thought I should check in and make sure you're still coming." He paused and Owen winced. Was he that predictable that Sam was certain he'd bail at the last minute? The thing was, Owen hadn't been planning to skip out on the birthday dinner he'd asked for a month ago. It was past due and needed if Owen was ever going to consider being able to move on in any area of his life. Now it mattered more than ever.

But then Kris had dropped this…this *bomb* on him that needed to be defused.

Sam seemed to sense his silence. "You *are* coming, right?"

"I want to," Owen choked out. God, how many people could he disappoint in the span of a day? A week? His lifetime? It was getting too high to keep track of. The numbers of people he saved didn't make a dent.

"Listen, brother. Because you need to hear this."

"I already know what you're going to say. That it isn't my fault and all that crap, but that didn't stop the way Mom and Dad reacted. I just don't know how they'll ever look at me like anything other than the guy who hurt you. And they're not wrong for that."

Sam didn't respond right away.

"You done?"

"Yeah," Owen said, properly chastised.

"Good. Because that's not what I was going to say. But

you make a valid point." Owen opened his mouth to reply but Sam cut him off. "It isn't your fault, but not for the reasons you think. Yeah, the kid that left the water boiling while he ran off to talk to some girl should've been watching me. But he isn't here anymore. In fact, I'm pretty sure he disappeared that day and never came back. Am I right?"

Owen nodded even though Sam couldn't see him.

"I'll take your silence as a yes. Which brings me to what I wanted to say before you so rudely interrupted me." Sam's voice was light, but his tone was serious. He rarely let emotions dictate his day—life was too short, according to the younger Rhys sibling —but when he did, he had a damned good reason. Owen guessed what Sam was about to tell him qualified as one of those reasons.

"You deserve to be happy, Owen. Like, stupid, in love with life, happy. So you made a mistake when you were a teenager? Who didn't?"

He agreed about the mistake, but he didn't deserve anything but a lifetime of repenting for what he'd done to Sam and his folks.

"Except my mistake almost killed you and even though it didn't, it still maimed your whole shoulder and torso."

"And? I traded skin that probably would have had Dad's teen acne issues for some perspective. To be honest, I'm pretty sure I came out on top of that one. So take a hard-earned look at what really matters in life and listen to me."

Owen braced himself.

"Okay," he said, his voice barely above a whisper.

"Forgive them. I know you think they need to forgive you, but they already did. That day. Mom told me when I woke up that she worried she'd lost both her sons that night, but I came back to her. You never did. And buddy, it's time."

Hot, heavy tears slid down Owen's face before he could register the matching heat that had built up in his throat and chest.

"Then why did they tell me they were disappointed with me for how I was living my life?"

"They didn't. They told you they were concerned about your lifestyle and your choices not because they were disappointed, but because they cared. And it had nothing to do with the accident. Man, you were screwing up left and right and they still stood by you. Remember the time you came home plowed, and Mom rubbed your back the whole time you puked in the toilet?"

No, he didn't.

"No," he whispered.

"Well, I do. And I've been watching them see you change your life for the better and finally start to relax."

"Because I'm not a screwup anymore?"

"No, because you're letting yourself off the hook and doing work you love. All they ever wanted was for you to be happy and they knew you weren't when you were drinking every night and sleeping through every beautiful Cali day. But I know something they don't."

"What's that?"

"You're doing work you love, but you haven't let yourself off the hook at all, have you?"

"No," he whispered again. How could he?

"Well, you owe me that. You hear me? If you sacrifice yourself for some of my old skin, how do you think that'll make me feel? You think I can live with that?"

Holy—

Owen took a deep breath of the salty air and let it cleanse the infected parts of his heart that had been necrotic since Sam's accident. His brother was right. How many years had he wasted?

"And one last thing."

Could Owen hear any more and keep what little control he had over his emotions intact?

"Okay," he said, hesitating.

"You've been so distracted for so long from things just as important as your career in giving you a life you can be proud of. And they're worth opening up for, Owen. You deserve them. All of them."

"Such as?"

"That's for you to decide. I'm just here to get you off your ass and thinking about it."

"Thanks?" Owen said.

Sam just laughed. "My pleasure. So, give dinner with the folks some thought and get back to me in the next hour or so. 'Kay?"

"Yeah. I'll text you when I'm home. And Sam?"

"Um-hmm?"

"Thanks."

Sam didn't even say goodbye; he just hung up, leaving Owen to work through more stuff he wasn't prepared to tackle. His parents, yes, but also how to approach Kris with more than a weak apology.

Because she hadn't done anything but what was right for the hospital while he'd been the one acting like an entitled, self-serving prick.

He ran home, showered and found himself at her office door in a matter of half an hour.

He knocked and went in when she announced the door was open.

"Owen," she said. Her chest rose and fell and she held tight to her desk. This was the first time they'd been alone together since he'd blown up on her. So much had changed. So much he needed to say.

"Kris."

But now she was an arm's length away and he was forced to reckon with the way she made him *feel*.

Out of control. Wild with passion. Turned on as hell.

But more importantly, hopeful for the first time in his adult life. He'd make the clinic partnership work with her, even if he had to forego the rest of what he wanted. Because even though Sam's speech had woken Owen up, it didn't change the fact that Kris was his boss.

"Dr. Rhys," she said, shaking her head and failing to keep the emotion out of her voice. "How can I help you?"

He ignored the flash of her on top of his desk, legs spread for him and how he might help them both. Self-serving, indeed. Even his libido was a jerk.

Normally, Kris was composed, methodical to a fault. Yet, her chest rose and fell with an unchecked emotion he'd never seen in her before. The exposed skin on her chest was flushed with heat and small beads of moisture dappled the pink flesh. Goddamn, he hadn't thought she could be more attractive physically, but knowing he was the cause of the fury simmering beneath her surface made him want to press her against the wall and let their emotions clash against each other.

Not that it would be remotely appropriate.

She's your boss, he reminded himself. *And she hates you.*

"I'm sorry," he said, simply, taking a step around the desk and closer to her. Her lips opened in surprise and didn't settle back into the frown she'd worn.

"Oh." She clearly hadn't been expecting that from him. "What are you sorry for?"

For not kissing you the minute we looked at each other with longing in the ED. For pushing you away instead of drawing you in. For making you feel like you needed to be two parts of the same person to be fully seen.

But he couldn't say that. Not yet.

"For making a fool out of us both on Saturday when I didn't know my place in the hospital. And for taking it upon myself to try and make my way the only way when it's clear that wasn't the best move." He closed even more of the space between them. She didn't move away, but her shoulders tensed and she worried her bottom lip between her teeth.

Did she have any idea of the effect she had on him? His body was losing the battle to keep her at arm's length.

"Thanks. I just… I don't understand why you wouldn't listen to my explanation. We were making good headway and I promised you. I don't break those, Owen."

Owen shrugged and shoved his hands into the pockets of his slacks. And took another step toward Kris like they were engaged in a sexy game of Mother May I.

"I know. I guess I just wanted to be right. I wanted to make you and my brother proud and I got lost along the way." She opened her mouth to reply but he shook his head.

"Kris, I'm sorry. You don't need to defend your position. I was wrong."

She took a gentle half step in his direction and for the first time since they'd met, it seemed they were headed toward the same goal. If only he could replace the tension she carried due to stress he'd caused with another kind.

"Then tell me," she said. His brows closed together in confusion. "About your brother."

Oof. This was it; the thing that had been holding him back, the secret he'd carried like oversize luggage since he was a teenager. Was it really as simple as sharing it with someone he was falling for?

He took a fortifying breath and dove in.

"When I was a teenager, I watched my younger brother, Sam, in the summers while my folks worked. I was supposed to be making lunch but the neighbor girl I had a crush on came by and I went to talk to her out front. I—I don't even know how long I was out there, or how it happened—"

He gulped back a wave of emotion. Even after all this time, he could still pinpoint the moment he'd known he'd messed up, that it had all gone wrong. His brother's screams of pain punctuated the silence. Maybe that was part of why he worked so hard. On one hand, if he did, it assuaged the guilt of causing so much pain, but the other, more selfish reason was how it filled the spaces so he didn't have to face what he'd done. Good God, he'd messed up, hadn't he?

A realization rose like bile in his throat. He didn't keep everyone away because he didn't want to be forgiven; he pushed them away so he wouldn't have to forgive himself. A small tremor shook in his chest, rattling every wall he'd built.

Kris kept his gaze and nodded. He exhaled out a breath laced with fear.

"Sam wanted to help, I guess. But he pulled the pot of boiling water down on himself."

She gasped but didn't move. She simply…stood beside him as he relived the worst moment of his life.

"So now you know why I do what I do and why I can't stop my work at the clinic."

She nodded and inched closer. "I do. And I'm so sorry for what happened to you both." *Both? No. It happened to Sam.* "And I have my own reasons for the hard lines I draw at work."

"The doctor?"

"James? Yes. Also my parents and my mentor, Alice. But we can talk about them another time. The point is, I haven't gone through what you have, but I understand and am grateful you told me."

His body pulled toward hers like a magnet. Where there'd been fear she'd reject him after knowing the worst thing he'd ever done, there was now a need to be nearer to her.

Don't—his brain tried. *She's still the boss. You can't be with her.*

The words seemed shallow and stale, much like the loaves of bread down in the cafeteria. He no longer believed them so he forced his brain to consider what his heart hadn't.

Dating her would undermine what she's doing at the trauma center. She needs to be seen as professional to get her funding.

For the first time in his adult life, he was making a decision not guided by guilt or fear, but what someone he cared about might need. But was it enough to override the overwhelming desire he had to touch her, kiss her, be with her? His stomach flipped over itself, an occurrence that had never happened to him, not even once. It wasn't uncomfortable, so much as new and unexpected.

"Okay. So what do we do now?"

"I buy you flowers and take you out to dinner to apologize." Apparently, desire won out. The errant curl framing her face was tempting enough to try and tuck behind her ear, but if he did, would he be able to stop there? Touching any part of her would be giving in to the temptation that had been pulsing through his muscles every day he was around her. Even when he wasn't...

Her cheeks pinked.

"I don't—"

"Like roses, I know. You're more of a daisy-and-wildflower woman."

She laughed. "I'm glad you remembered. But I was going to say I don't know if we should go to dinner. Not yet. You have to learn to let go of your control, Owen. You have to let people care about you and their jobs at the same time without pigeonholing them."

He understood... God, did he ever... But did she mean let go of the control that was keeping him from cupping her cheek in his hand, drawing her in and tasting her like he sorely wanted to?

Teasing the idea, he shrugged another couple inches back toward her. The jasmine scent held him captive, cutting off the ability to resist this frustratingly entrancing woman. Hope joined the fight against logic when she didn't back away from him.

"Let go of *all* my control?"

He was close enough to see her throat as she swallowed, to see the pulse in her neck and hear the sharp intake of breath she made.

"Not...*all* of it. Just the control that gets you in trouble."

"What if I like trouble?"

Her smile said he'd made worse choices than the cheesy line.

"I want you, Kris," Owen said.

"We really can't," she whispered, looking down at their feet, which were touching. "I mean, I want to, but you and I have to set some ground rules first, and then talk about—"

He tipped her chin up so she could meet his gaze.

She opened and shut her mouth and when she licked her lips in anticipation, he couldn't stop his body or the lack of control he had over it. He bent over her and captured her mouth with his. She didn't pull away and instead, she reached around his neck to bring him even closer. One of them moaned with pleasure but he couldn't be sure who.

In fact, the only thing he could be sure of was the feeling of absolute rightness that washed over him as her lips—as soft as he'd recalled—were pressed against his.

This was *good*. Better than good.

It was what he never knew he always wanted.

It was coming home after too long away.

But she's right, you—

His subconscious tried to speak before Owen shut it up by teasing Kris's lips open. He didn't need that kind of negativity while he explored Kris's mouth and his hands settled on hips he'd longed to know the feel of every time they sashayed past him.

As her tongue tangled with his, he was treated to another anticipated desire met; he finally knew what the infernal woman tasted like—mint and vanilla. He growled with desire. God, there was no going back now. He wanted that taste imprinted on his tongue, on his heart forever. He wanted everything he consumed to taste like mint and vanilla.

When he moved his hands up along her back, the strength in her shoulders surprised him, but it shouldn't have. She'd been the strongest woman he knew since the day she'd infuriated her way into his thoughts, so why should her body be any different? The kiss picked up in intensity as his hands migrated around the base of her head. She purred as Owen's fingers laced through the soft tendrils of her hair and he smiled at the soft sound so unlike the tough woman it came from.

The smile was just enough to break the vacuum in both time and space their joined lips created.

"Wow," she said. Her lips were swollen and her curls wild. "That was—"

"It was," he agreed, though to what he wasn't sure. It was… Incredible? Yes. Intoxicating. Um…yeah. The best kiss of his life? Absolutely.

"But I should…" She gestured to her desk, but it had nothing on it. "You know. Get back to work."

He nodded, agreeing to that, too. His mind was fuzzy, still replaying the aftereffects of the kiss back for him.

"Believe it or not, that's not why I came here."

Her soft laugh was about what he'd expect for a lame attempt at a joke like that.

"I'm glad you did," she said. But she was behind her desk then, which might as well be a thousand miles from him.

"All right, well, I'll talk to you later?"

"I'd like that," she said, taking her bottom lip between her teeth. An overwhelming desire to pull her lip into his mouth, to taste her again, welled up in his chest, but he ignored it.

When she pulled a laptop out, he took it as his cue to leave. But so much was unsaid, unresolved…

It's fine. You have time. This…this is a good development. It was…wasn't it?

As soon as her office door closed behind him, the fog lifted and his pulse quickened. Good God, what the hell had he done?

He'd kissed his boss. It was problematic on so many levels, but only one stood out to him.

I kissed @ladydoc.

Before he thought through what to do next—either apologize and beg to keep his job or kiss her again and never stop until she told him to—he needed to let her know what he knew. Because right now, she only wanted half of him, and he wouldn't go into something as risky as opening his heart to someone without them knowing exactly who he was.

Three strides into his mission, he stopped where he was and whipped out the device.

Hey, there. Sorry for the delay, but I had some things I needed to consider and take care of before I replied. I have a couple ideas about your predicament with your staff member. You can always talk to me—that's what friends are for. But... I'd like to do it in person. How does Saturday sound? Four o'clock at Lake Hollywood? If you haven't been, it's a good but chill restaurant with a killer happy hour.

When his phone showed the three little dots for five straight minutes, he couldn't help but worry. Kris, a.k.a. @ladydoc, was conflicted. Was it because she'd changed her mind about liking her "colleague"? Finally, a new message popped up.

Sounds good. Looking forward to it. See you then.

As he hung up and added the date to his calendar, the day loomed over him. The rest of the weekend was going to be the longest of his life as he waited on Saturday to come around.

CHAPTER TEN

KRIS RAN A FINGER along her swollen bottom lip. It was tender to the touch after Owen's teeth had grazed against it.

That kiss...

She shook her head. The encounter had been everything she'd thought it could be—hot, passionate and enough to make her rethink her life. It made what happened with James seem like a teenage crush. Which was exactly why it couldn't happen again. She was Owen's boss, for crying out loud. What she'd done wasn't just irresponsible, it was damning to her reputation and could derail *everything*.

So, she'd done the only thing she could think of after she left his office—she agreed to @makingadifference's text asking to meet up. Then she could tell Owen in person who she was— both physician and woman, hospital administrator and orphan.

Why did you do that? Are you hoping he'll be pissed that you kept who you were—and that you knew who he was—a secret for so long?

No. Of course she wasn't. Because that would be silly. What would she gain from making Owen or @makingadifference mad?

If he's hurt or disappointed, I won't have to decide what to follow—my heart or my head.

The answer was as certain as a terminal diagnosis, albeit with less at stake. Still... . She was shutting down her emotions like Alice had taught her to do, but in doing that, wasn't she trading her agency? Because her heart wanted him—in all his iterations. But her head reminded her persistently and pervasively what she had to lose if she followed that line of thought. Leaving it up to him was easier, but made her weak at the same time.

Then choose. Tell him who you are now and decide what you want to happen. And fight for that.

It wasn't that simple. Something nagged at her, but she tried to ignore it. It scratched, though, until she had to listen.

He still wants the online version of you, just not you.

Because that was always how it went for her—she lost the people close to her because they died, or they used her, or they chose something—or someone—else. Owen had kissed her, but he still wanted to meet @ladydoc. It'd always been @ladydoc, which was why it didn't matter what Kris wanted. She and Owen couldn't work because she was both people and he only wanted half of her.

Well, it looked like work was it for her. Alice would at least be proud.

Her pager went off, calling her to the ER. No rest for the weary. Or those perpetually turned on by a colleague they should absolutely *not* be thinking about.

At least whatever the emergency was would get her mind off Owen…and off the surprisingly soft touch of his lips on hers.

Knock it off, her brain tried.

Off how his hands on her waist had been firm, leaving behind a heat that still pulsed where his fingers had lain.

I mean it. This isn't healthy.

Oh, and the tangy sweetness of the coffee she tasted on his tongue, a taste that even now left the dull ache of a coffee craving that she knew darn well wouldn't be satisfied by a cup of the stuff.

You're hopeless.

She was. She wanted him. Wanted his taste, his touch, his warmth… But those were the last things she needed.

Hadn't she learned anything from James?

Finally, her brain rejoiced.

She took off down the hallway, grateful for her ability to jog in the pumps she wore. Alice used to tease her mercilessly about being "one of those women," but Kris had taken it as the joke it was intended to be. In all the ways being a boss and checking her emotions at the door was stifling, at least she got to play with the wardrobe aspect of the gig. Now that she was back in the states and with a disposable income for the first time in her life, it was fun to feel accomplished and feminine.

The ER was the only place that didn't ring true, though. When she arrived, the incessant beeping, yelling and staff's constant sprinting between rooms registered a chaos that was anything but delicate.

Kris made her way to the nurses' station and talked to the charge nurse on call.

"Hey, Kelly. I got a page. What's up?"

As the CMO, staff usually emailed her or dropped by her office to talk. A page meant an emergency with one of the patients she oversaw for specific reasons.

Kelly didn't stop pointing out where each nurse should go as new patients came in through the sliding doors. She was as efficient as anyone could be in the mayhem, keeping the ER riding the thin line between havoc and busy but organized.

"Haley paged you to trauma one. It's Remy." Haley was the day nurse who'd been there the longest.

"Remy? But we discharged him."

Kelly shook her head and jutted her chin toward the trauma bays in the back of the ED.

"He's back. Infection and fever."

"Thanks, Kelly," Kris shouted as she ran through the throngs of people. She arrived at the room at the same time Owen did and her skin erupted with goose pimples at the sight of him again so soon after being held in his arms. God, working together was going to be impossible, wasn't it?

"Dr. Rhys, they paged you, too?" she asked as she gloved up. He did the same and nodded, his eyes focused and jaw set. She recognized the struggle to keep his composure in his eyes because she felt the same challenge brewing beneath her ribs, in the jolt of energy surging between their bodies that they were both trying—and failing—to ignore. Their kiss had been too intense to just be thrown aside like it hadn't occurred.

Yep. This was going to be impossible, all right. But she was a professional and he'd made his stance clear.

"They did. Remy deteriorated when he got home. Who discharged him? He needs constant attention with those wounds or they'll get infected. Hell, that's probably why he's back."

Kris frowned as she checked Remy's chart. Sure enough, his fever had spiked to one hundred and three point four and his heart rate was through the roof.

Dammit.

"Dr. Magnusen discharged him last night."

Owen shook his head, but relaxed as he went farther in the room past the nurses hooking Remy up, to where his parents waited.

"Mr. and Mrs. Young, I need you to wait outside. We'll take the best care of Remy we can, and a staff member will keep you updated, but you can't be here."

"Please," Mrs. Young begged, her eyes lined with tears barely hanging back from falling. Kris knew from experience once they started, they may never stop.

"Mrs. Young, why don't you two follow me? I'd like to introduce you to Kelly, our charge nurse. She'll let you know what's going on back here as often as she can, okay?" Kris said.

"You're in good hands with Dr. Offerman," Owen added.

Kris sent him a smile she hoped conveyed that she was grateful, that she'd left the kiss behind her. He was holding true to his promise to be professional, and that was all she could hope for. She brought the Youngs to the nurse's station and ran back to the trauma bay.

When they were alone with Remy, Kris got to work setting up a line for an IV while Remy moaned in pain. The poor kid. He had a long road ahead of him.

"Dr. Rhys, I'll let you take the lead. I'm a peds doc, but this is a surgical case in your area of expertise."

Owen didn't look at her, his focus on Remy's burns instead. "His shoulder's infected and it's likely spread to his bloodstream. Give him two of vancomycin and increase fluids. This bag needs to be changed every fifteen minutes. Let's put him under with two of Versed. I don't want him to feel any of this."

"Okay. I'm on it."

He nodded but wouldn't meet her gaze. She let her own wander down his body, noting the rigid intensity of his movements. His shoulders were tense but his hands fluid, belying the world-class surgeon he was. But what would it take for him to fully relax?

She inserted the PICC line, careful not to touch the burn area.

Owen's gaze met hers and in it, she saw the pain she'd witnessed last time they'd worked on Remy, but laced with remnants of the way he dove into the depths of her eyes in his office.

"He's going to be okay," she said. "We won't let anything happen to him."

"I know."

Did he? His eyes were so sad around Remy.

See? This is one of the reasons why you wanted to put the brakes on things. You know too much about your subordinate to keep things professional.

Ah yes, but that didn't change *wanting* to know everything about him. Or wanting *him*, period. Alice would have a field day with Kris's internal struggle.

"I'm done. What can I do to help you debride?"

"Get a kit and start on that side."

Kris nodded, wishing she didn't know just how to do that.

Too many times she'd been in the same position in Angola with a child in need of dead skin being removed.

Kris got to work on one of Remy's shoulders while Owen worked on the other.

"There's inflammation here," Kris said, pointing out patchy areas of swollen, hot skin.

This poor kid, she thought again.

"Here, too. Jill, we need a tray of Xepi. Bring us both one, actually," Owen said. That was a good call. It would help the wound heal quicker, too. Owen's shoulders relaxed and his whole demeanor shifted to one of concentration rather than pinpointed focus. It looked good on him, but then so did everything she'd seen so far.

What would it have been like to meet him outside Mercy? she wondered, not for the first time. *I wouldn't be his boss and my trauma center wouldn't be dependent on his expertise.*

But then she'd miss moments like this, surrounded by his brilliance and calm. It was a double-edged sword, having Dr. Owen Rhys on her staff.

The fluids worked almost immediately, as did the IV antibiotics, and within an hour Remy's pulse had gone back to normal. His temp went down two and a half degrees as well, the best they could expect for now. That didn't change the fact that Remy still had months, if not years, of therapeutic healing to endure before this was behind him. That is, if it ever was. The scarring was another battle he'd have to face and from what she saw in Angola, kids weren't generally kind when it came to deformities no matter where they were from.

"He'll have significant scarring," she said, apropos of nothing.

"Yeah. And kids can be assholes. I wish he could take karate or something so he can beat anyone's ass who teases him."

"Not that I think violence is the answer, but I agree. I hate thinking how cruel his peers will be."

"At least he can hide most of this under a shirt. Some kids aren't that lucky."

She let that sink in. That wasn't a flippant comment; it was laced with experience tied to his brother's injury. The insight into the man opened up a place in her heart that had been closed off to him before.

She wanted to ask more, but that would be inviting him in, something she'd already decided was off-limits. It didn't stop her from wanting to know more, do more, *be* more with him. *Ugh.* If only she didn't know just how that would end.

A pleasant quiet settled over them while they worked. It wasn't awkward or remotely tense. Whatever had been zinging back and forth between them in his office had faded, leaving a calm in its place. It was…nice.

"I can get someone else in here to do this," Owen said, breaking the silence after some time. She realized she'd been working on the same piece of skin for a few minutes while she bit her bottom lip in determination. She must look ridiculous.

"No, I'm fine. I don't mind the work, and I'd rather keep my eyes on Remy this time around."

"I get that." A few seconds passed as Owen's face looked like he was considering saying something else. Finally, he took a deep breath and dropped his gaze back to Remy's exposed flesh. "I like working alongside you, Kris."

Her breath hitched at his informal use of her first name. "You're different with him. Is he the first kid you've helped since Sam?"

"He… He is," he said. "But I'll be fine working with kids. I just need to get used to it."

He debrided a three-inch-long section of nonviable, necrotic skin, then tossed it in the trash by his side. Remy's shoulders— the burned parts, anyway—were almost all exposed red flesh at this point. To any onlooker, it would be gory and horrific, like a bad Stephen King flick. But Owen and Kris knew it was the best-case scenario for Remy; if his skin was red and pink with blood flow, he'd heal.

The more alarming case in the room was the doctor with unhealed trauma of his own.

"Do you want to talk about it?"

"Please don't take this the wrong way, but no, I don't."

He didn't trust her. He trusted @ladydoc but wouldn't share details with her.

He'd kept her at arm's length all this time.

Isn't that what I wanted?

On paper, yes. Distance meant she could keep her professionalism around him and not worry what giving in to her emotions would mean. But…

She hadn't expected that distance to hurt. Like, *a lot.* A physical ache pulsed in her chest, which she hadn't anticipated.

Because you care about him.

Of course she did. That was a given.

So, where did this—the unexpected ache and the missing him while he was right in front of her—leave her?

With a glance around the ER, at the collection of art she'd adorned the walls with acting as reminders of all the places she'd been, it was obvious. She was in the same dang place she always was. At work, helping others at the cost of putting herself last.

At least she could put it all to bed on Saturday when she met up with @makingadifference, a.k.a. Owen. Wasn't life so much simpler when the two weren't conflated, when the screen between them acted like a protective barrier to her heart?

Oh, Alice, she thought, sending up a silent prayer to the woman who'd helped bring Kris back to life the last time a man had almost ruined her career and obliterated her heart, *what should I do?*

Nothing but silence answered her plea. Kris was left to figure this one out by herself and hope that someday she'd learn not to fall for men who would take everything she had without giving anything back.

CHAPTER ELEVEN

A FULL DAY in the trauma bay was a helluva way to spend his thirty-eighth birthday. Not that he had much to celebrate, anyway.

Owen worked without standing up to stretch for the next three and a half hours. It was mind-numbing, taking dead and infected tissue from a wound and cleaning it up. Luckily, he had enough on his mind to distract him so that his hands could concentrate.

It wasn't like Owen hadn't messed up before; in fact, for a while there, he was practically making a career out of it. But he'd had the opportunity to come clean with Kris today, and he'd choked. He knew why, instinctually. He'd already shared too much and he wanted to talk to his mom and dad before he told her anything else.

But that meant, you know, calling them. Why was it like a heavy stone hammer struck his hand every time he reached for his phone to do just that? The science was simple: he had unresolved trauma around his past that was screwing up his future, a.k.a. Kris. All he had to do was—and this was the impossible part—*resolve it*.

He groaned, glad the nurses had other patients to take care of so he could parse through his mistakes in the quiet of the private trauma bay. Only the steady beep of Remy's monitor reminded him where he was and why fixing things with Kris was necessary. He didn't just want her, the woman. He wanted to be her colleague, her partner in coming up with innovative ideas for the trauma center and his clinic. In screwing up with the woman, though, he'd messed up his other chances, too.

After kissing her, no less. His jaw ticked with the pressure of grinding his teeth in frustration.

She makes me feel like I'm the injured flesh and she's peeling away my defenses.

Defenses he'd labored tirelessly to build after Sam's accident. Patient after patient he'd saved with one singular goal—atone for the sins of his past. But he'd started a race with an ever-moving finish line and the worst part? He was no closer today than he was the day he saved his first patient.

Kris, with the help of Sam, helped him see that he might need to step off the racecourse entirely and stretch before figuring out what to do next, but the momentum propelling him was a force of nature indeed.

Owen pulled the last of the infected skin from Remy's shoulder and placed it in the bag below him. All that was left was cleaning off the exposed flesh and bandaging it so Remy could begin to heal. If things went smoothly, the kid would have scarring, sure, but nothing terribly visible outside a summer T-shirt.

If only extracting Kris from his thoughts was as surgically simple. Instead, her necrotic way of picking through his bricks-and-mortar walls of grief left him vulnerable and susceptible to making bonehead moves like he'd been making. She was efficient, too. If she weren't, he wouldn't have kissed her.

His mind replayed that moment—the precise second her lips had touched against his and branded him with her unique taste and feel. The damned thing of it was, he didn't mind replaying the kiss. In fact, like a true moron, he wanted more of them. Just one had shifted his world off its axis and dammit, *he'd liked it.*

So how come he felt so awful?

Because the kiss changed things. You like her. You want to do this right.

He did, a lot. But he needed to figure out what "right" looked like for both him and her, even though every cell in his body told him to chase her down and tell her how he felt. No, he had to wait for Saturday to see if he'd blown it altogether.

Owen twisted his mouth into a scowl as he positioned the first bandage on Remy's shoulder. The child looked peaceful in sleep, unaware of the chaos circling his hospital bed or the difficulty that would follow him home.

What Owen wouldn't give to be anesthetized through next week so he could come out of his date with @ladydoc with the clarity he needed.

A nurse came in and checked the saline bag hanging beside Remy's bedside. She changed it without much effort and looked back at Owen before she left.

"He's doing well," she commented.

"He is. He's a fighter—that's for sure." Owen laid the last bandage and pulled the sheet over Remy's chest.

"So are you. I don't know many plastic surgeons who would do as much to help a child as you have with him. We could use more caring physicians like you."

Owen smiled and thanked her, but the truth grew until it took over the rest of the space in the room once the nurse left.

He was caring, sure, but it stemmed from guilt more than anything.

It was one of many secrets he was keeping from Kris, each of which kept his heart safe.

His brother was one of the secrets close to his chest. He could tell Kris more about why Remy's case unsettled him, but what would she say if she knew his greatest wound?

That he caused the accident, yes. That he saved people to atone for his guilt, obviously. She already knew that. But what would she say when she knew the reason he kept pushing her and everyone else away: because a man with so many faults didn't deserve to be happy and she made him just that—*happy*.

But then there was the other complication even if he could put the rest aside. She was his boss and in coming to care for her, he wanted her to succeed. She'd been burned by another doctor who used her before, and he wouldn't do that to her, even inadvertently by chasing what he knew he couldn't have.

Owen took the stairs up to this office instead of the elevator. He needed the burn of exertion to stave off the constant pelting of thoughts about Kris that were pounding against his skull. If only he could separate the woman from the position. Things would be a helluva lot easier if he could have met Kris like he did @ladydoc—outside Mercy.

Once he was in his office, he pulled up his patient schedule. He had two more consultations, then the rest of the evening and weekend off. Owen whipped out his phone in case Kris had tried to contact him.

Nothing. Instead, he was greeted with three missed calls and two texts from Sam.

What the...?

The first text explained the frenzy.

Okay, fine. You wanna ignore me? Just remember I'm much more tenacious than you.

He'd completely spaced and hadn't gotten back to Sam about this weekend. Dammit. The second text was more foreboding than the first.

If you won't come to us, then we'll come to you. See you soon, brother.

Yeah, right—why would they come all the way to him? Owen dialed Sam's number but it went straight to voice mail.

"Come on," he mumbled, dialing again. Just like the first attempt, it barely rang before sending him to leave a message, which he did.

"Hey, Sam. Sorry I didn't get back to you. You wouldn't believe what I've been up to here, but to call it a circus would be giving P. T. Barnum a bad name. Anyway, call me back when you get this. I'm…" He paused, squeezing his eyes shut as he got out the next bit. "I'm not sure I'm coming to SLO this weekend, so tell Mom and Dad, please. Also, explain that last text you sent. Because pretending to come down here with the folks and then ignoring me would be a crappy joke. Love you anyway."

He hung up, and put his phone away. Today made med school seem like a kid's camp. At least it was almost over. He'd go up next weekend, no matter what.

Owen threw himself into work for the next two hours. Both his consults were for simple breast enhancements that were scheduled for the following week. They didn't bring him any satisfaction, but at least they weren't rife with emotion, either.

Gathering his briefcase and discarding his lab coat, he felt the week finally catching up with him. Exhaustion set in and he resigned himself to taking the elevator down to the lobby. Birthday or not, all he wanted was a beer, his couch and maybe some true crime TV to take his mind off the past month. Hell, the past year.

Just as the elevator doors were about to close, a hand slid in, opening them back up. Kris appeared and joined him. Her eyes registered a flash of surprise before settling back to indifference, but there was no missing the pink of her cheeks that took longer to fade.

"Dr. Rhys," she said.

"Dr. Offerman."

When the doors shut on them, the small space filled with her scent and Owen held his breath. Because he was a goner when it came to fortifying against the vanilla snaking around his neck.

All he needed to do was extend a finger to be touching hers. A step to the right would put their arms side by side. A diagonal move toward the front of the elevator and he would be facing her, close enough to pick up where their kiss left off earlier.

Beer. Couch. TV. Beer. Couch. TV, Owen repeated.

Anything to stave off the images of his mouth on hers, or the fire that had raced through him when he'd finally gotten his hands on those curves hidden beneath her suit. He just had to hold out till Saturday.

"I shouldn't have kissed you," she said. In the confined space, the words seemed bigger. "I'm sorry."

"You don't have to apologize. I want to talk to you, and I definitely want to kiss you, but I need to clear a few things with some people first before I share more about Sam. My folks and I need to clear the air and then...then I'll tell you anything you want to know, okay?"

Kris turned to face Owen and he regretted commenting. Because faced head-on with her beauty and nowhere to run, her pull on him was overwhelming. He tried to swallow, but his throat was dry.

"Oh. Of course." For some reason, the way her brows pulled together with hurt didn't do a damned thing to assuage his yearning for her. "I just want you to know you can talk to me. I may be your boss, but I could be a friend, too."

Did his body move closer to her? He couldn't tell, but somehow, she seemed half a breath from him—close enough he need only lean in and his lips would collide with hers.

And no, she couldn't be a friend. Because as a colleague he was equally inspired and challenged by her, and as a woman, she turned him on in every way imaginable. If they added friendship to that, he'd be powerless to stop his feelings. He meant what he'd said to her: that he wanted to share whatever she wanted to know, just maybe it was safer to not label that "friendship."

But nothing could happen either way until he mustered the courage to call his parents. And even then, could he be sure that talking to them was enough to change a lifetime of self-loathing and regret?

"Thanks," he hedged.

Okay, now he was sure of it. Somehow another inch of space closed between them. Inhaling her scent on each breath was like doing a hit of some medical paralytic he hadn't heard of yet. It froze him in place, restricting his thoughts only to her. What she would feel like beneath him, their clothes no longer the barrier they were now. Knowing every inch of her as they claimed each other for their selfish pleasures...

He gulped in whatever air he could, but it only made things worse. She was an infection, a disease that would kill its host, but damn, what a way to go.

When she turned to look at him, the slight movement displaced a few curls from the smart ponytail at her nape. The sedative holding him hostage loosened enough for his hand to tuck one of the curls behind her ear. The softness of her skin woke him up completely and before he could allow his mind to give him a reason not to, his mouth found hers. His hand didn't move except to tangle in the curls beneath her hair tie at the base of her neck.

She moaned and he swallowed the noise by deepening the kiss.

The electricity that had been jumping back and forth between them all day—both positive and negative charges—surged as their tongues met.

Just as Kris's hands gripped Owen's waist, a loud *ding* interrupted them. They shot back like the efflux of energy had shoved them apart.

The elevator doors opened to the bright lights of the lobby and he squinted. Had they always been so intense? Owen had trouble gaining his bearings. He was heading home, wasn't he? From work. From a surgery that had taken most of the day. It was his birthday, right?

"I'm… I'm sorry," he managed between ragged breaths. Because no matter how logically he looked at the situation, all he really wanted was to scoop Kris up in his arms and carry her home.

"It's okay. You're right, we just can't—"

"There's the man I've been looking for," a familiar voice called out from the middle of the lobby. Owen's attention to the woman next to him didn't wane, but he glanced up to see where the voice was coming from.

"*Sam?*" he asked, incredulity masking the tempered lust from moments ago. Sure enough, his brother—and his parents—walked toward him, throwing off his equilibrium. Halfway to him, his parents stopped, as if they were unsure of what to do next.

They shouldn't be here.

In the ten years he'd worked at Mercy, he couldn't recall his folks ever stepping inside the automatic doors of the entrance.

But…they were there. Heat pricked his eyes. Kris was beside him, her interest seemingly piqued. Her scrutiny made him feel like he was under a microscope. He'd wanted this moment, but now that it was here—he could barely breathe.

"One and the same. I told you if you wouldn't come to us, we were coming to you, big brother." He hadn't believed it, but Sam was always doing the impossible and making it look easy. His brother came up and clapped Owen on the back, and Owen couldn't help but smile. As odd as it was seeing Sam in this context instead of riding a wave off the sunny central California coast, it was so damn good to have him there.

And Sam was right; he wouldn't have been able to ask for it, but having them make the trip forced Owen's hand. He couldn't turn them away if they were in front of him. His heart raced and skin went cold with nerves.

Sam's smile was all mischief and unbridled joy. His brother had endured so much and still found the ability to smile through life. Except, it took a second to see that Sam's smile was aimed at Kris, who hadn't moved since they left the elevator.

"Hi. Since my big brother is too rude to introduce us, allow me." He stuck out his hand, which Kris took. "I'm Sam, the better-looking Rhys brother."

Sam lifted Kris's hand to his lips and kissed it. Owen groaned but Kris just let loose a laugh.

Well, hell.

"Sorry. Kris, this is Sam. Sam, this is my boss, Dr. Offerman."

The formality felt odd on his tongue, especially since that particular organ had been inside her mouth just seconds ago.

"Call me Kris. It's nice to finally meet someone in Owen's family. Maybe you can shed some light on why this guy is the way he is," she teased.

It'd been meant as a joke, but Owen stiffened under the weight of what having Sam and his parents there might mean. The truth of his distant and recent pasts were on a knife's edge of being revealed. And then what? Kris would never look at him the same again.

But she knows enough now and is still here. Giving her that chance is what vulnerability is. You don't get to decide how she reacts, just what you tell her.

Then what?

He'd worked so hard to keep his guilt separate from his life, but maybe…maybe without anything else to hold on to, he'd clung too tightly. Still, letting go scared the life out of him.

"Oh, we'd love to." Sam glanced between Owen and Kris and his gaze sharpened. Sam had always had a knack for sussing out what was going on without much difficulty. The knowing smile he tossed Kris said he'd caught on to the mutual attraction between her and Owen, who tensed. "Why don't you join us, Kris? We're taking this guy out since it's his birthday. Come to dinner with us."

"Oh, she doesn't want to—" Owen tried, desperation tugging at his chest.

"I'd love to. Thanks for the invitation." She turned to Owen and despite all the emotions piling up at his feet, he was struck anew by her beauty. The flush on her cheeks hadn't dissipated since their kiss, and her lips were swollen and full. *Jesus.* "And happy birthday, Dr. Rhys."

The way she said his name, even though it came with the honorific, was laced with sex and lust, and damn did he want to take her to bed.

Forget the truth. Forget home. Any bed would do.

"Great. Let's get the folks and head out. I heard Penelope's is still in business. Sound good?"

Owen just nodded. "Sure. Great."

Owen risked a glance up at the mention of their folks. They hung back, his father's face stoic and unreadable, but his mother's an open book as it always was. Her bottom lip trembled and pressure built in his chest.

Not only was this the first time he'd seen his folks in years, but Kris now knew it was his birthday as well as what he hoped from this moment. God, why had he shared that with her?

Because I didn't expect them to show up mere seconds later.

If he didn't send her on her way, she'd see his attempts at reconciliation in real time. Undoubtedly, a thousand questions would follow, questions he wasn't sure he'd have answers to.

He felt the beginnings of a storm brewing and he was too exposed to escape unscathed.

But instead of battening his emotional hatches, he left them open.

When the three of them made it to where Roger and Rebecca stood, a flurry of emotions crashed against the wall around Owen's heart, threatening its stability.

"Hi, son. It's good to see you," his father said, reaching out with both arms for an embrace rather than his usual hand-shake. Owen's chest rumbled, shaking dust and rubble from the wall. He bit his bottom lip as he hugged his old man for the first time in a decade or more. Too damn long, either way.

It felt so good that it seemed wrong at first, like the joy from such a simple gesture was undeserved. But he let himself feel it like Sam had asked him to. And, God, it was...

Perfect.

Overdue. Needed.

When he pulled back, his mother was there, tears already dampening her cheeks. She crushed herself against her son, and as he held her against his chest, Owen was struck by how small she really was. How fragile.

The last of his resolve evaporated and his body shook with grief and years of guilt and pain for all the time he'd lost out on with them. His crew, his family, his people. His reasons for living and working the way he did.

His own tears fell, as did mutterings he'd waited a long time to say.

"I'm so sorry. So damned sorry."

His mom just shushed him and squeezed tighter around his waist.

"Shh. I missed you."

A beat of silence fell over them until Sam spoke up.

"Well, don't just stand there. Penelope isn't getting any younger, and neither are you, bro. What's this, your thirty-sixth? Seventh?"

"Thirty-eighth," his father chimed in.

Good thing, too, since Owen couldn't make a sentence to save his own life.

"Right. Let's go, folks. Time to celebrate the old guy."

Sam led the charge out of the hospital lobby and as soon as the warm night air hit them, Owen could finally take in a breath. Kris watched him, but her face was kind, her smile soft.

Celebrate.

When was the last time he felt like doing that? It'd been too long; that was for sure. Now, though, an unfamiliar sense of peace settled in his chest amongst the detritus of the wall that had crumbled, leaving his heart free and on display.

He may not have asked for this—for any of this—but he was going to go with it and see where it led. Because storm on the horizon or not, he'd rather dance in the rain than hide in the shadows anymore.

Yeah, this was gonna be a birthday to remember; that was for damned sure.

CHAPTER TWELVE

KRIS FOLLOWED SAM RHYS and his parents to the restaurant. Of course, Sam had insisted his brother ride with her, so there Owen was, in her passenger seat, and for the life of her she couldn't deny it felt like he belonged there. If only she could get her brain to shut up.

Stop being his boss and maybe I will, it shot back in retort.

"Get lost," she mumbled.

"What was that?" Owen asked.

"Um…nothing. Sorry. Just thinking out loud." She tried for a smile, but this whole thing was just too odd. Two months ago she'd taken the job at Mercy with the perception that Dr. Owen Rhys would stand in the way of her goals for the hospital and needed to be handled. Now, mere weeks after starting her new position, she was on her way to dinner with him and his family after sharing not one, but two kisses that day. Kisses that had unraveled her good sense. And then there was the utter strangeness of seeing him cry in the lobby.

God, how was she going to make it until Saturday without sharing who she was? It would change everything; that much was certain. But how and what would change? He enjoyed her friendship online and they clearly had a physical connection in person. But would he want *her*—the CMO, the boss, the woman, the orphan—in *all* of her iterations?

And if he did, what did she want? Kris's heart slammed against her ribcage. Had she ever asked herself that question? She'd done what she needed, sure. But what about what she desired?

The doctor to your right fits the bill, her heart answered.

She didn't disagree.

"So, it's your birthday?" she asked.

Duh. Any other gems in there you want to embarrass us with?

Sheesh. Her subconscious was salty tonight. Maybe a hint she should listen more to her heart in general.

"Um…yeah. I guess it is." He shot her a lopsided grin and her stomach flipped over on itself. It took every available cell of resolve to keep her eyes trained on the road in front of her.

"Why didn't you say anything?"

She could feel his gaze and knew the moment it shifted away from her.

"The day of my birth isn't exactly a reason to break out the champagne."

Something cracked inside her chest. Even Alice's persistent advice was silent at Owen's admission. What in the world had happened after Sam's accident to make him feel that way?

"Does this have anything to do with the way your parents reacted when they saw you?" Kris risked a quick glance at Owen and he nodded.

She waited, the air heavy but not tense.

"Would you believe we haven't spoken—really spoken—since the accident?" he asked, finally.

"Never?"

"Not once. I don't blame them—what I did was horrible."

"Oh, my." Little locks fell into place, some from Owen, some from @makingadifference, each clicking loudly in her heart.

Kris had never been so thankful to see the car in front of her slowing down with their turn signal on, indicating they'd arrived at the restaurant. She pulled into a spot as quickly as she could and unclipped her seat belt before grabbing Owen's hands in hers.

"Owen, I'm so sorry. For all of you. But maybe ask them why they've kept the distance on their end instead of assuming?"

"Yeah, I guess it's now or never, huh? Them being here means it can at least get better from here."

"I think so. They showed up for your birthday, so that must mean something."

"How so? I mean, what makes today any different?"

"I can't imagine your parents have wanted to spend even a day away from you, let alone your birthday. Maybe they couldn't come until now."

His thin-lipped smile made it seem like he was a world away, lost in memories. "Yeah, they used to go big on birthdays."

"My parents always made such an event out of mine, too." She smiled, imagining her parents showing up in her room with her birthday cupcake every year. To eat sweets had been a rare treat in her house, but before breakfast? Unheard of. Except on her special day.

"What happened to them?"

Her smile fell. "They died when I was a teenager. A car accident on the way home from vacation. When they left, I—" She swallowed her fear about sharing this pain with anyone. But she cared for Owen, which meant she had to. He deserved to know, when he was opening himself up to her. "I didn't think it would be the last time we spoke. I'd thrown a fit about something—probably wanting to see my friends or something as pointless. What I wouldn't give for a chance to fix things with them."

"Oh, Kris. I'm so damn sorry. Is that when you went into foster care?"

"Yep. Which is a trauma for another day, but my point is,

I'd give anything for my parents to share one more special day with me, even under strained conditions."

"Okay. I hear you. Thank you for telling me. It means a lot. And we're coming back to the foster care. I want to know it all, Kris."

"Of course." Surprisingly, she meant it.

Owen let out a laugh that lightened the mood. "Sam is going to be impossible now that he finally got his way. He's been begging to get us together for years now." Then he grew serious. "But I still don't want them to be here if he dragged them."

Kris squeezed his hands and he didn't take them back, so she counted that as a good sign. "They didn't look like they'd been forced to make the trip, Owen. But I can't imagine this is easy on them, either."

He shrugged. "Hence the reason I don't do much celebrating on my birthday. I'm pretty sure they want to put the accident and the rift it caused behind them, but that doesn't mean they forgive me."

"Have you asked?" He shrugged. "It makes sense now."

"What does?"

"Remy, your need to keep your patients out of the news, your desire to work at the trauma center—all of it."

"Maybe. But not wanting to share the story isn't about my own shame, but because a reporter hounded Sam after his accident—he even snuck into his hospital room to snap a picture when my parents took me to school. We had to take him to court to get him to back off. Unfortunately, the money I got to start the clinic was from Sam's settlement when the reporter was fired."

"Oh, my goodness. I'm so sorry—I didn't know."

Owen nodded. "That's my fault, not yours. I want to share everything with you, but I need to get through this dinner first. And I'd like to hear about your parents more. If you wouldn't mind sharing them with me."

"Sure, I'd like that." Her weak smile barely moved her

lips. "They were amazing. I wish I could have told them that, though. How much I appreciate all they did for me."

"I'm sure they knew how you felt. One argument can't have ruined your whole relationship."

She raised her eyebrows and gestured toward the restaurant with her chin.

Owen smiled. "Touché."

It was nice to think about and talk about her parents again, even if the ache their absence caused didn't abate. Bit by bit, Owen had distracted her from the pain, smoothing it over with his crooked smile and complexity. Hearing his trauma around family helped her see that she didn't need to forget what had happened to her to move on, but find a way to learn from it and trust others in spite of the pain of potential loss.

Kris's gaze migrated to the door of Penelope's as his family went in without them.

"You know, after seeing what you did for Remy today, I'm not convinced you couldn't help your brother minimize his scarring. Even after all this time. You know, being one of the best plastic surgeons in the state and all."

Her compliment teased a half smile from Owen which in turn made her stomach do flips like she'd just won the Edison.

"I'm sure you meant to say *the country*."

"Did I? I'm not sure," she teased. "I actually think I might have you confused with someone else."

He laughed and it took all her restraint not to lean over the center console and kiss him.

Again.

Good grief.

"I'll bet you do."

"Anyway, what do you think? Maybe Sam could be our first patient in the new *completed* trauma center?"

Owen's smile fell along with Kris's heart. "No. I don't think so. To be honest, Sam wouldn't let me if I tried. And, God, have I. I wish it were different because then maybe some of this guilt would go away."

"Oh, Owen," Kris said. She'd been led around by her own ghosts for most of her life and they were no closer to giving her any peace. With this in mind, she pulled his hands toward her until she and Owen met in the middle of the cab. After wrapping her hands around his neck, she pulled him into a kiss that was unlike both of the previous kisses in its tenderness and intimacy. It had the same effect on her, though, igniting her stomach like it was filled with fire starter instead of chyme.

She might be his boss, and this desire wrong for more reasons than it was right, but they were people first. And as a woman, she wanted the man across from her to know how she felt about him.

He pulled away, leaving her wanting more—far more than would be appropriate in the front seat of a Mercedes-Benz G-Class in a restaurant parking lot.

"We should head in," he said. His gaze burned into hers, and in this light, his eyes looked like cut granite.

"Yeah. Your family…"

"Can wait. But if we do this, I want to do it right."

He hopped out of the car and came around to open her door for her.

If they did this…

Did that mean they were going to? What would happen Saturday, then, when he found out who she was?

"So, I've heard good things about this place." She tried for a subject change, but the idea of kissing him into oblivion somewhere private still dominated her thoughts. "A…uh…a friend recommended it to me for breakfast. Apparently they have the best eggs Benedict in the county."

"They're an institution. You won't find better. They do a mean steak sandwich, too," Owen said, giving her a weak smile.

An institution. You won't find better.

@makingadifference had told her as much. She bit back her own smile.

"Awesome. Hey, if the server comes, can you order me a glass of Malbec? I'm going to wash my hands real quick."

"Sure. But I'm not at your Malbec and call, you know."

He smiled and she shook her head. In the ladies' room, she washed her hands like she'd said but also met her own gaze in the mirror. If she did this, the family dinner, the kissing, the sharing of her own family, she was making a commitment to this man. Not like they'd be married next month or anything, but she was saying *I'm in.*

Whether he made his own in return was out of her control and that had to be okay with her if she continued.

She breathed in like Mercy's head of obstetrics, Kelsey, had taught her. It was okay. She was ready to let someone in. Maybe she hadn't been when she met Owen, but little by little, he and @makingadifference had whittled away at her resolve to keep everyone at arm's length. He was worth the risk.

Kris made her way to the table. A hush came over what seemed like a stilted conversation as she sat down between the brothers. Owen's gaze met hers for a brief second and the pain in his eyes had turned them a stormy gray.

"Hey," he whispered, taking her hand under the table. "Everything okay?"

She nodded, believing it for the first time.

"Please say you brought some jokes or something to liven things up, Owen," Sam whispered over Kris. She shot their parents a glance, but they were talking to a server about appetizers and didn't seem to notice their side conversation.

"I told you they weren't ready for this," Owen hissed back from behind his water glass.

"Yeah, well, what do you want, a medal for being right? I did my part in getting them here."

Owen glared at his brother. "So, how was the flight?" he asked, turning to his folks.

"Fine. Smooth and on time. Best you can ask for these days," Roger said.

"Good. Good." Kris squeezed Owen's hand hoping to share some strength with him. "So, how long are you in town?"

"Sunday," his mother replied. She fiddled with her wine-glass and looked down at her lap.

"So, Dr. Offerman, how long have you worked at Mercy?" Roger asked.

"Just about two months."

"Wow. You must still be settling in, then. Where are you from?"

"The Midwest by way of Angola. I came here from a two-year stint at a trauma center over there."

"Impressive," Roger said. "I always thought Owen would get into that kind of medicine, but I guess life has a way of changing our plans, doesn't it?"

"Dad, he actually—" Sam started.

"I agree," Owen interrupted. "Which is why I've been working at a clinic Sam and I designed to help kids with burns or birth defects for the past ten years. I know it doesn't solve what I did, but—"

Kris shut her eyes against the hurt vibrating over this family. She'd seen it in the ER too many times—families infighting or ignoring each other instead of letting their pain rest on the shoulders of those they loved most. Grief did horrible things to people. But in Angola, they sat with it, out in the open, until everyone was healed. It was part of the practice she hoped to institute at Mercy—a family trauma therapy center attached to the ward.

"You two have been working together?" his mom asked.

Sam's smile was off-center, too. His cheeks were painted red, the whole look giving him the appearance of having been caught stealing his dad's liquor.

"Yep," Kris said. "And now Owen is using those skills to help me open a new, world-class trauma center at Mercy. It will help young folks and civil servants get the care they need that medical insurance doesn't always cover. We'll be able to help young men like you, Sam."

The table fell into a hushed silence reminiscent of the mornings Kris spent running along the roads in Africa. The sun wasn't quite over the horizon yet and the air was still with promise. And danger, like now. She'd gone and mentioned the one thing too big to sit between bottles of wine and calamari appetizers, but it was the one thing they needed to talk about if they were ever going to move on.

"What are you doing?" Owen asked under his breath.

"Shh. Let her talk. This needs to happen, brother."

Kris continued. "In fact, he saved a kid's life today by debriding his burns and getting rid of the infection underneath. You should be proud of him—he's one of the best doctors I've met."

If this is a joke, I hope the punch line's funnier than this, Owen complained to himself.

"We *are* proud of him," Roger said. Then, turning to Owen, he added, "we just wanted to be a part of it all. Everything we know about your work we hear secondhand from Sam, except the clinic, and we didn't even know you were seeing anyone. It breaks our hearts that you won't talk to us, son."

Rebecca sniffled and nodded, tears sliding down her cheeks.

"I—" Owen said, his own voice cracking. Kris squeezed his hand again letting him know she was there. Whatever she was to him outside this place, she was in his corner right now. "I thought you hated me."

Rebecca let out a sob. "I could *never* hate you."

"But you never forgave me," Owen said. His voice was so quiet it was almost impossible to hear.

"I did—of course I did…the minute after it happened. I just didn't know how to talk to you. How to encourage you to want more when you were so bent out of shape, but I shouldn't have given up trying. I'm sorry, Owen. I'm so very sorry I wasn't there for you, too."

Owen coughed, then his voice became thick with emotion. "It wasn't your job to be there for me. You needed to be there for Sam, and you were."

"We needed to be there for both of you," Roger said. His eyes were lined with moisture, too, and he clung to his wife's hand with a ferocity that made Kris jealous. No matter what they'd been through as a couple, as a family, they had each other to fall back on.

But this wasn't about her. Her job at that moment was to be there for Owen.

"I was terrified I'd lose a son that day and…and I did. Just not the one in the ER. But the part that breaks my heart the most is that you thought you'd lost us." To anyone eavesdropping on their table, it wouldn't seem like much of a celebration at all, but Kris could see the tenuous strands binding this family were getting stronger by the minute. It may not be the birthday gift Owen expected, but it was what he needed. "Owen, I'm your mother. You'll always have my love and you never needed my forgiveness because you didn't do anything to be forgiven for. It was an accident, and your father and I have come to peace with that."

"I have, too," Sam said, smacking his brother on the shoulder. "Plus, this scar pulls more ladies than my sparkling personality, so…" The whole table collectively sniffled at the same time and then burst into a fit of laughter at the inadvertent mood lightener.

"Okay," Sam continued, slapping the table. "I know this place is supposed to be bougie, but I think we need some birthday shots."

"As much as I'd like to pretend this is my twenty-first birthday, I need to get Kris home. Then maybe we can meet up tomorrow," Owen said. "I'd like to spend more time together."

The whole table agreed and after they said their goodbyes and made plans for the next day, Owen and Kris headed out.

"Thank you," Owen said when they got outside. "You made that bearable. Hell, I even enjoyed myself." He pulled Kris into an embrace and though he didn't kiss her, the way he held her against the wall of muscled flesh in his chest made her world feel like it was on fire and spinning out of control. She was never out of control, but this was…okay. Better than okay. It was just what she'd been avoiding, but for all the wrong reasons.

"You're welcome. I'm glad I was there."

"Same. But let's get out of here. I have plans for you."

She shivered but followed his lead, her hand tight in his.

They got to Kris's car and Owen opened the passenger-side door.

"I'd like to drive," he said. His eyes were still a slate gray, still dark like a storm was on the horizon, but they were no longer filled with sadness or grief. Instead, a heat made them out to be liquid mercury. If she spent any longer staring into them, she'd fall in their depths and be unsavable.

She tossed him her keys and nodded.

"I wish I'd known it was your birthday—I would have brought you a gift."

The skin from Owen's earlobe to the base of his neck turned a pale pink, then a deep red. That she had that effect on him gave her a surge of what Alice used to call "*Lady Boss CMO confidence*," which she usually reserved for board meetings with the rich old men who ran the hospital.

"You're the only gift I need. I want to unwrap and enjoy you, Kris."

She swallowed hard, the confidence shrinking but leaving room for her hungry libido to weigh in.

Lady boss CMO indeed. More like sex-starved teenager.

"Where are we going?" she asked. Her voice was huskier than she knew it could be. Her skin prickled with anticipation as he put the car in Reverse and treated her G-Class like a Formula 1 speedster.

"My place." As if to punctuate the end of his statement with purpose, he put a hand on her thigh, moving the hem of her skirt up so his palm rested on her bare flesh. She spread her legs enough to allow space for the desire building between them and Owen took the opportunity to slide closer to the part of her that throbbed with want.

She just nodded again, unable to formulate the myriad of questions nagging her into actual words. Only the thrum of their bodies and the need that drove them both.

As they sped down the highway toward Playa del Rey, a small voice in the back of Kris's mind reminded her that she still had to tell Owen she knew that he and @makingadifference were one and the same.

With Owen's fingers sliding along the seam of her lace underwear, she didn't care near as much as she should. All she wanted right now—consequences be damned—was the man to her left, whoever he was.

CHAPTER THIRTEEN

OWEN THREW THE CAR into Park and was at Kris's door in a flash. He tore it open and she squealed with delight when he bent down, lifted her up and carried her across the gravel driveway to the front door.

"You think I'm being chivalrous, but this is purely a selfish move on my part. It would take you half the night to traverse that stretch and I want you in my bed right damn now."

Kris's smile fell, and in its place were two flushed cheeks and a bottom lip tucked between her teeth. Goddamn, she was sexy.

And brilliant and kind and driven and—

He cut himself off before his brain could conjure the part where she was his boss or he'd overthink what they were about to do and he *really* wanted to do it.

Still holding her in his arms, he put in the keyless entry code for his front door and whisked her through it. Just past the entryway, he set her down and leaned her against the wall. Dipping his chin, he pressed his lips to hers, trying to fight against the insatiable urge he had to take her then and there. God, he wanted her, but more than that, he wanted this to be good for her.

She gazed up at him with wide eyes filled with a longing he could match.

"I don't want to talk about what this means, or anything so serious, but promise me we can still work together after tonight."

"I promise," he whispered against the soft curve of her neck. They were going to burn each other up when they finally gave in to this. The way her skin was stained a pale blush at first, then deepened into a rose red, made him want to forget his previous thoughts and strip her bare right there in his foyer.

The knowledge that she was his at least for the night filled him with desire and a sense of propriety he'd never experienced. He peppered her neck with kisses until he reached the tender spot just below her ear, where he sucked until she gasped and tangled her fingers in his hair.

"Oh, God, you feel good," she whispered.

It was a quiet enough murmur that it might've been said only for her. But, Christ, did it turn him on.

"The things I want to do to you, Offerman." Just when he thought her cheeks couldn't turn any darker red, she went and proved him wrong. He itched to kiss the deep maroon and see if it was as warm to the touch as it appeared.

"Do them. Do them all," she said, arching her back. He set her down on the leather sofa, slipped a finger underneath the strap of her blouse and slid it down over her shoulder. He trailed the finger down the shape of her bell curve, drawing goose pimples out on her skin as he went.

"You're stunning."

She shook her head so he dipped down and kissed the top of her breast peeking out from black lace. She may not believe how sexy she was, but he could show her how he felt, what he desired.

Her lace bra was hot as hell, but thoroughly in the way of what he wanted to do with his tongue. He pulled it down until her breast was freed. Cupping the small of her back, he drew her in to him, then kissed the soft flesh around her nipple until it hardened for him. He flicked the diamond bud with his tongue, then drew as much of her into his mouth as he could.

She moaned and hooked a leg over his, before pulling his hips against hers.

Owen bit back a groan of pleasure. "Holy hell, Offerman. If you keep that up, I won't last long."

"We have time. I want to feel you now. I want you inside me."

We have time.

Did she mean tonight, or something longer, more permanent? Need coursed through him but he shut his brain off. Overthinking wasn't in the cards tonight.

He still had a lot of work to do and so much more about her to discover.

Kris tucked herself into the space between his legs. She inhaled sharply, and thoughts of everything else slipped away. The proximity of her body did something to his defenses, disabling them from the inside.

A growl unfurled from his chest made of wanting and a sharp need.

He moved up her chest, tracing her skin with kisses, then cupped her cheeks and bent to kiss her, soft at first. As her body fell into his, he couldn't contain his desire any longer. Her tongue found his and tangled with it and his growl turned feral.

Jesus. He liked this woman—a lot. He wanted her in a way that had him trashing all the rules he'd made for himself regarding dating, sex and...*love.*

A warmth spread from his chest outward as that word swirled around in his heart, deepening the kiss and feelings that had been brewing for some time. Their online friendship boiled over into what they were doing in that moment, confusing the issue even further. When she pulled away, his lips ached with the loss.

She slid from underneath him, stood up, and started unbuttoning her blouse. He reached out to help but she shook her head. He craved to have his hands, his mouth, his body on hers, but this slow tease held its own attraction.

She dropped the shirt at her feet and then unzipped her skirt. Watching her shimmy out of it left Owen's mouth dry.

Hurry, he wanted to tell her at the same time he wanted to ask her to slow down.

"Follow my lead," she said, her voice thick and sultry. He only nodded and removed his shirt, then his slacks. When she was left in nothing but her heels and the matching black-lace-bra-and-underwear set, and he wore only his boxer briefs, she crooked her finger at him, calling him over. He moved without hesitation, taking her in his arms, finally feeling her flesh against his. It was every bit as perfect a sensation as he hoped it would be.

They fit…in more ways than one.

From that point on, the night spread before him as a bounty of love and passion that came out in rich emotions.

The warmth and wetness of her mouth as it took the length of him in.

The way her breasts tasted like salt and honey.

How he'd slid inside her and found home and heaven in the same place.

He'd come almost immediately the first time they made love, but like she'd promised, they had hours for him to make up for it and he meant to take his time with her the next go around.

And that he did. He'd started at her temple, kissing her softly along the crown of curls he'd longed to feel between his fingers. Then he'd trailed kisses along her cheeks, her collarbone and her breasts, where he'd stopped and appreciated them each individually. He'd sucked on them until Kris writhed in pleasure beneath him, moaning each time he flicked her nipple with his tongue.

God, he could have stayed there forever, but her taut stomach with enough curve to make the trip interesting called to him. So, he'd traveled south along her ribcage, tracing it with his tongue until her hands fisted in his hair.

"Owen," she called out. His name on her exhale of wanting was all the motivation he needed to keep working across the expanse of her.

When his lips pressed against the inside of her thigh, she screamed out. "Yes. Oh, my God, yes."

"This?" he asked, kissing her a centimeter higher and closer to her center.

"Yes, that's it. It. Feels. *So. Good.*" Each word of the last sentence was punctuated by a sharp intake of breath.

"What if I do this?" he asked again, riding his tongue along the edge of her sex.

"Oh! Please…" she begged him.

"What? Tell me what you want."

Her hips bucked and her hands pulled his head into the part of her that he tasted and wanted to dive into.

"You. I… I want you."

He nodded, thrusting inside her folds, sucking and pulling until she cried out and clenched around him.

"I want you inside me," she gasped. "Now."

Owen didn't need another invitation. He tore open another condom and sheathed himself, then slid inside her slick walls again, this time intent on lasting long enough to bring her to another orgasm. He'd wanted few things in his life, but those he'd desired he'd gone after with a dogged pursuit.

Loving Kris was no exception.

They spent the next three hours alternating between love-making and short fits of sleep until, inevitably, one of them would curl into the other. The moment their bodies touched, it was like a fuse was lit. They were off again, exploring and teasing pleasure from each other.

Finally, sated enough to let her sleep, Owen rolled out of bed to get some water.

A heavy truth settled over him. He…cared about her. Maybe even…*loved* her. Maybe not even maybe. He loved her, plain and simple. It was not like the discovery was an immediate hammer that had dropped, but more a gentle nudging from the moment he'd first replied to @ladydoc. Backed by their months-long friendship and faced with the challenges she posed, he'd grown to respect her first, then befriend her, but all the while he'd wanted her.

How am I ever going to stop loving Kris now that I've started?

If she turned him away on Saturday, he'd be heartbroken. It would be her prerogative to tell him to go to hell; after all, he'd kept something from her that he should have shared the minute he knew. And yeah, he should have. But when? Only now, now that they'd both come clean about their pasts, both opened up to the other, could they fully see one another for who they were.

Would it be enough?

He grabbed a glass from the kitchen, the question an insatiable curiosity, his growing feelings a blaze that couldn't be put out. When he walked back into the room, he was struck again by how much he wanted her in every way possible.

Kris's bare skin stretched out the length of the bed. Her legs were crossed like she'd been worrying her feet together while she slept. Her arm was draped on her head, exposing the sides of her perfect breasts—breasts he'd had in his mouth and hands just moments ago. God, she was beautiful. And intelligent. And sexy. And not to mention one of the most driven people he'd ever met.

He let himself appreciate all of her now, knowing it was the only way to love her—as the sum of her parts.

He traced the silhouette of her and she purred in her sleep. It took restraint he didn't know he was capable of to not slide his hand around her waist and tease her awake so he could make love to her again. Heck, after their night, he wasn't sure how he'd concentrate on anything else again—he wanted her with a singular focus that sent heat surging through his extremities.

But there was still so much in the way between them.

Though she knew his truth and had still come home with

him, would she be patient as he parsed through his guilt and worked to put it behind him?

All he wanted was to curl up with her and pretend the world didn't exist until all those kinks were ironed out. But life wasn't that easy, was it?

Risking waking her up, Owen bent to kiss Kris's shoulder. A small smile rose on her lips, but she didn't rouse. He sighed.

Another problem, the one that kept him up after Kris had softly snored against his chest, was the woman waiting to meet him that afternoon for coffee, a woman he'd shared so much of his life and dreams and trepidations with. And vice versa. A woman who knew about his brother, his clinic work, *everything*.

@ladydoc. That she and Kris were the same person made him feel like the universe had seen what a crap deal he'd been dealt and did him a solid.

And he'd effed it up, of course.

How could he tell her he'd known about her the whole time without it seeming like an excuse? The last thing he wanted was for her to think he'd been interested in another woman. He needed her to believe he already knew that @ladydoc was the same person he'd fallen for at work.

He hadn't really thought through this part of the plan, had he?

Oof. It was a mess.

Because he'd never felt so intensely about anyone like he did for Kris, which meant he ran the risk of losing something he actually cared about. He got out of bed and pulled on some boxers. In a few hours, he was supposed to meet up with her and tell her who he was and ask for time to blend the two versions of themselves and get to know each other as full people. Full people who cared about each other and wanted to see what a future together might look like.

He snuck back in and kissed the base of her neck. A shiver rolled up her back and she smiled. So did he, knowing he had that visceral effect on her. Jotting down a note explaining he had to see his family, then meet up with a friend at four, he felt the familiar weight of expectation pressing down on him again.

His patients, his brother, his parents, his guilt, even Kris—everyone needed something from him and if he allowed vulnerability in his life again, he was sure to disappoint someone.

But if he learned not to let that get in the way of growing, of getting better, it would be okay. As he gazed down at the naked woman beside him, a woman who as of now still had the power to shape his career and claim his heart in the process, one thought nagged him.

If only he'd figured out answers to these existential questions before he'd fallen so hard in love with her.

CHAPTER FOURTEEN

KRIS GOT HOME on Saturday afternoon with a pep in her step she normally lacked. Excitement that they were finishing the drywall on the trauma center on Monday was there, of course, but it was overshadowed by the start to her weekend, which was...*hot*.

First, there was The Kiss she'd shared with Owen in his office. She put her fingers to her lips, which were still tingling from the encounter. Good grief, was it one of the most spectacularly world-shifting kisses she'd experienced? True, her worldliness lay more in her career and travels as opposed to men, but she knew enough to know that kiss with Owen was special. It'd done the trick to make her forget about Alice's advice to her after she'd been burned by James, that was for sure.

Of course, the elevator had helped, too. The tension between Owen and Kris was enough that a circus performer could traverse between them without support.

Sheesh. She'd thought she was a goner after that first kiss, but after meeting his family and getting to know what made Owen... *Owen*, it was a done deal. Dinner was enough to make her reevaluate her rule against showing emotion and letting a man who could influence her career into her heart. Combining that with the knowledge that he was the person behind the online avatar @makingadifference, she was almost powerless to the blossom of feelings sprouting in her chest.

And then Owen had taken her home.

Her cheeks flushed at the memories of their lovemaking sessions that had lasted through the night and into the predawn until they'd both collapsed with exhaustion. They'd talked, made love and shared intimacies she'd never shared with anyone, her parents' and Alice's losses, especially.

Pressing her palms to her skin, she felt the heat brimming beneath the surface. It'd been perfect, but...

But the next morning, things shifted. Hot turned to cold and no amount of replaying it made sense to her.

Owen had cuddled up against her when she'd fallen asleep, but she'd woken to a note from him saying he had somewhere to be and would connect with her at work the next day. She'd glanced at her watch but it was only ten in the morning. He wasn't set to meet his folks until noon.

Also why hadn't he said anything to @ladydoc about being involved with someone?

Because he doesn't think he is, her heart warned. No, that couldn't be true. They'd shared more than just a physical passion the night before. For him not to text @ladydoc and cancel their afternoon date said it wasn't enough, though.

Because of her self-imposed, Alice-made rules, she'd never been forced to second-guess herself, and she had to say, she didn't like doing it now.

Kris had slid back into her skirt and shirt and checked her phone for messages just in case it'd chimed and she'd missed it. All she discovered was that her battery was about to die. Charging her phone when Owen was touching her in places she'd thought were dormant, if not extinct, hadn't been her first priority.

After Kris got home she did some work finalizing the details with the funding request she'd received from the governor's office. When her alarm beeped at three o'clock, she looked up as if from a daze. She hadn't realized it was already time to get ready and head out for her date with @makingadifference. She changed into shorts and flip-flops, opting to walk.

She hoped it would clear the doubt that had settled like fog in her mind. She headed out the door, grabbing her ID and credit card at the last minute. The instant the bright afternoon sun landed on her shoulders, she smiled. She needed to do more of this. All she'd done was work since she got to LA.

Aside from the food recommendations @makingadifference had given her, she hadn't explored the city or its surroundings. As she made her way down San Vicente toward the water, she ticked off a list of places and things she wanted to do while she lived here. She forced her subconscious to only provide stuff a single woman could do since she'd been given no indication the thing with Owen was more than a one-night screw-fest.

A damn thrilling screw-fest, but anyway...

If he didn't want more than her online persona, he wouldn't get any of her. In fact, the only reason she was keeping the date was to tell him as much in person. She wanted it all or nothing. Nerves flitted across her skin, chilling her despite the sun, but she countered them by thinking through the list.

Hiking to the Hollywood Sign topped it, and it was definitely something Kris could do alone.

Of course, she'd be silly if she didn't visit the Hollywood Walk of Fame.

But more than the touristy stuff, she really wanted to see the Venice Beach Boardwalk and Huntington Botanical Gardens. The outdoorsy, less populated places spoke to her heart, but they'd also be nice to experience *with* someone.

Don't think of Owen—don't think of Owen, she willed her mind.

Ugh.

What else was she supposed to do in this situation? They'd worked in opposition to one another for almost a full month, but then, one day, she'd realized the barrier she'd imagined between them wasn't actually there. And then they'd hopped right into bed together. At which point, he'd left her without so much as a word of explanation.

He used you and left you, like they all do, her subconscious tried.

But she shook the thought away.

That's not true. You know him both as Owen and @makingadifference. You know he's a good guy. And you're not that scared young woman anymore. You can take loss.

Not that she wanted to lose Owen, but she would survive it now that he'd helped her grow and trust again.

Regardless of why he'd left her alone that morning, at least knowing and loving him had opened her up to experiencing emotions, even the ones that felt less than awesome. She'd always care about her career, but she desired a full life with a love and friendship she could count on and she would always have Owen to thank for that.

Kris rounded a corner and picked up her pace. The ocean breeze ruffled her hair and her thoughts calmed. She was so close to the boardwalk and a glimpse of the Pacific Ocean. The part of her that had loved the ocean since she was a little girl giggled and urged her on, faster and faster until the buildings disappeared behind her and a panoramic view of the dark blue water spread out in front of her like a gift.

Yep. She needed to do this more often. Preferably when she wasn't headed to a double breakup.

Up ahead, at the entrance to the beach path was the restaurant. She slowed and took in a fortifying breath.

"Here we go. It's now or never."

She approached the restaurant with the same caution as she had around the wild boar in Angola. When all the outdoor tables were in view, she sighed. She'd beat Owen there.

"Okay," she muttered to herself. "Get comfortable so when he arrives you'll have the home court advantage."

She glanced at her phone. It was one minute past four. Hmm… He was late. And neither he nor @makingadifference had messaged her.

Her nerves intensified as she sat and ordered a basket of bread and an iced tea.

Maybe he was standing @ladydoc up, but then what would she do?

She sipped at the tea, growing more and more concerned with each minute that passed.

Eleven minutes past. Crap. How is this happening?

She dialed Owen but the call went to voice mail. Kris squeezed her eyes shut against the heat building behind them. "Owen," she said when the beep prompted her to leave a message. "Can you call me as soon as you get this? Even if you and I were just a…a fling, I'm going to ask that you find a way to work with me on the trauma center."

She hung up and sipped her drink again, desperate to focus on the sun glinting off the water in front of her, on the kids laughing and splashing in the surf at the tide's edge, on the feel of the sand tickling the skin between her toes. These were the reasons she'd decided to take the CMO gig in Southern California. Because look at this place—it was magnificent.

A little girl with blond ringlets and an iridescent green-and-purple bathing suit ran by Kris, giggling with her arms outstretched toward the water as she kicked up sand and salt water in her wake. The sheer innocence was a joy to watch, but it hurt, too. Kris had never really had the ability to let go and embrace the world with open arms like that. Not even as a child.

The one time she had was before Africa and it had almost cost her a career in medicine. Now she'd done it again and the inevitable loss loomed in front of her, blocking the sun and warmth from reaching her.

She shivered as her server approached the table.

She covered her iced tea glass. If she added any more caffeine to her already frayed nerves, she'd be up all night. "I'm fine, thanks," she said.

"Can I take these?" the server asked, indicating the second set of silverware on the bistro table.

She nodded. "Um, yeah. I don't think I'll be needing them."

The twentysomething woman's eyebrows went up as if to say, *Yeah, this happens all the time.*

Her phone chimed. She greedily snapped it up and swiped open the text from the board secretary.

On time for the closing document signing. Just got word from the governor.

Kris sighed. A month ago that would have been the only news she wanted—that her dream was happening and would be funded for at least ten years, with an option to renew after assessment in a decade's time. And no pimping out the patients for a docuseries, though some patients had asked to do solo interviews when they heard the show was canceled. Sharing their stories was important to them, and she'd granted their requests.

But now...

Now all Kris wanted was something from Owen, even if it was just closure. No, that was not all she wanted. She wasn't in the habit of lying to herself and wasn't about to start now. She loved Owen and wanted him, but short of that miracle, she wanted to move on.

Come on, she chided herself, *when will you learn?*

She checked her watch again. Four thirty-five.

He's not coming.

Heat burned the backs of her eyes. She slipped a twenty-dollar bill from her purse and left it on the table for the tea and bread and stood up to leave.

A block away, the tears began to fall at the same time her phone rang again.

Great. Now she was sobbing.

This time she checked the caller ID and when Owen's name

scrolled across her screen, she almost didn't answer. He'd made his point. They were colleagues, nothing more. Not even on-line friends.

But her heart slammed against her chest, urging her to see why he was calling.

"Hello?" she asked.

"Kris. Hi. Where are you right now?"

"By the boardwalk. Why?"

"How close to the restaurant, Kris?" Seagulls squawked in the background on the other line at the same time they did so over her head.

She froze. He was close. And she almost missed the fact that he hadn't mentioned which restaurant.

Did that mean...?

No. Because he would have said something, surely. But her breath was trapped in her lungs and her fingers shook as she wiped under her eyes.

"I just left. I was stood up by a friend."

He sighed. "Which direction did you go?" he pleaded. He sounded out of breath.

"North. Why do you care?"

Heavy, quick footsteps fell behind her. She stopped and turned around, and though she recognized the strong, delectable body, his face was partially obscured by flowers.

They were stunning—exactly what she'd order herself if she were the type of woman to do that. Daisies were sprinkled amongst a bed of lupine and mariposa lily, the local flora she'd appreciated on her drives to Mercy each morning.

"Because you weren't stood up." He paused, hanging up the phone and catching his breath while she lost hers. "These are for you," he said, a tentative smile on his face. He held out the flowers, which, on closer examination, were a little crumpled and disheveled like they'd been through battle to get to her. There was a card attached.

A rose by any other name...

"They're beautiful, but the card's a little cryptic."

He just smiled, his breath calming as he stepped toward her.

"Wait…" She started to reply but stopped. It hit her with full force then. She looked up, tears in her eyes.

Daisies and wildflowers. Not roses.

She'd only ever told one person about her favorite flowers. Not James, not Alice. Not even @makingadifference, who she was supposed to be there to meet.

That meant—

He knows it's me. That I'm @ladydoc.

"I'm sorry I wasn't there to meet you on time, Kris," he said before she could make sense of what it all meant. "My dad and brother had their second flat tire at the botanical gardens so we had to take in the rental to see why. It turns out there was a sharp sliver on the rim that was causing them."

"There weren't phones?" she asked, then winced. "Sorry."

"Nope." He pulled another phone out of his pocket and the screen was shattered. "I just couldn't find your contact info without bringing it to a cell phone repair place. Turns out I needed a new one." He shrugged and gave her a timid smile while he waved the new phone.

Her reply got stuck in her throat making it hard to breathe.

"How long?" she whispered finally. He took the hand not holding the enormous bouquet. Her pulse went wild and erratic and her breathing wouldn't regulate.

"Have I known? A while. But you don't look very shocked, either."

She grinned and bit the corner of her bottom lip. "Yeah, I might've known, too. What does it mean, that we both knew?"

"Well, I learned from my good friend @ladydoc not to give up on something you believe in, and I believe in you, Kris. So I don't care what it means that I fell for you twice, just that I don't want to live without either of you."

He winked and took the flowers from her hands and put them on the bench beside them. Good thing, too, since she couldn't concentrate on anything but him. When he took her hands in his this time, she didn't pull away.

"You really fell for me twice?" she asked. He bent down and softly brushed his lips against hers.

"I did. I fell in love with your brain first and your drive after that. Along the way, I learned how addicting your body is, but it's your heart that's had me all along. Your one, beautiful heart that's big enough to house Dr. Kris Offerman and @ladydoc in the same stunning body. Basically, it's always been you, in all your iterations."

With that, he kissed her again, this time with all the passion they shared. The world went on around them, people dodging the flowers and kissing couple as they made their way through the busy boardwalk. It was part of the magic of their city, that they held a small corner of it along with all the other people they'd get to help with the trauma center and clinic.

Finally, she broke off from the kiss.

"Okay, Rhys. I'd love to spend a couple minutes getting to know each other. Why don't you pull up a chair and we can talk," she said, using the same phrase as the first day she met Owen Rhys. Had that only been two months ago?

"As long as you make me a promise."

"I'll consider it."

"When it works, which it will, will you—all of you—be mine? Forever?"

Kris let that word—*forever*—dance on her tongue. She'd never had forever with anyone and she had to admit, a lifetime with a love like Owen would be pretty darn great.

"Deal," she said, reaching up on her toes to kiss him back. He picked her up and twirled her on the crowded sidewalk as she squealed.

I told you you'd find happiness in LA.

Okay, Kris thought. *I hear you, Alice. And thank you for making sure it all worked out.*

And it did. Oh, how it did.

EPILOGUE

Two years later

KRIS PARKED THE CAR and took Owen's free hand in hers. He smiled and brought it to his lips to kiss.

"Are my ladies ready to go to work?" he asked.

She nodded, rubbing her swollen belly. Only another month and she and her husband would be welcoming their newborn baby girl into the world. Thank goodness they had a rock-star team led by Dr. Kelsey Gaines to help with the birth because Owen had been a hovering mess since Kris discovered she was pregnant. He doted on her every need and had only agreed to let her go back to Mercy this late in her pregnancy because the joint trauma-center-slash-recovery-center ribbon cutting was that afternoon.

"We are. Will you ever get used to that?" she asked, pointing to the sign above the entrance. The Samuel R. Rhys Trauma and Recovery Center, it read. A small press pool had formed, but she didn't worry about welcoming them in. This was a story they were all happy to share.

"I won't. But I'm grateful the hospital agreed to do it."

"Well, when you merged your plastics clinic and agreed to fund a portion of the center, they kind of had to."

"It didn't hurt that Sam stared down Keith like that," he said.

She laughed. "No, that didn't hurt at all. Oh, Owen. Have I

told you how crazy you drive me?" she asked. Her words were light and filled with the love she felt for this man.

"Have I told you how much I love you?" he asked in response.

"You have, every ten minutes."

He kissed her, and like it had the first time they kissed, and every time since, her stomach flipped with desire.

"And I always will. Every day for the rest of our lives."

With that, the couple—soon to be a family—walked hand in hand into the place they'd built from scratch, determined to share that love with everyone who walked through its doors.

* * * * *

COMING
SOON!

We really hope you enjoyed reading this book.
If you're looking for more romance
be sure to head to the shops when
new books are available on

Thursday 28th
March

To see which titles are coming soon, please visit
millsandboon.co.uk/nextmonth

MILLS & BOON

MILLS & BOON®

Coming next month

FORBIDDEN NIGHTS WITH THE PARAMEDIC
Alison Roberts

He wasn't about to put any pressure on her, but he wanted Jodie to know that, if he had seen behind her mask, she could trust him not to use it against her or even mention it.

That she could trust *him*.

Maybe his lips curved, just a little, but it was Eddie's eyes doing most of the smiling and Jodie caught her bottom lip between her teeth.

Eddie was still holding her gaze. Or maybe Jodie was holding his. Maybe it didn't matter because something bigger was holding them both. The air in this small room with its shelves so tightly packed with medical supplies and the heavy, security door firmly closed seemed to be getting heavier. Pressing down on them.

Pushing them closer together.

Neither of them said a word. They didn't seem to need to. By whatever means, whether it was body language or telepathy, apparently the desire was expressed, permission sought – and granted.

Jodie slowly came up onto her tiptoes. Eddie bent his head just as slowly, turning it in the last moments, just before he closed his eyes and finally broke that contact, so that his lips were at the perfect angle to cover Jodie's with a soft, lingering touch.

When he lifted his head, he found Jodie's eyes were open before his. Maybe she hadn't closed them at all? Because of their soft, chocolate brown colour, he could also see that her pupils were getting bigger fast enough to tell him that she had liked that kiss as much as he did. That quick intake of her breath suggested that she wanted more.

Eddie had played this game often enough to be an expert. He knew there was an easy way to find out…

This time, the kiss wasn't nearly as soft and her lips parted beneath his, her tongue meeting his almost instantly.

Oh, yeah…

She wanted more.

So did Eddie. But not here. Not now. Not just because they'd be breaking all sorts of rules and it was a bad idea, anyway. No…he had a promise to keep to someone else and Edward Grisham never broke a promise.

He broke the kiss, instead.

'I have to go,' he said.

Jodie's gaze slid away from his. 'Me, too. We're done here.'

But Eddie was smiling as he turned away. He spoke softly but he knew that Jodie would be able to hear him perfectly well.

'I'm not so sure about that,' he said.

Continue reading
FORBIDDEN NIGHTS WITH THE PARAMEDIC
Alison Roberts

Available next month
millsandboon.co.uk

Copyright © 2024 Alison Roberts

afterglow BOOKS

Introducing our newest series, Afterglow.

From showing up to glowing up, Afterglow characters are on the path to leading their best lives and finding romance along the way – with a dash of sizzling spice!

Follow characters from all walks of life as they chase their dreams and find that true love is only the beginning...

OUT NOW

millsandboon.co.uk

OUT NOW!

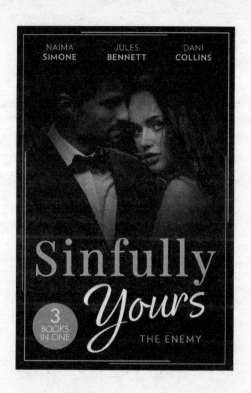

Available at
millsandboon.co.uk

MILLS & BOON

OUT NOW!

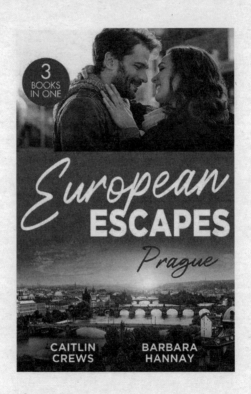

Available at
millsandboon.co.uk

MILLS & BOON

OUT NOW!

Available at
millsandboon.co.uk

MILLS & BOON

OUT NOW!

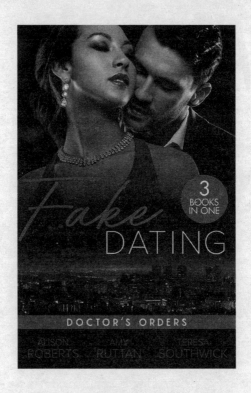

3
BOOKS
IN ONE

Fake
DATING

DOCTOR'S ORDERS

ALISON
ROBERTS

AMY
RUTTAN

TERESA
SOUTHWICK

Available at
millsandboon.co.uk

MILLS & BOON

LET'S TALK
Romance

For exclusive extracts, competitions and special offers, find us online:

f MillsandBoon

X @MillsandBoon

⦿ @MillsandBoonUK

♪ @MillsandBoonUK

Get in touch on 01413 063 232

For all the latest titles coming soon, visit
millsandboon.co.uk/nextmonth

MILLS & BOON

THE HEART OF ROMANCE

A ROMANCE FOR EVERY READER

MODERN
Prepare to be swept off your feet by sophisticated, sexy and seductive heroes, in some of the world's most glamourous and romantic locations, where power and passion collide.

HISTORICAL
Escape with historical heroes from time gone by. Whether your passion is for wicked Regency Rakes, muscled Vikings or rugged Highlanders, awaken the romance of the past.

MEDICAL
Set your pulse racing with dedicated, delectable doctors in the high-pressure world of medicine, where emotions run high and passion, comfort and love are the best medicine.

True Love
Celebrate true love with tender stories of heartfelt romance, from the rush of falling in love to the joy a new baby can bring, and a focus on the emotional heart of a relationship.

HEROES
The excitement of a gripping thriller, with intense romance at its heart. Resourceful, true-to-life women and strong, fearless men face danger and desire - a killer combination!

From showing up to glowing up, these characters are on the path to leading their best lives and finding romance along the way – with plenty of sizzling spice!

To see which titles are coming soon, please visit

millsandboon.co.uk/nextmonth

GET YOUR ROMANCE FIX!

Get the latest romance news,
exclusive author interviews, story
extracts and much more!

blog.millsandboon.co.uk